...vels.

music, wine, horses, architecture and the English countryside.

Visit the author's website at www.cynthiaharrod-eagles.com

The Foreign Field

Cynthia Harrod-Eagles

sphere

SPHERE
First published in Great Britain in 2008 by Sphere
This paperback edition published in 2009 by Sphere

Copyright © Cynthia Harrod-Eagles 2008

The moral right of the author has been asserted.

A CIP catalogue record for this book
is available from the British Library.

ISBN 978-0-7515-3770-3

Typeset in Plantin by Palimpsest Book Production Ltd,
Grangemouth, Stirlingshire
Printed and bound in Great Britain by Clays Ltd, St Ives plc

Papers used by Sphere are natural, renewable and recyclable
products sourced from well-managed forests and certified
in accordance with the rules of the Forest Stewardship Council.

Mixed Sources

Product group from well-managed
forests and other controlled sources
www.fsc.org Cert no. SGS-COC-004081
© 1996 Forest Stewardship Council

FSC

Sphere
An imprint of
Little, Brown Book Group
100 Victoria Embankment
London EC4Y 0DY

An Hachette UK Company
www.hachette.co.uk

www.littlebrown.co.uk

To Peggy Hughes, friend of the Morlands,
with much love

Author's note: In 1917 the Russians used the Julian calendar, which was thirteen days behind the Gregorian calendar used by the rest of Europe. Therefore, in this book, dates mentioned while the action is in Russia are given according to the Julian calendar. Thus the 'October Revolution' of the 25th of October, Russian style, happened on the 7th of November by English reckoning.

THE MORLANDS OF MORLAND PLACE

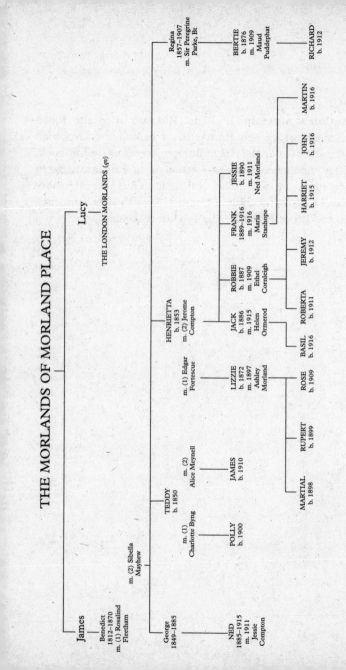

THE LONDON MORLANDS

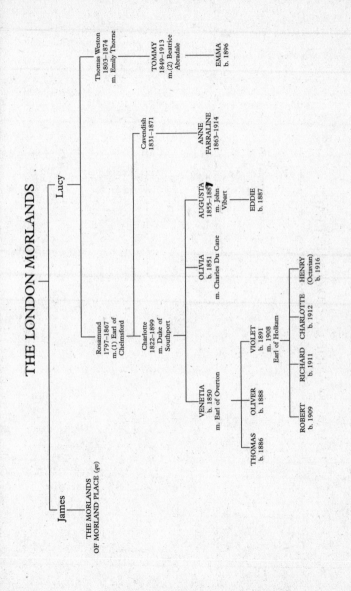

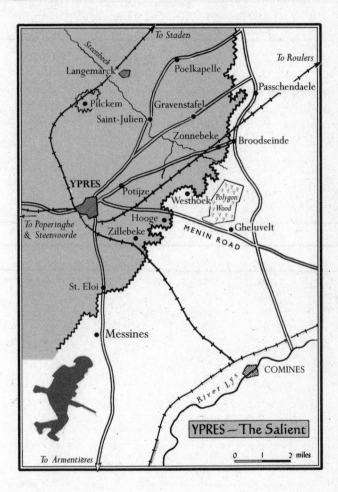

YPRES — The Salient

BOOK ONE

New Year

Take up our quarrel with the foe:
To you from failing hands we throw
The torch; be yours to hold it high.
If ye break faith with us who die
We shall not sleep, though poppies grow
In Flanders' fields.

John McCrae: 'In Flanders' Fields'

CHAPTER ONE

January 1917

The journey, like all journeys in wartime, was tedious. The train moved slowly, with frequent unexplained stops, often being diverted onto a siding to allow military traffic to pass. And it was crowded – there were even people standing in the first-class corridors, officers going back from leave. In second class, the heating worked only fitfully. At times the bitter cold from outside seemed to seep in like creeping death; at others the compartment was as steamy as a jungle, and Helen sweltered in her thick travelling clothes. She was large with child and could not keep struggling in and out of her outerwear, even had there been elbow room to do so.

The air smelt of sulphur, and everything was grubby: there was dried-out orange peel on the floor and smuts on the antimacassars. Cleaning standards had certainly declined as the war went on, with so many people going into war work. To add to Helen's trials, her year-old son, Basil, had recently discovered the delights of crawling, and objected passionately when restrained. The nursery-maid she had borrowed for the journey – from the wife of the wing commander at the flying school – was too excited about the whole expedition to be much use.

Still, Helen had known how it would be before she started. Having been brought up in the philosophy of 'what cannot be cured must be endured', she had packed sandwiches, plenty to read, and her knitting bag, and determined to make the best of it, despite her aching back and swollen ankles.

Her mother-in-law, Henrietta, had been doubtful about her making the journey at all so late in pregnancy, but there was no help for it. Jack was in France with the Royal Flying Corps, and her sister Molly, who had helped at her last lying-in, was now working as a clerk in the Ministry of Munitions and could not get leave. Mother could not leave Daddy, who was unwell, and in any case she was too elderly and nervous to be much relied on.

It was the last straw when her excellent nursery-maid, Becka, had left to work in the aircraft factory. Helen could hardly blame her. Not only would she earn much more, but she would be working with other young women, whereas at Downsview House there was only the cook, who was old, and the housemaid, who was half witted. And it was two miles from the nearest village. The spectacular views over Salisbury Plain, which so enchanted Helen and Jack, did not weigh with Becka at all.

With only weeks to go before her confinement, Helen had found it impossible to replace Becka; and since Mrs Binny and Aggie could not do their own work *and* look after Basil and a new baby, the only thing to do was to go 'home' to Morland Place. Uncle Teddy was delighted, of course, and had wanted to send his motor and chauffeur for her. But the heavy winter weather had made many country roads impassable; and, as Henrietta pointed out, if Helen had to travel on the main roads via London, she might as well be on the train. At least the train was sure to get through. Teddy, alerted to the possibility that the motor might get stuck somewhere, with Helen in labour on the back seat, gave in gracefully. Jack was pleased about it, anyway. Helen had wanted to give birth in her own dear home, but Jack was glad to think she would be at Morland Place with every attention and comfort around her.

The worst bit, Helen reflected, as the train came sighing

4

and huffing into Waterloo, would be the struggle across London to King's Cross. Because of the unreliability of timetables, she had had to leave plenty of time between trains, but porters were fewer, older and less obliging than before the war, and taxicabs harder to find. And there was the question of Basil's napkin: it could hardly be expected to continue its rearguard action indefinitely. She would need the privacy of the station hotel to effect the change.

As the train lurched to a halt, everyone jumped up and began scrambling down their baggage, jostling to get out first and secure a porter. Helen, too large to compete, gave up hope and sat tight with her charges until the rush subsided, noting rather grimly that no-one offered to help her. Cleanliness was not the only casualty of wartime rail travel. By the time she finally stepped down from the train, there was hardly anyone left on the platform. She looked round hopelessly for a porter, and was immediately accosted by a smart young man in a chauffeur's grey uniform.

'Mrs Compton?' he enquired, touching his cap. 'I'm Perkins, madam, from Lady Overton's. Her ladyship's compliments, and will you please to take luncheon with her at home? And I'm to take you to the station afterwards and see you onto your train.'

'However did she know I'd be here?' Helen wondered, but she guessed the answer even before Perkins gave it.

'I believe Mr Edward Morland telephoned to her ladyship and arranged it all, madam. Is this all your luggage, madam? Oh, no, don't you trouble, madam, please. I can manage it if the girl can carry your little boy.'

So Helen had only herself to get along, and soon found herself in the cradling comfort of a large motor-car, being whisked through the streets of London with as much expedition as the traffic would allow. The noise and crowdedness were almost a shock to her after two years in the country, and Mabel's eyes were out on stalks. It was a foggy day, and everything was so grey that the occasional splashes of red, of pillarbox and omnibus, were a welcome relief to the eye. The snow in the streets had been worn to grey-brown slush by wheels and feet, and was banked up unattractively at the edges of the roads and pavements. Though it was the middle of the day, the street-lamps were lit, each wearing a fuzzy halo of fog, and at the busy junctions policemen directed the traffic with torches.

But the welcome at Manchester Square could not have been warmer. The door was opened by Ash, the late Lord Overton's former manservant, and two maids, one of whom whisked Basil and the girl away while the other showed Helen to a bedroom where hot water, towels and all other conveniences awaited her. Much as Helen adored her young son, it was blissful to have him taken over by someone else. He had just begun to express his sorrow and rage over the disruption to his life in the only way he knew.

Refreshed, she was shown into the drawing-room, where a wonderful fire was leaping under the chimney. It glowed on the polished legs of furniture and glinted cheerfully on silver and glass, making the day outside look even dirtier by contrast.

Venetia, Lady Overton, came towards her with both hands outstretched. 'Welcome, my dear. You must be so tired. Come and sit by the fire. Did you find everything you needed upstairs? Luncheon will be served directly. I've told them to lay it in here – I hope you don't mind. I thought it would be cosier and, frankly, these days one has to economise on fuel *and* effort. The servant problem gets worse all the time.'

Venetia was tall for a woman, and very thin – bony as an old horse was how she described herself. Her hair was still thick and luxuriant, though quite white now, and she wore it in the old-fashioned style, wound on top of her head like a crown, which made her look taller. Though she was in her sixties, she worked harder now than she ever had. Her step was vigorous, her eyes bright, her face firm, and the hands that pressed Helen's and led her to the fire were strong and capable.

'I hope you don't mind my kidnapping you,' she said. 'Teddy's idea was that I should lend Perkins to take you across London, but when I knew how much time you would have between trains, I thought it would be nicer to bring you here for luncheon. Stations are dreary places to wait, and station hotels are so crowded.'

'How can you think I would mind?' Helen smiled. 'I feel as if I have been rescued from one of the circles of hell. I hope Basil isn't making a nuisance of himself?' she added, with a last surge of conscience.

'Don't worry about him. I have two perfectly capable maids upstairs looking after him and your girl. I'm sure you must have had enough of him by now, after being confined in a railway compartment with him for so many hours.'

'He was rather like a bee in a bottle,' Helen admitted. 'It's wonderful to be relieved of all responsibility for a while.'

Venetia gave her a glass of sherry and sat down opposite, looking at her with satisfaction. 'I kidnapped you with the intention of getting to know my godson's wife a little better, but remarks like that make me feel I know you already. There's too much sugary sentiment about children. I adored my own, but I should have gone mad cooped up at home with nothing to do but listen to their unedifying noises.'

'I haven't really had much choice in the matter lately,' Helen said.

Venetia glanced at her maternal shape. 'How long to go? Three weeks? Four?'

'Four,' Helen agreed.

'You look well. I suppose you didn't mean to have another so soon?'

Helen managed not to blush at such a direct question, reminding herself that Venetia was a doctor – one of the first lady doctors ever to qualify – and also that intellectual briskness had already been praised. 'In wartime, things sometimes don't go as planned,' she said, with a fair attempt at insouciance.

'I should recommend you not to have another for a year or two,' Venetia said. 'Incessant child-bearing is not good for the general health. Besides, you have a mind and a brain. Tell me about flying. I've achieved many things in my life, but I've never once left the surface of the earth.'

So Helen told her about her former job, delivering new aircraft from the factory to the RFC units. She had had to give it up, of course, when she became pregnant. 'People tell me I'm still performing valuable war work by having babies,' she concluded, a touch wistfully.

At that moment Ash and a maid came in with trays, and luncheon was set at an oval table by the window. Outside the fog swirled, condensation dripped from the bare black trees, and the occasional motor and horse crept miserably by down in Manchester Square. But inside, in the warmth and brightness, Helen delighted in a meal that had not required any decisions from her, and conversation with another intelligent human being. It made her realise how lonely she had been in the last few months, shut up in a house in the country with the servants and a small child.

They talked of Venetia's work: as well as operating at two hospitals, she sat on several committees, and ran her own charity, which provided X-ray ambulances to the Front. Then conversation drifted on to affairs in general.

It was fascinating to Helen to hear Venetia talk about public figures with a casual intimacy. To Helen they were just names in the newspaper, but Venetia had been on the inside all her life. On her own account, or through her late husband, she seemed to know everyone in Westminster, the Court and Horseguards. Helen revelled in the conversation: stimulation such as this had not come her way in many long months.

She asked about the inside view of the way the war was going and got a prompt answer.

'Haig feels that if the weather had held off a few more weeks he could have broken through last year on the

8

Somme,' Venetia said. 'The Germans were exhausted, their supplies and reserves stretched to breaking-point. It's a pity they've had these winter months to recuperate. The greatest uncertainty is the situation in Russia. Their losses have been terrible, but it's essential they continue fighting and divide the German effort.'

'And will they continue?' Helen asked. Venetia's eldest son, Thomas, was in Russia, a military attaché to the Court of St Petersburg.

'Who can tell?' Venetia said, and changed the subject rather abruptly to the servant problem – something everyone in the country had experience of, from one side or the other. 'I shall be losing Perkins next week, and my butler, Burton, went at the New Year. I'd had him for so long it was like an earthquake below stairs! I asked Ash to stay on when Overton died to help Burton, and to valet Oliver when he's home – very light duties. Now he'll be the only male servant in the house. I hope his health will stand it.'

Just then Ash himself came in to clear, which was the signal that time was getting on, and Helen must prepare to resume her journey. She felt rested and invigorated by her visit, and thanked Venetia warmly.

'Don't thank me, my dear,' Venetia said. 'You've reminded me what intelligent female company can be. I hope we shall meet again.'

Perkins took them to the station, found their reserved seats, helped them in and saw their luggage stowed. Helen parted from him with regret. But she only had to endure the rest of the journey. They would be met at York, and after that everything would be done for her. She would not need to lift a finger at Morland Place until the baby was born.

The train pounded north through the increasingly empty countryside, and the early dusk slipped into darkness. Putting her face to the window, Helen could see a black-and-white world, acres of snow under a black sky, black trees laden with white, as though the branches had been iced like

9

Christmas cake. It was a silent world, where men and women were indoors, all the animals were stalled, and small birds and beasts had taken shelter in hedges and holes. From time to time they passed through a station, its roof heavy with snow, its platform empty but for a lonely porter with a lamp. The lights of the train fled alongside, flicking up the cuttings and dropping down the embankments. Here and there a yellow square in the blackness marked an isolated cottage snugged down for the night against the bleakness all around.

But inside the compartment the smeary warmth of the steam heating built up a pleasant fug, and the rhythmic pounding of the wheels lulled the senses. At last Helen, Basil, Mabel and the new baby all slipped into a doze. Just before her eyes closed finally, Helen noted that it had started snowing again, and she thought of Jack in France, and hoped he was sitting cosily by the fire in the mess drinking tea. At least when it snowed he could not fly, which kept him from harm's way. But God help the poor men in the trenches, was her last thought.

Coming out of the line near Bapaume, Bertie didn't mind the snow. It softened the wounded landscape. There must be plenty of parts of France that were still beautiful, but of course he never found himself in them. Everywhere he was sent was spoiled, a ghastly waste of churned mud, shattered tree stumps, ruined houses, and the litter of destruction an army always leaves. Even the villages behind the line, where they went on rest, were battered by the passage of thousands of careless men and their machines. It was a condition the eye grew accustomed to, so that he hardly noticed it any more; but there was a part of the mind or the spirit that continued, dimly, to protest at the unrelenting ugliness.

But the snow laid a soothing hand over things, covering the scars, easing the jagged edges, giving at least the illusion that all was clean and white. And tonight his unit was finishing its time in the line, and he had fifteen days at rest to look forward to. 'Rest', of course, was a misnomer: generally there was far more sheer hard work done out on rest than in the line. But it meant proper food, proper beds, some little luxuries – and, best of all, the chance to get clean.

There was no point in even trying to keep louse-free in the line, even when in reserve. The close proximity of so many men and the appalling dirtiness of the trenches and dug-outs made it futile. But almost thirty months of war still had not resigned him to it. He had got used to monotonous food, and tea out of a petrol can, and damp cigarettes. He had got used to shaving in cold water, wearing damp clothes, and living in a hole where he could not stand upright. He had even got used to stepping on rotting body parts when he went out on patrol; and he rarely even thought about the constant threat of death from sniper bullets and whizz-bangs and all the other jolly toys the enemy tossed over. But he *could* not get used to the feeling of vermin on his body. He would sooner share his bed with a rat (and that had happened too – they wanted warmth as much as any creature) than his clothing with the common *pediculus humanus humanus*.

As soon as they got back to billets, he would set Cooper, his servant, to boiling as much water as humanly possible. Then he would strip everything off and get into it, and *stay* in it until he resembled a prune. In his dunnage back there he kept a set of clothing that never went near the trenches, so had never known the patter of tiny feet. The lust to be clean was stronger in him when he came out of the line than any desire for decent food or good wine.

The house where the officers billeted did not have a bathroom – that would have been too much to ask – but it did have an enormous hip-bath which Cooper lugged up to Bertie's room, and which held him comfortably under water from chest to knee. He had finished the urgent business of washing, and was stewing peacefully when Cooper came in bearing a tumbler of brown liquid and a bundle of envelopes.

11

'I hope that's not cold tea,' Bertie remarked.

'Whisky, sir,' said Cooper. 'Not the sort *we*'re accustomed to, but beggars can't be choosers. Brickett, Colonel Scott-Walters's man, reckons 'e knows where 'e can lay 'is 'and on some proper gin, though, so we shall see.'

'I can't see Brickett letting you have any,' Bertie said. '*You* wouldn't give *him* any if you'd found it.'

'There's ways and ways,' Cooper said, with mysterious dignity. 'Brickett and me understands each other. A wangle here and a scrounge there. Don't forget *we* still got the only bottle o' bitters in Picardy, sir, so if the colonel wants pinkers, Brickett 'as to sort 'imself out, don't 'e? Anyroad, don't you trouble *your* 'ead about it,' he concluded, with the implication that a mere officer's intellectual equipment wasn't up to solving the problems a batman had to face. 'You just drink your whisky.'

Bertie accepted the glass and sipped. It made his eyes water. 'Aah! You are a saint in human form, Cooper. You deserve a knighthood at least for this.'

Cooper was a man who loved a grievance, and was not to be bought off by idle compliments. 'Pair of boots that fitted proper would do me,' he said. 'You want to see my blisters.'

'I don't, I really don't,' Bertie assured him.

'The Lord Jesus never walked on as much water as me,' Cooper sniffed. 'Letters 'ere for you.'

Bertie eyed them. 'Anything official?'

''Ow long 'ave I been with you? I left *them* in yer room. These 'ere are the personal ones.' He handed them to Bertie, then stepped out to retrieve the can of hot water he had put down to open the door. 'Mind your legs, then.' He poured the hot water in – there was just room for it – and Bertie felt the delicious warmth creep round him. 'I'll have a bit for your shave after,' Cooper went on, 'but you'd better not be long, 'cause it won't stay 'ot, and Major Fenniman's bagged the rest o' the copperful. Dinner in 'alf an hour, give or take, and the major's come up with a nice bottle o' port,

12

which 'e hinvites you particular to share – 'e says don't ask where it come from.'

'I shall be more than happy to know where it's going to,' Bertie said, and waved Cooper away. 'Ten minutes, and then you can shave me.'

'It'll be a cold shave, then,' Cooper said. 'Can't keep the water 'ot more'n five. It ain't reasonable in this weather.' And he stumped out.

Bertie sorted out the letter from his wife, Maud, and read that first. She had been carefully trained in the art of female letter-writing, which meant her lines were beautifully straight, her handwriting elegant, and she made a little matter go a long way. Her letters were always long, without actually communicating anything very much at all – except an underlying current of faint discontent.

Bertie learnt that eggs had almost disappeared, the price of milk was beyond reason, and butter had become un-obtainable. Since she refused to have margarine in the house, she had been forced to serve biscuits instead of bread and butter when Lady Wolfitt came to tea.

He sighed. If only she would take little Richard and go down to live at Beaumont, his estate in Hertfordshire, she could have all the eggs, milk and butter she wanted. But then, of course, there would be no Lady Wolfitts to have to tea. Maud was London born and disliked the country. It would have been cruelty to force her to go.

He learnt that Mr and Mrs Weedon (who on earth were they?) had closed up house and gone to stay with Mrs Weedon's sister in Sussex. That meant there was an empty house on both sides now (oh, yes, they were the next-door neighbours). It made Maud nervous when there were Zeppelin warnings. She could never get used to the thought of the Germans flying over her head in the night, and having no neighbour to turn to in an emergency made it worse.

He read that her Red Cross branch had raised twenty pounds at their last drive, which wasn't as good as the Victoria branch, but with so many empty houses what could one expect? He read that Mrs Betteridge (no, even after some thought he had no idea who she was) had heard her nephew, a very promising boy, had been killed on the Ancre. Little Richard seemed to have one cold after another. Nanny had left quite suddenly to go to work for Mrs Monkton in Brook Street, and Maud had had the greatest difficulty in replacing her. The new nanny was too young, in Maud's opinion, and did not look very healthy, but there was simply no choice these days. The only other candidate had had a shocking accent, and looked as if she *drank*.

Bertie thought for a moment of Richard, their only child, who was almost five. He had been two when the war started, and since then Bertie had been at home for only a few weeks out of the two and a half years. Whenever he had leave, there was a shy boy to win round all over again, a boy who hardly knew him, about whose life he knew desperately little. His son was growing up without him, and whatever happened hereafter, he would never get back these years of Richard's life.

He took another gulp of the punishing whisky, and went back to the letter. Ah, here was a piece of news that meant something to him. Lord Manvers was planning to visit London again in March, and would no doubt spend some time at Pont Street. Manvers had been a business acquaintance of Maud's father, but Bertie had also known him in India, where they had both kept studs. Manvers bred racehorses and Bertie polo ponies, but since they had sold them to many of the same people, they had met often on the English social circuit out there. Bertie had always liked him. Manvers, on his recent visits home to look for breeding stock and buy clothes and saddlery, had befriended Maud, and Bertie was glad of it. He was a kind and capable man, and now that Maud's father was dead she had no older man in her life to look up to.

But now, it seemed, he was leaving India and moving permanently to Ireland to set up a stud, only breaking his journey in London. He was finding the climate in India trying, and business was declining. Because of the war, many of his best customers had gone to the Front, and others were not buying as they once had.

Bertie knew Manvers had relatives in Ireland. Perhaps he had got to the time of life when he wanted his own people about him. Bertie thought it would be nice to visit him there after the war. He was vaguely glad that Manvers was moving closer to home.

He did, however, have one unworthy pang of jealousy, when Maud added that Manvers had not forgotten his promise to teach Richard to ride next time he visited. Richard had been too young to ride when the war started, and since then Bertie had not been home for long enough at a time to give him lessons. Lord Manvers, a civilian, was free to come and go as he pleased, while Major Sir Perceval Parke, Bt, was the property of the British Expeditionary Force. Bertie could not help feeling that if anyone was to teach little Richard to ride, it should be his own father; and that it would have been tactful of Maud to say so. But tact had never been Maud's strong suit. This damned war . . . !

He put the letter aside and picked out the envelope in his cousin Jessie's handwriting: a letter from which he anticipated much more pleasure, if a great deal more pain. He was still engrossed in it when the door opened and Cooper came in with the can of shaving water and a martyred expression. 'Shave, sir,' he stated rather than enquired. 'Dinner's near-on ready.'

Bertie folded the letter to read again later – in bed, perhaps, if Cooper had been able to scrounge a decent lamp for him. French candles, these days, were practically all animal fat. He rubbed his hand over his chin and thought of the exquisite pleasure of shaving with *hot* water, followed by a meal that actually tasted of something, eaten at a proper table, without danger of interruption from shells or alarms. It was interesting how this hardship business narrowed your focus and made you appreciate things you would once have taken for granted. The war had its compensations, after all. An absurd, and probably unwarranted, cheerfulness broke over him, like a very small wave over a rock.

'Oh, it's not such a bad old war sometimes, eh, Cooper?'

'If you say so, sir,' Cooper said repressingly. 'It's the only one we got, any'ow.'

The imperial family was at home, in the Alexander Palace at Tsarskoye Selo, fifteen miles south of St Petersburg. It was their principal residence, where they spent the larger part of the year, though the seaside house at Livadia in the Crimea was their favourite place. The Tsar, who had come home early for Christmas, seemed in no hurry to go back to Stavka, the army headquarters at Mogilev; and where the Tsar was, Venetia's son Thomas must be also.

His position was an unusual one. He was a serving officer in the British Army, but his post, as military attaché and diplomatic liaison, placed him half-way between the Tsar and the embassy; while the privileged access he had to the Tsar and the way he was treated gave him rather the status of an old family friend. It made him invaluable to the British government; but he hoped he was useful to the Romanovs, too. Nicholas and Alexandra had both treated him very kindly over the years. The very fact that he was *Colonel* Lord Overton was due to imperial favour. He was a soldier who had never fought. He had come to Peter – as those who loved the city called it – long before the war began, and his rapid promotions had followed in recognition of his services to diplomacy, not in battle.

Occasionally he thought rather wistfully of the life he might have led had he not caught Nicholas's eye; of the companionship of serving in a battalion; of the satisfaction of risking your life for your country. Even his younger brother, Oliver, was at the Front – with the RAMC, but in the firing zone all the same. There was a deep vein of loneliness in him, for

16

his life had been given to serving a foreign court in a foreign country. He loved Russia and the Russians, spoke the language like a native, had read more Russian books than the average Moscow *literatus*, was deeply, hopelessly in love with a Russian girl – but it was not his country. He wondered sometimes if he would ever be able to go home.

But his place, for the foreseeable future, was here in the heart of the Romanov family; and he was surprised when one day an important visitor came to Tsarskoye Selo without his knowing anything about it in advance. The visitor was a smooth-faced, balding man in civilian clothes – which fact alone made him stand out in a palace where almost every man was in uniform – and he spoke a rather stilted, accented English. He was received with obvious affection by the Tsar and Empress, and was whisked away by them into the private suite.

Thomas was not introduced to him, nor asked to help entertain him, as he normally would have been, and it worried him. There was something of haste and secrecy about the business, something almost underhand. Fond as he was of Nicholas and Alexandra on a personal level, he did not trust their political instincts one whit, and the Tsar's decisions, untempered by outside advice, were almost invariably bad. Thomas needed to know who the visitor was and why he was there, but he could not think of any way to find out.

Later that day he was passing down one of the corridors in the east wing when he came across the youngest grand duchess, Anastasia, playing with her dog, throwing a ball along the passage for it to fetch.

'What are you doing here, Anastasia Nicholaevna?' he asked her, with mock sternness. The family's rooms were in the west wing; and this was the hour of lessons.

She looked at Thomas under her brows and stuck out her lip. 'Nothing.'

'Did you run away again?' he asked, with sympathy. She was the tomboy of the family, restless, unruly, always in trouble, and famous for escaping from lessons to do more congenial things like climbing trees or fishing. 'What was it this time?'

'French translation,' she said, with an indescribable grimace. Then she looked up at him with a beguiling smile. 'You won't tell, will you?'

He laughed at the rapid transformation of her mobile features. 'My lips are sealed,' he said solemnly, making a cross on his mouth.

'Thank you. Then I won't tell about you idling here instead of working,' she teased.

'I have nothing to do,' he said. 'Your father and mother are with a visitor and haven't asked for my services. I wonder who he can be?'

He only said it idly, but she said at once, carelessly, 'It's Uncle Ernie.'

'Are you sure?' Thomas asked, surprised. 'Uncle Ernie' was Grand Duke Ernst of Hesse; and Hesse, as part of Germany, was at war with Russia.

'Of course I am,' she said, surprised in her turn. 'He's Mama's brother. How could I not know him? I like him. He always gave us sugar mice when we were little. He didn't bring any this time, though. I suppose he thinks we're too old for them,' she concluded wistfully.

'But I wonder what he's doing here,' Thomas mused to himself, with a worried frown.

'*I* know,' Anastasia said, lowering her voice importantly. 'It's a secret mission. That's why there isn't a state dinner.' She threw the ball again and the dog scampered away, claws skidding on the marble floor. 'Cousin Willi sent him to try to get Papa to make peace.'

'My God,' Thomas breathed. 'Cousin Willi' was the German emperor, Kaiser Wilhelm.

Anastasia looked anxious for a fleeting moment. 'You won't tell? It's supposed to be a huge secret.'

'Of course I won't – and don't you tell either,' he warned her.

'*I* shan't,' she said. 'I'm good with secrets.'

'You told me,' he pointed out.

'Oh, but you don't count. You're one of us.'

'How did you find out, anyway?' he asked. 'About the secret mission?'

'The servants always listen at doors, and they tell me everything,' she said. 'There isn't much that happens that I don't know about.'

Thomas pondered this, and supposed it was probably true. She did have a closer relationship with the servants than the other children. And there was also the possibility that she did some listening at doors herself, in her frequent absences from the places where she ought to be.

The dog scampered back and presented the ball graciously to Thomas, who retrieved it and handed it to Anastasia. 'Well, you won't tell anyone else about it, will you?' he urged.

'Of course I won't. I'm not a *child*,' she said scornfully. And then, in her mercurial way, she changed tack. 'When you go to Peter next, would you get me some more of the nice paper from the English shop in the Nevsky Prospekt? *Pleease*, Thomas Ivanovitch. It's so much better than ours. I'll paint something for you if you do. A nice picture for you to keep.'

Thomas promised he would, and detached himself hurriedly so that he could go away and think about what he had learnt. It was a serious, potentially a disastrous, situation.

The war was going desperately badly for the Russians. The death toll was appalling, and the bitter weather and food shortages were hitting hard. But it was vitally important to Britain that Russia remained at war with Germany, because if she made peace, Germany would be able to transfer all her Eastern Front troops to the Western Front.

For exactly the same reason, Germany was desperate to get Russia *out* of the war, and to this end, there was no stratagem they would not consider. For instance, it was perfectly well known to British Intelligence that the German government was secretly fomenting socialist revolution in Russia, giving money and aid to leading revolutionaries in return for the promise that, if they succeeded in toppling the regime, they would make peace as soon as they came to power.

So it did not surprise Thomas that the Kaiser should have sent Hesse to make peace – secretly, monarch to monarch, as it were, and behind the backs of both governments. While the Kaiser wanted Russia out of the war, he naturally would prefer another means than Red revolution: after all, the Tsar was his cousin – and, besides, revolution had a nasty habit of spreading, like an infectious disease. There was already a strong left-wing movement in the Chancellery, which was threatening his own throne.

No, it was not surprising that the Kaiser had secretly sent Hesse; but it was madness for the Romanovs to have received him. Grand Duke Ernst was a high-ranking officer in the German Army, and to be treating with him was nothing less than high treason on the part of the Tsar. Some elements in the popular press already believed Alexandra was a spy, just by virtue of her German birth. If the fact of this visit by her brother leaked out, it could be desperately dangerous for the family.

Thomas spent an unhappy day and a sleepless night worrying about what he should do. Britain needed Russia in the war, and as a British officer it was his duty to pass on what he had learnt. On the other hand, he hesitated to expose Nicholas and Alexandra when they had both been so kind to him, and he was a trusted friend of the family. Besides, if it got out, it might precipitate the very trouble that the secrecy was meant to avert – scandal, revolution and the toppling of the regime.

Yet if Nicholas *were* thinking of making peace, it was Thomas's duty to warn his government. All night his mind revolved the problem helplessly.

The next morning the visitor left, and Thomas received a summons to attend the Tsar in his private office. He started there with leaden feet, wondering what on earth he should say or do. He didn't officially know about Hesse's visit, so he couldn't broach the subject with Nicholas; but to take the information to his intelligence liaison without warning Nicholas seemed a betrayal of friendship. For once, his unique position seemed more of a burden than a privilege.

As he was crossing the upper hall, he was waylaid by Anastasia, who was hiding behind a Nollekens bust on a plinth. She drew him into an empty ante-room, and pressed a silver-wrapped chocolate into his hand.

'What's this?' he asked, amused.

'I saved it from dinner last night, to thank you for not telling.'

'There was no need – but thank you,' Thomas said. He tucked it into his pocket. 'I'll have it later. I have to hurry to your father now.'

'Papa might be a bit cross,' she warned him, 'because he didn't like Uncle Ernie asking him to make peace.'

He resisted the urge to ask her how she knew. 'He said "no", then?' he suggested hopefully.

'Of course he did,' she said proudly. 'He said he would never make peace while a single foreign soldier remained on Holy Russia's soil! He said he's a soldier himself and he's proud of Russia's armies, and they will never yield and neither will he. It made Mama cry a bit, because she loves Uncle Ernie, but she loves Papa and Russia more, so of course she was on Papa's side. So Uncle Ernie's gone, now,' she concluded. 'He left early this morning.'

'Yes, I saw the carriage from the window,' Thomas said, relief making his knees feel a little weak. He had often had cause to deplore Nicholas's stubbornness, but thank God he had stood firm on that point, at any rate.

The Tsar did not mention the visit or its outcome to Thomas, and for once seemed to understand the importance of keeping the whole thing secret. Thomas, therefore, felt it would not compromise the Romanovs for him to do his duty and pass the information to the British Intelligence

21

Service. Indeed, it might even do them credit, as showing them able to stand firm against the calls of family.

On his next trip into Petersburg – Petrograd, they were supposed to call it now, because it sounded less German, but it never came easily to his mind – he sought out Lieutenant Rayner, his liaison.

Rayner listened carefully, then said, with a certain amused sympathy, 'Have you been fretting about this? There was no need, old chap. We've known about it all along. We tracked Hesse every step of the way, from northern Germany, through Norway, Sweden and then Finland, right down to the gates of Tsarskoye Selo.'

'I thought it was supposed to be a secret mission,' Thomas complained, feeling a little foolish, with a schoolgirl his only source of information.

'The Russian legation in Oslo is extremely permeable,' Rayner said. 'We have a man there who knew all about it well beforehand. Besides, these Hesses love to chatter, and they have relatives everywhere. But we weren't worried about it. There was never any danger Nicholas would yield to the Kaiser, even via Uncle Ernie Hesse.'

'Well, so it proved – and very glad I am about it, too.'

Rayner frowned. 'We're not out of the woods yet, though. Nicholas is stubborn, but there is one person who can sway him.'

'You mean the Empress?'

'Someone who has the Empress's ear – and who has a lot more influence with her than a mere brother.'

'Rasputin,' Thomas said flatly. He hated the very sound of that man's name.

Alexandra's infatuation with the *staritz* was not only alienating the general public, but dividing the imperial family. The Tsar's mother had gone to live in Kiev rather than share Petersburg with 'that creature'; and just recently the Tsar's favourite cousin, Grand Duke Sandro, had stormed out after a flaming argument that had been clearly heard through the doors of the private quarters: 'I realise *you* are quite ready to perish, but you have no right to drag your relatives with you down the precipice!'

Sandro and other family members – along with most government ministers and many senior generals – believed some degree of constitutional reform was necessary to avert the threat of revolution. But Rasputin, through the Empress, urged Nicholas to be obdurate, encouraging his natural bent to be an absolute ruler and to refuse any measure of reform, however slight.

Government circles hated Rasputin for his interference and flagrant bribe-taking. Outside these circles, he was hated for his drunken debauchery. The problem was that the Tsarevitch's illness was kept strictly secret from all but the closest family, so no-one understood that Alexandra reverenced Rasputin for his ability to bring the boy back from the brink of death. She regarded him as a genuine holy man sent by God. And Thomas had seen how in her presence, and that of the Tsar, Rasputin behaved modestly and reverently. They had no idea how he was outside the palace, and how it revolted people to know a man like him was received at all, let alone had influence. The general public believed Alexandra and Rasputin were lovers, fellow devil-worshippers and German spies. The filthiest cartoons and most scurrilous gossip were freely circulated about them.

It frustrated Thomas unbearably to be aware of both sides of the situation, but to be unable to do anything about it. Even his privileged position within the inner circle did not permit him to speak frankly to Nicholas; and if he had, Nicholas would not have listened. The Emperor was well-meaning, kindly and of unimpeachable personal virtue; but he was also stubborn, autocratic and not very bright – a fatal combination in a ruler

To Rayner, and to the British government, Rasputin's evil lay not in his personal habits, however unsavoury they were, but in the fact that he was anti-war, spoke out against it in public on every possible occasion, and through Alexandra had influence over Nicholas, the man in whose sole power it was to end it.

Rayner said, 'The madman calls publicly on the Emperor to make peace. At the moment Nicholas is not inclined to listen, but if the Tsarevitch should have another bad turn, and Rasputin "saves" him again . . .'

Thomas saw. 'It would give him fresh influence.'

'I could see him claiming that it was a sign of God's will that Nicholas should make peace,' said Rayner.

'Yes, it's just the sort of thing the rascal might say.'

'And Nicholas might just believe him,' Rayner concluded, frowning.

'You think it's a serious possibility, then?' Thomas asked.

'More than that: a logical inevitability. Sooner or later, it *must* happen – unless the boy dies. Even then his influence over the Empress might remain. She'd want spiritual comfort in her grief, wouldn't she?'

'Then what's to be done?' Thomas said

'Rasputin must go,' Rayner said. 'The damage he does is beyond counting.'

'But how would you persuade him? He's too mad to reason with. And you could never outbribe the imperial family.'

'I wasn't thinking so much of persuading,' said Rayner, with a certain grimness. Then his expression cleared, and he grinned at Thomas. 'Sooner or later, someone will assassinate the brute. That's inevitable too.'

'It's been tried before,' Thomas reminded him. 'And failed.'

'My dear colonel, don't tell me you believe he has divine protection too?'

'Too?'

'It's what he claims,' Rayner reminded him. 'But don't worry. He may think he's a demigod, but he's mortal, like the rest of us.'

CHAPTER TWO

Through her many friends in high circles, Venetia had obtained government funds for her charity, along with an official title – director of Mobile Radiological Services – and an office. It was in an annexe of the War Department, Winchester House in St James's Square, and from there it was only a step across the square to Fitzjames House to visit her daughter Violet.

On the steps one afternoon she met Sir Frederick Copthall, Violet's oldest friend, just coming away. He looked rather like a melancholy bird, his shoulders hunched in his greatcoat against the penetrating cold, but he straightened them when he saw her. He assumed his top hat purely for the purpose, it seemed, of raising it to her, but his 'Mornin', Countess!' did not resonate with his usual cheerfulness.

'Good morning, Freddie. You've been visiting Violet? How are things?'

'Not awfully merry and bright,' he admitted. 'Left her in tears, in fact. Well, she sent me away – wouldn't have left otherwise. I'd just come to tell her I've been called up.'

'Oh, Freddie, not you too!'

'Fact.' He seemed rather bewildered by it. 'Can't think what they want with me. Never been any use at anythin' at all. Got to report to the Trainin' Reserve at Hounslow. Don't even know where Hounslow is.'

'It's out to the west of London.' She tried to put it into a context he would understand. 'Not far from Windsor.'

'Ah. You know it, then.' The news seemed to make him glummer, as if perhaps he had hoped no such place existed, and the whole thing was a hoax.

'They'll probably make you an officer,' Venetia said encouragingly.

He thought a moment. 'Probably better if they did,' he admitted. 'Never been able to shoot straight. As likely to shoot the chappie next to me as Jerry, if they let me loose with a rifle. Can't go so far wrong with a pistol. I mean, it don't swing about in the same way.'

'You'll look extremely handsome in uniform,' Venetia said.

'Think so?' He brightened slightly, but then it faded as he remembered. 'Hate to leave Violet, though, especially the way she is at present. Wish I could stay around to try and cheer her up.'

'I'll talk to her,' Venetia said. 'It's high time she got a grip on herself. And it was very naughty of her to make it harder for you to go.'

'Oh, no,' Freddie said, shocked at the idea that anything Violet did could be wrong.

Venetia patted his arm. 'You run along, Freddie. And don't worry about Violet.'

'Can't seem to help it,' he said, raising his hat to her again. 'Well, cheer-oh, Countess. Pip-pip!'

Fitzjames House was silent and dark, with too many shutters closed and drapes undrawn. It smelt cold and unused, slightly musty. Venetia could only hope the nursery floor was warmer and brighter, for Violet had not sent the children down to the country this time.

It was Violet's own maid, Sanders, who admitted Venetia – sign of a disordered household – greeting her with evident relief and the news that her ladyship was sitting in the small rear parlour. Venetia dismissed Sanders and found her own way there. It was slightly more cheerful, in that there was

26

a fire lit and the drapes were open, though Violet, her face buried in a handkerchief as she sat weeping on the sofa, was in no condition to appreciate the daylight, such as it was on a grey January day. Her two little Pekingeses, Lapsang and Souchong, were curled up together in an armchair looking depressed.

Venetia sat beside her daughter and put an arm round her, but she could tell from the quality of the sound that the tears were almost done. In a moment, Violet emerged from the handkerchief. She was so beautiful that even prolonged weeping did not make her look ugly, but it was not true to say it had no effect. Her grief since her lover Octavian Laidislaw had been killed at Pozières had aged her: she looked like a woman now, no longer a girl. Her eyes were red and swollen, and she was pale and drawn – an effect increased by the stark black she insisted on wearing.

'I met Freddie on the steps,' Venetia said, as Violet looked at her at last. 'I'm sorry, darling. You'll miss him.'

'It's so awful,' Violet said, in a shaky voice. 'Everyone goes away, but I thought there'd always be Freddie. Now they've taken him, and he'll be killed too.'

Venetia tried never to lie to her children. The death toll among officers was far higher than among ordinary soldiers, and there was more than a chance Freddie *would* be killed, so she couldn't say the contrary. Instead she went on the attack. 'It was very wrong of you to make it harder for him to go, given that he had no choice in the matter. He hated leaving you in tears.'

'I couldn't help it,' Violet said, in what was close to a sob. 'He's been so good to me, and now . . . Oh, Mummy, it's going to go on and on until they're all dead, isn't it?'

'Nonsense,' Venetia said briskly. 'They're not all killed. If they were, the war couldn't go on anyway. And the Germans were badly hit last autumn. Haig thinks they'll be beaten this year. But I don't want to talk about that. I want to talk about you. What are you intending to do?'

'What do you mean?' Violet said, startled out of her thoughts.

'You haven't sent the children down to the country.'

'The tutor left, and it seemed like too much effort to try and find another. So I decided to stay here, and keep them with me. I hate Brancaster, anyway. It's so horribly cold in the winter. I'm sure it isn't healthy for them.'

'You could go back to Shawes.'

'It's too far from London. And there would still be the tutor problem. They can go to school here. Why, Mummy? *You* brought *us* up in London. Why shouldn't I do the same? I'll take them down in the summer, of course, the way you used to take us.'

'Very well, but if you want to stay in London—'

'It's what Holkam wanted,' Violet said bitterly. Any mention of her husband's name, these days, was bitter. It brought Venetia to the point.

'He wanted you to appear in London from time to time in order to cultivate an appearance of normality. And you agreed it was the best thing. But you never go out, you keep the shades drawn, and you dress yourself from head to toe in black – which, by the way, almost no-one does any more. It's not considered patriotic.'

'Patriotic!'

'Thousands of other women have lost men. You're not a special case. *I* don't wear mourning for your father.'

'But it's my fault Laidislaw's dead! If it hadn't been for me, Holkam wouldn't have had him killed.'

'You're not to say such things! It was the Germans who shot Laidislaw, not your husband.'

'But it was Holkam who had him sent into the trenches.'

'Violet, I've been patient with you because I know how much you loved Laidislaw. But I'm close to losing my temper now,' Venetia said grimly. 'Even if it were true – and you have no evidence to support it – that Holkam had Laidislaw called up out of turn, what difference would that make?

28

He would have been called up eventually. All men of the right age are liable to conscription, as you know perfectly well. My God, you've just said goodbye to Freddie Copthall! Sooner or later Laidislaw would have had to go, and then he would have been subject to the same risks as anyone else. *And*,' she added tellingly, 'as a man of spirit, he wouldn't have had it any other way.'

Violet looked down at her hands, twisting the wet handkerchief in her lap. 'What is it you want me to do?' she asked, almost too low to be heard.

'I want you to behave yourself. Get rid of all this black, dress normally, resume your usual occupations, go out and see people, and be seen.'

'I can't!' she cried.

'You can! Listen to me. I'm not asking you to be gay. It's not expected – the war gives you a perfect excuse to be as serious as you wish. But you must be seen. Visit a few friends, rejoin a few committees, attend a few functions. The whole point of your being in London was to give the appearance that everything was normal between you and Holkam, so as to kill the old scandal.'

'I don't care about the scandal,' Violet said despairingly. 'I don't care about Holkam.'

Venetia closed her hand about her daughter's wrist so tightly that Violet gasped and looked up at her in surprise. 'You agreed to do it for the children's sake, don't you remember? It's absurd even to talk about a *rapprochement* if you won't take those few extra steps to regain your public position and retrieve your reputation. Whatever you think of Holkam, you must do that for the children's sake.'

'You're hurting me,' Violet said, in a small voice. Venetia released her. She rubbed her wrist and sighed, a long, deep sigh that seemed drawn up from the centre of the earth. 'You're right,' she said at last. 'I know you are. It's what Freddie's been saying for weeks.'

'Freddie has more sense than is generally realised.'

'But it will be so hard,' Violet went on, 'to go out and face people, knowing they're talking about me behind my back.'

'They won't be. Memories are short, and everyone has more important things to think about. As long as you behave as if nothing has happened, it will be forgotten.'

'It will be hard to do it alone,' Violet sighed. 'I wish Freddie hadn't gone.'

'I'll help you all I can,' Venetia said.

It seemed like the working of Providence, given that Violet was at last trying to get herself into the right frame of mind to go back into society, that the next day she received a telegram from Emma Weston, asking if she could come and stay. She sent an enthusiastic reply: 'Come as soon as possible and stay for as long as you like.' And only two days later, there was Emma in person, on the doorstep with her maid Spencer and a mound of luggage.

'Is it really you?' Violet cried, coming out into the hall to meet her.

Impulsive Emma flung her arms round her. 'It's really me! I've escaped!' She pulled off her hat and gloves and thrust them at Spencer, who was waiting patiently to remove her coat. 'Oh, I shouldn't say that! Uncle Bruce and Aunt Betty are so very kind, and I do love them – but it does feel as though I've escaped from durance vile!'

Violet felt her spirits rising irresistibly. Emma's smile and vivacity seemed to light up the gloomy hall. Even the Pekingeses came running forward, plumy tails waving, to be scooped up and hugged – 'Dear little doggies!' – and put down again. 'I can't tell you how horrid Scotland has been, especially now with all the snow. Oh, that railway journey! I'm worn to a shadow. But even before that, Uncle and Aunt were doing everything they possibly could to get me married off before I came of age. I know they thought they were doing it for my own good, but I was so afraid I wouldn't be able to hold out and I'd end up marrying someone dreadful.'

There was no help for it – there must be talk now, and showing to rooms would have to wait. Violet led Emma into the small parlour and ordered tea to be brought. 'But why would they want you to marry someone dreadful?' she asked.

'Oh, not really dreadful, but their idea of a suitable husband is not the same as mine. Poor Uncle Bruce!' She smiled ruefully. 'He absolutely hates entertaining and going to parties and so on. If it were up to him, he'd never leave Aberlarich. The only things he likes doing are shooting and fishing, and even those he prefers to do quite alone, except for his gillie – who's quite the most silent man I've ever seen, by the way, just like a lump of granite, except not so exciting. But in the good cause of getting me married off, Uncle has been dragging me round every house-party and theatre and card evening and review and I don't know what else, having to stand there talking to people, and smiling until his poor face aches.'

'Oh, Emma!'

'It's true. They were so afraid that as soon as I came of age I'd come to London and be taken in by some fortune-hunting rogue. But, oh! The men they've been thrusting at me!'

'What was wrong with them?'

'*Dull!*' Emma cried. '*Impossible!* There's one in particular Uncle favours, Lord Knoydart: he owns thousands of acres bordering Loch Nevis and the Sound of Sleat, the emptiest, most storm-lashed country you've ever seen! Just the sort of place Uncle Bruce adores, of course – nothing but rocks and heather as far as the eye can see. I was really afraid I'd end up accepting him, because Angus Knoydart is frightfully good-looking and really rather sweet, only *very* shy and tongue-tied, and imagine being shut up for ever in Knoydart Castle with a man who never talks to you! But he was so smitten with me it was hard to keep refusing him – so awfully

31

like kicking a puppy, you know. I had to keep reminding myself it meant staying in Scotland, and being married to a man who wears the kilt.'

'Don't you like kilts?' Violet said. 'They're much admired in London. Officers from Scotch regiments are quite a prize at dinner parties. Don't you think the kilt is very becoming, and terribly romantic?'

'No, I don't,' Emma said feelingly. 'I know it's probably very wicked of me, but I simply can't *bear* them. I feel such an idiot dancing with a man who's wearing a skirt! If anyone's going to wear dresses in my house it will be me. Men should wear trousers, and that's that.'

Violet found herself laughing, for the first time in six months. 'Poor Emma. But you held out.'

'I did, but I felt an awful beast, especially when the time came to tell them I was going to London. I kept putting it off, because it seemed so ungrateful, and I knew it would break their hearts. But it had to be done. They were terribly disapproving and worried. Of course, once I was twenty-one they couldn't actually stop me, but it felt like taking advantage of them.'

'Your uncle couldn't stop your allowance, I suppose?' Violet asked. Apart from the moral pressure, that was the usual way women were kept in check. She knew Emma's father had left her a vast fortune, but it had been under Lord Abradale's control during her minority.

'My father wrote in his will that once I reached twenty-one I was to have a greatly increased allowance,' Emma said. 'The solicitor came down to explain it all on my birthday. It has to be paid to me direct, so Uncle can't do anything about it, and it's so generous I shall be able to live in good style until I come into my fortune. *That* doesn't happen until I'm twenty-five, which I think is the only thing that reconciled Uncle to my leaving: he comforts himself it will be four more years before a fortune-hunter can get his hands on everything. I think he hopes I'll get scared in London and go running back before then.'

'Well, I'm so very glad you're here,' Violet said. 'What are your plans?'

'Clothes first,' Emma said. 'You will come with me and help me? I've been away so long I don't know what people are wearing – except that all the skirts I saw on my way here in the taxi looked *very* short. It did look queer just at first, but rather exciting in a way. How long are you staying up, by the way?'

'I'm going to live in London permanently,' Violet said. 'Except for going down to the country in the summer, of course. And you're welcome to stay with me as long as you like.'

'Wonderful! *Thank* you, dear Violet! Poor Uncle Bruce would be terribly shocked if I set up on my own and, really, I didn't like the idea myself. I'd much sooner live with you. We'll have such fun!' She caught herself up. 'But of course I don't mean to do nothing but enjoy myself. I firmly intend to do some war-work, as soon as I've decided what's best to do. That's my main reason for wanting to be in London.'

'And what are the others?'

'The other reasons? Well, there's one other important one.'

'Major Fenniman?' Violet hazarded.

Emma coloured a little. 'You guessed.'

'I saw you with him when he and Bertie visited. I thought there was something between you.'

'It's hard to know if there is,' Emma said, 'when I've had so little time with him. That's why I want to be in London. If he comes home on leave, I'll have a much better chance of meeting him here than in Scotland. Because I *think* I'm in love with him, but how do you tell when you're hundreds of miles apart? And when you can't even write to one another because you're not engaged, and you can't *get* engaged because you never see each other?'

'It is a problem,' Violet admitted. 'But he seemed very attracted to you.'

'Do you think so?' Emma said, turning to her eagerly. 'Because I'm thinking of doing something, and I want your opinion about it. Now I'm of age, do you think it would be very shocking if I wrote to him? I know Uncle would never countenance it, but now I'm a grown-up I can make my own decisions, can't I?'

Violet considered. 'I don't suppose there would be any harm in it.'

'He wouldn't think me *fast*?' Emma said anxiously.

'No, I don't believe so. If he loves you, he'll be glad of your letters. And if he did think you fast, it would mean he doesn't love you.'

'Dear Violet, how clever that sounded,' Emma said, impressed. 'I hope you're right.'

Violet pressed her hand. 'Things are different now,' she said. 'Nearly three years of war has changed everything. The old rules don't apply any more. When the men are going to the Front and you may not see them for years, letters and visits on leave are all you have. You have to seize what you can, while you have the chance.'

'Yes,' said Emma seriously, 'and I'm so afraid that he may get killed before we ever have time to get to know each other. That would be the worst thing of all.' She saw Violet's eyes fill with tears. 'Oh, Vi, I'm sorry. What a tactless thing to say.'

Violet shook her head, then found her voice. 'No, you're right. At least I had my love. You deserve to have yours.'

'You've never spoken about it,' Emma said shyly. 'I sort of thought I wasn't supposed to know about it, but I couldn't help knowing.'

'You were in the middle of it, but everyone was trying to protect you.'

'And then Uncle Bruce dragged me away, just when I might have been able to be some comfort to you.'

'You wanted to stay?'

'Of *course* I did. You're my friend. I wasn't shocked,' she said

earnestly, 'only very, very sorry that you were in trouble.'
They were silent a moment, and then Emma said, 'Would
you tell me about it now? If it wouldn't hurt too much. I'd
like to know the whole thing, so I can understand.'

And so, with a sense of letting go of something, Violet told
her. It was the first time she had spoken in this way of Laidislaw,
of their love, of his death, of their child. Freddie had known
almost everything, but it had never been discussed between
them. But Emma was the perfect audience – young, eager,
sympathetic. Violet told; and in telling it seemed as if she were
drawing a terrible thorn out of her breast, one whose pain
had been sickening her for months past. In a way, she regretted
its passing, because it was all she had left of him, and part
of her wanted it, though it destroyed her, as a way of keeping
him near. But once she had begun the process it could not
be stopped. She let him go, seeming to see him drift away
into the darkness that lay beyond the warm precinct of the
cheerful day: her lover, her perfect love, growing faint, fading,
until the vibrant reality of him was only an after-image –
bright on her mind's eye, but flat, two-dimensional, like a
photograph. It was over. She would never see him again.

She paused, to discover that Emma was crying, and that
made her cry, too. But they were not the desperate tears of
only a few days ago. The agony of grief had softened into
sorrow.

'But you have the baby,' Emma said, through her tears.
'I am right, aren't I? Oh dear, is that a terrible thing to ask?
But the baby—?'

'Yes,' Violet said. 'Of course, no-one must ever know.'

'I swear I shall never say a word to anyone. Oh, Violet,
how can you bear it?'

'I don't know,' Violet said, with bleak honesty. She remembered her mother's words. 'But thousands of women have
to, and thousands more will before this war's over. My father
was killed – Jessie's Ned was killed – Octavian was killed.
There's nothing to be done about it.'

Emma shook her head, unable to speak.

'So I think you should write to Major Fenniman,' Violet concluded.

Everyone was saying this was the coldest winter in memory. Jessie sat on the edge of her bed and looked down at her snow-stained boots, and watched her breath cloud the air. She was just beginning to realise how tired she was. She had come off night duty a few hours ago. At supper – beef sausages with cold potatoes, and cold rice pudding with jam (hearty enough to fill you up, but strange eating at half past eight in the morning) – the senior night sister, Sister Thompson, had read out the changes, one of which was 'Nurse Morland to go on day duty tomorrow morning.'

When she had first come to the No. 1 London General, she had heard other nurses say they dreaded having to go 'on nights'. But in the event, she had enjoyed it. Once she had got used to living upside-down, it meant she was free to go about during the daytime. Night nurses were supposed to be in bed by eleven, but the assistant matron never bothered to check. As long as she took a few hours' sleep in the afternoon, she found she could manage very well, and she had enjoyed the freedom to visit shops or restaurants or see friends every day.

And not least of the benefits was that night nurses had their own accommodation, in huts right there in the hospital grounds, each in her own room, tiny but blessedly private. But this morning she had had to transfer her things back to the hostel, which was a two-mile walk from the hospital, up the steep side of Denmark Hill – every step of which was felt at the end of a long shift. Here her private space was just a scrap of a cubicle, screened off from the other five inmates in the room by a washed-out curtain. And the room was freezing, with the penetrating cold of a house where no fire had been lit in years. She would have to wear many layers and heap her coat on top of her bed that night to get warm enough to sleep.

But that was not the worst thing about going back on days. In the ward at night there were only two nurses – a senior certificated nurse and a junior, who was either a probationer or a VAD – which meant that all the nursing work had to be done by them together. It was not possible for the senior to shut the junior out from proper nursing on the grounds that she was 'only a VAD'. Jessie's senior had been a youngish woman, friendly and open-minded, and they had shared the work with a real sense of comradeship. Jessie had learnt a lot from her, and together they had coped with several crises, which had advanced both her experience and her confidence.

But Sister Thompson had said that Jessie was to go to Ward Five tomorrow morning, one of the wards housed in huts in the grounds. Ward Five was under the command of Sister Cartwright, and Sister Cartwright did not like VADs. Many of the trained nurses, particularly the older ones, resented the influx of amateurs into their profession. Sister Tudor was probably the worst. Jessie's best friend Elizabeth – 'Beta' – Wallace was presently suffering on days under Tudor, who hated VADs so much she would do anything in her power to humiliate them. Cartwright was not petty and spiteful like Tudor, but she did not regard VADs as proper nurses, and gave them only cleaning and tidying jobs. Even at busy times they would not be allowed so much as to take a temperature. Jessie could foresee months of frustration ahead of her until the stately machinery of the hospital rotated her into a different ward. All the real and valuable experience she had accumulated would count for nothing, and she would be scrubbing floors and dusting lockers while men she might have helped waited for a busy nurse to get round to them.

She was aware with one part of her mind that the accumulated tiredness of night duty was affecting her, but still, as she sat on her bed and the cold of the house sank into her bones, she felt weary and depressed. The war seemed

37

to have been going on for ever, and there was no end of it in sight. Her husband, Ned, had fallen at Loos fifteen months ago; her brilliant brother Frank had died at Gommecourt last July, his promise snuffed out in an instant. Jack – the brother she had always felt closest to – was out there now, pitting his flimsy aeroplane against German 'Archie' – anti-aircraft fire – and their fighter aces. And Bertie – ah, but it was well not to think of Bertie if she could help it.

Tomorrow she would be back on day duty, under a woman whose sole purpose in life, as far as Jessie was concerned, would be to thwart her every attempt to be useful to the war effort. Life was grim.

But then her sense of proportion asserted itself and she jerked herself back from self-pity. What hardship did she have to bear, compared with the men at the Front? No-one was shooting at *her*. And she had not taken up nursing to please herself. She stood up, stretched her aching body, and then had a happy thought. The house was quiet – everyone was out, or on duty – which meant she could get a fair turn in the bathroom for once. She collected towel, sponge-bag and book, and at the last minute remembered a half-bar of chocolate concealed in her trunk. To lie in warm water with something to read and something to eat seemed to her just then the greatest pleasure on earth.

And she had the whole day to do as she pleased, for she could sleep tonight. Beta would have her three hours off this afternoon. If she got out on time, and they were lucky with the trams, they could catch a matinée up in Town: perhaps *Nuts and Wine* at the Empire – something light and frivolous to cheer them up. Even if they had to leave before the end, because Beta had to go back on duty, it would be worth it. Or if they could not make a matinée, they could at least have tea somewhere. Food at the hospital was plentiful, but it was rather lacking in refinement, and sometimes the soul yearned for buttered scones and fancy cakes. Luxuries could still be had if you were prepared to pay enough. As she climbed into the bath she decided she would be waiting at the hospital gate in a taxi when Beta came out, so as to make the most of their time. Neither of them was dependent on their tiny wages, and what was money for if not to buy comfort and convenience?

Edward 'Teddy' Morland, the Master of Morland Place, had come to family life late, after a long and agreeable bachelorhood, but he had embraced it wholeheartedly. Now he liked nothing better than having a house full of his nearest and dearest and, being a rich man, was able to indulge his taste. As well as his wife Alice, his little son James and his sixteen-year-old daughter Polly by his first marriage, Morland Place was home to his widowed sister Henrietta, her son Robert with his wife Ethel and four children, and her son Frank's widow, Maria, with her baby Martin.

To add Helen, Basil and her baby-to-be was, in Teddy's view, not merely no trouble at all but positively right and natural. The Morland Place nurseries took up a large part of the upper floor of the old house, and had been designed to hold the vast families of Plantagenet and Tudor times. Modern families, however expanded, could never outgrow them. And Nanny Emma, who had brought up Henrietta's children and was now happily working her way through the next generation, had similar views on family to the Master's. Far from regarding more children as an imposition, she could not wait to get her hands on them. Poor Maria, whose marriage to Frank had consisted of one week's leave in Brighton, before he had had to go back to France and be killed at Gommecourt on the first day of the battle on the Somme, had only his posthumous son Martin to comfort her. But, as she complained gently to Helen, she hardly felt like his mother any more. Babies belonged to Nanny Emma and her maids, and mothers, except when they were actually nursing, were superfluous to requirements.

'I sometimes dream about being able to set up a home

of my own away from here, and looking after Martin myself,' she said to Helen. 'But of course it's impossible.' Frank's death had left her with nothing but the tiny widow's pension, and nowhere else to go. Then she sighed and remembered her blessings. 'It was very kind of them to take me in, though,' she said. 'What would I have done otherwise?'

'They would never have let you starve,' Helen said, and admitted, 'It is a comforting knowledge to have at the back of one's mind, should the worst happen.' She crossed her fingers as she said it, a childish habit that had come back since the war began. Even mentioning the possibility that something might happen to Jack required a propitiation of the Fates.

Maria pretended not to notice. She understood completely. 'I'm very grateful to them. I wouldn't want you to think otherwise.'

'I know,' said Helen. 'And at least you have some useful work to do.'

Maria had been accustomed to work before she married Frank, and could not bear to be idle. It had taken a great deal of persuasion to make Uncle Teddy accept her as his secretary, but his previous two had gone off to war and it was almost impossible to find a replacement. Now she worked every day in the steward's room, ordering his personal affairs and taking care of the estate accounts. Even though Teddy also had a land agent, a steward, and a commercial secretary, who worked from an office in York and took care of matters concerning the drapery business, there was plenty for Maria to do. The last two incumbents had left things in a mess. She was secretly pleased about that, because it made her indispensable to Uncle Teddy, and helped him forget that she was the wrong sex to be a secretary.

Just after Helen arrived, the household at Morland Place was depleted by the departure of Lennie Manning. He was an American cousin of the Morlands who had been convalescing at Morland Place from wounds taken at Gommecourt.

He had been pronounced fit for light duties at his last medical board, and now was recalled to barracks in Scarborough. Helen was sorry not to have had more time to get to know him, for he seemed a very nice fellow and a good conversationalist – something to be valued by a woman tied to the sofa by her advanced pregnancy. Lennie went off cheerfully, still limping slightly, but looking forward with a young man's enthusiasm to a life of activity and, he hoped, excitement and glory.

Uncle Teddy had said he reckoned Lennie would be passed fit enough to be sent out to France in the spring with the new drafts; an idea not wholly appealing to Polly. At sixteen she had enjoyed having a young man about the house, especially one who was an authentic hero (he had been given the Military Medal for his actions at Gommecourt); and most especially one who was in love with her. For the first few days, Helen was likely to have Polly flop down into a chair nearby at any time of the day and complain that she had nothing to *do*. The post-Christmas doldrums and Lennie's departure were compounded by the heavy weather, which made riding impossible. As her contribution to the household's welfare, Helen set herself to amuse Polly with conversation, cards and games, until the fit passed.

It didn't take long. Polly soon remembered that she had friends to visit, Red Cross classes to attend, and wounded officers at Heworth Park to read to. In addition she worked for a few hours each week in her father's drapery business in York, learning the ropes, for it was an empire that would one day be hers.

Then there was the ongoing duty of every young woman to cheer up officers home on leave from the Front, by chatting, dancing and, if necessary, flirting with them – and in a place like York, which had so many soldiers passing through all the time, it was a duty a conscientious girl never got to the end of.

So Polly vanished back into her own world, and Helen

sank into the pleasant lethargy of her advanced pregnancy, happy to sit with her feet up on a footstool and a dog or two dozing nearby, working her way through the general sewing-basket, and being visited by whichever member of the household happened to be passing. It was one of the strengths of Morland Place that there was always something going on, and one never wanted for company.

One of Maria's regular tasks was to sort through the post when it arrived in the morning. Before the war, in the days when a few letters and packages were all that could be expected, this had been the butler's job. But nowadays there was a whole bagful every morning, what with the expansion of Teddy's businesses, various war committees, and his involvement in the York Commercials regiment, not to mention the large number of adults living at Morland Place, all with their own correspondents. It would be Maria's business to deal with Teddy's personal and estate letters anyway, so she had suggested to Sawry that the bag might just as well come straight to her, and she would do the sorting. Sawry was happy to pass the duty to younger and more willing hands. With the last footman having left, and only untried boys to augment the female servants, he was having to do more and more about the house himself, and he was not getting any younger.

Therefore it was Maria who found the official call-up letter for Robert in the post one morning. Teddy was out about the estate, so she couldn't check with him, but she guessed from the envelope what it was, and handed it to Robbie at the breakfast table with some trepidation. She went on to give Henrietta a couple of letters and put one from Jack by Helen's plate – she was not down yet. By the time she had dropped a small heap of invitations by Polly, Robbie had got the envelope open and was making explosive noises.

The original Military Service Act had covered only single

men between the ages of nineteen and forty-one, but an amendment to the Act in May 1916 had extended it to married men. At the time, Robbie had assured his wife Ethel that married men would never be called up. In the earliest days there had been some sort of commitment – he was sure he remembered it – that no married man would be called before all the single men had been taken, and that day, he reasoned, would never come. Even if the war went on for years, there would be more boys all the time reaching the age of nineteen, and they would make up the numbers.

But now here it was in black and white. He was to report to the office of the local Training Reserve unit for a medical examination on Tuesday next, and if he was declared fit he could expect to be summoned on the first of the next month.

'This is ridiculous!' he exclaimed. 'It's outrageous! I'm a married man with four children. How can I possibly be expected to leave them and traipse off to France on a whim?'

'Not exactly a whim, dear,' Henrietta said anxiously.

'Well, *you* don't support this nonsense, do you?' he demanded angrily.

Henrietta looked unhappily out of her depth, and Maria stepped in. 'Jack's a married man,' she pointed out. 'Frank was a married man.'

'That's completely different. They were volunteers. And Frank was still single when he went in – he married you afterwards. It's a different matter *forcing* a married man with my responsibilities to abandon them willy-nilly just because – because—'

'There's a war on?' Polly said, without looking up from her letters.

'Oh dear,' Henrietta said, under her breath.

'You can appeal,' said Ethel, who had taken the letter from him. 'Look, it says here at the bottom where to write to.'

'Well, of course I shall appeal,' Robbie said.

'You must,' Ethel said, putting the letter down with an

air of determination. 'They promised they wouldn't take married men. *Promised.*'

'Besides, I can't be spared from work. We're short-handed already, and the girls they're taking on are no use at all. My work is of the first importance to the nation and I shall point that out to them in no uncertain terms.'

He and Ethel continued to mutter about the subject between themselves until Robbie eventually had to leave to go to work at his bank in York.

When Ethel also had left the table and Polly had gone off about her own business, Maria said, 'You know, I'm not sure there are any grounds for appeal. Banking is not a starred occupation.' For the sake of Henrietta's maternal pride, she did not add that Robbie was only a deputy branch manager.

Alice looked at Henrietta and said kindly, 'Perhaps he won't pass the medical examination.'

'He's very well,' Henrietta said.

'Oh, I didn't mean he should have anything serious,' Alice said. 'Just some minor fault or other, enough to keep him out. Flat feet, perhaps, or weak eyes, or bad teeth.' She dredged these up from conversations with friends.

Henrietta sighed. 'Robbie doesn't have flat feet. He reads without glasses. And all my children have excellent teeth.'

She got up and left the table, and went about her daily tasks, feeling wretched. She had no hope that Robbie would get out of it – as Maria had said, his was not a starred occupation. So she would have another son at the Front. Another soul to worry about, along with Jack and Bertie and Lennie. Frank was dead – the words even in her head made her ache, and unconsciously she put her hands to her chest as if to stop the pain leaking out. And it had been bad enough all this last autumn worrying about Jack, when the RFC was taking such heavy losses on the Somme. Five hundred and eighty airmen had been casualties: it sounded a small number against the thousands lost by the rest of the army, but as a proportion it was tragically high. In the spring it would start again, and she would have to wait day after passing day, never knowing when a telegram or a letter might come, as it had come for Frank; and before him, for Teddy's son Ned, dead at the battle of Loos. Sometimes she wondered how England could sustain the collective weight of fear and pain of all her women. She didn't want to add Robbie to the list of those she suffered for.

When Robbie came home that evening he had evidently spoken to someone during the day, and had finally accepted that his job would not excuse him from conscription. He was a little more subdued than he had been in the morning, but no less determined, especially with Ethel egging him on. He fulminated some more at the dinner table, and Ethel complained bitterly that she knew a lot of single men who hadn't gone – a *lot*! – and why didn't the government get after them, instead of persecuting honest fathers of four? What would become of her and her poor children if they tore Robbie away from her?

Teddy was not at the table, being a guest of the regiment that evening, so there was no-one to bring the pair to order. Henrietta sat in silent wretchedness, while Maria and Helen did their best to introduce other topics of conversation. When the meal reached its conclusion, Robbie flung down his napkin and said, 'I'm going to talk to Uncle Teddy when he gets back. I'm sure he can do something. He knows everyone. And don't tell me people of influence can't get their own people off. Lord Lambert's son hasn't gone!'

The party broke up. Maria caught Helen's eye and read the message in it; but she had already determined to do something. She slipped out under the general movement and, finding Robbie in the staircase hall, lighting up a cigarette, invited him to come to the steward's room for a moment, as there was something she wanted to say to him in private.

Robbie eyed her in surprise, but followed her. When he

had closed the door behind him, she turned to face him and said, 'I don't want you to ask Uncle Teddy to help you escape the call-up.'

He looked even more surprised. '*You* don't want? What the devil is it to do with you?'

'He was talking to me today about how difficult recruitment is, because even with conscription, so many people are appealing or just not turning up. The courts are clogged with prosecutions of people who haven't answered their call-up.'

'You can't equate *my* case with—' Robert began indignantly, but she carried on over him.

'Then there are the half-million or more who claim exemption, on top of one and a half million men already starred. The army simply can't get enough manpower. Numbers are always falling behind what the generals plan for.'

'I don't see what that's got to do with me.'

'Don't you? You're strong and healthy, and your job can be done by someone else. But you're still trying to get out of it.'

He coloured. 'I don't like that phrase, "get out of it". I'm willing to do my bit, like anyone else. I just don't see why I should go when so many single men haven't. And if Uncle Teddy can use his influence—'

'You can't ask him,' Maria interrupted. 'You mustn't! For God's sake, don't you see? He's lost Ned, but he never tried to stop Ned going. He was proud of him. And he loved Frank like his own son, but he never tried to stop Frank going. If you ask him, you're as good as telling him that they were fools for getting themselves killed. You can't do that.'

Robbie was silent, very red in the face, staring at her with new thoughts plainly going through his mind.

'Do you think your brothers were fools?' she asked him quietly.

'No,' he said. 'No, of course not. I just—'

It was Ethel, of course, terrified of losing him, who had stopped him seeing things as he should. Ethel was too completely a woman to see any side to war but the danger and death. But Maria had a man's mind, and understood the concept of honour.

Now Robbie began to think. Frank, little Frank, dead. Jack risking his life in those damn flimsy aeroplanes. Ned, who had grown up with them like another brother, dead, his body never found – probably never would be found, blown to bits by artillery shells.

Rob's children up in the nursery: what would he say to them in the future when they asked him why he wasn't a soldier like their uncles? Frank's fatherless boy – how would he explain to him? It was his duty to go, his duty to the children – yes, and to Ethel – and to the rest of his family. Better to die doing his duty than live to see them look at him askance, and be ashamed of him. Better death than dishonour.

Maria saw him straighten his shoulders, saw the heightened colour fade from his face, and knew she had prevailed. For a moment she thought of Frank, and wondered if she had signed his death-warrant. She was woman enough for that. But in wartime it was not possible to think like that. Or, if it was possible, it was simply not advisable.

'I won't appeal,' he said. 'It will be hard, leaving the children, but – I won't say anything to Uncle Teddy.'

'I'm sure you're doing the right thing,' said Maria.

They went back to the drawing-room, where he announced quietly that he would accept conscription. Ethel stared, then burst into tears and ran from the room. The others murmured their approval of his change of heart, and he bathed a few moments in the warmth of it, before going to find his wife.

She was in their room, sitting on the bed, weeping. She stood up when he came in, but anything she was planning to say died on her lips when she saw his face. There was no arguing with that expression; and while she passionately did not want him to go, she thought he had never looked so dignified or so handsome. A sort of acceptance came into her heart, cold and comfortless, and as inevitable as death.

He kissed her, wiped the tears gently from her face, and then, putting an arm round her waist, said, 'Come with me.'

'Where? Why?'

'You'll see.'

He led her to the nursery, where, in the dim glow from the night-light, they stood at the foot of each bed in turn, and looked for a long time at their sleeping children. Roberta, Jeremy, Harriet and baby John: so beautiful when they were asleep, so tender and helpless. He thought his heart would burst with his love for them: he could feel it like a physical pain in his chest.

'It's for them,' he whispered at last. 'Dear?'

He felt her nod. 'All right,' she said.

'It's worth it,' he said.

Not if you get killed, Ethel thought fiercely. But she said nothing, knowing it was pointless now.

At the end of December, Rasputin's battered body was found under the ice of the river Neva. Some days earlier he had been invited to spend the evening at the palace of Prince Felix Yussoupov. Yussoupov was a handsome young man, heir to the biggest fortune in Russia, and related by marriage to the Tsar. He was also completely dissolute, leading a life that was politely described as 'Bohemian' but which, according to the British Intelligence Service, embraced every debauchery. He and Rasputin were friends and shared drunken, drug-fuelled orgies. Rasputin loved rich people, particularly rich, immoral people; and Yussoupov, who was homosexual, seemed erotically infatuated with the *staritz*.

On the evening in question Yussoupov and Grand Duke Dmitri, the Tsar's cousin, gave Rasputin enough poison, so they said, to kill ten men. But the *staritz* shrugged it off;

so they shot him three times in the back; and then, when he still refused to die, they stabbed and clubbed him repeatedly, and finally threw him into the river.

The story was too good not to get out – and there were always enough drunken friends hanging around the palace, to say nothing of tattling servants, to make sure that it did. Besides, Yussoupov made no attempt to conceal it. He and Dmitri boasted about the plot both before and after the event. To anyone who asked, they gave a new version of the affair, each more lurid than the last. They even spread the story that the fingernails on the body were found to be broken from trying to claw through the ice, proving that he had still been alive when he was thrown into the river, despite the poisoning, shooting, stabbing and beating. They were popular heroes for killing the madman, so the harder he had been to kill, the more credit it was to them to have succeeded.

Thomas wondered often what had persuaded them to do it. In his many interviews, Yussoupov claimed it was pure patriotism on his part. Thomas knew something about him, and thought it was just as likely to have been a drugged fantasy, or the degenerate's perpetual search for ever more extreme thrills. He did not believe, as the peasantry seemed to, that Rasputin had been so difficult to kill: more likely Yussoupov and Dmitri had been too drunk and drugged to do it efficiently.

This view seemed to be borne out by the autopsy results, of which he obtained a copy from Intelligence. There was no sign of poisoning, the stabbings had been superficial, and the three shots in the back had caused only minor injury. However, the *staritz* had been dead when he went into the water, because he had also been shot once in the head, a shot that would have caused instant death.

This last piece of information caused Thomas much thought. The bullet recovered from the head, the report said, was of a different sort from the others – a kind only used in Webley revolvers. As Thomas knew well, the only people in Europe who used Webley revolvers were British Army officers.

He remembered Rayner saying to him, 'Rasputin must go,' and he wondered. A single shot to the head certainly looked more like a Secret Service killing; and a drunken orgy late at night would give all the cover needed for the deed. Furthermore, he recollected that Rayner had been at Oxford with Yussoupov. They knew each other very well.

Thomas put his wonderings aside, however, aware he would never know the truth of it, and accustomed now to the fact that nothing in Russia was ever quite what it seemed. Rasputin's body was buried quietly, early one morning, in a Petersburg cemetery – the Empress had wanted it returned to his native Siberia, but the prime minister had warned against any such public show of favour, in the current climate – while Yussoupov and Grand Duke Dmitri were banished from Petersburg.

Thomas suspected that the Tsar might have been glad to have the problem of Rasputin resolved; but Nicholas was certainly shocked by a blow so close to himself and his family. And Alexandra was prostrated with grief. Her belief in Rasputin had been complete, her trust in his judgement unquestioning: she had believed him a sincere friend in a world that was rapidly becoming more hostile. Now 'they' had killed him, and 'they' would surely come for her next. She was taking Veronal for her arthritis and migraines, narcotics to help her sleep, and drinking endless pots of strong coffee, which she believed was medicinal. The combination made her ever more nervous, tearful and depressed. In this atmosphere, the Tsar further delayed his return to Stavka, and Thomas, of course, remained at his side.

Gradually something of equilibrium returned. Nicholas and Alexandra seemed to retreat into the safety of their own secret world inside the private quarters of the West Wing: the world of Sunny and Nicky, devoted lovers, and their beloved children. It was a world of plain food and solid, middle-class comfort; a world of punctual meals, keeping diaries, knitting, card games and photograph albums; of family pets and family jokes; where even the servants addressed the family by name and patronymic – no 'highnesses' or 'majesties' – and everyone had his nickname.

In its way it was utterly beguiling, and Thomas, despite his knowledge of the world outside, felt its drowsy charm. The sitting-rooms, with their knick-knacks and family photographs and over-stuffed furniture, seemed to exist sealed off from time, unchanged since the 1880s. They might have been the rooms of an ordinary Edwardian English country gentleman – which was what, Thomas supposed wryly, Nicholas really wished he could have been. Seldom could an absolute ruler have demanded less from life: Heal's furniture, afternoon tea, and unquestioning obedience from his people.

As January turned into February, the Tsar still lingered at Tsarskoye Selo. In Petersburg there were strikes and riots. The food and fuel shortages caused by the war were compounded by the bitterest weather in memory: in the extreme cold, locomotive boilers burst and railway tracks were buried under huge snowdrifts, preventing the movement of vital supplies. Both in the cities and on the Front, men starved.

But the Duma reconvened, and its noisy debates were no more revolutionary than before. Rasputin's death seemed, to most of those in the upper circles, to have drawn a sting, and everyone hoped things would settle down again. Sir George Buchanan, the British ambassador, told Thomas that he believed there was no immediate danger. And Thomas wrote again to his mother that the situation seemed to be stabilising, and that the dread spectre of revolution seemed to have retreated a few paces.

CHAPTER THREE

At the end of January 1917, the Speaker's Conference, which had been in session since October 1916, published its recommendations for reform of the electoral system. The speed and secrecy with which it had done its work were proof of the importance, for the war had thrown up a dangerous anomaly. Britain had never had conscription before, relying on a volunteer army. But now that conscription had been brought in, it became apparent that many, if not most, of the men who were being sent to the Front did not have the vote. It was not acceptable to force men by law to go out and die for their country when they had no say in how the country was run.

The Speaker's Conference was also to consider how to tidy up various other problems in the franchise and voting systems. So an open letter had been sent to the Prime Minister before the conference began, urging that votes for women should be on the agenda. Since there were several staunch supporters of the female franchise among the members of the conference, Venetia and others like her, who had spent half a lifetime trying to further the cause, had some hope that this time things might be different.

'The war *has* made a difference,' her friend Millicent Fawcett had said to her, back in October. The two women were much of an age, and had been on many a march together. In 1901 they had travelled to South Africa as members of the commission of inquiry into the Boer women's camps, a strenuous trip that had confirmed to each the other's sterling qualities. 'Women have proved they can do the same work as men, in every field but the actual fighting. In fact, the war couldn't have been carried on without us.'

'You mean that we have shown we "deserve" the vote?' Venetia said.

'If you like to put it that way.'

'It's a point,' said Venetia. 'But here's another one: as long as there was a qualification for men before they could vote, women could be hidden away in it. But if *all* men have the vote, regardless of any qualification, simply by virtue of being born male, then it becomes starkly apparent that women are being denied purely on account of being born female.'

'Which is the case,' said Millicent.

'Yes, I know that, and you know it, but I don't think our lords and masters in Parliament assembled will care to have it put into those words. It's a logical monstrosity – an intolerable nonsense.'

'It always was, my dear,' said Millicent. 'But you have such a nice, lawyerly way of putting it, why don't you go and say it to Mr Asquith? You know he likes you.'

So Venetia had gone to see the Prime Minister at Downing Street, and put the point to Asquith, to which he had replied, 'I agree.'

Venetia felt as if she had pushed hard at an open door. He had always been an implacable opponent of the women's vote. 'You agree?'

'If it were not for the war,' he said, 'we might have left the whole election question alone, and I wish to God we could have. But as it is, since we *must* look at the soldiers' vote, the women's vote will have to be dealt with as well.'

She smiled slowly. 'My dear Mr Asquith, can you mean that you have changed your mind?'

He did not smile back. 'No, I still think the women's vote will be bad for the country; but I'm of the opinion that it cannot be resisted now, and a sensible man does not fight the inevitable.' He paused a moment, looking reflectively into the fire. 'You will remember as well as I do what a time we had between 1910 and 1914 with the militants. The last thing the country can bear is a resumption of that sort of thing while we're fighting a war.'

The militants hadn't gone away, only put their energies into war-work; but if universal male franchise were brought in with nothing for the women, Venetia could imagine the consequences.

After a moment Asquith looked up at her, a faint frown between his brows. 'Tell me, why do you *want* the vote?' His tone implied it was something a sensible women like her should avoid.

She selected her words carefully. 'When I was a young woman, fighting to be allowed to be a doctor,' she said, 'I could not see the point of the vote. I wasn't interested in it. Besides, I had to struggle with every fibre of my being to qualify as a doctor. Now I flatter myself that even my male colleagues recognise I am every bit as good a doctor as they.'

'Well, perhaps some do,' Asquith said drily.

Venetia smiled and went on. 'Women now face fewer difficulties in becoming doctors. But there are many other spheres in which they still may not even begin to use their abilities. I have come to see that if women are ever to be accepted as equals, it can't be fought out case by case. It has to begin with political equality. Without the vote, we are classed with the animals, not as human beings.'

He nodded thoughtfully. 'Well, you may tell your friends that the conference *will* be considering the woman question. And I hope,' he added, eyeing her cautiously again, 'that I shan't be badgered to death the whole time it is deliberating.'

'No, I promise you'll be left alone. After all, you have a war to run.'

In the event, Asquith had been ousted in December 1916, and Lloyd George was now prime minister. He was widely believed to support the cause, but Venetia did not trust him. Many times in the past she had been thwarted by him, when he had made large declarations of support, and then done nothing, or even voted against.

At the end of January 1917 Mrs Fawcett came to see Venetia with the first news of the conference's recommendations. She was pleased and excited. 'I think we really have done it this time, Venetia, my dear.'

'The conference has recommended votes for women?'

'Yes. Well, it's not everything we wanted, but it's a good start. They've recommended the vote for all men over twenty-one, or over nineteen if they're on active service. And for women, they've proposed the vote for ratepayers and the wives of ratepayers, with an age limit of either thirty or thirty-five.'

Venetia was taken aback. 'But that's absurd! Only property owners? And it's a ridiculously high age limit. That will eliminate half the female population.'

'Yes, I know,' Millicent said. 'And, of course, the reason they've put in limits is that they're afraid women voters will be the majority. But, Venetia, consider – this is something we *can* have. It's far, far better for us to support an incomplete measure that we *can* win than to stand out for a perfect measure that we have no chance of winning.'

'Oh, Milly,' Venetia said. 'I had such hopes this time. And the very women who most need the vote – working-class women – won't benefit at all.'

'But we must regard this as simply the first instalment,' she said firmly. 'Once the principle is established, it will be easier to secure the extension of the vote. If we hold out for a universal female franchise, we may end up with nothing.'

'Oh, I know you're right. And of course it's foolish to expect the men to give up their privileges all at once.'

Millicent leant forward. 'But don't be glum, my dear.

It's vitally important that we stand together on this – all the women's movements and all our leading women. It will greatly strengthen our case if I can assure Mr Lloyd George that, if a Bill is brought on these lines, it will receive unanimous support.'

'Provided the lower of the age limits is chosen,' Venetia added.

'Yes, of course. I shall put that in.'

'But will it go through, Milly?'

'Yes, I believe it will, if we all do our part. We must go round to every Member, the pros *and* the antis – make sure of the pros, and try to persuade the antis. If the Bill goes in with the Prime Minister's support it will certainly carry, but it's important that it should have the largest possible majority before it goes up to the Lords.'

'Yes, of course. That's where the real battle will lie.'

'And I hope we can count on your support, Venetia dear, to speak to as many of the peers as you can. The individual approach is so important.'

'I won't be able to give it a great deal of time,' Venetia began.

'I know you are busy,' Millicent said, 'but – not give time to the most important thing that has happened in our lives?'

'Of course, you're right,' Venetia said. 'I shall *make* time.'

Mrs Fawcett rose to go. 'The last barricades are going down. We have some hard work ahead of us, but this time we shall see victory!'

'What a warrior you are, Milly,' Venetia laughed. 'You make me ashamed. I shall help all I can: if we fail, it won't be for lack of my effort.'

'But don't I tell you? We shan't fail this time,' said Mrs Fawcett.

The Germans had ceased U-boat attacks on neutral and non-military craft in May 1915, after the sinking of the *Lusitania* – an act that had so inflamed American public opinion, the Germans had feared it might bring them into the war. But by the beginning of 1917 the war was going so badly for Germany that she decided to resume unrestricted U-boat attacks on the 1st of February, in the hope of wearing down the British, starving them out, or both.

Almost at once there were American losses, of goods and lives; and in England the price of wheat and beef – the majority of which was imported – began to climb steeply.

At Morland Place Helen's second baby was born without any untoward incident. Dr Hasty looked in, but Nanny Emma and Henrietta did most of the work, and Helen was happy to put herself in their experienced hands. The baby was a girl, rather small, but perfectly formed. Nanny Emma immediately pronounced that she would be a beauty, and was shocked that Helen laughed and said she was 'Rather squashed, poor thing, but can only improve.' To Nanny Emma, all babies were beautiful – and all mothers ought to think so.

Henrietta was inclined to be tearful, in a happy way. It was a particular delight to have Jack's child born here, where she herself had been born. Teddy had the house bell rung for the newcomer – 'She's a Morland by blood if not by name!' – and regretted they did not have a resident chaplain so that she could be baptised at once in the chapel.

'What *are* you going to call her?' Polly asked. She had been out riding and had come to see Helen on her return, bringing a bunch of the first snowdrops, which she had found under the birch trees up by the Monument, a folly built by a previous Morland. Helen put them to her nose and savoured the faint, sweet scent, and admired their hopeful green flèches – green against white, symbol of spring breaking through winter.

'Jack and I talked about it when he was home. We decided if it was a girl, she should be Barbara.'

Polly considered, and found she had no associations whatever with the name. 'Oh, that's nice,' she said vaguely. Then,

'I suppose it goes with Basil. I say, do you think Jack will get leave because of it?'

But he didn't. Matters were at a critical point out there, the RFC was desperately short of men, and he couldn't be spared. He wrote of his joy, sent his blessings, and said that he hoped to have a few days at home in some weeks' time.

The birth weariness passed, and Helen was soon feeling well enough to balk against the convention that kept her in bed. Nanny Emma was adamant that if she got up too soon her insides would slip. 'Moi old ma knew a woman that got up too soon to goo out an' feed the hins, an' all her insoids slipped down to the bottom of her stummick. She never could sit down again! Had to eat her dinner kneelin' down, loik she was a-prayin'.'

In the face of such dire warnings, Helen remained in bed but begged the household members to come and talk to her as often as possible. Maria was good company, and came when she could spare the time from her office work. She told Helen that the new baby was queen of the nursery. 'She's quite supplanted my poor Martin,' she said. 'Nanny Emma's got no time for him now – and as for Ethel's little John, he might not exist.'

'Oh dear, I hope I'm not causing a disruption.'

'Nanny Emma loves a new baby, that's all. Martin and John are too old to enchant any more,' said Maria. 'The trouble is that the nursery-maids feel the same. They almost fight over Barbara when Nanny's out of the room.'

'How is Basil?' Helen had only seen him for a few moments: brought in to visit her, he had stared at her – unfamiliar in the high, white bed – then turned his face away.

'Oh, he's surviving. He's still something of a novelty to the girls, so he isn't quite so neglected as the others.'

The effect of this neglect revealed itself before Helen was out of bed: six-year-old James, who was already too much for the girls to handle, used the opportunity to get himself into trouble. On the first occasion he only got into a pantry, ate a jar of gooseberry jam followed by a jar of pickled onions, and made himself sick. On the second he tried to investigate a chimney in one of the empty guest rooms, and caused a soot fall, with unpleasant consequences to himself as well as the housemaids.

'He has an enquiring mind,' Teddy defended his son to Henrietta. 'And what do we keep a pack of women in the house for, if not to clean up?'

'I'm not complaining about the mess,' Henrietta said patiently, 'but you know he swallowed a lot of soot. It can't be good for him.'

'Boys swallow a lot of everything before they grow up,' said Teddy, blithely. 'It never hurts 'em. Soot, mud, grass – I once swallowed five tadpoles because Georgie dared me! Boys have iron stomachs. Snips and snails and puppy-dog tails, you know, Hen!'

He was less sanguine about the third incident. James managed to get out of the postern – the rear door, which was at the foot of the nursery stair. He went across the drawbridge, slipped on the ice at the end of it and went up to his waist in the moat. It brought him howling back into the house, where he was chafed, changed and chastened, and had slaps and hot soup administered by Nanny Emma, who pronounced him none the worse for his adventure.

But Teddy was shaken. 'He might have drowned. Supposing he'd fallen right in and couldn't pull himself out?'

He still sometimes had *that* dream about the *Titanic*, where he was in a boat among the frozen dead, floating in their life-jackets, their faces and eyes white with frost, rime thick in their hair . . . They hadn't drowned, those fifteen hundred victims. He could never wholly forget, and his dreams took him back all too often.

On the back of fear rode anger. 'How could the maids let him out of their sight? What the dickens do I pay them for?'

59

Helen was downstairs by this time, and felt her part in the débâcle. 'I'm afraid I've disrupted everything by coming here, and giving your girls two extra charges.'

'Nonsense, m'dear,' Teddy said, taken aback. 'I didn't mean to pass blame on *you*!' He changed tack. 'It would never have happened if someone hadn't left the postern unbolted. It's *always* kept bolted. The boy couldn't have reached the bolt so he wouldn't have got out. Someone will pay for this carelessness.'

But Ethel joined in the debate. She had been rather fretful since Robert left. Though he was only at the training camp at Ripon, she was anxious in anticipation of his going somewhere more dangerous. Besides, she missed him. No-one but him had ever much consulted her opinion or considered her requirements, and she felt her loss of consequence in the household. So she said, more sharply than she might otherwise have done, 'The fact of the matter is that James is too big for the nursery. The maids can't control him any more.'

Teddy said. 'If they did their job properly there'd be no difficulty.'

'But, Uncle, with Helen's two, there are eight of them now,' Ethel said. 'And you haven't taken on any more nursery-maids.'

'Well, that's easily remedied,' Teddy began.

Henrietta winced, and murmured, 'Not *easily*.' It was so hard to find the right sort of girl, these days.

Ethel was not to be distracted. 'James ought to go to school.'

Teddy looked surprised. 'Nonsense, he's only a little fellow.'

'He's six years old,' Ethel pointed out remorselessly. 'He ought to be doing his letters. I try to teach him when I teach Roberta hers, but he doesn't heed me.'

Maria asked, 'Where do you usually send boys? Is there a school nearby?'

'There's St Edward's down by the south road,' Henrietta answered her.

'But Morland boys don't go to school,' Teddy said. 'They have a tutor at home.'

'Well, if he doesn't do one or the other, he'll soon be quite out of control,' Ethel said. '*I* can't do anything with him.'

Henrietta said, 'I hadn't thought about it, but of course he's ready for a tutor, Teddy dear. And little Jeremy will be five this year.'

Polly brightened. 'Perhaps you ought to look for a nice young man, Daddy, to come and teach them.'

'All the young men are being called up,' Maria pointed out.

'Why not an older man?' Helen said. 'Wisdom and experience, that sort of thing?'

'James is a lively, spirited boy,' Teddy said. 'He needs a man in the vigour of life, not some doddering greybeard. I know my son, and he wouldn't respect a man who couldn't keep up with him.'

'It seems like an impasse,' Helen said. 'If he's young enough to suit you, Uncle, he'll be young enough to suit the conscription board.'

'Perhaps,' said Maria, tentatively, 'you could find someone with some slight defect, who's been rejected for military service.'

Teddy frowned at the thought of having someone less than perfect for his boy; and then he brightened. 'Or someone wounded. A soldier hero would be just the thing, as long as his wound wasn't disabling. A lost finger or something of that sort would do. It would be good for the boys to have someone who'd been to war to look up to.'

Henrietta said. 'But, Teddy, the tutor at Morland Place has always been in orders, and acted as chaplain as well.'

'Well, that's all right. I'd be happy with a cleric.'

'Oh, it would be nice to have services in the chapel again,' Henrietta said. 'I remember when Mama was alive . . .'

'All right,' said Teddy. 'Leave it to me,' he concluded. 'I'll make enquiries and see what comes up. I'm sure we can find the right sort of person, with a little luck. It may take a while . . .'

'Not too long, I hope,' Ethel said. 'The next thing you know, James will start leading my Jeremy astray.'

Teddy bristled at this idea, and said no more. Helen, seeing his annoyance, changed the subject by asking Polly what she had been up to that day, at the same time as Alice began talking to Henrietta about the very dull doings of her friend Mrs Winnington, so the moment passed.

Teddy would have been in no great hurry to find a priest, had it not been for Ethel's urging. He had quite enough to do without adding to his work. The nursery suite, of day nursery, night nursery and schoolroom, was tucked away at the back on the upper floor, so the children of the house were normally well out of the way and no trouble to the master. As for James running wild, now the fright of the moat incident had dissipated, he felt that a little of *that* did a lad no harm. It was only because he had been confined to the house so much lately that he had got into mischief. Once the good weather came he would be out and about the estate all day. To learn its ways and get to know his own people were the essentials for a future Master of Morland Place. Formal education came a long way behind. When the war was over, Teddy thought vaguely, and things settled down, that would be time enough to start the boy cramming under a tutor. He didn't want his son's spirit crabbed by too much frowsting over books.

But once the idea had been planted in Ethel's mind, it flourished there. It was so redolent of the Great House to have a chaplain-tutor – so much more distinguished than sending the boys to a local school. Besides, you never knew *what* they might pick up there, mixing every day with God-knew-who: a bad accent, or bad opinions. Suppose they were exposed to conscientious objectors, or even *socialists*? So every time she saw Teddy she asked if he had found anyone yet, and the easy option of forgetting was denied him.

As in many things, he turned first to his old friend Colonel Bassett, with whom he had been responsible for setting up the local Pals battalion, the York Commercials. Old 'Hound' Bassett knew just about everyone, and Teddy had a good opinion of his common sense. The Hound in turn made enquiries of *his* old friend, Colonel Gresham, whose family Henrietta and Jessie had visited when they stayed in Scarborough at the beginning of the war. Gresham's son Erskine was serving with the Green Howards, and through him, Teddy was made aware of a young man who had been an army chaplain in the same regiment.

'I think he may be just what you're looking for,' said the Hound. 'He's young, but not too young – thirty or thereabouts. Comes from a good family, good academic record at Cambridge and so on, but best of all, he's had a first-rate war. Volunteered right at the beginning, back in 1914. Since then he's seen bags of action, twice been mentioned in despatches. Doesn't hang about safely behind the lines, y'see, but always goes right into the trenches with the men. Young Gresham says his colonel thought the world of him, and so did the men.'

'How come he's not still in uniform?' Teddy asked.

'Poor feller caught a packet at Serre. He was with his battalion in the line when a shell fell into the trench. Dug-out collapsed and he was buried. Battle going on, of course, so it was hours before he was rescued. Physical injuries not too severe – broken arm, I believe, collar-bone, ribs, that sort of tackle. But that wasn't all. He was buried alive, y'see, shells exploding, terrible noises all round, not knowing if anyone knew he was there. His nerves were affected so much he was invalided out. Ha-hmph.' Straying into these grounds unsettled Bassett, who cleared his throat and then blew his nose. 'Shell-shock is what they call it, I understand. Not his fault – no blame attaches to him at all. Lot of first-rate chaps getting it, these days.'

But would he be safe with the children? Teddy wanted to know. He wouldn't suddenly go off his chump and run amok?

'Good God, no,' Bassett said, looking rather shocked. 'He's not doo-lally or anything of that sort. Just a bit on the nervous side. Starts at loud noises. Occasional nightmare, that sort of thing.'

Teddy could not argue with nightmares.

'Army's all washed up for him now,' Hound went on, 'and a parish is out of the question at present. Doesn't want to give up orders, so he's thinking of teaching. But Colonel Gresham says the MO thinks a school might be too much of a strain. Too much hurly-burly. What he needs is a quiet billet, good food, country air and so forth. Females around to pet him. Build him up, so to speak. As for the rest, he's just the sort to give young boys the right ideas. Excellent war record, brave as a lion.' He paused for thought, and added, 'Mrs Gresham's met him, and says he's a very nice boy. Had him to tea, apparently.'

This final accolade tipped the balance. Teddy interviewed the young man, and without further delay engaged Denis Palgrave on a month's trial. He had very little to pack and no arrangements to make, so it was all decided very quickly, and there was nothing more to do but for Henrietta to take off the dust sheets in the priest's room, have a fire lit, air the mattress and make up the bed.

'The room hasn't been used for such a long time,' she said. 'It smells a little musty to me. I hope he won't mind.'

'He's been in the army, my dear, and at the Front,' Teddy said. 'He'll have been used to a lot more hardship than a bit of damp.'

'I hope he won't have lice,' Ethel said, half pleased with the fact of a tutor coming, half annoyed that she had not been involved in the selection.

'Good Lord, no,' said Teddy. 'He's been back from France six months. What can you be thinking about?'

The next day Palgrave arrived in a taxicab from the station, with all his worldly possessions in a carpet bag and a small valise. He had dark hair and a very pale face – his soldier's tan had worn away in hospital – and was rather on the thin side, hollow of cheek, but otherwise there was nothing to suggest there was anything wrong with him. Henrietta liked him at once. He had a quiet voice and a gentle air, but there was a soldier's directness in his gaze and a firmness to his mouth. He thanked her for taking him in, shaking her hand and smiling into her eyes, so that before she knew where she was, she found herself mentally vowing to feed him up, and to get that shirt away from him so that she could mend the frayed collar.

He praised the priest's room and said he hadn't had anywhere so commodious to live since he had left his father's house. He admired the schoolroom, and if he looked a little doubtfully at some of the books, Teddy soon assured him that whatever he needed to teach James and Jeremy, he should have. And he was struck to silent awe at the beauty and antiquity of the chapel. 'I had no idea it would be like this,' he said to Henrietta, who was showing it to him. 'How old is it?'

'The same age as the house, which was built in 1450. The date is carved over the main house door.'

'Nearly five hundred years,' he breathed reverently, his eyes roving over the details of the architecture.

'The statue of Our Lady over there is said to be even older,' Henrietta said, pleased with his appreciation. 'There's a legend that if something bad is coming to the house, she weeps real tears.'

'I expect there are lots of stories about a house this old,' he said.

'Oh, yes, and—' She was about to add, *and there are lots of ghosts, too*, when she remembered his shell-shock, and that he was subject to nightmares. Better not mention the ghosts just yet, she thought.

He was taken to meet his future charges, and Henrietta was pleased to see that he genuinely seemed to like children. He had an easy manner, and was soon squatting among them while Roberta and Jeremy competed for his attention, and two-year-old Harriet tried to climb onto his knee. James held a little aloof at first, with *I don't need a tutor* writ large on his face, but as heir to Morland Place he could not tolerate the others hogging the new man's attention, and soon he was to the fore, asking Palgrave about the trenches and his adventures.

At dinner that evening he seemed rather tired, which Henrietta thought not surprising, given how many strange faces there were around the table. She hoped it would not be too much of a strain on his nerves: it occurred to her it was not exactly the 'quiet billet' that Teddy had said he was seeking.

Ethel wanted to talk about Robbie and her children, and also to probe his genealogy: Palgrave was a good name and she wanted to know if he was one of the Suffolk Palgraves, in case he had any influential or titled relatives. Henrietta and Alice were more restful dinner companions, merely smiling and exuding goodwill, and Helen thought the best she could do for him was to emulate them: the crowd in the dining-room would be bewildering for anyone, let alone a man with shattered nerves. But Maria started talking about books, and he responded so eagerly and with such erudition she found she could not stay out of the ensuing conversation for long.

It did at least have the benefit of deflecting Polly, who had been ready to be smitten by him, given that he was young, handsome, and had been at the Front. She had only wanted encouragement from him to begin a crush; but she had nothing to say on this particular subject, so she left him alone for the present and talked about horses with her father instead.

The following morning when Henrietta came downstairs, early as usual, she saw the chapel door was ajar and smelt the pungent-sweet odour of freshly lit candles. Going to the door, she saw Father Palgrave in his cassock kneeling before the altar, on which the candles were burning and the altar-furniture was laid out. The sight warmed her heart, and she stepped quietly forward through the door. She was sure she had made no sound, but he turned his head and saw her, and smiled a welcome. No arrangements had yet been made about what services he would hold, and when, but he invited her with a look to join him, and together they made his first celebration of his new cure. For Henrietta it was like a balm being laid over a hurt she had forgotten she had. She was sure this young man had come to them by more than chance.

And afterwards it occurred to her happily that now they could have a proper christening for little Barbara, as soon as Jack had leave.

It was from Arthur Bigge, Lord Stamfordham, that Venetia learnt about the telegram that later became known as the Zimmerman Note. Stamfordham was almost her exact contemporary, but as the son of a Northumberland clergy-man he had been far below her circle in their respective youths. They had got to know each other when he became assistant private secretary to Queen Victoria, in the days when Venetia's late husband had been an equerry. Through the years of their various Court service, their friendship had ripened, and lately they had been drawn closer by sadness – his only son John had been killed in action in 1915, and Venetia's husband had been lost at sea in 1916, when his ship hit an enemy mine.

It had become his pleasant habit to drop in on her when-ever his duties allowed, and towards the end of February he brought her the extraordinary story of the German foreign secretary's telegram. Arthur Zimmerman had cabled the German ambassador in Mexico, Heinrich von Eckardt, instructing him to propose an alliance between Mexico and Germany. If Mexico would declare war on the United States, Germany would give her money and support, and would guarantee the return of the territories in New Mexico, Texas and Arizona that the USA had seized in the Mexican War.

The idea, of course, was to keep the Americans so busy on their own border that they would not have the time or energy to join the war against Germany.

This explosive suggestion had been routed to von Eckardt via the German ambassador in Washington.

'But how did we get hold of it?' Venetia asked, pouring more tea.

Stamfordham chuckled. 'You know, of course, that since we cut the Germans' transatlantic cable, the Americans have been allowing them to use theirs?'

'And a damned disgrace it is,' Venetia said. 'How long can we tolerate the United States' so-called neutrality?'

'We may not have to much longer, I suspect,' Stamfordham said, amused at her passion. 'What Germany didn't know, because America didn't tell them, is that there is a relay station in the cable at Land's End to boost the signal – I think that is the correct expression – for the long leg across the Atlantic. And what America didn't know, because *we* didn't tell *them*, is that we have been intercepting the messages going through it.'

'Arthur, how delightfully underhand!' Venetia said. 'Have a macaroon.'

'Neutrality can only be taken so far,' Stamfordham acknowledged, selecting one. 'The Americans should never have allowed the telegram to pass. Their agreement with the Germans was that the route should be used only in relation to a search for peace terms, which would automatically entail that any cables sent through it should be *en clair*. But Zimmerman's telegram was in cipher.'

'Indeed? Then how do we know what it said?'

'Because it was in a code that our chaps in Room Forty at the Admiralty cracked some time ago. Of course, we can't let the Germans know that, or they'll change the code. And, for obvious reasons, we can't let the Americans know we're monitoring their cable, either. So we had to make up a story about how we got hold of it: that the telegram was deciphered by the Mexican embassy, and then both copies were stolen or lost.'

'That'll be easy enough to believe. I imagine things are pretty chaotic down there.'

'At any rate, we hope the whole matter is incendiary enough to bring the United States into the war.'

'I should hope so, indeed. They'll be furious that the Germans used their embassy in Washington to relay the thing.'

'Quite. And American public opinion is very anti-Mexican at the moment, with all those cross-border raids, so there'll be plenty of spleen to work on. Venetia, my dear, your cook makes the best macaroons in London.'

'Thank you, Arthur. Do have another. They were Overton's favourite, and Mrs Cannon keeps making them – out of habit, I suppose, because I can't possibly eat all she makes.'

Stamfordham took another, and went on, 'The other inflaming circumstance is that the telegram makes specific mention of the resumption of unrestricted submarine warfare.'

'Tactless,' Venetia commented.

'The last paragraph suggests that the ruthless employment of German submarines will compel England to make peace in a few months,' said Stamfordham. 'Those are the actual words – "ruthless employment". Our American cousins won't like that, not after *Lusitania*.'

'So what happens now?'

'Room Forty sent it to Walter Page at the American embassy – unofficially, just to prime the pump. Of course, Page wanted to believe it was a forgery by our intelligence wallahs, because the whole thing will be so embarrassing to Washington. But having given him just enough time to digest it, Balfour, as Foreign Secretary, requested an official meeting with him – which happened yesterday – and gave him the text in cipher, in German, and in the English translation. He gave our concocted story of how we came by it, and invited Page to check the telegraph office records for the date in question – because, of course, the German embassy in Washington sent it to Mexico by public telegraph. That gave independent confirmation. So now Page has reported the whole thing to President Wilson, and we shall see what we shall see.'

'They can't ignore it, can they?' Venetia asked anxiously.

'Not with the U-boats attacking shipping in the Atlantic as we speak,' Stamfordham said. 'The question is, how much help will the Americans be when they do come in?'

'What do you mean? Their resources are huge,' Venetia said. 'In manpower alone—'

'Ah, yes,' he said, 'but how much of it will they commit? Unless they are wholeheartedly determined to beat the Germans, it could amount to nothing more than a token gesture. As I see it, it's a race between American shipping losses sufficiently inflaming the Americans, and our shipping losses crippling us.'

'*We* will never make peace,' Venetia said, 'no matter what the German foreign secretary thinks.'

'Dear Venetia,' Stamfordham smiled, 'what a rock you are! Tell me about your ambulance scheme. Is it going well?'

'So well that I'm taking on more staff,' Venetia said. 'Thanks in part to you, Arthur – your idea of giving the ambulances popular names and inviting everyone of that name to contribute is really capturing the public imagination. I have a Margaret almost fully subscribed now, and a Hilda and an Edith well on their way.'

'I'm glad to have helped,' he said. 'When does the good ship Peggy slip her moorings?'

'Next month. I shall probably go over to Paris and have a launching ceremony of some kind – *pour encourager les autres*, you know. Besides, the illustrated papers like that sort of thing, and it will be useful publicity.' A thought struck her. 'Arthur, do you think you could persuade His Majesty to do something for us when he next visits the Front? Shake some hands, have his photograph taken with one of our ambulances, something of that sort?'

Stamfordham considered. 'I don't see anything against it. I could mention it to him, and if he seems agreeable we could see whether we could work it into the schedule.'

'Would you? It would do us so much good with the middling sort. They do so love the royal touch.'

'Presumably the date of your launching ceremony can be adapted to fit in with HM's diary?'

'Oh, nothing is fixed yet. It can be at any time that is convenient to you.'

'Then I shall certainly see what may be done.'

One morning in late February Bertie was leading a patrol to investigate what had seemed over the last few days to be unusual activities behind the German line. The Germans had been firing off a lot of shells by day, more than their routine 'hate'. Their snipers had been extremely active, too, breaking the unwritten rules that had evolved over the winter, that the carriers bringing food to the trenches should not be attacked, and that latrines were sacrosanct. Bertie had lost several good men. Besides, knowing that one might be picked off while answering Nature's call was very demoralising all round.

Such an increase in busyness might simply be the outward and visible sign of a visit by top brass, who tended to object to the cosy understandings that developed between enemies facing each other for any length of time. But there had been a lot of transport coming and going behind the German trenches, too, and the Hun scout aeroplanes had been aggressively determined to stop the RFC flying over to take a look, on those few occasions when weather permitted the kites to get up.

Then, last night, after a frenzied bout of artillery practice, it had all gone quiet, except for some rifle fire, which, to Bertie's experienced senses, did not seem quite right. 'It's too regular, and it seems to be coming from only a few places,' he told Fenniman. 'I think it's decoy fire, meant to give us the impression that all is as usual.'

'I agree,' said Fenniman. 'But with the flying patrols grounded, the only way to find out is to go over there on foot.'

Bertie grinned at his friend. 'I suppose this is the point where I "volunteer", is it?'

'I *could* send someone more junior,' Fenniman said. 'A patrol like that is a captain's command, but all our captains are still wet behind the ears. It needs someone with enough experience to make deductions from the evidence. And to know what to do in an emergency – because there's no knowing what may happen.'

'I can't tell you how much that reassures me,' Bertie said.

'Don't take any unnecessary risks,' Fenniman said, 'but find out everything you can. It takes maturity of judgement to carry out orders like that.'

'Unprincipled flattery,' Bertie said, and went off to pick his men.

So, in the darkest of the early hours he set off with a dozen men to creep down the observation trench. This was one that, over time, they had sapped out into no man's land to where a clump of willows grew beside what had once been a small stream, a tributary of the Ancre. The ground there was very wet, and the trench was unpleasantly boggy, sometimes flooded, but the willows, though they had been blasted down to stumps, gave just a little cover to men wriggling out of them, and it was a short crawl from there to the remains of a hedgerow that ran along the top of a sunken lane. The Germans had known about the route for a while, and there was always danger from snipers there, which was why it was best to use it at the darkest of times. On this night the moon was two hours off rising and, with the sky overcast, there was not even a glimmer of starlight to expose them.

The end of the trench was filled with a foot of wet slush, but the ground underneath it was still frozen enough to make a firm bottom. Bertie halted his men and listened in tense silence. It was not the sort of clear night that carried sound well but, even so, from out here he should have been able to hear something from the German line. The silence was absolute. He signalled to the man behind him, waited while the sign was passed silently back, and then pulled himself up by the willow stumps, sliding out on his stomach onto the cold ground. He listened again, then got up and dashed in a crouch across the open ground to the shelter of the hedge. That was the most dangerous part, but there was no alarm, no sniper shot, no brattle of machine-gun woken from its doze. Once into the sunken lane, there was cover and a degree of safety.

Slowly the patrol made its way towards the German line, in a crablike progress, across and forward and across again, making use of the natural features of the terrain and various shell holes for cover. The Germans had been investing a ruined village, where there had been vicious fighting on the 1st of July last year and all through the autumn. The British had never managed to dislodge them, and apart from the area immediately in front of the British line, it had not been possible to retrieve the dead from the many attacks. So as they neared the village they had ghastly company. In places the dead lay so thickly it was not possible to avoid treading on them; but all of them were used by now to crawling over corpses while out on patrol. It was the severed body parts Bertie liked least: there was something gruesome about a leg still in its trouser, puttee and boot, or a uniform sleeve with a hand protruding from it – always with the fingers slightly curled as if grasping after the life that had been snatched away. Entire corpses troubled him less. They called them the quiet soldiers; and they gave cover. Almost, they were friends.

As they neared the edge of the village, still unchallenged, they were crossing ground no patrols had covered before, as he knew when he began to discover corpses with their identity discs still in place. He stopped the patrol again to listen, but all up ahead was silent. The lightest breeze had got up, blowing from the German line towards them, and it brought no sound but the faint whisper of the barbed wire. It was thinning the clouds, however, revealing a pinprick star here and there, which would make them more visible. He had to decide now whether to go on or not, whether it was the 'unnecessary risk' that Fenniman had warned against. As he debated inwardly, he heard an owl call 'kee-wick, kee-wick' from somewhere in the village; but there was not another sound. He began to feel very strongly that the place was deserted. It was not possible for hundreds of soldiers to make no noise at all. The owl called again, from a little nearer. It seemed a friendly sound, reassuring.

He rose cautiously to a crouch, and employed his field-glasses, but they revealed no movement, no smoke, no light anywhere. He signalled to his men, and carefully at first, then with increasing confidence they crossed the last open ground towards the ruined village. The men spread out in line, guns at the ready, but there was no challenge, and soon they were climbing over the heaps of rubble and burnt timbers that were all that was left of the village. The Germans had gone.

They picked their way through, examining the evidence the enemy had left behind, of their machine-gun posts, their dug-outs, their command rooms; the places they had had their food and ammunition dumps; their sniper positions; the roads that had been cleared leading to the rear. The men were fascinated by this glimpse into the life of the faceless enemy they had stood opposite for so many weeks. Even their rubbish was interesting, and what they had left behind was eagerly gathered up for souvenirs and trophies to show to their mates back in the line. A German helmet with a shrapnel hole in it; a broken bayonet blade; a uniform button, a shoulder flash, a spent cartridge. But there were richer pickings: unopened tins of food, half a packet of cigarettes, magazines (in German, of course, but one could always look at the pictures), furniture and ornaments and bits of kit. In one dug-out Cooper found a whisky bottle a quarter full and a bag of oranges somehow forgotten; in another a pound of candles. Oliphant found a cigarette lighter; Kittery a clock. Neither worked, but they might be mended, mightn't they? Baxter found a shaving-mug with a regimental badge on it. Hodges found an ashtray made from a shell case and a photograph in a leather frame of an elderly couple.

They wandered, upright and untroubled now, through the deserted village as the moon rose, picking over the remains of an occupying army and, beneath them, of the native people before them, who had been displaced by the war. In the ruins of someone's sitting-room Bertie found a whole shelf of books, and made himself leave them; and he told Maxwell to put down a brass scuttle half full of coal. In the wavering moonlight the scene had an enchanted look to it, as though it had been frozen and might come to life again. But there was no sound or movement other than their own, and they saw no living thing except a couple of cats, wary and keeping their distance, and once a rat, coming out of the rubble and sitting up for a moment on a jutting end of a beam, scenting the air, before it whisked away into hiding again.

It was time to go back. Bertie made them spread out in a line across and collect any tags they found on the bodies. If they could relieve the mystery for even a dozen mourning families, it was worth doing. He thought of Ned, whose body had never been found because the place where he fell

75

had been overrun by the Germans. Probably they would never know what had happened to him. So many bodies were simply missing, either blasted into unidentifiable fragments by artillery, or so trampled into the mud by the passage and repassage of armies that they were buried too deep ever to be found again. Jessie would never know how she had become a widow. He thought with sharp pain for a moment of Jessie, then turned his mind resolutely away. They reached the willows again, dropped back into the trench, somewhat hampered in some cases by their booty – he had not been able to prevent all the unsuitable foragings – and trotted back to the line.

'They gorn! Ole Jerry's gorn!' Huckstable shouted, as soon as he reached the front-line trench. 'Look at this, wot I got!' He waved a walking-stick and a battered pewter tankard in one hand, and slapped the damaged helmet on top of his own with the other, grinning wildly as face after face popped up and out and round the corners with wide eyes and open mouths to hear the news. The rest of the patrol crowded in, and Huckstable actually capered in his delight at being the first with the news. 'They've bleedin' gorn!'

The news was passed by more official methods to Headquarters, and the next day the RFC was able to put up some scouts to verify that the Germans had not only abandoned the village but had moved back more than eight miles.

As the days passed, more reports came in and, collated with the RFC observations, they began to show that something extremely serious had been going on all through the winter. The 'unusual activity' in the rear, which the scout pilots had noticed as far back as October, was now explained. The Germans were retreating to a new line, between six and thirty miles to the east, cutting off a huge salient. This shortened the line they had to hold, and allowed them to concentrate their men, which would go some way to solving the problem of manpower shortage resulting from their losses on the Somme and the Ancre last autumn. It was a superb tactical move, consolidating and strengthening their position, for the loss only of a salient of territory that would have proved harder and harder to defend once the campaigning season opened fully.

And they had had all winter undisturbed to dig trenches on their new front line – the sort of deep, well-fortified, comfortable trenches the Germans liked. The impregnable sort. It was a terrible blow. The campaign on the Somme had seriously weakened the Germans and destroyed many of their positions. The British had flattened their defences, driven them out from their comfortable bunkers and into temporary trenches, forced them onto the back foot and made them defend a wide, loose and vulnerable line. Haig's army had spent the whole autumn, and a torrent of blood, softening the enemy up for the fatal blow. Now what they had achieved in those six months in Picardy had been snatched away, as lightly as the wind scattering chaff. They had thought they would break through this spring and have the Germans on the run. Now they had to start all over again. Bertie had difficulty in hiding from his men his depression at the thought.

CHAPTER FOUR

At the end of February the Tsar received a telegram from his staff at the Front requesting his urgent return to Stavka. He showed it to Thomas. 'Now, what do you suppose it can be that requires my urgent personal attention?'

'Perhaps with the loss of morale among the troops, your presence is needed to rally them,' Thomas began, but stopped abruptly when he saw the tell-tale crease appear between Nicholas's brows.

'Russian soldiers are the bravest and best in the world. There is no loss of morale in *my* army. If you cannot speak to more purpose than that, Lord Overton, you had better not speak at all.'

'I beg your pardon, sir,' Thomas said, with suitable abjectness. 'I spoke without thinking.'

'So it seems.'

He seemed to want another answer, so Thomas tried him with: 'I imagine your presence is being sought because there are matters of strategy that only the Tsar can decide.'

'That seems quite likely,' Nicholas said, his frown disappearing. 'I think we had better go. We shall leave tomorrow.'

The news did not please the Empress. Thomas saw her already pale face whiten further when the Tsar told her. 'Cannot you possibly stay with us?' she asked him, in a low but urgent voice. 'Nicky, I do not think you should leave us at such a time as this.' There were riots in the city, and assassination rumours stalked the palace corridors.

'No, I must go,' he said airily, and Thomas saw that he had grown just a little bored with the soft female life at Tsarskoye Selo, and wanted a taste of the masculine grittiness of Stavka and soldiering again. But then, always sensitive to his wife's moods, he put on a show of reluctance, and added, with a rueful shake of the head, 'I can't think what it is that requires my presence, but it seems they can't decide anything without me. I'm sorry, my love.'

'You must do your duty, of course,' she said stiffly.

Now that he had had time to think, Thomas suspected that the ministers and generals were trying to get the Emperor away from his wife, because he was always more malleable and open to argument out of her company. It was certainly what Sir George Buchanan thought, as he said plainly when Thomas went into Petersburg to make his adieux later that morning.

'If they can't get him to make some concessions there'll be the dickens to pay, but it's no use talking to him when he has the Empress at his back, telling him he's Peter the Great. Get him on his own, and there's a chance. He's got to give the Duma *something*. That chap Kerensky's been making speeches again, and he has a big following in Petersburg. If Nicholas won't treat with him, he'll have worse fellers to deal with presently. At least Kerensky's a gentleman – or the Russian equivalent of one.'

'Do you think there's immediate danger of revolution?' Thomas asked, trying to conceal his anxiety.

'Oh, no,' Buchanan said. 'There's a lot of unrest in the city, but it's low-level, unorganised stuff – mostly protests about the food shortage. Of course, that's what the political wallahs will harness when the time comes. But I think we still have some leeway. I'm not cancelling my holiday in Finland, anyway.'

Thomas finished his official business, made some purchases

79

and sent some letters, then went back to Tsarskoye Selo to prepare for departure. He was invited to dine and spend the evening with the imperial family in their private quarters. It was not an unusual event, but on this eve of departure he felt the compliment of it. Usually he was required to make a fourth at bridge with Nicholas and Alexandra and her lady-in-waiting, Anna Vyrubova, or would discuss the war with the Emperor and other guests, usually cousins or close friends. But tonight there was only him and Vyrubova with the family.

Nicholas sat apart on the sofa with Alexandra. They talked urgently in low voices with their heads together, and were not to be disturbed. Tatiana was playing the piano; Marie, on the far side of the room, was sewing and talking to Anna Vyrubova; and Anastasia and Alexei had gone to bed. That left Olga, sitting alone on another sofa, sticking new photographs into her latest album.

It was good, Thomas thought, to see her out of nurse's uniform for once. As soon as the war began, the Empress, Olga and Tatiana had undergone training to become certificated nurses, and since then they had laboured almost every day in the war hospital that had been set up in the old Catherine Palace opposite. And he knew they spared themselves nothing, from washing the filthy, lice-ridden bodies and picking maggots out of festering wounds, to helping in the operating theatre. With his own eyes Thomas had seen the Empress of all the Russias carrying away a severed leg to dispose of it.

Marie and Anastasia were considered too young to do proper nursing, but they were patrons of another, smaller hospital, where they went to read to the soldiers, write their letters, and take them little gifts of tobacco and cakes bought out of their pocket-money.

So almost every time he saw Olga she was in uniform. The Russian nurse's headdress was particularly severe and nun-like, covering the whole head down to the eyebrows, and fastened like a wimple under the chin, so that only the face showed, peeping out of the small space in the stiff, white cotton. The severity made the Empress look more drawn and tired than ever. Tatiana's perfect features were enhanced by it, as a picture by its frame. But Olga, he thought, looked like a beautiful, trapped animal.

Tonight, though, she was in an evening dress of grey-blue lace over silk, her soft, fawn hair piled and pinned in grown-up fashion, with pearls around her neck and at her ears. She looked lovely and womanly; and vulnerable and alone. He ached for her. She was the most intelligent of the girls, the most sensitive, the best-read. She had an enquiring mind, which it was often his pleasure to inform; but the more she knew, the more it seemed to set her apart from her family. Tatiana was her mother's favourite and very close to her; plump, pretty Marie was her father's pet; and Anastasia and Alexei had each other. But Olga was no-one's special Olishka.

Her relations with her mother were cool. Olga had seen the disaster of her mother's worship of Rasputin. She had heard how he behaved outside the palace; moreover, she and Tatiana had had to endure his sly touching and pinching and stroking when they grew of an age to be interesting to him, knowing that they could not complain to their mother. Olga alone had remonstrated with the Empress, tried to make her see the truth. But Alexandra would not tolerate criticism from one of her own daughters, and repulsed her angrily. Since then, Olga had retreated into herself, lonely and frustrated. The Empress called her 'sulky' and 'difficult' and complained there was no dealing with her.

Thomas felt for her isolation, which made fertile soil for fear to grow in. Nicholas and Alexandra did their best to keep their daughters in ignorance of the dangers of their world, but it did not work with Olga. Her grave, troubled expression drew more accusations of sulkiness, and drove her more into herself. Harmony only returned on those occasions when Thomas had seen her revert deliberately to innocent, happy childhood again. When she romped with 'the children', as she called her younger siblings, her laughter tore at his heart.

She was grave tonight. He walked across the room to her, received the invitation of a look, and sat down beside her, as if to help her with the photographs. If they kept their voices down, their talk would be as near to private as was possible in a grand duchess's life.

'So you are leaving tomorrow,' she said. 'I wish you need not go. I wish you could stay here with us.'

'I have no wish to go.' He longed to comfort her. He could never hope for more. 'Perhaps we will not stay away long,' he suggested.

She looked at him quickly. 'Do you know something?' And when he hesitated, 'I would never ask you to betray a confidence, Thomas Ivanovitch. I know there are things you cannot tell me.'

'I don't think your father would go if he thought he was leaving you in danger,' he said carefully.

'No, I suppose not. But I hear things, you know. Riots in the city. The people are hungry.' She made a small movement of her shoulders. 'They think we live in fabulous luxury, like sultans. I have no money, but if I had any, I would give it to them. But would it make any difference?'

'You give far more by nursing the soldiers,' he said. 'Anyone can give money, but to give time and effort – to give oneself—'

'When I'm nursing, I'm glad to be helping. That's all I care about. But afterwards, in bed at night, I wonder if, when the time comes, anyone will remember it to our credit.' She smiled faintly. 'I suppose that's wrong of me. But I feel sometimes as if we were all in a great heavy lorry that's running away downhill towards a precipice, and the brakes are broken, and the doors are locked so we can't get out.'

'It's not as bad as that,' he said. 'Nothing like as bad.'

'Isn't it?'

'No,' he said firmly.

She inspected his face for sincerity, then sighed a little. 'Mama thinks that now they have killed Father Grigori, they will try to kill her next, but why should they? If he's gone, surely the worst must be over?'

'I hope so,' Thomas said.

'Only hope so? Poor Mama, what has she ever done to deserve to be hated so?'

He thought of Alexandra's unwavering devotion to virtue and duty. She was narrow and stubborn and wrong-headed, of course, but she did nothing for her own glory. Not that it helped: wrong things were not made right by good intentions. But how could she have been any different? She was trapped by her nature and limitations, and by the times. In another age and another country she might have done very well, been respected for her virtue, if not loved; but a very different set of qualities was needed now in both Emperor and Empress, which they were incapable of supplying.

He couldn't say any of this to Olga. Instead, he said, 'A war lets loose so much hatred, it can end up anywhere. Like the debris from an explosion, it doesn't choose whose head to fall on.'

For a moment she looked into his eyes, and he had the feeling she was reading the thoughts he had not expressed. Then he saw a faint blush begin, and she bent her head, hiding her face, and began turning the pages of the album.

She paused at a photograph from a day in December. Thomas remembered that day very well. It had been very cold, very bright, and they had gone out – all but the Empress – for a walk in the snow. Alexei had brought his sledge, and the big ones had taken turns at dragging it. There had been much laughter and some incontinent throwing of snowballs. Olga, who had a good eye and a surprisingly strong arm, had got Thomas in the back of the neck with one, which had shattered and gone down inside his collar. He remembered how she had stood laughing at him.

In the photograph Olga and Tatiana were dragging the sledge, with Alexei on it, his booted feet flown up in the air as they jerked forward. The photograph was in black and white, of course, but someone – probably Anastasia – had been hand-colouring it. There was a craze for that at the moment. He remembered that the girls had been in matching suits of a pink-purple tweed called 'heather mix', with hand-knitted mufflers round their necks, and round fur hats. Anastasia had got the colours just right; and she had touched in the faces and hands quite delicately. But nothing could match the brightness of the eyes he remembered, or the fresh faces, cold-stung, dusted rose on ivory, the pink lips and white teeth of their laughter.

Olga said, 'Do you remember this day?'

'Yes, very well,' he said.

'I've never seen a sky so blue. Something like that can make you think the whole of your life has led up to it, that the reason you were born at all was one day to see a sky that colour.' She laid a finger on the photograph. 'And there you are, Thomas Ivanovitch.'

There he was, in the background. Anastasia had coloured his greatcoat in a suitably drab khaki, but had not bothered with his face or hands. One of his hands was stretched out, as if he had been gesticulating as he spoke. And while he watched, Olga laid the tip of her finger over that image of a hand, and stroked it. He felt the shock of the gesture run through him like electricity, just as he would have felt it if she had touched the real hand with her own.

'Do you have snow like that in England?' she asked. Her hand was back in her lap. Had he imagined the whole thing?

'Hardly ever,' he said.

'Snow is very Russian, I think. Will you miss the snow when you go back to England? But you must miss England,' she went on, without waiting for him to answer. 'I know, if it was me, I would be terribly homesick.'

'Yes, I miss it,' he said.

'And your family. Oliver and Violet.' She remembered their names. During long summer days on the terrace at Livadia he had told her about them. 'And your mother, the doctor. It must be wonderful to have such skill to help people. And to be allowed to do it.'

'She wasn't, at first. She had to fight very hard for the right.'

'But she was free to fight,' Olga said. 'I shall never be free.' He couldn't deny it. 'I would love to see England. I was supposed to marry the Prince of Wales, once, did you know?'

'Yes, I knew.'

'Mama thought it would be nice for me to be Queen of England. She always loved England. But Great-Grandmama decided against it, I don't know why.' Great-Grandmama was Queen Victoria, of course.

'The Prince of Wales isn't married yet,' he said. 'Perhaps when the war's over—'

'It's too late,' she said. 'I don't think I will ever marry now. Who will there be left to marry when the war's over?'

He didn't answer that, taking her point. If not the Prince of Wales, she might once have been married to one of the numerous German princelings of Queen Victoria's enormous family. But Germany was the enemy now.

'Anyway,' she said briskly, 'I don't want to leave Mama and Papa and the children. But if I *had* to leave them, England would be the place I'd choose. It's such a gentle country. Even kings are safe. Great-Grandmama used to go about with nothing but an ordinary policeman to guard her. And he didn't even have a gun, just a rolled umbrella.'

Thomas laughed. 'Where did you get that idea?'

'Mama told me. Besides, I know it's true because when we visited the Isle of Wight we stayed in a dear little house without any soldiers, just a plain-clothes policeman hiding in the bushes. Nastya used to take him out buns and biscuits. She felt sorry for him. She thought he lived in there all the time.'

Thomas laughed. He could imagine Anastasia doing it.

'Then one day the four of us – Alyosha was too little then – slipped out all alone to go and look at the shops. It was very naughty of us, but we'd never been out on our own *anywhere*. It was exciting at first, but then we were recognised and a lot of people crowded round, and we were rather scared. But a policeman came and told them, quite kindly and nicely, to step back – and they did. He didn't have a gun, either.'

'He would have had a truncheon under his jacket,' Thomas said.

'Yes, but he didn't use it, don't you see? He didn't even have to take it out. He just *asked*. English people are kind to their kings and queens,' she concluded.

'Well, most of the time, perhaps,' Thomas said, smiling.

She turned to a clean page and began selecting photographs to mount. 'Tell me some more about your family,' she said. 'Tell me something you and Oliver used to do when you were young.'

So as she arranged the photographs, he told her about fishing trips and cricket matches, passing her sticky-paper hinges when she needed them. When he mentioned his father, she looked up suddenly. 'It must have been dreadful to lose your father like that. How can your mother bear it?'

'I do worry about her being alone, now Oliver's at the Front. But she keeps busy, that's the thing.'

'You must wonder whether you ought not to go back,' she said musingly, not as if it was a question but something she had discovered. 'I know you've extended your tour of duty several times. I'm glad you have. It makes everything seem much better, knowing you are looking after Papa and

– us. I keep dreading that you'll come and announce you're going. Of course, I know you will one day.'

'No,' he said, looking down at her. Her wide, grey-blue eyes were like those of a bayed animal. He felt hollow inside for fear of what might happen to her. 'I won't go. Not until you don't need me any more.'

'I shall always need you,' she said, so quietly that he was unsure he had heard her correctly.

Venetia was surprised to receive a visit from Lord Derby, the war secretary, at her office in Winchester House.

'I wonder if I might consult?' he asked her. 'Is there somewhere we might talk privately?'

'Of course,' she said, a little puzzled. Lord Derby and her late husband had worked together when Overton was at the War Office, but she couldn't think what advice *she* could give him. 'Come into my private office.'

It was a very small room off the main office, but at least it was her own – Winchester House was filling up rapidly and she was lucky to have moved in when she did. It contained little more than a desk and two chairs, but it was enough to invite Derby to sit down, and take the other seat herself.

He settled himself, and began, 'How much do you know about this new Women's Auxiliary Army Corps?'

'I didn't know there was one,' she said, with surprise.

'There isn't, as yet. So you haven't heard anything about it? Well, it *is* supposed to be pretty hush-hush.'

'So I imagine,' Venetia said with faint amusement. 'I suspect there will be violent opinions on both sides. Whose idea is it?'

'I believe it was General Lawson who first raised it with the adjutant-general. He pointed out that women were doing excellent work in the ammunition factories, and there was no reason why they shouldn't do more to help the army in France. The adjutant-general took it to Geddes, and of course he's bound to look at anything that might ease the manpower shortage.' Sir Auckland Geddes was director general of National Service. 'And Geddes brought it to me.'

'Is the shortage so critical?' Venetia asked.

'I wouldn't consider it for a minute if it wasn't,' said Derby, bluntly. 'Frankly, the idea of large numbers of our women out in France, with the ghastly sights they might witness and the danger to their safety and modesty – well, it horrifies me. Nursing is one thing, but to be making a regular army of them . . .'

'But surely no-one is suggesting that women become involved in actual combat?' Venetia said, shocked.

'Indeed not,' said Derby warmly. 'That is out of the question. It will be the end of civilisation itself if women ever go to war.'

'And the end of the army?' Venetia suggested.

'That too. No, the idea is that there should be a uniformed corps to help out with clerical work, administration, cooking – possibly driving and vehicle maintenance.'

'Well, I don't see anything against that. Those are jobs women are already doing here, at home. And the FANYs are doing them in France.'

'Quite so. But—'

'Yes, I can see that setting up an actual women's army could cause difficulties.'

'Ah! I'm glad someone agrees with me. Macready wants them treated exactly the same as the men.' Sir Neville Macready was the adjutant-general. 'The whole thing would be so coarsening to women's sensibilities that it doesn't bear thinking about.'

'Then why aren't you quashing the idea?' Venetia asked shrewdly.

He looked uncomfortable. 'Every woman employed as a cook or clerk releases one man for front-line duties. Our losses in the autumn campaign last year were severe, and Haig wants every man possible for his big push this year.

I can't reject the idea out of hand, but I do think there are grave problems we need to consider.'

'I can see two right away,' Venetia said. 'For one thing, how do you impose military discipline on women, especially those who have never been in employment? They don't have the same *esprit de corps* as men. They tend to resent it.' She gave a faint smile. 'It's hard enough getting housemaids to do what one wants.'

'And the other?' Derby prompted.

'I'm wondering what would happen to women in uniform if they were captured by the enemy.'

'Yes, that has been exercising me, too,' said Derby. 'It would be necessary to keep them well behind the line to avoid the danger of capture—'

'But then that would dilute their usefulness. Quite.' Venetia waited, but Derby seemed lost in thought, so at last she prompted him, 'What was it in particular that you wanted to ask me?'

Derby looked up, called back from his reverie. 'Oh – yes, of course. I beg your pardon. I wanted to ask you, if we do go ahead with it, whether you would consent to lead it.' Venetia was so surprised that she did not immediately speak, and he went on, 'You see, Geddes and Macready both want a Mrs Chalmers Watson to be the head – do you know her?'

'I know *of* her. She's a medical practitioner in Edinburgh, isn't she?'

'That's correct. She also happens to be Sir Auckland Geddes's sister.'

'I didn't know that. But is she not suitable?'

'I have only met her twice. She seems a sensible, energetic woman; but I am convinced that a venture such as this ought to have a titled lady at the head of it. It would confer a certain weight and distinction, which might overcome some of the resistance that's bound to arise. And you are eminently suitable, if I may say so. Your particular experience is so apposite, and you know so many people in the government and the War Office, and society in general. Everyone likes you, Lady Overton, and admires you. You could carry arguments where others might fail.'

'You are too kind,' Venetia said, dismayed, 'but really, Lord Derby, I don't think—'

'Dame Katharine Furse and Mrs Fawcett both think you are the right person. Yours was such a tactful influence before the war, during the suffragette militancy – and there are bound to be a great many arguments of that sort, about equality of treatment and so forth. A women's army corps will be a great step forward for the women's cause, but it needs careful handling, and you will be listened to, where I fear a lesser woman might not be.' She drew breath to answer, and he smiled and fired his last shot. 'And Lord Kitchener admired you, you know.'

'I am grateful for his good opinion, and yours,' Venetia said, 'and I wish the venture all possible success. Anything that goodwill and my verbal support can do is yours, but—'

'But you will not take the position?' he said, plainly disappointed.

'I have far too much to do with my own work, and my little operation here is dear to my heart. I couldn't give it up now. And apart from that,' she added, preventing any interruption, 'I am simply too old. All those arguments, the blinkered obstructions, the mutton-headed objections – going over the same ground all over again – frankly, Lord Derby, the very idea makes me feel exhausted. You have come to me twenty years too late.'

'If you are really decided, then I mustn't keep you any longer,' he said, rising. 'Thank you for hearing me, anyway.' She accompanied him to the door, and he turned to shake her hand, and said, 'You would have made a wonderful head of the women's army.'

'I can't see myself as Boadicea,' she laughed, 'but I'll take it as a compliment.'

'May I consult you again, as various matters arise? I should find it most useful.'

'Of course. My opinion, for what it's worth, is always at your service.'

'And in return, if there is any little thing that my influence in the War Office can help you with . . .'

'That seems a fair exchange,' she said.

Violet had not thought she would enjoy going back into society. She anticipated cold looks, snubs, whispers, even hostility; but her mother proved right. Her affair with Octavian Laidislaw had been last year's scandal. Now he had disappeared, out of sight was definitely out of mind. He had been comprehensively forgotten. Violet's baby was universally attributed to her husband: if anyone had doubts, they were not foolish enough to air them. After all, many a society lady's child had been conceived outside the marriage bed: what mattered in these cases was that her husband acknowledged it. As long as he did, life could go on as normal. And Holkam had done so, promptly and publicly.

Besides, Violet was rich, beautiful and good-natured. She had always been well liked, and she returned to society in the company of the pretty heiress, Emma Weston. Violet's absence, which to her had been a monumental, guilt-charged thing, appeared to everyone else to have been the normal retirement of pregnancy and childbirth. Now Lady Holkam was back, with her elegant clothes and her two smart little dogs, and a lively young woman at her side: a rather dull Season looked like being transformed. Why should she not be welcomed? Within days, the knocker of the gloomy house was busy with messengers, and the postman brought sheaves of invitations – 'just like the old days', as Sanders said to Spencer, with not a little relief on both sides.

Violet had always been quiet, and if she was quieter, and smiled less, the change was not remarked in the sparkling company of Emma, who carried all before her. Her occasional abstraction and sad smile only made her seem more romantic and mysterious. They touched something in the hearts of officers home on leave, so that she had almost as many admirers as Emma, though they were of the quiet sort, happy to devote themselves to Lady Holkam's comfort; to pick up her glove or bring her teacup without needing more in return than a thank-you, and perhaps one kind look from those violet-blue eyes.

Despite the deep well of sorrow in her, it could not be said that Violet had no pleasure from her ventures into company. It was a relief from the sombreness of the house, and a distraction from her own thoughts. Emma was always a pleasure to be with, and it was good to see her enjoying herself and making such a mark. And there was always the comforting knowledge in the back of her mind that she was doing this for the children, to ensure their eventual acceptance into society.

One evening, at a *soirée* given by Princess Androvsky, Violet met her cousin Eddie Vibart. They had grown up together in the same nursery – his mother, Violet's aunt Augusta, had abandoned him when he was two years old – but of late years had not seen much of each other. Now he came up to her with a look of great pleasure, took both her hands, kissed her soundly, then stood back to look at her. 'You are as beautiful as ever. Dearest Violet! Why is it one never sees any of the people one really likes these days? This damned war . . . How is the new baby?'

'Thriving. And thank you for the present you sent.'

'Oh, it was just a trifle. Sorry it was rather late after the event, but I didn't hear about it until I bumped into Holkam in Amiens. He seems to have done well for himself – practically in Haig's pocket. Smart fellow! Haig's the coming man. I say, it *is* good to see you. I had no idea you'd be here.'

'It's good to see you, too,' Violet said. She examined him

as he beamed down at her. Despite being clean-shaven, he bore a striking resemblance to the late King Edward, with his rather bulging, pale blue eyes, distinctive nose and small mouth. He was losing his hair, too, though he was only four years older than her. He had become an officer as soon as the war broke out, and was now with Headquarters Staff of the XIV Corps. 'You're a major now,' she noted. Like most women, she was getting used to recognising the insignia of rank. 'Congratulations.'

'Oh, it's nothing. It's rather a lark, really, this soldiering business. A bit more "oof" to it than Court life, anyway! I was getting rather tired of all that hanging about, I can tell you. Oh, but I say, did you know I was engaged to be married?'

'No, I didn't. How wonderful, Eddie.'

'Well, it's all a bit new to me. Only popped the question a few days ago. Still can't quite believe it myself.'

'Who is she?'

'Lady Sarah Montacute – Talybont's daughter. Do you know her? She's one of the Queen's maids of honour. The Queen thinks the world of her.'

'I have met her. We came out in the same year. But I don't really know her.'

'Oh, she's wonderful!' Eddie said enthusiastically, and Violet was happy to see that it was a match of the heart. 'Can't think what she sees in me. She's bags cleverer than I am, and a real beauty.'

'You're very nice-looking yourself,' Violet assured him. 'And being clever isn't everything. When will the wedding be?'

'Some time this summer, we hope. What with the war and all, we don't want to wait, and the Queen's agreeable. You must come, Vi – promise you will!'

'Of course I will. And what then? Where will you live?'

'Oh,' he said, looking a little conscious. 'Well, we're being given a house in Piccadilly. The thing is, she outranks me rather a lot, so to save embarrassment I'm being given a peerage. I'm going to be Lord Vibart of Flaunden. It will all come off at the King's birthday.'

'That's wonderful,' Violet said. 'Congratulations.' She understood by this that the house was also being given by the King. So the stories about Aunt Augusta and King Edward – she had always wondered about them – might be true, after all.

She was going to ask more about his plans, when he caught someone's eye across the room, and said, 'Oh, look, I shall be in trouble if I don't get back to my duty. Have you met the prince?'

'Prince Androvsky?' she said, puzzled. 'I thought he was in France?'

'No, the Prince of Wales,' Eddie said. 'Didn't you know he was serving with the XIV Corps? I've been told off to look after him, keep him out of mischief, that sort of thing. He's a very good fellow. Come and be presented.'

Ah, thought Violet, that explained a great deal. Eddie was not just a Court supernumerary, but was the appointed companion of the heir to the throne. Eddie took her hand on his arm and a path opened magically for them through the crowd to where a small, very slight young man in uniform stood smoking a cigarette with rather nervous, jerky puffs and talking to an admiring circle of females – one of whom, she noted, was Emma. Despite the immediate company, the prince greeted Eddie with a glance of what looked like relief.

'Sir, may I present my first cousin, Lady Holkam?'

Violet curtsied slightly and the prince offered his hand to shake, giving her a quick, comprehensive look of interest, as though assessing her against an internal template. He had the family pale blue eyes, but the cast of his features was unmistakably Queen Mary's.

'How do you do, Lady Holkam?' he said pleasantly. 'I suppose it was your husband I met with General Haig last year?'

'Yes, sir.'

'He's a lucky dog! What wouldn't I give to be close to the action? They won't let me go anywhere the least dangerous, you know – and poor Vibart here is set on me like a watchdog to see I don't stray.'

'I'm sure my cousin doesn't mind at all. When we were children together, he never much cared for playing soldiers,' Violet said.

The prince laughed, but again there was that quick, appraising look. Violet was used to her beauty being remarked, but the room was full of beautiful girls, Emma not least among them. It must be something else about her that intrigued him. She did not care enough to wonder further about it. She thought him pleasant enough, but since Laidislaw she was indifferent to all men. He might have the rest of the females in the room in a flutter, but to her he was simply another man who wasn't Octavian. The three of them talked for a few minutes, and then Princess Androvsky decided her guest of honour was being hogged and came to break it up. The prince and Eddie were towed away to another part of the room, and soon afterwards left the party, without her having the chance to speak again to her cousin.

Emma joined her as soon as the prince moved away, eager to know all that had happened and what had been said. Violet answered her patiently but with indifference. 'Really, you are making such a fuss about it,' she said at last.

'But it was the Prince of Wales,' Emma insisted. 'The heir to the throne!' Violet shrugged minutely. 'Well, you must be the only woman in the room who wasn't thrilled by him,' Emma said. 'Perhaps that's why he looked at you in that way.'

'What way?'

'I'm not sure how to describe it. Interested, but puzzled. Perhaps he was wondering why you were immune to his charms.'

'I'm a married woman,' Violet reminded her.

'So is Princess Androvsky, but she's been fawning over him like anything! Didn't you think him awfully handsome?'

'He's more your age than mine,' Violet said, answering the thought behind the words.

'Oh, but I'm a commoner. I'd never have a chance with him,' Emma said.

Lady Ravenna Worseley, one of Emma's friends, joined them at that moment and sighed, 'He's gone. Why did he leave so early? Don't you think he's just the most charming creature? I mean, even if he wasn't a prince and heir to the throne, I'd still think him splendid, wouldn't you? Every woman in the room is in love with him.'

Violet, whose love was dead and buried in a foreign field, felt she couldn't bear any more of the subject, and said quickly, 'How is your war-work going, Lady Ravenna?' She had no idea what it might be, but every young lady of note had her war-work.

Lady Ravenna raised an eyebrow at the determined change of direction, but said, 'Oh, very well, thank you. Why don't you come along and see for yourself, Lady Holkam? You too, Emma. There's a convoy coming in tomorrow and we shall need every helping hand. Do come – the dear fellows are so pathetically grateful for anything one does. Victoria station, ten o'clock tomorrow morning. I know it's rather early, but it *is* important work.'

Under Emma's urging, Violet went with her next day to Victoria station, where they discovered a small group of young women, Lady Ravenna among them. They were dressed warmly in tweeds and furs against the continuing cold, and some of them puffed daringly on cigarettes. Some plainly dressed women of the middling sort were also with them, wheeling trolleys on which stood steaming urns of tea, stacks of mugs, and trays of buns. They were waiting for the hospital train from Dover.

Ravenna greeted them eagerly. 'I'm so glad you came. It's

such important work! Look, in this box are cigarettes. Take a packet each, and you can give each man one, and light it for him. Do you have a cigarette lighter? Oh, well, you can have this one. I have another. And there are boxes of matches over there. Or if you prefer you can do the tea – a mug each, and a bun if they're hungry. They mostly like a lot of sugar in their tea, but we are rather short of it, so just put in one spoonful. And don't on any account take the spoon away from the trolley. We only have half a dozen left. They just disappear, I don't know how.' She broke off, and said, her voice rising in excitement, 'Here it is!'

The train appeared, steaming slowly in, and drew to a gentle halt so as not to shake the passengers, sighing out great gales of steam. The doors opened with a fusillade of bangs, and a mass of people began to descend. Ravenna's group went eagerly into action. Violet had witnessed this sort of scene before, and went forward with them in a spirit of resignation, not expecting to be moved in any way by the encounter. She put a mug of tea into the hands of the first man she came to: his forearm was bandaged and his uniform sleeve had been cut to the elbow to accommodate it. He said, 'Thank you,' and she heard his voice shake, and looked up into his face for the first time. He was very young, fair, with blue eyes and a vulnerable mouth; his head was bandaged under his cap. His face was drawn, with pain or shock, or both; and as their eyes met and he tried to smile, she knew he was on the verge of tears. Whatever he had been through, he was home now, and a woman was being kind to him: it was that, she knew with a sympathetic flash, which was unmanning him.

Her own tears rose in a knot in her throat. She patted his hand in lieu of words and dragged herself away, biting her lips for control. He was Laidislaw to her; they were all Laidislaw. She shouldn't have come. And yet, foolish though it was, Ravenna's group *was* doing something important. She saw it as she went on, mechanically handing out the

97

small boons. It wasn't the tea and the cigarettes, it was the reminder of home, of the women – their mothers or sisters or sweethearts – they had done it for. It was reassurance that their suffering was for a reason.

On another part of the platform, Emma had gone into the fray eager to do some good, and expecting pleasure from the encounter, as encounters with men had almost always brought her pleasure before. But as she got close to the soldiers, a desperate shyness reddened her cheeks and lowered her eyes. They were not men as she had always met them before, polite, restrained, drawing-room clean, and held in check by the silken threads of social niceties. These men were dirty, and she could smell their bodies; their faces were rough with sprouting bristles. They had just come from a place where there were no women, and where they did things only men did – things fierce and physical and foul. Their masculinity seemed to Emma to reek from them like a miasma, and she was afraid of them: not that they would harm her, but that she would be forced to know something she was not ready to know, something about the real nature of mankind and its flesh, its urges, its primal force.

But they spoke to her politely, thanked her in gentle voices. Seeing her confusion, even the ordinary soldiers forbore to exercise that loud, rough teasing they usually employed towards women; and she was touched by their consideration. Gradually the fog around her cleared and she began to see them. The walking wounded were dispersing and it was the worse hurt she was meeting now: men on crutches, men being supported between two friends, men on stretchers. Their shocking wounds were like a physical attack on her senses. Her hands shook as she handled cigarettes and lighter.

She knelt clumsily by a stretcher to find that the occupant's head was massively bandaged, leaving only one eye, mouth and the end of the nose uncovered. That one eye looked at her helplessly, like that of a bullock trussed for slaughter. The hand resting on the outside of the blanket was also heavily swaddled; the other arm ended above the elbow in a bandaged stump.

'Would you like a cigarette?' she asked, and her voice was no more than a whisper.

The one eye only stared with what seemed to her a desperate appeal. She couldn't tell what he had been before, but he seemed young. 'Would you like a cigarette?' she asked again, and felt all the inadequacy of what she offered in the face of his terrible wounds. She pulled one out with shaking fingers and held it up so he could see it.

'Yes, please, miss,' he whispered.

She was going to put it between his lips, and then, fearing for his weakness, put it between her own, lit it, sucked to get it going, coughed out the smoke, and placed the end gently to his mouth. His lips took it, but he did not seem to have the strength to suck. Then the one eye closed, and she saw him take a pull on it. As the cigarette sagged with his outbreath, she caught it to stop it falling on his blanket, and waited helplessly for his eye to open, for some signal that he wanted it again.

But a nursing sister tapped her on the shoulder, and said briskly, unsmilingly, 'We're taking him now.'

She rose, and two orderlies came, one to either end of the stretcher, and picked him up. His eye was still closed. The cigarette burnt uselessly in her fingers. Was he dead? Had he just died while she watched him?

'Where will he be taken?' she found voice enough to ask. 'Where will they all be taken?'

The sister had been moving away, but stopped now and looked at Emma consideringly, as if gauging the sincerity of her wish to know. 'The acute ones go to the nearest available hospital. The others go to different places. We try to send them to a hospital near their home, so their families can visit, but it isn't always possible.' And then with a nod she turned away, stepping quickly down the platform about her known duty.

Emma watched her, feeling helpless and useless. One of Ravenna's friends touched her arm. 'You don't need to do the ordinary soldiers unless you want to. Some of them can be a bit rough. You can stick with the officers if you like.'

Her rough soldiers had said nothing to her but 'Thank you, miss.'

'No, I'll do them,' she said. 'Is there another train coming?'

'In half an hour. Are you staying?'

'Oh, yes,' said Emma, 'I'm staying.'

CHAPTER FIVE

On the 23rd of February, the day the Tsar and Thomas went back to Stavka, the situation in Petrograd began to fall apart. It was International Women's Day, and the streets were packed with marchers, and the crowds who had gathered to watch. But a bakers' strike had led to a shortage of bread and to some bread shops being closed. Queues became bad-tempered and disturbances broke out. Meanwhile a strike of textile workers, mainly women, had joined the marchers; and presently the discontented workers from the huge Putilov armaments factory decided to join in too. The addition of these men, organised and militant, changed the mood of the demonstration, and tension began to rise in the city.

A rumour got about that the capital had only three days' supply of flour, and the next day strikes broke out in every quarter, and huge crowds filled the streets, milling slowly, converging on the city centre. Militant elements infiltrated the mass, trying to turn it into an anti-government riot. In fear of provoking running battles in the streets, the Duma gave orders that the police were to take no action against the protesters, and that the Cossacks, who were usually called on to restore public order, should not carry whips.

By Saturday the 25th, tens of thousands of workers were on strike, and their absence from their posts brought the city to a virtual standstill. The streets were packed with demonstrators, and the Cossacks were assuring them they would take no action. Students and militants were egging the crowds on to more violent action, and there were riotous outbreaks and some accidental deaths. The Duma went into emergency session and finally, in desperation, the chairman, Rodzianko, sent a cable to the Tsar at Stavka, saying that the government was paralysed and incapable of restoring order, and begging him to 'summon a person whom the whole country trusts, and charge him with forming a government in which the whole population can have confidence'.

The Tsar would not believe that the situation had deteriorated so quickly. He was inclined to believe Rodzianko was exaggerating. He despised the man, anyway, and had never liked having to have a Duma at all. Moreover, he had other troubles on his mind. There was an epidemic of measles among the troops at the Front, and some of them, wounded, had taken the infection back to Tsarskoye Selo. On the evening of the day he had left, Olga and Alexei went to bed with high temperatures, and by the next morning the doctor had diagnosed measles. The Empress telegraphed the news, and the next day cabled that Tatiana had gone down with it, and Anna Vyrubova as well.

Thomas discovered that the measles at home exercised the Tsar far more than the situation in Peter. He was naturally concerned – measles was a serious matter – but he said many times that it was good for the children to catch the disease while young. It was much worse for adults; he hoped they would *all* get it now, and have it over with.

Thomas listened and nodded, but he could not feel so sanguine about Olga. The Tsar might think of her as a child, but she was twenty-one years old; and the complications of measles could be grave, even fatal. But Nicholas continued simply to say he hoped that there would be no complications, without seeming really to feel it would be any other way.

Thomas attributed this confidence to his overall good

mood. He said he felt well and rested away from Peter, without ministers to bother him and 'fidgety questions' to tax his brain. There was nothing in particular for him to do at Stavka, and Thomas suspected again that he had been lured there to get him away from his wife – who, in a letter she had slipped into his luggage for him to find when he got to the Front, urged him to be firm and let the Russians 'feel the whip', because that was what their Slavic nature longed for.

The Tsar spent his days receiving, showing himself to chosen units of the troops, writing long letters, and having dinner with the generals. In the evenings, when he had completed his diary, he confessed himself somewhat at a loss because there was no work for him and no family around him. Thomas played dominoes with him, and endless games of cards, while outside the snow fell thickly, increasing the silence and Thomas's sense of isolation. The Tsar might be feeling rested, but he was feeling as though he had fallen down a hole, while vitally important things were happening up on the surface.

In Petersburg, Sunday the 26th brought a new development. In barracks in various parts of the city there were around two hundred thousand soldiers, many of them raw recruits, plucked unwillingly from their families and farms by conscription. Others were front-line troops recovering from wounds and sickness, with a good salting of old hands and bad characters who had wangled barracks duty rather than going into combat. It was an explosive mix, into which the revolutionaries had deliberately introduced their agents, murmuring sedition. These soldiers now spilled out onto the streets and joined the protesters, and when ordered to form ranks and control the crowds they refused.

By the Monday, order had broken down. All but a handful of military units had either expelled or murdered their officers and 'gone over to the people'. The government ministers had fled or were in hiding, afraid for their lives. Huge crowds surged through the streets, looting and setting fire to government buildings. They charged the Winter Palace, and occupied the Peter and Paul Fortress, releasing the prisoners held there.

Rodzianko, the Duma president, urged the Empress to flee with her sick children – Anastasia had caught the infection too, now, leaving only Marie to help nurse them – but she refused to go. She would not leave until the Tsar joined her, she said. By the end of the day the railway into Tsarskoye Selo was cut off by rioters, and the local soldiers had run away. The Duma quickly sent a force of marine guards still loyal to the Tsar to defend the palace, but the imperial family and their household were effectively prisoners.

That evening, the news from Peter filtered through to the Tsar. 'It's very bad, being so far away, and receiving news only in scraps,' he complained. 'I think I must go back. What do you think, Thomas Ivanovitch?'

'Back to Petrograd, sir?' Thomas asked doubtfully. He did not think there was anything the Emperor could do in Peter that he could not do here. He imagined Nicholas showing himself to the mob and appealing for order, and it was not a convincing picture.

But Nicholas said, 'No, to Tsarskoye Selo, of course.'

Home, Thomas thought: he wanted to go home to his wife and children. The husband and father were to the fore, the absolute monarch slumbered on. Much as Thomas longed to see Olga and find out how ill she really was, to be there to protect her, he was not sure, from what he had heard, that they would be able to get through. If that was the case, the Tsar would be safer here. Things had deteriorated so quickly, and with the city garrisons gone, there was nothing to stop the disorder spreading into the countryside. Suppose the train were attacked by a mob? Nowhere outside the nuclei of disciplined troops at the various headquarters would there be anyone who could be relied on to defend him. With that thought, Thomas had a hollow feeling in his stomach that this was the end after all: that these were not just temporary disorders, but the revolution they had talked about for so many years.

He tried to express this to the Tsar, for it was his duty to keep him safe if possible, but at the first hint of a contrary opinion the frown line reappeared. Nicholas listened for a moment, and then interrupted. 'No, I think we must go,' he said. 'We will go tonight, after dinner. See to it, if you please, Colonel.' There was no arguing when he called him 'Colonel' rather than 'Thomas Ivanovitch'.

Their train set off in the blackness of one o'clock the following morning, the 28th of February.

On that day, the Duma met in the Tauride Palace and instituted a Provisional Committee, with the task of taking control and ending the desperate state of affairs in the capital. It issued a proclamation to that effect, confiding that the people and the army would give their support to the task of creating a new government that would reflect the aspirations of the people.

In another part of the Tauride, the Soviet of Soldiers' and Workers' Deputies had their headquarters. The threat of their presence was almost palpable, and they alone had any chance of controlling the mutinous soldiers of the city garrisons. If the Duma were to have any hope of taking control, they must have the soldiers on their side. Before the day had ended, the Duma had agreed to a union with the Soviet, and that union was in all but name the government of Russia.

Meanwhile, the imperial train had stopped at Malaia-Vichera to take on water, where railway officials told the Tsar that the line ahead was occupied by rioting troops and it was not possible to get through. Nicholas, angry that he had not been better informed before, ordered the train towards Moscow; but at Dno they learnt that the whole of Moscow had gone over to the revolution. After consulting with Thomas and a map, he gave orders to go instead to

Northern Headquarters at Pskov, where the troops commanded by General Ruzsky, he felt, would be loyal. Thomas had pointed out that from Pskov it was only a day's journey to Tsarskoye Selo.

But when they arrived at eight in the evening, General Ruzsky hurried on board at once to say there was no way through. The train could proceed no further. The Tsar, who before had been restless and anxious, seemed stunned to apathy by the news. For the first time, Thomas heard him mention the unmentionable.

'If the revolution succeeds, I shall abdicate voluntarily,' he said, staring out of the window at the snow. 'I'll go and live at Livadia,' he added, after a moment. He had always loved Livadia best of his palaces. 'The Crimea will be good for all of us. The children will need sunshine. Dr Fedorov says a change of climate is absolutely necessary after the measles.'

When Nicholas had retired, Thomas went out to try to find out more. In General Ruzsky's outer office he met a friendly adjutant, who had been party to some of the telegrams coming and going between Peter and Pskov, and was more than willing to talk about them.

'The Duma wants a constitutional monarchy, like yours in England,' he said. 'They think it's the only way to prevent terrible bloodshed – and also win the war. So far, the main bodies of troops outside the cities haven't heard about any of this, but if they once get a whiff of republican talk, all will be lost. The Duma thinks they can be rallied in the name of saving Russia from the Germans, but the soldiery need someone tangible to follow, or it will be every man for himself. The Tsar's name won't work any more – not this tsar, I mean.'

'So – what then?' Thomas asked, though he had guessed.

'His Majesty will be asked to abdicate in favour of the Tsarevitch.'

'But he's only a child.'

'Under the regency of Grand Duke Michael.'

The Tsar's brother was very popular. Abdication in his favour was a lot less bad than many of the alternatives Thomas had imagined. With Michael in charge, the family's lives would be safe. 'What news from Tsarskoye Selo?' he asked. 'His Majesty's children were ill.'

'I've heard nothing,' the adjutant said. 'I'm sorry.' He hesitated. 'It's likely that the Duma will prevent any news from the family coming through until this matter is settled. As a form of leverage.'

'Yes,' said Thomas. 'I see.' Things had degenerated so far, then, that they could think of using such a despicable black-mail on their ruler.

But on the 2nd of March, the Empress did manage to get one letter through to her husband, sending it by hand since the telegraph from Tsarskoye Selo was cut off. Thomas watched the Tsar reading it, and saw his face crease with pain, but then revert to the blankness it had worn since he had woken that morning.

Thomas dared to ask if there were news of the children. Nicholas stared a moment, then roused himself to say, 'They are all very ill, with high temperatures. But Dr Botkin is there. And they have the best nurse in the world in their mother.' He sighed and looked again at the letter, and it almost seemed as though he was going to offer it to Thomas to read. Then he folded it and set it aside. 'Tell me, Thomas Ivanovitch,' he said abruptly, 'do you think the situation is capable of recovery?' Thomas hesitated too long. 'You do not wish to give me your opinion, which tells me you think things have gone too far. Tell me the truth. I am surrounded on all sides by treachery, cowardice and deceit. Let me at least have an honest opinion from you. You are not Russian – you have nothing to lose.'

'I think things have gone too far, sir,' Thomas said.

Nicholas stared into his eyes a long time; Thomas tried to hold steady. The Tsar looked exhausted, he thought, and somehow shrunken; but perhaps that was only Thomas's perception of the situation. The ruler of half the world was nothing more now than a mouse in a trap. He had nowhere to run, no idea what to do next. He might give orders, but who would carry them out? He must have longed for it all to end.

'Thank you,' he said at last. 'I think so too.'

General Ruzsky and other dignitaries came after breakfast and talked about the situation. Words and cigarette smoke seemed to fill the carriage, choking thought. During the day, telegrams came in from the commanders-in-chief, including Grand Duke Nicholas, the Tsar's respected and loved Uncle Nikolasha. All the advice was the same.

'It seems my abdication is necessary,' he said to Thomas at last. 'The crux of the matter is that I must take this step for the sake of Russia's salvation, and to keep control of the army at the Front. Nikolasha,' he gestured with the telegram in his hand, and his lips quirked in what looked like a grimace of pain, 'begs me on his knees, he says, to go.'

Thomas nodded. He could think of nothing to say. The Tsar had always been kind to him, treating him rather like a favoured cousin. His advancement had been due to Nicholas's personal patronage, and he had been given a privileged place in the heart of the imperial family. His judgement might condemn the Tsar's actions as a ruler, but as a man he had done much that Thomas was grateful for.

'I never wanted the throne,' Nicholas said suddenly. 'I always wished I could have been a private gentleman. Perhaps now I can fulfil my dream. I should like to have a farm – perhaps in England. I think I should be a good farmer.'

'Yes, sir,' Thomas said. For a giddy moment a golden prospect opened before him: Nicholas a gentleman farmer in England, and Olga no longer a tsar's daughter, no longer out of his reach. A wealthy earl might be considered good enough for the daughter of a deposed monarch. Marriage, children, normality – oh, it was a sweet dream, a glittering prospect!

Nicholas seemed suddenly to come to a decision. 'Bring Dr Fedorov to me,' he said.

Thomas brought the doctor in, and was about to go, but Nicholas said, 'No, stay, Thomas Ivanovitch. We have no secrets from you now.' And he turned to the doctor. 'Tell me, Sergei Petrovitch – your honest opinion. Is my son's condition incurable?'

The doctor's eyes flickered enquiringly towards Thomas, not knowing which way the Tsar's mind was moving. He sought carefully for words. 'It is incurable, sir. But, nonetheless, it has been known for sufferers to reach an advanced old age.' He studied his master's face, and went on, 'Yet they are always at the mercy of accident, as you know, sir. Sometimes a considerable fall may have no bad effect; at other times, the slightest blow may cause serious harm. Life on those terms must always be uncertain.'

'Uncertain, yes,' said the Tsar. He stared, frowning, into the distance for a moment, and said, 'Then it is quite clear that Alexei can never fully serve his country in the way an emperor must. In that case, there can be no argument for separating him from us. With us, with his family, he has the best chance, does he not, Sergei Petrovitch?'

'Undoubtedly, sir. There is no substitute for a family's care.'

'And I could not bear to part with him. I shall abdicate for him, too,' the Tsar said decidedly. 'Mishka shall have the throne and carry on the dynasty.'

Having made the decision, the Tsar seemed to feel no more doubts about it. In that same blank, rather dazed way, he discussed the wording of the instrument with Ruzsky and the adjutant-general, Count Fredericks, while Thomas wrote and corrected to their dictation. Then the Tsar said, 'Type it out for me, Thomas Ivanovitch. Will you do that for me? I would rather it was you.'

A little while later, when the document was brought to him, he read it through and then signed it without hesitation, as if it were the most ordinary piece of daily business. Thomas took the paper back from him to dry the signature, and his hand trembled, knowing what he had there. It was raw history, and he felt rather sick, as though he were holding a lighted stick of dynamite.

In the evening the representatives of the Duma arrived. Nicholas received them politely, told them of his decision, and handed them the signed and witnessed document. Thomas thought there could never have been such a significant act completed in such a prosaic manner. The Duma members, Guchkov and Shulgin, seemed shocked, almost incapable of taking the paper from the Tsar's hand, and had no words for several minutes. They had got what they wanted without argument, without even asking for it, and only now did the enormity of the business come home to them, rendering them shaken and speechless.

They stared at the Tsar as if trying to understand what he felt at that moment; but Thomas guessed that Nicholas had, in truth, accepted the inevitable much longer ago than anything he might have said or done would suggest. He had perhaps hidden the knowledge from himself, but in his heart he had known it would come to this long before Thomas had reached that conclusion. Signing the document was unimportant, because it came a long way after the fact for him. He shook hands with the two men and sent them away with a kindly farewell; and as soon as they were gone, he retired alone to his carriage and the train started off on its way back to Stavka at Mogilev – for until word spread it was still impossible to get through to Tsarskoye Selo.

During the night, as the train worked its way south again and the rhythm of the wheels utterly failed to send him to sleep, Thomas pondered that document, that sheet of typed paper. He had doubts of its legitimacy. How could the Tsar abdicate on his son's behalf? As soon as Nicholas abdicated – from that very instant – Alexei became tsar, and from then on, only he could give up his throne. He hoped no-one loyal to Nicholas would try to make trouble on that account.

But when they reached Mogilev, they heard news that made the point academic. Grand Duke Michael had renounced the throne. He had been visited by some of the more revolutionary members of the Duma, who both brought him the news, and warned him that they could not guarantee his safety. He had long been suspected of having republican leanings – one reason the Duma thought he would be acceptable as regent – and had shown his feelings when the mob rushed the Winter Palace, by countermanding the order to fire on them. He had said then that he did not wish to shed a single drop of Russian blood; now he said that he would take power only if the people voted it to him by universal suffrage. His abdication manifesto gave the power back to the Duma in the form of the Provisional Committee, now to be called the Provisional Government. When he signed the short document on the 3rd of March, three hundred years of the Romanov dynasty ended without a whimper.

Maria worried about Father Palgrave. He seemed cheerful enough whenever she met him during the day, but he did not seem well. His pale face had a taut, dry look, and his eyes were shadowed with lack of sleep, the skin around them tight with strain. Settling into this large household, learning his way around, coping with so many new people: it must be putting a strain on his nerves.

Henrietta was worried because his appetite was poor – Maria saw her looking anxiously at his plate at mealtimes – but if ever she tried to raise the subject with him, he turned her gently and skilfully to a new topic. He was widely read and had a quick intelligence, and there was no subject on which he could not entertain.

Maria too quickly found the points beyond which he would not talk about himself, and hesitated to push at them.

She had no right; and in a house so well populated, privacy was a thing to be cherished, whether of the person or the mind. In the course of things they spent quite some time together. As the other 'outsider' at Morland Place, she felt the best able to explain the house and its customs to him. Furthermore, despite the fact that she did not need any help, Teddy wanted him to help her in the office. It was traditionally one of the chaplain's duties, and Teddy was a great traditionalist. Maria suspected that, in the back of his mind, Teddy did not expect her to keep doing the job for ever. She was a woman and it was not a woman's job. And if she did stop doing it, it would be as well to have the chaplain ready trained to take over.

Maria could have told Teddy that it was impossible for Palgrave to tutor the children, care for the souls of the household and perform the functions of secretary – the latter were too complex and extensive now. But she had learnt the things there was no point in arguing about with Uncle Teddy; and besides, she liked having Denis Palgrave to herself now and then, for there was no-one else in the house on the same intellectual level. She enjoyed talking to him, more than she had with anyone she had met since Frank.

Her brief marriage had taken up so little of her life that sometimes it seemed like a dream. Frank, brilliant mathematician, with an illustrious academic career ahead of him, had been briefly translated into Frank the tender lover and kind, adoring husband. And then he was gone. If it had not been for Martin, she might doubt it had ever happened. They had been so much in love, but now she could hardly remember what he looked like. Sometimes she felt that it was Henrietta who had really lost him: she had borne him, reared him, loved him through his childhood until he became the young man she was so painfully proud of. His photograph, in uniform, stood on the table in the drawing-room, and it was Henrietta who put fresh flowers in the vase in front of it. She had so many memories of him; Maria had only a few passionate nights in Brighton, and a pathetically thin bundle of letters from the Front. She loved him still, and there was a place in her heart, sealed off, which would always be his. But he was slipping away from her, ineluctably, day by day. Sometimes she was almost jealous of Henrietta's sorrow; but when Henrietta came to her to talk about Frank, Maria, who was not a patient person by nature, heard her out.

But losing Frank, and now having even his memory slip away from her, left Maria lonely – more lonely even than before she had met him. Then, earning her living, she had been in control of her own life to a small extent; now she was tied to Morland Place, and yet could never feel she really belonged here. Often, at night in the privacy of her room, she would cry herself to sleep, trying to draw Frank back from the recesses of her memory, longing to feel his arms round her and hear his voice. If she could have conjured him properly, it would have comforted her, just a little. But she could never make him real.

One night in March, she was sitting up in bed reading. It was cold and blustery and the house was full of restless noises, creaking and sighing as it eased its ancient bones. Her shutter did not fit quite snugly: it strained outwards against its catches, whistling faintly as the wind dragged at it, then thudded sullenly back against the frame. The wind hooned in the chimney, and a draught she could not identify made her candle suddenly dip, sending bat-shadows fleeing up the walls into the dark corners. Somewhere something was making an irregular tapping noise; she heard footsteps where there could be none, and sometimes voices muttering.

She told herself it was just the wind searching into the cracks and crannies, tugging at the house to see what might come loose. You are too old and too sensible to believe in ghosts, she told herself sternly – but she wished she did not know so many stories of the spectres who were supposed to walk Morland Place. She tried to concentrate on her book, but Spinoza's *Tractatus Theologico-Politicus* did not grip the imagination like the horrors that lurk in the dark of every mind.

And then she *did* hear footsteps. She tried to dismiss them as imagination, but her senses told her, even as the hair began to rise on her scalp, that they *were* footsteps. They moved uncertainly in the passage outside her room, not going steadily in one direction as they would if it were one of the household, but wandering now here, now there. There was a muttering voice, too, starting and stopping. She turned her head towards the door, finding a strange reluctance in her neck muscles. The door knob – was it moving? She feared so much to see it stealthily turn to let in – God knew what! – that her flinching eyes told her it was, indeed . . .

She took a furious grip on herself. It was the candlelight that was moving on the polished metal of the knob. *And there were no such things as ghosts!* The only way to settle it was to go and look. She very much did not want to leave the warm safety of her bed, but at last she got up, put on her dressing-gown and picked up her candle. As she neared the door she realised that there was a thread of light under it, coming from outside. Whatever was out there, it had a candle too. Did ghosts use candles? *There are no ghosts!* She heard the muttering voice again. With her mind and her body completely at odds, she put her hand to the door knob.

She opened the door and stepped out into the passage. Her head jerked round to the left, towards the nursery, and she would have screamed, except that her throat went rigid. Coming towards her, with a slow, uncertain step, was the ghost. It carried a lighted candle. Her throat strained to make a sound, any sound, and her hand came up in a warding-off gesture, but she could not move from the spot.

Then it moved its candle a little to one side, and she saw, with a swoop of relief that was almost sickening, that it was the chaplain. He was in his night clothes, but he had put on his boots, which accounted for the footsteps. But what was he *doing*? She was about to address him, when it occurred to her that his behaviour was very odd. He was moving back and forth, up and down, pausing here and there, almost as if he were miming some small, daily domestic action. And now and then he spoke in a low, blurred voice. She could not catch his words.

She found her voice at last. 'Have you lost something?' she asked. She could not account otherwise for his dithering movements.

He turned towards her and walked a few steps closer, and stopped, and said, 'What the dickens are you doing here?'

She was offended by his vehemence and his frown, but then realised that, oddly, he was not looking at her, but past and over her, as if at someone much taller standing behind her. Cold fear ran down her spine and she jerked round – but there was nothing there.

He said sharply, but in that same curiously muffled voice, 'I don't care what he said.'

And it was then that she realised he must be sleepwalking. She must have seen an illustration in a story or magazine, for she had always thought sleepwalkers kept their eyes shut and walked with their hands stretched out in front of them. But Palgrave's eyes were open, and he was moving and talking naturally, though as if in a place and among people she could not see.

What to do? Hadn't she read somewhere that you mustn't wake sleepwalkers for fear the shock would kill them? But he couldn't be left wandering here, especially not with a lighted candle. Perhaps she could enter the world he was in, and guide him back to bed that way. But where was he?

He said, 'You should be at your post. I'll have to report you for this.'

He must be back in the army, she thought. On an impulse, she said, 'I have a message for you,' and added, 'sir.'

He looked at her invisible alter-ego, then turned his head sharply back to look behind him. 'Put out that light!' he whispered harshly. He blew out his candle and flung himself to the ground, grabbing her arm and pulling her down too. The bare floorboards hurt her knees as she landed. He was lying, his arm over his head, the other hand holding her down, and she felt him shudder convulsively. 'God, that was close,' he said. 'They're noisy tonight. Some poor soul got it that time.' He moaned. 'Will it never end? Stay down!' He jerked at her again as she tried to get up.

'It's all right,' she said. 'It's stopped now.'

He released her and raised his head, but she could see he was flinching spasmodically, as though reacting to sudden loud noises. 'Don't you hear it?' he said.

'It's a long way off. Not near here.' She tried her ruse again. 'I'm a messenger. They want you at – at Headquarters,' she said. 'I'll show you the way.'

And, for a wonder, it worked. He stood up, looked vaguely around, but when she said, 'This way,' he turned and walked with her. For a miracle, her candle, which she had dropped, had landed right way up and was still alight. She picked it up, and his too, and walked back down the corridor towards the nursery. 'It's all quiet now,' she said, hopefully.

'Can't you hear the guns?' he said, and moaned again.

'No, it's all right, that's thunder. The guns have stopped.'

She crossed the day nursery, the candle flame distorting the shapes of the furniture. The rocking-horse in the corner seemed to rock; there was a red glow still in the fireplace. His cold hand grasped her wrist, and she felt his fingers trembling. Pity seared her heart. Bad enough to have to serve in that terrible place once, but to be trapped by his mind into going back there night after night! She didn't know why, but it touched her unbearably that he had put on his boots.

He walked with her steadily, and did not speak any more. He seemed weary. Perhaps natural sleep was coming back for him. Across the schoolroom, and there was the open door of the priest's room. She had never seen the inside of it. It was austere – a bed, a chest, a small wardrobe, a writing-desk and chair, a carpet covering the centre of the floorboards – the furniture Morland Place had provided. There was nothing on the mantelpiece, nothing on the walls. He seemed to have no possessions.

She didn't know how to get him into bed, but he sat on the edge of his own volition, and took off his boots. Then he looked towards her and said, 'I'm going to turn in, Franks. Wake me half an hour before stand-to.'

For a flinching moment she thought he had said 'Frank'. It must have been his batman he was talking to. She said, 'Don't worry, I'll call you. Go to sleep now. It's all quiet. Everything's safe.'

He got into bed, pulling the covers up, closing his eyes, and instantly was utterly still. She waited, listening to his breathing, until she was sure he was sleeping. His cheek on the pillow looked thin, but his tousled hair and surprisingly long eyelashes made him look young, and his mouth in relaxation was vulnerable. Poor young man, she thought.

But now she realised that her feet were bare and she was feeling very cold. She put his candle back on the nightstand, and left him, closing the door gently behind her.

'Is there something wrong?' Palgrave asked.

Maria blushed and bent her head again to the account book. 'No, of course not,' she said. 'Why should there be?'

He hesitated, afraid of offending, but said, 'I beg your pardon, but you seem to be staring at me rather a lot. Did I miss something when I shaved this morning?'

She blushed even deeper at the thought of him shaving – the only man she had ever seen doing that was Frank, in that strange, fairytale week at Brighton. It had seemed a very intimate thing to witness.

She summoned her courage and asked, 'I was wondering – whether you slept well last night.'

He didn't immediately answer. Then he said, 'You must have some reason for asking. Was I shouting in my sleep?'

'I wouldn't have heard you if you did,' she said. 'The priest's room is too far from everyone else.'

'At the hospital,' he said, watching her steadily, 'I frequently woke people up by shouting. Sometimes I even woke myself. I had nightmares, you see.'

'Do you still have them?'

'Sometimes,' he said. 'Sometimes they are more like – very exhausting dreams. Full of hard work and worry and—'

'Danger?'

'What happened?' he asked.

'I found you sleepwalking,' she said. She did not feel the truth would hurt him now. 'At least, I assume that's what it was. You were walking about in the passage by the nursery, talking to yourself. And you seemed to think there were shells going off.'

'I woke you up? I'm sorry,' he said.

'You have no memory of it?'

'No. In fact, I thought I slept rather better last night. I haven't been sleeping well since I came here.'

'You were sleeping quietly when I left you,' she said.

'You got me back to bed?'

'I said I was a messenger come to take you to Headquarters, and it seemed to work. At any rate, you followed me back to your room and got into bed.'

'I'm sorry you should have been put through that,' he said, looking down at his hands. 'I had no right to come here, with my wretched nerves the way they are. I shouldn't have taken the position. But I wanted it so much.'

'Please don't apologise,' Maria said, upset by his distress. 'It isn't your fault. And I didn't mind at all. I was only sorry you seemed so disturbed. I was glad to help you – if I did help.'

'I think you must have,' he said, looking up again with a wry smile. 'I certainly feel more rested than I did yesterday.'

'Who is Franks?' she asked.

'My servant – in the battalion.' He looked a query.

'You spoke about him – or, rather, to him.'

'He was a very decent fellow. One of the old sort – I was lucky to get him. He looked after me like a mother.'

'Where is he now?'

'He was killed a couple of days before I caught my packet.'

'I'm sorry. It must have been dreadful for you.'

'Well . . .' he said, but did not finish the sentence, looking down again at his hands fiddling with a pencil. His mouth was drawn down, and she thought there must be lots of things he felt he could not tell her – yet. Then he sighed and said, 'I had better give Mr Morland my notice.'

'No, why?' she cried. 'You mustn't!'

'He won't want a person in my condition looking after the children.'

'But he knows about your condition.'

'Not the sleepwalking.'

'That doesn't make any difference. Really, you mustn't go. The children are starting to love you. Aunt Henrietta would be dreadfully hurt if you went now. And Uncle Teddy would feel betrayed. They're both determined to feed you up and make you well.'

'They are kind people,' he said, with an infinity of regret.

'Don't you think the nightmares will go away once you get used to being here, when you're rested and happy?'

He smiled faintly. 'That's the theory. It doesn't seem to be working so far.'

'But you must allow yourself time to settle in. It's all still quite new to you. Once you get used to everything, I'm sure you will be better.'

'You're very kind,' he said, and she thought there was a slight easing of the strain that had come back into his face. 'But this sleepwalking—'

119

'I've been thinking about that. Of course, it may not happen again. It was windy last night and there were lots of strange noises – shutters banging and so on. Perhaps that disturbed you.'

'I can't depend on it never being windy again.'

'No, and I *am* worried about your walking about at night with a lighted candle. But you went back to bed all right when I spoke to you. How would it be if we asked Aunt Henrietta to have one of the servants sleep in the schoolroom for a while? Then, if you did walk, there'd be someone to take care of you. I'd do it myself,' she added, blushing again, 'but—'

'No, that wouldn't be proper,' he said. 'And I wouldn't ask it of you.'

He still seemed doubtful, so she said, 'Why don't we speak to Uncle Teddy about it? I'm sure he'll say that this is nothing for you to resign over. You *want* to stay, don't you?'

'Very much,' he said, looking at her. 'I really can't tell you how much.'

As Jack put his head round the day-nursery door, Basil's face lit up with a beaming smile. It was tremendously flattering. The boy hauled himself up by the leg of the chair beside him, and took several bandy-legged steps towards him before the force of gravity tugged his well-padded behind back to the floor. Jack was as impressed with the achievement as Basil himself. The last time he had seen his son, he was only just beginning to crawl. Probably the competition in the nursery, and the roughness of the floorboards to young hands and knees, had accelerated the development.

'Come on, then, come to Daddy,' he encouraged, bending and holding out his arms. Basil was only too pleased to demonstrate his new prowess, rose again to a man's commanding height, and staggered forward like a drunken sailor; until Jack, seeing he was about to go down again, darted forward and swept him, giggling, into the air.

Later, when he and Helen went out for a walk to get some privacy, he said, 'He's amazingly heavy. I don't know what you've been feeding him on, my love, but I almost strained myself lifting him up.'

'He has big bones,' Helen said. 'I think he'll be tall. And what do you think of his little sister?'

'She's beautiful,' Jack said, with obvious sincerity. 'I didn't tell you at the time, but I thought Basil was pretty strange-looking when he was born.'

'He was a little squashed, that's all. Hardly surprising.'

'As you say. And he straightened out all right. But Barbara is lovely from the beginning, like a little porcelain doll. And how are you feeling?'

'Astonishingly well,' she said. They were strolling slowly up the slope towards the Monument, with Jack's mongrel Rug running out ahead, shoving his nose ecstatically into every bush and clump of grass, sucking up the new smells. Helen put her hand through Jack's arm, secretly alarmed at how unused her legs had become to exercise. 'It was so much easier this time than last.'

'You look well,' he said.

'You look thin. Don't they feed you in the RFC?'

'I'm not thin, it's just that you're not used to all my muscles.' He patted his midriff. 'Pure Adonis.'

She laughed. 'Speaking of Adonis,' she continued, 'what do you think of the new tutor?'

'He seems a decent sort of chap. Damned shame about what happened to him. Is he managing all right, with the nerves and so on?'

'I think so. He's all right as long as there are no sudden loud noises.'

'Well, that rules out going back to the Front,' said Jack, wryly.

'That's why Uncle Teddy's so pleased. He's tired of training young men and then having them called up. Anyway, there's a programme at the moment of feeding him up and getting him well. Uncle Teddy thinks it's important for him to get fresh air, so he's taking the boys on lots of "nature walks". They're out of doors half the day. I don't think many letters and numbers are being learnt, but of course that suits young James and Jeremy very well.'

'But Palgrave is educated all right, isn't he? He seemed a clever chap when I spoke to him.'

'Yes, he's quite an intellectual. Maria has befriended him, and when they get talking I don't understand one word in three. I think she was pining for mental activity. It's nice for her to have someone like that to talk to.'

'Yes, she must miss poor Frank.' He sighed. 'I still can't believe he's gone. And Ned, too. It's foolish, but I keep thinking that when the war ends they'll come back – as if there's some place where they're all waiting for it to be over.'

They reached the Monument and sat down on its steps. Helen was glad of the rest. It was probably too far to have come for a first walk, but it was worth it now, to sit with him in the breathing silence of the countryside, with no-one else near. There was no sound but the wind, and far off, only just in earshot, the tremulous murmur of sheep calling to their young. Lambing season was under way. Rug finished his exploration of the immediate neighbourhood and came back, jumped up onto the step beside Helen and lay down, his forepaws across her lap. The snow was gone, though it was still very cold. The sky was uniform grey, but high enough not to portend rain. A brisk little wind moved her hair and sent exploring fingers down her neck, and she pulled her muffler closer.

'Cold?' Jack said, in quick concern.

'No. Enjoying the air, and the long horizon. I've been cooped up indoors too much.'

'Yes, I get restless if I'm indoors for too long.' He pulled off his hat, and let the wind ruffle through his hair. Helen glanced sideways at him as he squinted into the distance, and thought, with a little quickening in her stomach, that he was still the most handsome man she had ever known. She loved him more than ever, and how was that possible?

'I miss the sky when we can't get up, day after day,' Jack went on. 'It's silly, really, considering going up means Archie and enemy fighters and having to shoot at people, but I still miss it with one part of my mind.'

'I know what you mean,' she said.

'Do you?' He looked at her, and just doing so made him smile. She was so unutterably dear to him, that simply to look at her face was a warm pleasure that nothing else came near. 'Do you miss your old job?'

'Yes, I do.' The wind had blown one of Rug's ears inside out. She righted it gently, and the dog smiled up at her. 'And that was something I wanted to talk to you about. By the end of the month, I shall be recovered enough even for Nanny Emma to admit it.'

'I suppose you'll want to go home, then?'

'In fact,' she said, watching him carefully, 'I was thinking about *not* going home. Basil loves it here, and I do think it's good for him to have other children to grow up with. And Nanny Emma and the girls are so wonderful with him and with Barbara. What would you think if we all stayed here – just until the war's over and you come home?'

There was no doubting Jack's approval. 'I think it's an excellent idea. In fact, it was what I was hoping for – though if you'd wanted to go home, I shouldn't have said anything. But I'll feel much better about leaving you all, if I know you're here and being looked after.'

'Ah,' said Helen, 'but you've only heard part of the plan. I shouldn't *be* here and being looked after – not all the time. I was thinking, if you don't mind it, of going back to my old job.' She let the surprise sink in a moment and then went on, 'I really want to do my part to get the war over with, and it *is* important work.'

'More important than ever now. We'll be getting a whole

123

fleet of new machines this spring and summer, and someone has to deliver them from the factory.'

'You see, I'd be happy to leave the children here while I was away,' she explained, 'but I couldn't leave them at home with only a nursery-maid, and no-one to keep an eye on her.'

'No, that wouldn't do at all.'

'I'd come back here in between jobs, of course, and see them. I might have to stay a night at home sometimes, depending on the circumstances, so I could keep an eye on the house, too.'

'You'd need a motor-car,' he said.

'Yes, I think so. But what we save on housekeeping ought to pay for the running.'

'It's a good job Uncle Teddy's rich, or I should have a terrible conscience.'

Helen laughed. 'Offer to pay him for our keep. I dare you!'

'No, thanks. I don't want my head bitten off.'

Rug sighed and placed his nose where his paws already were. Helen stroked his head – so rough, and the ears so surprisingly velvety. 'So do you approve? Can I do it?'

'Yes, of course you can. Did you think I'd play the heavy husband and forbid you?'

'You might think I ought to be a good little wife and mother and stay at home.'

'You ought to know me better than that,' he said, with mock reproach. 'I love your strong, independent mind. And the sooner this war's over, the sooner we can be together again, so anything that helps win it is a good thing.'

She sighed with pleasure. 'You are such a *satisfactory* person to have as a husband.'

He kissed her, holding her cold face between his hands, and the kiss prolonged itself until Rug gave one of his huge, noisy yawns to remind them of his presence. They broke apart, smiling. 'We'd better go back,' Jack said. 'Don't want you catching cold.'

Rug leapt up, barked once and started off down the track home, looking over his shoulder to make sure they were following. Jack and Helen linked arms and Helen leant against him gratefully as they walked.

'What did you mean, "speaking of Adonis"?' Jack said suddenly. 'You don't think Father Palgrave is an Adonis, do you?'

Helen pretended to look at her watch. 'Your head is running half an hour late, my love,' she advised him.

CHAPTER SIX

At Stavka, the ex-Tsar did not seem to be in any hurry to go home. He was calm, even cheerful, but he did not speak about the abdication. His mother came to visit him from Kiev, and there were various uncles and cousins serving at the Front, who came to see him too. He played host in the imperial train, gave dinners, played bezique. Seeing him so settled, and in no apparent hurry to move, Thomas left him there and went back to Petersburg to consult with Sir George Buchanan.

Buchanan received him gravely. 'Well, this is a state of affairs!' he said. 'I can't believe it happened so quickly. How did you leave him?'

'Very calm,' Thomas said. 'I think he must have resigned himself to it long before the event.'

'Hmm,' said Buchanan. 'Well, things are quietening down now in Peter. It's a miracle it all happened almost without bloodshed. The Duma has made some Devil's pact with the Soviet, but the Soviet at least can keep the troops in order. I've spoken with Guchkov, Rodzianko and some of the others – Milyukov's the new foreign minister, by the way – and they're all very keen to carry on with the war, thank God. And the generals evidently think they have a better chance of winning it with the Duma and its industrial backers than with Nicholas, or they wouldn't have advised him to go.' He offered a cigarette.

Thomas accepted and lit it. 'Have the Duma said anything about His Majesty?'

'Not a word. Frankly, they all seemed rather dazed. I don't think they expected him to go so easily. As I see it, it gives us a small window of opportunity, before the rougher elements wake up to what's happened.'

'To get him out of the country, you mean?' said Thomas. He was glad Buchanan had come to the point so readily. On his journey up from Mogilev he had come to the conclusion that the ex-Tsar ought to be got out as soon as possible.

'Exactly. At the moment, nobody has thought about what to do next, but when they do, they will see him as an embarrassment; and soon after that, as a threat. We need to remove him before that stage is reached. Where does he think he will be going?'

'He wants to stay in Russia,' Thomas said. 'At first he talked about being able to help the new government with advice, and about serving out the war as an ordinary army officer. However, I brought him to see that wouldn't be possible. Now he hopes to go to England, and return to Russia when the war's over and live at Livadia.'

'Well, I think we had better try to get him away to England directly from Mogilev, if possible,' Buchanan said. 'Once he's out of the country, it will be easy enough to move the Empress and the children. The Russians won't care about hanging on to them if Nicholas is gone.'

Thomas shook his head slowly. 'I can see that would be best, but even I don't believe he would agree to it. He'd feel he was deserting his wife and children – particularly when the children are ill. He would never save his own hide and leave them behind.'

'He'll make it much harder to save their hides if he joins them,' Buchanan said. 'Once the Russkies have got the whole family locked up together at Tsarskoye Selo, it becomes a very different hand of cards.'

'I see that,' Thomas said, 'but . . .'

'Do what you can to persuade him,' Buchanan said. 'I'll get the diplomatic ball rolling. I suppose you are going straight back to Mogilev?'

'If you think it advisable. How are things at Tsarskoye Selo?'

'Quiet at the moment. There's a Red guard around the palace – rough fellows, but they seem to mean no harm to the family. I think at the moment they're just enjoying themselves being top dog.'

'The children? How are they progressing?'

'The boy is on the mend – amazingly, he seems to have weathered it best of the lot. The eldest girl, Olga, has developed complications, and she's pretty sick. Tatiana and Anastasia aren't quite so bad, but they've high temperatures. Marie is still healthy, fortunately. She helps her mother with the nursing. And the Empress's friend, Lily Dehn, joined them shortly before they were cut off. She's a sensible woman.'

'Yes, she'll be a great help.' Thomas hesitated. 'I suppose I can't go and visit them before going back to Stavka?'

'I wouldn't recommend it,' said Buchanan. 'I don't suppose the guards would dare offer insult to a British officer, but with revolutionaries there's no relying on their temper, and it would strain our resources to have to rescue you at this particular moment in time. Besides, there's nothing you can do for them. You will be more use to them all if you go back and persuade Nicholas to let us smuggle him out. Let the women look after themselves for the moment. Sick-nursing is women's work, anyway.'

So Thomas had no choice but to go back to Mogilev, where he felt a hopeless task awaited him. He had had plenty of experience of Nicholas's stubbornness, and he knew there was no possibility in the world of persuading him to leave the country without his family. And the children could hardly be moved until they were well. It was a race between their recovery and the revolutionaries' realisation of their power.

There was a window of opportunity, but how long before it was slammed shut?

Bertie had come home on leave, and found his son Richard still with that troublesome cough. 'Surely it should have gone by now?' he said.

'Dr Buller says it's bronchitis,' Maud said, 'caused by the cold he had before.'

'Bronchitis? I thought that was what old people get.'

'No, children get it too.'

'Well, what's he doing about it?'

'I have some medicine. And he says it will go away when the warmer weather comes.'

'That's not good enough. Listen to the child! Send for Buller, and I'll talk to him myself.'

'There's no need for that, dear,' Maud said. 'Dr Buller told me not to worry, and I'm not going to. He knows what he's doing. Everyone says he's the best doctor for children. Lady Cunningham has him for her boys.'

This was recommendation enough for Maud, but Bertie did not know Buller at all – he had come onto the scene since the war began. 'I still think I should see him.'

'I don't see any point in that,' Maud said calmly. 'He saw Richard only yesterday, and he's not going to tell you anything different today. You mustn't worry so. Don't you think I'm capable of caring for my own son?'

Put like that, he could not argue further. Instead, he said, 'Why don't you take him down to the country? I'm sure London can't be good for him. A spell at Beaumont would set him up – clean country air and so on.'

'I couldn't possibly go,' Maud said. 'I've far too much to do, with all my war-work, and John Manvers coming at the end of the month. Besides, I don't think Beaumont would do him any good at all. It's horribly cold and damp down there at this time of the year, and damp air is the worst thing for bronchitis. And he'd be bound to play in the mud or fall in the stream and get soaked to the skin. You encourage him to behave like a gypsy down there,' she said with mild reproach, 'so I wouldn't be able to stop him.'

The last time he had taken the boy to Beaumont, they had built a camp together in the woods, and both had got covered with mud. Bertie smiled at the memory. Maud did not understand the smile and her fine brows drew together.

'You may think it makes him manly, but getting wet and cold would not be good for him, and I would sooner he *wasn't* so manly and *didn't* get sick. In London I can keep him warm and dry and there's no temptation for him to wander. The new nanny collects him from school and brings him straight back here, and then he plays by the fire. And if there happens to be a fine day, we go for a nice walk in the park.' She patted Bertie's hand and concluded, 'It's best to leave these things to a mother's care. I know what's best for my own child.'

So he had to give in. But it was he who heard Richard coughing during the night, and got up to take him a drink of water and a spoonful of honey. Maud did not stir, and the new nanny did not appear at the door of the room until Bertie was already by the bedside; then, seeing him, she went away at once back to bed. But apart from the cough, the boy seemed lively enough, and in the end he had to assume that the doctor did know what he was doing.

Jessie had received word of Bertie's leave in a letter from him a few days beforehand.

I hope I shall be able to see you, but I shan't know what has been planned for me until I get home. You know I *will* come if I can. If your duties don't allow you to get away, if it has to be only a few snatched minutes together, at least I will get to see you.

Jessie knew the difficulties. He might know only at the last moment that he was free, and by then it might be too late for her to arrange the time off.

He went on,

Fenniman is coming home too, but not at the same time. He will be arriving just as I am leaving. Things seem to be going on quite nicely between him and your Miss Emma. I didn't tell you, by the way, what a delightful development it seems to me that young women are now going to take the lead in affairs of the heart! Fenniman tried not to be shocked when she first wrote, but soon came round to my point of view. If women are to do all the unpleasant jobs while men are away, it's only right they should be allowed to take the initiative and tell men what they think of them. But I do hope it doesn't end with ladies leading on the dance-floor. I don't think any amount of practice would enable me to dance backwards.

I saw your cousin Oliver, by the way. His unit has been rotated down to Picardy, and I got a very civil note from him, inviting me to dinner in Amiens. We dined in a hotel – three of us, for he brought his friend, Lord Westhoven – a lean, handsome young dog, blast him! But very nice, and pleasantly well-read. We had a good long conversation that hardly touched the war, which was a relief to all. I can imagine what sights they have to deal with every day, operating so close to the Front. It was a good evening, though I was tired to death when it began, and ended it positively light-headed. Oliver was in expansive mood and the hotel happened to have a stock of champagne – a dangerous combination.

It will be a relief to get away from here for a few days. We are following up the Germans, of course, and that means endless digging of new trenches. Now the snow has gone and the rain has come instead, I live in mud, breathe mud, eat mud, smoke muddy cigarettes. I long to be able to walk without several pounds of it weighing down each foot. Sometimes when I find my foot sunk yet again almost to the knee, the effort of pulling it out seems almost too much, and I toy with the idea of just giving up and staying there until it's all over. If only we could get a week or two of good, drying wind!

I long to see you, even if only for a few moments, just so that I remember what the world can be like without the mad normality of war. That's almost the worst thing – that one gets used to the insanity, until one starts to forget that things were once different.

On the day that would be the second day of Bertie's leave, Jessie was already engaged to go with Violet to a supper party at the Cunninghams'. Jessie had been surprised to be asked, since she barely knew them, but Violet had begged her, because Emma was engaged elsewhere that evening, and she hated to go alone. 'I'm not quite used to people yet, and I don't know who else will be there. I'm not brave without Freddie or Emma beside me. Please say you'll come.'

Violet's eyes were anxious, and Jessie relented. 'But I have nothing to wear,' she said.

'Oh, it won't be terribly smart,' Violet assured her.

'Your idea of "not terribly smart" and mine are very different,' Jessie objected.

'I mean that lots of people won't be in evening dress. That's why it's a supper party and not a dinner party. Just a costume would do. I'd lend you something of mine,' she concluded apologetically, 'but you know it wouldn't fit.' Jessie was taller and bigger-framed than her.

So Jessie had sighed and said, 'I'll go out and buy something. I suppose I ought to have one smart outfit, even though I am a nurse.'

So the next day she had used her three hours off to travel up to Oxford Street to buy something ready-made at D. H. Evans. It was a strange feeling to buy clothes again: just the smell of the department, of new cloth and clean carpet and a hint of expensive perfume, took her back to another world, before the war. The sales assistant was inclined to look down on her nurse's shabbiness, until her voice and her confidence and her indifference to price proved her a lady. Then the woman became almost too helpful, for Jessie did not have time for a long trying-on session. She quickly chose a two-piece costume of rose-fawn silk-and-worsted mixture, trimmed with blue braid, which fitted well enough, and rejected the assistant's offer to have some small alterations done.

Then, since hems were now a full eight inches off the ground, which tended to draw attention to the feet, she visited two more departments and bought herself a new pair of shoes – black kid with a double bar – and a decent pair of stockings. When she left the shop, burdened with her purchases – for she could not have them delivered to the hostel – the brief warmth of pleasure dissipated, and she felt almost guilty at having enjoyed the transaction, at a time of war when men were dying at the Front.

But the pleasure of it came back when she was dressing herself on the day. It was so nice to put on new, clean clothes. She had washed her hair, glad that it was naturally curly, for curled hair was the fashion at the moment, and struggled with a scrap of looking-glass and inadequate light to pin it up. There was nothing much she could do about her red, cracked hands. She had rubbed them all over with Vaseline the night before and worn cotton gloves to bed, but the difference was hardly noticeable.

Still, she felt pleased with herself as she drove in a taxi-cab over to Violet's house. For a wonder it had not been difficult to get her afternoon off on the chosen day. Sister Cartwright had a harmless passion for the high life – or what she supposed it to be, from what she read in the illustrated papers. When persistent questioning elicited that Nurse Morland would be going *with* Lady Holkam *to* Lady Cunningham's, Sister Cartwright could not have been more helpful. She even said she would let her go off a bit early, so that she could go home to wash and change. It all seemed too easy, and Jessie was prompted, suicidally, to demur. 'Are you sure you can spare me, Sister?'

Cartwright gave her a mildly astonished look. 'Spare you? Of course I can. You're only a VAD.'

At Fitzjames House, Violet examined her appearance and pronounced her blessing on the costume – 'Very smart, and a lovely colour!' – but with a hesitancy in her voice that made Jessie smile inwardly. 'You can speak your mind,' she said. 'Tell me what's wrong with it.'

'Nothing, nothing at all,' Violet said, blushing. 'The costume is lovely, but – would you be offended if I were to lend you a different hat? Hats are wide-brimmed this year, and yours, well—'

'Is old and shabby, I know,' Jessie said unconcernedly. 'My dear Violet, if it will make you happy to make me fine, go ahead.'

So Violet took her upstairs and provided her with a wide-brimmed black felt (which Jessie privately thought hideous, like a Boy Scout's hat) and, since they had plenty of time and Jessie really didn't seem to be offended, she got her maid to re-dress her hair.

'Rather a waste of time, since it will be covered by the hat,' Jessie remarked, sitting before the looking-glass in Violet's room, and contrasting it with her facilities at the hostel.

'You'll be taking off the hat.'

'Then I don't need a smart one,' the devil in Jessie argued.

Violet would not be baited. 'It's never a waste of time to have one's hair properly arranged,' she said reprovingly. And then she caught Jessie's eye, and they both laughed. They had not laughed together in a long time, and something eased in both of them. 'Oh dear, you must think me very foolish,' Violet said. 'What do these things matter now?'

Jessie smiled at her, feeling the old love. 'That's what I thought when I bought the costume. But I was wrong. We must never start thinking things don't matter any more. That would mean they had died in vain. It was life the way it used to be that they went to war to defend.'

Violet had not followed. 'Costumes and hats?'

'No, darling, but a world peaceful and safe enough for us to have the freedom to care about costumes and hats.'

'I see,' Violet said doubtfully. But she understood, in a wordless way, what Jessie meant. When they were ready to go, she built on her sartorial success by offering Jessie a fur to complete her outfit, and Jessie, to please her, accepted. The addition of a fur lifted any costume into a different realm, and she felt very grand as she followed Violet into the motor. Well, why not? A little finery and foolish pleasure just for once in a while wasn't going to hinder the war effort, was it?

Everyone seemed to have arrived at once, and the entrance hall of the Cunninghams' house in Piccadilly was crowded. Violet and Jessie waited their turn to be relieved of their wraps, and by then people had started to go upstairs and the crowd had thinned. Jessie turned from the maid who had taken the borrowed fox piece, and the first person she saw was Maud, looking killingly smart in a cherry-coloured two-piece piped with black, and a wide-brimmed hat trimmed with cock's feathers. And if those aren't new, Jessie thought ruefully, remembering her own twinge of conscience, I'll eat my borrowed hat.

Maud had seen her, so she went across at once and shook her hand, aware of the cool eyes appraising her. She never knew – had never been able to tell – what Maud was thinking: she was always the same, polite, correct, remote.

'How do you do?' Maud said. 'I didn't know you knew the Cunninghams.'

'Slightly. I came with Violet.'

'Oh, is she here? How nice.'

Jessie wanted to ask if Bertie was there, but could not. Her mouth was dry. It was always difficult to be in company with Maud – even more so if Bertie was also present – and to ask or not ask seemed equally impossible, equally redolent of guilt.

Fortunately, Maud said, 'Bertie is home on leave – did you know?'

Which made it natural to ask, 'Is he here?'

'Yes. He met Colonel Wetherby on the steps, and – ah, here he is.'

There he was: so tall, so solid, so much more real to Jessie than all the women her life was populated with. His masculinity seemed to fill the space, and the drabness of his uniform only emphasised it: he had the splendid, substantial presence of a horse, where the women seemed mere butterflies, frail, decorative and ephemeral.

Violet joined them at that moment, and there were greetings all round, polite exchanges, and it seemed some time before it was Jessie's turn with Bertie. But at last she was licensed to look at him, to offer her hand and have it taken in his, to exchange the permitted kisses of a cousin. His hand was warm and strong, and so alive that the awareness of hers in it was like being connected to the engine of the earth itself. She saw that the skin of his face was rough and reddened by the winter weather, his lips were slightly chapped, and his other hand was bandaged. He seemed thinner, and the hair at his temples was grey. But most of all it was from the way he bore himself, from the tension about his mouth and eyes, that she knew it had been bad out there. Then he smiled, and his blue eyes burned into hers, and she felt hollowed out with perilous joy simply to be in the same room with him.

'You look tired,' she said. She should not have said anything so intimate – or, at least, not in the way she said it – but she couldn't help it.

'It's been a busy time,' he said. 'But you – you're well?' His eyes searched hers with a dozen messages he could not speak aloud.

'Yes, of course,' she said automatically. 'But your hand – you're wounded?'

'Oh, it's just a scratch,' he said. 'A shell landed nearby and I got hit by a piece of shrapnel. The sawbones stitched me up. I wasn't going to let it spoil my leave.'

'He won't let me look at it,' Maud said.

The sound of her voice shattered the bubble in which, for a few precious seconds, Jessie had been alone with Bertie.

'I should think not, indeed,' Bertie said lightly to his wife, and offered his arm. 'Should we go upstairs? Almost everyone else has gone.'

Jessie passed the evening in something of a daze. There was a fine supper, daringly in the Russian buffet style, where everyone helped himself, but Jessie could hardly have told what she ate or drank. There was lively conversation, but much of it went over her head unheeded. Wherever Bertie was in the room, her eyes were drawn to him. She hardly saw anyone else – it was as if a bright mist obscured everything but him. Sometimes he looked across the room at her, and there was a flood of feeling, as though they had touched. She stood at Violet's side, and took what she could of him while she could, in foreknowledge of famine to come.

Violet was much in demand because the news had just arrived of the Tsar's abdication and everyone wanted to know more about it and hoped she might have heard details from her brother that were not yet widely known. But she could only say she had not heard from him yet. 'I'm sure he will write when he can. He must be very preoccupied at the moment.'

'But what will happen to the Emperor now?' everyone wanted to know.

It was hotly debated. Most people thought he would come to England, because the King was his cousin. The Kaiser was also his cousin, but Germany was obviously impossible.

'But why not Denmark?' someone asked. The Emperor's mother was a Danish princess, sister to Queen Alexandra.

And then someone else said, 'I hope they do go to Denmark. We certainly don't want the Romanovs here. Nicholas was a bloody tyrant. I have no sympathy for him.'

'But the Empress – and the children . . .'

'*She* was worse than *him*, from what I've heard. I agree with you – it would look bad to be giving them asylum.'

'The children can't be blamed. Poor things. I saw the grand duchesses once – so pretty and sweet.'

'They should go to Switzerland. That's the place. They'd be in no-one's way there.'

'*He* should go to prison.'

'But the King would never allow it.'

Bertie managed to come over to them, and Jessie turned to him like a flower to the sun. Violet abandoned the Romanov conversation without regret, and said, 'It's good to see you, Bertie. I'm glad we met like this. I expect you have a great many things to do while you're home, or I'd invite you to come and visit.'

'I'm afraid Maud has arranged rather a lot of engagements,' Bertie apologised, 'but I was hoping to call on your mother. How is she?'

'Oh, just the same. Busy, you know.'

'Her X-ray ambulances will be needed when the campaign season starts again.'

His eyes turned to Jessie as he said that, and they exchanged the look of knowledge. She drew a breath, thinking of the convoys and the shattered bodies, the terror of pain and the stink of blood. And his eyes were old with memories of things he had seen.

'I suppose that's why there are so many officers in London at the moment,' Violet said, from a place outside them. 'They're being given leave before it begins.'

'That's right,' said Bertie, dragging himself back. 'Will Holkam be coming home?'

138

'I haven't heard yet,' Violet said, and the cold indifference in her voice would have been obvious to anyone. She changed the subject. 'How is your little boy?'

'Not as well as I'd like. He has a troublesome cough that won't go away.'

'Oh, don't worry about it,' Violet said. 'Everyone's children have that. They pass it to each other at school. Robert's just started going to school and he came home with a horrid cold the very first week.'

Lydia Cunningham came up at that point and spirited Bertie away: even with a large number of officers home on leave, as Violet had remarked, men at social functions were still too precious for hostesses to allow them to be hogged. And that was the last chance Jessie had to speak to him that evening before she had to leave – early, so as to get back to the hostel before the door was locked.

She was tired to death when she got back, and dragged herself out of the taxi and up the stairs like an old woman. Her finery was horribly incongruous in the bare, ugly house and she felt the folly of it, and cursed herself for having bought it, for having accepted the invitation in the first place. She reached her cubicle and sat on the bed, staring emptily at the bare floorboards, and sank into depression.

Her friend Beta had heard her come in, and in a moment appeared before her with a warm woollen dressing-gown over her pyjamas. 'How was it? Gosh, you look lovely,' she whispered. 'Where did you get the fur?'

'Violet lent it to me,' Jessie answered. That was another thing – she would have to find a way to get it back to Violet. Just then, everything seemed like too much effort.

'What's the matter?' Beta asked, sitting beside her on the bed.

Jessie sighed. 'It made me see how ridiculous it is to be going to parties while the world destroys itself around us. The Germans are digging themselves in harder than ever, and all the suffering of last year was for nothing.'

Beta considered her. 'You need cocoa,' she said wisely. 'I have a tin of evaporated milk. Richardson's got a gas ring and a saucepan, and she's on nights. Come on, and I'll make us both some.'

Jessie looked up from the floor. 'She'll have a fit if she finds out.'

'She won't find out. Besides, this is an emergency.'

Richardson was a senior and had a room to herself. They closed the door and Beta rolled up Richardson's dressing-gown and stuffed it in the crack at the bottom of the door before lighting the gas mantle. 'Now, tell me all about the party. You may be *blasé* about such things, but I'm interested.'

While she boiled up the cocoa, she coaxed Jessie skilfully with questions, until it began to seem even to Jessie that the party had been a moderately enjoyable one – food, company, nice surroundings, the chance to wear something other than uniform. Jessie had never told Beta about her feelings for Bertie, but Beta had deduced from various things Jessie had said – and, perhaps more tellingly, not said – that there was someone she cared for, and that the situation was hopeless. Now, as she spoke about her cousin being there with his wife, something in her expression and her voice made Beta wonder if that was it. She would not ask, of course. To be in love with a married man was a hard enough thing to bear without anyone else knowing of it.

She brought the mugs over and sat beside Jessie on Richardson's bed. 'Mind you don't spill any on your costume. It's very pretty.'

'I suppose it is,' Jessie said. 'But what's the point of dressing up?'

'Every woman likes dressing up,' Beta said firmly. 'Especially when you spend the rest of your days in that hideous old uniform, with a collar round your neck like a dog.'

'Well, tomorrow we'll be in it again,' Jessie said, 'and not

140

even doing any proper nursing. I'll be back on Cartwright's ward, scrubbing floors because she doesn't think a VAD can do anything else.'

'And I'll be back on Tudor's, rolling bandages because she hates VADs. Golly!' Beta interrupted herself with such a jump that she almost slopped her cocoa over the rim of the mug. 'I knew there was something I meant to tell you, but it completely slipped my mind! It must have been the fog of gloom you brought in with you that confused me.'

'Well, what is it?' Jessie asked.

'It might just be the answer to our prayers,' Beta informed her. 'There's a notice up in the VADs' sitting-room, asking for nurses to volunteer for overseas posting. You have to be over twenty-three and have six months' service, so we both qualify. There's a list to sign if you want to be considered. What do you think?'

A light began to dawn in Jessie's mind. 'Overseas! Do you think we'd be sent to France?'

'I don't know. That's obviously where they're going to need nurses the most, but they may think we're too young or something. Wouldn't you want to go to France?'

'Of course I would! To do real nursing, right there at the Front, where it matters? To make a difference, to be really useful?'

'Well, we could ask for France,' Beta said. 'But even if it isn't France, it must be better than this. We won't be treated like housemaids, anyway.'

'How can you be sure?'

'Because they can't afford to waste us where there's a real emergency going on. So what do you think? Shall we sign? Do let's! I don't want to go without you.'

'Oh yes,' said Jessie. 'Let's do it. But we'll tell them we want to be posted together?'

'Of course. And that we want to be sent to France.'

'Assuming they want us at all.'

'Why ever not? Two intelligent young women with excellent records and valuable experience?'

'Oh, when you put it like that,' Jessie said. She raised her cocoa in a toast. 'To new beginnings.'

'And to being useful,' Beta responded, and they clinked mugs and drank. 'If it's France, it will mean being nearer to Alpha, too,' she said. Her brother Alfred was serving with the Royal Welch Fusiliers. When she was little, the nearest she could get to pronouncing his name was 'Alfa', and their parents had nicknamed them Alpha and Beta. 'Perhaps I may even get to see him more often.'

Jessie would not allow herself to think it might mean being nearer to Bertie.

The days of Fenniman's leave went by all too quickly, and despite the inclement weather, he and Emma managed to get out and see and do a great many things. They went to the theatre twice and to a couple of exhibitions, and dined in a restaurant, and Emma felt at first very awkward and then wonderfully liberated from restraints to be doing these things with a man and without a chaperone. They were invited to tea parties on most days, and to dinner parties, and with Violet to a ball, where they met Eddie Vibart again, still chaperoning the Prince of Wales around the social circuit.

But best of all for Emma were the times when they went out for a walk together, well wrapped up against the rain and the chilly March winds. It was only the Park, to be sure, but when she was deep in conversation with Fenniman, it felt as private as if it were her guardian's empty heathery acres they were treading. They talked and talked as though they would never stop, and Emma loved every moment. She had decided that she definitely was in love with him; she wanted only to know what his feelings were towards her. Despite the bold move she had taken in writing to him, and her unconventional (or so it felt to her) behaviour in jettisoning the chaperone, Fenniman was too much of a gentleman to take advantage of her. She sometimes wished he would – just a bit. Sitting so close to him in a darkened theatre or the back of a taxi, she wished he would at least take her hand.

When they went for their walks, he took her hand through his arm, and sometimes laid his own over it for a moment, but that didn't really count in her mind. But at last, in the taxi on the way home one evening, he did take it. She thrilled all over, and turned her face towards him. The street lights were low, because of a Zeppelin warning, so she could hardly see him; but on the other hand, it did give them privacy, and the wonderful thing happened. He kissed her. She trembled all over with the excitement of it; she smelt the male smell of his skin and his breath, felt the male firmness of his lips and ached and longed for – she hardly knew what. Because of her mother's death when she was very young, her father's abstraction, and the stern guardianship of the Abradales, she had only the vaguest idea of what men and women got up to after marriage. All she knew was that she wanted to find out, and to find out with Fenniman.

When the kiss ended, she sighed with perfect bliss. Fenniman heard her, and smiled to himself in the darkness. From the moment he had replied to her first letter – and it had taken him much serious thought as to what to say – he had known that this was where *she* wanted it to lead. He had been uncertain about his own feelings. He had liked her from the first meeting – indeed, how could anyone *not* like her? She was a sweet, pretty, well-brought-up girl, with the addition of a lively mind, a great deal of charm and an outgoing personality. It was very flattering that she had picked on him to prefer. But he had never considered himself in the market for a wife. Before the war he had enjoyed the bachelor routine of the regiment; now, the war itself was a disincentive, for life was uncertain for all of them. And his personal circumstances were not favourable to supporting a wife and family.

But Emma was independently wealthy, which modified the last objection. And being with her this past week had made him feel the disadvantages of the monastic life in the all-male environment. He was very attracted to her, to the extent that he thought about her all the time they were apart, and rushed eagerly to their next meeting each day. He didn't think he would ever feel quite contented without her again. There remained the objection concerning the war. But perhaps the very uncertainty of life demanded that one lived it to the full while one had it?

Enough of thinking. He decided in that moment to follow his feelings for once, and said into the dark, 'I would very much like to take you to meet my father. Would you?'

'Your father?' she said wonderingly.

'Yes. He lives down in Kent. We could go the day after tomorrow, if you cared to.'

Emma thought of the bliss of a whole day out with Fenniman, and did not get much beyond that. 'That would be lovely,' she said.

Violet lent her motor and her chauffeur Dawson for the outing. Trains were, in any case, uncertain these days, but she felt also that it would be as well to have an older and wiser head along with them. Dawson was elderly and of unimpeachable probity.

On the way down, Emma asked about his father, and learnt that the brigadier lived alone at Linton Hall, cared for by his former soldier-servant, Harrup, and a housekeeper, Mrs Eagan.

'They've both been with him for ever,' Fenniman said. 'Harrup was with him all through his military career, and he still keeps up mess standards. Makes the old boy dress for dinner every night and so on. And Mrs Eagan came when my mother died.'

'You were quite young then, weren't you?'

'Yes, twelve. But I was away at school, of course. From

the age of eight onwards, I was only at home during the holidays and my mother was already a shadowy figure. Mrs Eagan is much more real to me. Anyway, they do everything for Father, with just a charwoman and a gardener who come in. It's quite a small place – you're not to be imagining a mansion. Father bought the whole estate when he retired from the army, but bit by bit over the years he had to sell the land, and there's just the garden left now. It'll be enough to see him out, anyway.'

'Have you any brothers or sisters?' she asked.

'One half-sister. She's much older than me – the product of my father's first marriage – but she's married and lives in South Africa and I haven't seen her in twenty years. My mother had three before me, but they died in infancy.'

'Oh, how sad! So you're an only child, like me? I have half-brothers and -sisters too, but they're all much older than me, so it was just Papa and me while I was growing up.'

'Is it sad to be an only child? I don't know, never having experienced the contrary. But as I said, I was away at school, and then university, and then I went straight into the army, so I've always had lots of "brothers" around me, in that sense. The regiment has been my home now for a long time.'

Emma thought it seemed a lonely sort of life. She longed to make a home for him, and fill it with people of his own. But she must keep thoughts like that to herself for the moment. She asked, 'Why did you join the West Herts, and not a Kentish regiment?'

'Oh, we're not from Kent originally. That's just where my father bought his estate when he retired.'

'Is the West Herts your father's regiment, then?'

Fenniman smiled. 'No, not even that. Father was a cavalry man. But I'd followed him through prep school, Eton and Christ Church, and I'd reached the point of longing to rebel. A friend of mine at the House, Harcourt-Miller, was going into the West Herts because it was *his* father's regiment, so I went with him and joined the PBI – the Poor Bloody

Infantry. Probably broke my father's heart, though he's not one to let his feelings show.'

'Do you regret not joining the cavalry?' Emma asked.

'Not at all. The cavalry haven't had much fun out of this war; and if I hadn't joined the West Herts, I would never have met Bertie Parke. And,' he looked down at her tenderly, 'if I hadn't met him, I would never have met you.'

Emma blushed with pleasure, and found nothing at all to say.

Linton Hall was a pleasant surprise to Emma, for she had never seen a Kentish hall house before, and this was a particularly pretty one, set in charming gardens of about two acres, which ran down to a small stream at the rear. Fenniman explained it to her as they climbed out of the car. 'Originally there would have been three rooms, the hall in the centre where most of life was carried on, with the parlour at one end, which was a sort of bedroom and reception room for the master and mistress, and a service room at the other end. This one had fifteenth- and sixteenth-century additions, but the central hall remains – very handsome, but the dickens to heat in winter.'

They were greeted at the door by a tall, very upright, military-looking man, whom Emma took to be the brigadier, but who turned out to be Harrup. Fenniman introduced him just in time to avoid a *faux pas* on her part.

'Welcome, Mr Cedric,' he said reproachfully. 'It's been a long time since we had the pleasure of your company.'

'Not since the war began,' Fenniman said, to remind him that there was a reason for his absence.

Harrup received the rebuke with a sniff. 'Your father is in the parlour,' he vouchsafed, but got no further as Mrs Eagan appeared at that moment, wiping her hands on her apron, and introduced a warmer touch to the proceedings.

'My dear, dear boy!' she greeted him. 'What a treat to see you again!'

'Darling Eagan,' he said, and they embraced each other

warmly under Harrup's disapproving gaze. 'You're not a day older,' he concluded, examining her at arm's length.

'You look as if you could do with a good square meal,' she told him, her hands automatically tweaking at his jacket and brushing at his shoulders. 'Don't they feed you in the army?'

'All the time,' he assured her, 'but it's not the how much, it's the what.'

'Oh, you always were a fussy eater. Nothing was good enough for you,' she said.

'*Your* cooking was always good enough for me,' he said. 'But the greatest delicacy I get nowadays is grissoles.'

'Lord save us, what may those be when they're at home?'

'Meat balls, made with minced-up bully beef and hard-tack crumbs,' Fenniman said, with such mournfulness that Emma almost laughed.

'That's burgoo,' Harrup interposed.

'Just so,' said Fenniman, 'only rolled into little balls for the jollity of the thing.'

'Poor lamb!' said Mrs Eagan. 'Well, your dinner will be ready in half an hour, just time for you to talk to your father. And this must be Miss Weston. What must you think of our manners, my dear, chatting away and ignoring you? But we haven't seen this dear boy of ours for such a long time!'

'That's quite all right,' Emma said, shaking the offered hand.

'Now,' Mrs Eagan said to her, with a confidential lowering of her voice, '*would* you like to be shown upstairs?'

'Not at present, thank you,' Emma said, grateful for the kindness.

'Well, any time you do, just ring for me. Now, Harrup, why don't you take them in, and I'll take the chauffeur to the kitchen. I expect he'd like a nice cup of tea after that long, nasty journey.'

She took their coats from Harrup and all but gave him a shove; but he was able to recover the situation at once by giving them a quelling look and saying in the most butlerish tones, 'If you would kindly follow me, I will announce you.'

Fenniman fell in meekly behind him, but dropped Emma a wink that almost made her giggle.

The brigadier rose from a comfortable chair in a square, comfortable room to meet them. There was a good fire in the grate, books lining the walls, a few cherished old pieces of furniture, and a great many military mementoes on the available surfaces. It was very much a man's room. He was much older than Emma had expected – Fenniman was the child of his old age – and very dignified, with the upright carriage and fine whiskers of a cavalry man of the last century. He had the same cast of features and the same dark eyes as his son, which endeared him immediately to Emma, but there was no warmth in him. He was polite, courteous and considerate towards her, but she felt nothing coming from him, either towards her or towards his son. She felt again how sad Fenniman's upbringing must have been.

But despite the host's lack of warmth, it was a very pleasant day. They took a glass of sherry and warmed themselves by the fire for half an hour before being called through to the dining-room – very handsome, if rather chilly, with some fine military paintings on the walls and a number of silver cups and trophies on the sideboard and side tables. Mrs Eagan's 'dinner' – served by Harrup, who remained standing behind his master's chair all through in the old style – was excellent: a delicious pea soup, fillets of haddock in a lightly curried sauce, a shoulder of mutton with capers, and a dessert of cheese and rather wrinkled, but very sweet, store apples.

The talk was mostly between Fenniman and his father, and mostly about military matters and the war, but Emma was happy enough just listening. When the brigadier, of his courtesy, paid attention to her, she enjoyed it less than listening to them talk, for it was inevitable that his attention should express itself in a series of questions about her birth and upbringing. They had nothing in common, after all, apart from Fenniman. The old man hadn't been to London in twenty years, had never been to the theatre in his life, and read nothing but *The Times* and the *Morning Post*. However, he had a passion for shooting, as did Fenniman, and Emma knew a bit about that, having been taken to every shooting house party in Scotland by her uncle in his attempt to get her married, so that made a topic they could talk about. They had a pleasant discussion of the differences between English shooting and Scottish; and Emma answered the brigadier's questions about deer-stalking to the best of her ability, and with some exercise of her imagination.

After the meal, the brigadier showed Emma round the house, and Emma was so interested in the history and so admiring of everything that he went into greater detail than he might otherwise have, and even she could detect a slight unbending in him. They took a stroll outside, though the garden was March-bare and Emma had to take the beauty of the roses – of which the brigadier was obviously proud – on trust. Then they were called in for tea, which they took in the great hall, where the fire had been lit, with all the appurtenances of cake stands, spirit stoves and chafing dishes; and then it was time to go.

The brigadier bent courteously over Emma's hand, and said he hoped she would come again some time. And then he shook his son's hand with what, to Emma, looked like almost a convulsive pressure. Perhaps he was not as emotionless as he liked to appear, she thought with relief. 'Goodbye, Cedric, my boy,' he said. And then, clearing his throat awkwardly, he added, 'Take care of yourself.'

When they were in the car, tucked up under the thick rug and on their way back to London, Emma said, 'So your name's Cedric?'

Fenniman said, 'I was christened Cedric John, but I ditched the Cedric part at Eton, the first time I was roasted for it. But of course, in the army, one hardly has a Christian name at all. They still call me Cedric at home – as you now know – but everywhere else, anyone who has cause to call me anything other than Fenniman calls me John.'

'How strange that I never knew your name until today,' Emma mused.

'Now I suppose you will laugh at me. To distract your attention, I could tell you that my father's name is Algernon.'

'Is it really?'

'Oh yes. Young Algy Fenniman was quite a masher in his time. Or if I really wanted to be unprincipled, I could tell you that Bertie Parke's real name is Perceval.'

'I knew that already,' said Emma.

'He ditched it just as I did my encumbrance, wise man. But I do appreciate the sterling effort you displayed in not laughing about it in front of my father.'

'I wouldn't dare laugh in front of your father.'

'He is rather a dragon, isn't he? Though I believe he has a heart of gold – it has to be a belief, as I've never been privileged to witness it at first hand. He liked you, though.'

Emma glowed. 'Did he?'

'You would have known if he didn't. Those he disapproves of are left in no doubt of it. But I knew he would like you, or I shouldn't have taken you.'

'Why *did* you take me?' she asked, greatly daring.

He reached across the blanket and took her hand, and they looked at each other.

'Haven't you guessed?' he asked. 'I didn't quite intend to do this here in the car, but it's as good a place as any, I suppose. Emma, would you do me the great honour of being my wife?'

Emma's heart thudded almost painfully with the delightful shock of it. 'Oh, gosh, yes!' she said.

He grinned. 'Emphatic, if not elegant. You could call me John now, if you liked.'

'Yes, John, I will marry you,' she said, with mock solemnity, and was rewarded by only the second kiss of her life.

She liked it even more than the first. After it, they looked at each other for a long moment, until Fenniman laughed.

'Extraordinary! I can't think of a thing to say. I've never proposed to anyone before, so it takes me all unready. What happens next? I know you are over twenty-one, but I can't help feeling there ought to be someone I ask for your hand.'

'You ask me. I'm an independent woman,' Emma said.

'So you tell me. But it seems – well, odd.'

It felt odd to Emma, too. She had wanted to be completely free and independent, but now that she was, it seemed an unnervingly open space to exist in. She could almost hear the unchecked wind howling through it. It was rather frightening to think that she alone must be responsible for deciding her future.

'You could ask my uncle Bruce,' she said doubtfully, 'but—'

'But?'

'Well, supposing he said no?' She could imagine Uncle Bruce saying no. Fenniman – her dear John now – would not be his sort: he had no title or fortune.

'Not Uncle Bruce, then,' Fenniman said firmly. 'What about Lady Overton? Isn't she a guardian of yours?'

'Not exactly a guardian, but she and my father were cousins and he asked her to keep an eye on me.' Emma brightened at the thought. 'I'm sure she wouldn't say no. And it would be courteous to ask her.'

'I'm all for courtesy,' said Fenniman. 'And now, that being decided, come here, my lovely affianced. It's perfectly acceptable for engaged people to kiss, you know – at least, as long as it's each other.'

And laughing, Emma went to his arms.

CHAPTER SEVEN

On the 8th of March, in the afternoon, the imperial train left Mogilev for Tsarskoye Selo. Having said goodbye to his staff in the morning, the ex-Tsar had taken a long and emotional lunch with his mother and various other family members. There was no knowing when they would see each other again. A crowd of people had gathered to see the train pull out, and he waved goodbye from the carriage windows. Many of them were in tears.

Fortunately, the journey was quick this time. During the morning of the 9th, Thomas and Prince Dolgorukov, one of the Court officers, sat with the Emperor and let him talk – there was no talking *to* him in his unusual state, at once excited and depressed. He was inclined now to blame his generals for the abdication, and hinted that their insistence that he go was close to treason. And he complained particularly about General Ruzsky: he had been rough and inconsiderate, had badgered him and not given him a moment to think. He still seemed to hope he might live at Livadia as a private gentleman, and Thomas and Dolgorukov both tried, gently, to assure him that a sovereign who renounced the throne could not remain in the country; and that if he attempted to, events would quickly become tragic.

They arrived at Tsarskoye Selo a little after eleven in the morning. The motor was stopped at the gate by a sentry, who peered into the window, then made a signal to an officer waiting a little way off. The officer came no closer, but shouted in a loud voice, pitched to carry, 'Who is there?'

The guard shouted back, 'Nicholas Romanov!'

'Let him pass,' the officer shouted.

It was evident that this pantomime had been arranged to make sure the Emperor knew his new status. It seemed to Thomas petty and spiteful, and he saw that Nicholas felt it. At the door they were met by Count Benckendorff, the grand marshal of the Court, and the antechamber was full, with every staff member and friend who remained at the palace, their faces strained and eager. Nicholas shook hands with Benckendorff, and walked through the chamber stiffly, with his hand at the salute the whole time, but he did not say a word. Thomas guessed he was afraid he might weep if he spoke. He passed through into the private quarters, and the door closed behind him.

Now Thomas could make the urgent enquiry of the count: 'How are the children?'

'Better,' Benckendorff said. 'Much better – all but Grand Duchess Marie, who just started the sickness last night. I'm afraid it looks as though she may have it badly. But the others are recovering, though they are still lying in a darkened room – the light hurts their eyes. Dr Botkin says there is nothing to worry about.'

'Thank God,' Thomas said. 'And Her Majesty?'

'Bearing up very well. She can't understand this business, of course. Frankly, neither can I. We could never get His Majesty to make up his mind even to grant a constitution or appoint a responsible minister. Now he consents to an abdication without the slightest difficulty.' He shook his head. 'It passes me.'

'I don't think he really grasped at first that it was irrevocable,' Dolgorukov said. 'He thought they would all go to Livadia and he would be a sort of emperor by proxy.'

Thomas said, 'He still doesn't grasp the necessity of leaving the country as soon as possible. Can you speak to him?'

'Good God, yes, of course,' said Benckendorff. 'You saw that business at the gate? Things will get a lot nastier – and who knows how long this Provisional Government will last, or who will come after it? I will certainly speak to His Majesty as soon as I can. But you have seen Sir George Buchanan? What does he say?'

'He has sent a telegram to Mr Balfour, on Milyukov's behalf, to suggest that the King and the British government offer asylum as soon as possible.'

'I hope they don't take too long to think about it,' Benckendorff said. He turned his head abruptly as one of the sentries outside paused to stare in at the window, grinning insolently. Benckendorff shuddered slightly. 'You will use any influence you have to speed their decision?'

'Of course I will,' said Thomas.

Venetia was pleased that Emma wanted to 'ask her permission' to marry, for it showed affection and respect. She was equally glad she did not actually have a say in the matter, for she knew very little about Major Fenniman. She liked what she knew; but she suspected he had no fortune, and Emma would be very rich. She was pretty sure that the Abradales would not approve; but on the other hand, she thought Emma's father, Tommy, would have liked Fenniman, and probably wouldn't have cared whether he had a fortune or not. She didn't *think* Fenniman was after Emma's money: he was Bertie's closest friend, and she could not believe Bertie would be so deceived about a man with whom he had been in the closest of shaves. So she invoked Tommy Weston's spirit, crossed her fingers, and said she was delighted with the news.

Emma looked relieved. 'Oh, I'm so glad! I know I'm of age and don't need permission, but John – ' she looked conscious as she said the name '– and I both felt we wanted to ask *someone*.'

'And when do you plan to marry?' was the obvious next question.

They looked at each other. 'We haven't discussed that yet,' Emma said.

'Well, you're both independent and fancy-free,' Venetia said, 'so there's nothing to wait for.'

She said it as a test, and Fenniman came through with flying colours. 'I shouldn't want to hurry Emma into it,' he said. 'I'd like her to have time to change her mind – though naturally I hope she doesn't.'

'Of course I won't,' Emma said indignantly. 'I'm not a *girl*.'

'Pardon me, of course I was forgetting your great age,' Fenniman said teasingly.

'Well, we can't get married right away, of course,' Emma said, ignoring him, 'because John has to go back tomorrow.'

'And I don't know when my next leave will be,' he added. 'I imagine we shall have some hard campaigning this summer. I can't depend on getting away.'

'What about next Christmas?' Venetia said. 'You're bound to get leave, aren't you?'

'The war might even be over by then,' Fenniman said. And to Emma, 'But would you want to get married in the middle of winter?'

'We could make it the following spring,' she said; and then looked doubtful. 'But that's such a long way away.'

'It will soon pass,' Venetia said. 'You'll have the wedding to plan, as well as your war-work. And if you find you really can't wait, you can always bring the date forward.'

'Oh, yes,' said Emma, pleased with the thought. 'Shall we agree on that, then?'

'Whatever pleases you,' Fenniman said, smiling at her in a way that made Venetia feel better about the whole thing.

'But can the engagement be announced at once, in *all* the newspapers?' Emma added. 'I want everyone to know.'

'In that case,' Fenniman said, 'we had better go out right away and buy a ring, so that you can show it to everyone.

And afterwards we'll have a celebratory dinner at the Ritz. Lady Overton, will you join us?'

Venetia smiled. 'No, children, you go and enjoy the privileges of betrothal. You can dine alone together at a restaurant in perfect propriety now. But thank you for asking me. Run along now.'

It was a piece of happiness to lay beside the other things that were filling her mind. The main one was anxiety for Thomas. Her hope that the Romanov family might come to England was almost painful, for Thomas would certainly come with them, and then he would be home and safe and she would see him again, and he would never go back to that dangerous, troubled country. To have her son home, safe! But her fear that it would not come about was even more painful. Who knew what the revolutionaries might do? They might change their mind. They might lose control to a worse set. The Emperor and Empress were officially under arrest by the Provisional Government; a more extreme group might actually imprison them.

Lord Stamfordham told her about a meeting that had taken place in Downing Street on the 22nd, between himself and Lloyd George, Andrew Bonar Law – the chancellor of the exchequer – and Lord Hardinge, the permanent secretary to the Foreign Office. They discussed Sir George Buchanan's telegram, and whether it might be better for the imperial family to go to Denmark.

'Lloyd George was very much against it,' Stamfordham said. 'He said it was too close to Germany, and that there would be a serious danger of the Emperor becoming a focus of intrigue.'

'Yes, he might not encourage schemes of that sort, but one can't be certain the Empress wouldn't,' Venetia said.

'Indeed. So it was generally agreed that we *should* accept the family into England, as the Russians have proposed.'

'Oh, thank God,' Venetia said.

'You are thinking of your son,' Stamfordham said, 'but there is no reason why he shouldn't come home at once.'

'I know. But he won't leave them until they are safe.'

Stamfordham looked anxious. 'I think you should try to persuade him. The Russians want us to send a ship – which naturally we will agree to – but they want the departure to be from Port Romanov.'

'I don't know where that is,' Venetia said.

'It's in the far north, on the Kola peninsula.' He saw she still did not understand and said, 'In the same region as Archangel.'

'Oh,' she said, and her eyes were stark. From there it was a long and hazardous voyage all the way round the top end of Norway and down through the North Sea, two thousand miles of the coldest and roughest seas, with the added danger of being sunk by U-boats. Her husband had perished the year before on that very route, on his way to Russia, when his ship had been sunk by a mine. To have Thomas risk the same thing was an irony too far.

'If he travels separately, he can go by the quickest and safest route,' Stamfordham said. 'If he waits and travels with the imperial family he will have a much less pleasant journey of it.'

And perhaps not arrive at all, she thought. She wondered if that was in the Provisional Government's mind as well. The Romanovs would cease to be a problem to anyone at the bottom of the sea.

'I will try to persuade him,' she said, but with little hope. 'So, what was the conclusion of the meeting?'

'Lloyd George is sending a telegram tonight to say that we will receive the family, on condition it's made clear that the request came initially from the Russian government. Buchanan says that Milyukov is eager to get them out of Russia as soon as possible, because of growing hostility towards them from the extreme left, so we have every hope that they'll expedite the matter.'

This conversation left Venetia hopeful; but a day or two later came the news that the last of the grand duchesses had come down with measles, and could not be moved for at least a week, and she was cast back into anxiety.

She had reason to be. On the 30th of March, the King instructed Lord Stamfordham to write to Balfour expressing his doubts.

The King has a strong personal friendship for the Emperor, and therefore would be glad to do anything to help him in this crisis. But His Majesty cannot help doubting whether it is advisable that the imperial family should take up residence in this country.

After a hasty meeting at Number Ten, Balfour wrote back on the 2nd of April that it was not now possible to withdraw the invitation, and trusted 'that the King will consent to adhere to the original invitation, which was sent on the advice of His Majesty's ministers'.

But on the 6th of April, after a week of unfavourable discussion of the subject in the newspapers and journals, the King wrote again that 'from all he hears and reads in the Press, the residence in the Country of the ex-Emperor and Empress would be strongly resented by the public, and would undoubtedly compromise the position of the King and Queen'.

He went on to say that 'Buchanan ought to be instructed to tell Milyukov that the opposition to the Emperor and Empress coming here is so strong that we must be allowed to withdraw from the consent previously given to the Russian Government's proposal.'

Venetia learnt about it all from Lord Stamfordham when he came up from Windsor to a further meeting with the Prime Minister. He visited Venetia afterwards.

'The King wishes me to keep you informed because of your particular interest in the matter. But you understand that this is all top secret,' he said first.

'Of course, Arthur,' Venetia said. 'You know you may rely on me. Please tell me what's happening.'

He told her about the exchange of letters, and went on, 'The King expected to hear by now that the invitation had been withdrawn. Since he hadn't, he sent me to impress on the Prime Minister the urgency of the situation. He feels that if the Emperor and Empress come here, it will be dreadfully unpopular, and he personally will be blamed for it. The press seem to believe the invitation originally came from him.'

'And didn't it?'

Stamfordham hesitated. 'Not precisely. The government assumed that it was what he would want, and acted accordingly. But you've seen the newspapers. And now he's receiving letters from all sorts of people expressing their hostility and assuming the idea *was* his. He thinks it dreadfully unfair that he will be blamed.'

'Especially when he is the one with the most to lose,' Venetia said.

Stamfordham looked unhappy. 'Venetia, dear, don't be bitter. You must have heard the comments yourself. No-one wants them here. And London is a hotbed of exiled revolutionaries. Bringing the Romanovs here could touch off a tinder-keg. There are plenty of republicans in our own drawing-rooms, you know.'

'I know. And presumably Lloyd George knows. So why send the invitation in the first place?'

'The Russian government wanted it, and it's important to keep them happy so they'll stay in the war. That's why we haven't withdrawn the offer yet. The Prime Minister doesn't want to offend the King, but he doesn't want to offend the Russians either.'

'And what will happen now?'

'Balfour is drafting a telegram to Sir George today.'

'Withdrawing the offer? Oh, Arthur!'

'But don't despair,' he went on quickly. 'At the meeting

today the Prime Minister suggested the South of France might be a better place for the imperial family. He called in Painlevé – the French minister of war – to ask him if there were likely to be any objections. Painlevé said the French people have a high regard for the Emperor, because he's been their staunch ally for years.'

Hope revived painfully in Venetia's heart. 'So they might go to France?'

'Painlevé is going to raise the matter with the ambassador and get him to request the French government to make the offer. So, you see, there is no reason to despair.'

'Thank you for telling me, Arthur,' Venetia said, her emotions in turmoil. 'You will let me know if anything further develops?'

'Of course – as soon as I know, you shall.' He hesitated.

'What is it? You can speak freely to me, you know. What did you want to say?'

'Only that it might be wise for you to try to persuade your son to make his independent way home.' He saw her expression. 'Just as a precaution.'

'You don't think the French will take them,' she said.

'I hope they will,' he replied.

'That's not the same thing,' Venetia said.

While this was going on, some better news came from the other side of the world. President Woodrow Wilson of the United States had published the facts about the Zimmerman Note on the 1st of March, but the Hearst press had declared it a fake. Three-quarters of Americans were indifferent to the war anyway, so it did not arouse sufficient indignation to change their minds.

However, on the 9th of March, astonishingly, Zimmerman himself boasted publicly at a press conference that the telegram was genuine, and this was soon reported in the United States. Then on the 18th of March three American ships were sunk without warning by U-boats. Armed with this ammunition, the President met with the cabinet on the 20th, and they decided on war, to 'make the world safe for democracy'; on the 2nd of April he announced the decision to a joint session of Congress; and on the 6th of April 1917 America declared war on Germany.

Some days after the news broke, Henrietta received a letter from her daughter Lizzie in Flagstaff, Arizona.

You can't imagine the excitement! Everyone's in a ferment about the Zimmerman Note, especially here, because the Germans promised to give Arizona to the Mexicans. The idea outraged Flagstaffians! Previously most people were saying the war was nothing to do with us. They approved of Mr Wilson, saying, 'He kept us out of the war.' Now they talk of 'Germany's perfidy' and say Mr Wilson has let us down badly in Mexico. And once the U-boats started attacking our shipping, you would hardly find an 'anti' in a hundred miles. The majorities in Congress in favour of declaring war were 373 to 50 and 82 to 6, which is pretty conclusive. Everyone here is now saying, 'About time too', regardless of what they felt before.

Of course, our army is tiny, so now a conscription bill is being hurried through Congress – though not quickly enough for some of our hot-blooded young men. The McLeod boys set off for Canada last week to join the Canadian Army rather than wait. Everyone's in a state of high excitement, there are flags everywhere, and no-one talks about anything but the war and the wicked Germans. Betty's Restaurant has renamed sauerkraut 'liberty cabbage', which makes me laugh every time I go past. And Rosie's school principal has sent round a note to parents saying that German lessons are to be discontinued. But I heard a man after church on Sunday saying there ought not to be any more concerts of music by Beethoven,

Mendelssohn and so on, which strikes a sour note, so I hope things don't get unpleasant. Some of our cities have large numbers of people of German extraction, and it would be dreadful if there were attacks on them. We don't have any German restaurants in Flagstaff, though there is a shoemaker by the name of Hermann, but he's as American as the flag!

My greatest worry at the moment is that Martial is longing to volunteer. They're saying the draft will call for men between twenty-one and thirty-one, but they can volunteer from the age of eighteen, and Mart was eighteen last September. Naturally, Rupert eggs him on. He's not eighteen until November, so he's watching closely to see what precedent Martial sets. Of course I should be terribly proud if Mart did go and fight, but frightened too. And I do think he ought to finish college first. Ashley agrees with me that Mart should *not* go, but I don't feel he says it with his whole heart. He complains, in a wistful way, that he is too old to serve, and wishes he might strike a blow for democracy and the old country – of course he is half English by blood, which makes our boys three-quarters English, though that's not something I want to stress at this juncture! I think Mart is safe enough from temptation at Harvard until semester ends. But how we shall keep him through the summer I don't know. And two of his Boston cousins are within the conscription age, and if they are called up, as they may well be, or if they volunteer, I'm afraid my boy may be tempted beyond endurance.

Finally, I must tell you about Aunt Ruth, who has been staying with us for a while. She followed every bit of the debate in the newspapers, but would never give her opinion on anything, just pressing her lips tight if anyone asked. But as soon as war was declared, she said, 'Well, thank God for that!' I said, 'Why, Auntie,

162

I thought you hated war.' And she said, 'You bet I do, honey. War makes beasts of men, and destroys everything it touches. But I've got a hankering to see England before I die, and I can't go until this damned war is over. If I was a man, I'd go myself, and give those Germans a pasting until they hollered Uncle.' Hard to remember that Aunt Ruth is seventy-one years old, and weighs about ninety pounds!

Henrietta entered fully into her daughter's feelings. To see one's sons off to war was a very mixed joy; and when they were gone, it was an unmixed anxiety. It was strange to think of little Martial being old enough to go and fight. She hadn't seen any of them for five years. She wondered if *they* might make a visit when the war was over. It would be wonderful to see them again. With that thought she folded the letter and went off to talk to Tomlinson about the laundry.

After weeks of rain, it was good to have a dry day again. Polly was making the most of it. There was a cold wind – the penetrating sort they called a 'lazy wind' because it was too lazy to go round you and went straight through instead – but it was just what was wanted for drying out the ground. Polly was out riding on Vesper, with her young hound Kai running ahead of her. Bell, her old dog, had shown willing, but had left them after half a mile to go back home to the fire.

Despite the cold, there was a definite feeling that spring was on its way. The willows had a hint of yellow to their tresses as they swung in the wind, and there were little wild daffodils along the back lane in Knapton, though the wind was bending them almost flat. And when she passed Prospect Farm on the way to Low Moor, there were primroses under the hedges, pale and deckle-edged, nestling in their dark rosettes of leaves. Brown hens pecked in the lane, the wind ruffling their feathers madly. They fled in absurd panic before Vesper's dancing hoofs – even though she was four now, she never walked if she could dance. But the Prospect geese came hurrying officiously down to block her way and curse at her, and be affronted that she would not stop. As they hurried away again in an indignant wedge, Polly noticed how white they looked against the drying-lawn, proof that the grass was growing green again.

Vesper was fresh from not having had enough exercise lately, and Polly let her gallop across Low Moor and then over Marston Moor almost as far as Tockwith. That warmed them both up. She lost Kai on the way – the hound was fast, but not a stayer – but knew she would find him again some-where on the way back. When Vesper had got her wind, she turned her back and walked and trotted alternately to keep them both warm, crossing Moor Lane and Atterwith Lane, passing the straw-bale lambing pens, and sending the early lambs stotting away madly, like mechanical toys, to hide their eyes under their mothers' flanks. The breeze had been the wrong way before to carry the sheep's clamour; now she was among them it was loud, but yet something she hardly heard, a sound so familiar and natural to the place it was like the soughing of the wind in the trees. Vesper started to pull again, saying she had not had nearly enough, so Polly let her canter, passing round behind Rufforth Hall towards Harewood Whin. They jumped the Smawith Dike twice where there were firm places, but then they had to slow to a walk as they neared the Whin, for the ground was boggy.

Picking a way for Vesper, Polly decided to go through the Whin rather than round, to see if the wood anemones were out. She walked Vesper under the branches and the din of the wind against her ears dropped suddenly. The mare's hoofs were quiet on the beaten path, and there was no sound but the creaking of the saddle and the faint hooning of the high branches.

Suddenly Kai was there, bounding onto the path in front of them, grinning his pleasure at the reunion.

'Where have you been, old fellow?' she called to him. He bowed, waving his whip-like tail, then turned away, trotting a few feet and diverting down a side track, looking back beguilingly to make her follow. Then it was she heard a murmur of voices and, intrigued, she went after him. The side path was only just wide enough for the mare. Brush caught at Polly's legs and scratched the leather, and she had to duck her head under low branches. It led back to the brook, and as soon as she came in sight of it, she saw three figures lying prone on the grass, their heads over the water and their hands in it.

'Well,' she said, halting the mare, who was snorting with interest at the sight, 'you'll be in a nice state when you get home!'

All three scrambled up at the sound of her voice. There was a paraphernalia of fishing nets and jam-jars around them on the grass. Their sleeves were rolled up, their arms red with the cold, and two of them had dirty faces and untidy hair. She looked with sharp interest at the third person, for he was undeniably handsome, and his looks were enhanced for her by the fact that she could never get him to smile. He was always pleasant and polite, but remained reserved, which gave him an air of mystery she found romantic and intriguing.

'What *are* you doing?' she asked.

But it was James and Jeremy who answered, with a splurge of overlaid voices, and upheld jars, showing their treasures, which made Vesper blow with affront and walk backwards. Father Palgrave took a step forward and caught the rein. Normally Polly hated anyone touching her horse while she was in the saddle, but it brought him to her side and made him look up at her.

'It's a nature walk,' he said. 'We've been learning the names of the trees and other plants.'

'But what were you doing lying down in the dirt?' she asked, though she had guessed.

'We were checking on the progress of the frogspawn,' he said.

He looked up at her, no smile in his face or his eyes, no further words forthcoming, waiting for her to do whatever she would do next. She studied him a moment, wanting him to respond to her, as young, handsome men always did. The boys were still chattering away about what they had seen and done that morning, but she hardly heeded them. She was racking her brains for something to say that would interest Palgrave enough to break through that reserve, but infuriatingly she could not think of anything.

And then she realised that he was not going to advance the conversation, because he was *waiting for her to go*. She didn't know whether to be amused or insulted. She didn't want to turn meekly away with her tail between her legs; but fortunately Vesper solved the problem. She had been champing her bit, disapproving of this detour when she had been on her way home. Now she shook her head violently, making the bridle straps rattle, and in the middle of the shake she vented a mighty sneeze. Ropes of saliva and mucus whipped out and splattered everyone, but Father Palgrave caught the most, and it made him step back hastily and drop the rein.

Polly laughed. 'I'd better go. I don't want her to get cold.' She turned the mare away, then called over her shoulder, 'I hope you won't get into trouble when you get home! You're awfully dirty!'

Kai started to follow, then paused, looking back at the boys, wondering where the greater pleasure lay. But as the mare disappeared round the curve of the path, he made up his mind and bounded after her.

'She wasn't a bit interested,' Jeremy complained, peering into his jam-jar. 'She didn't even look, and these have got *legs*.'

'Girls are never interested in things,' James said, from the deep wisdom of a year's superiority in age. 'Not proper things, I mean.'

'But Polly used to be,' Jeremy said.

'She's grown-up now,' James said, as if that explained everything.

Perhaps it did, Palgrave thought, relaxing now that she was really gone. He had seen from his earliest days at the house that Polly was interested in him, and he knew how dangerous that could be. She was extremely beautiful, head-strong and passionate and, while not exactly spoilt, she was used to commanding everyone from her father down. And she was sixteen. It was an explosive mixture.

There were always women who were attracted to priests; and his position, as chaplain in an ancient house, would probably seem very romantic to some. He had been prepared from the beginning to be the object of crushes among the housemaids, and had decided on strategies to cope with that. But Miss Polly was an altogether more hazardous prospect. She was just of the age to fancy herself in love – indeed, girls of that age pretty well *had* to be in love with someone, and he was the only young man in the house. So he was doing his best to repulse her by never chatting or smiling. It did not come naturally to him – he was a sociable soul – but he did not want any complications to arise that might mean his having to leave. He loved Morland Place already, and he very much wanted to stay.

He was beginning to feel more settled, was sleeping better, and had some appetite for the excellent meals that were so regularly served. It had been hard at first to cope with so many people around him, to learn the geography of the old house, and to take up the variety of responsibilities that waited for him. In the hospital and the convalescent home, he had had no decisions to make, and the doctor had warned him that responsibility might tax his nerves. At first, at Morland Place, he had had the old nightmare every night, so that he almost dreaded going to bed. But since the time he had sleepwalked into Maria, the nightmares had gradually decreased in frequency. He did not now go to bed expecting one, so he slept better, which in turn strengthened him against the next night.

His employer, Mr Morland, could not have been kinder. He had positively urged him not to do too much book studying with the boys just yet, but follow plenty of outdoor pursuits. Palgrave thought he was right: you could not, after all, train a dog that had not had enough exercise. James had been difficult at first – resentful of male authority and inclined to show off his independence in front of the other children. But the strategy was working. Having let off steam, he was willing to do a modicum of work, and a warmth was growing up between him and his tutor. With all his naughtiness, Palgrave liked him more than Jeremy, who tended to be spiritless and complaining. The three of them were out of doors as much as the weather allowed, which was doing them the world of good. Palgrave's health was improving, James was running off his excess energy, and Jeremy was growing hardier. It was a sop to conscience that he improved the shining hour with instruction on the birds, beasts and flora, for what they were really doing was running about and having fun.

This holiday period would have to come to an end eventually – he had seen Jeremy's mother frowning at him when he came in with the boys, and knew she was restless for him to be running a proper schoolroom with the boys at silent attention and dusty books open before them. But even when that day came, he would not like his new home any less. He loved the house and the beautiful, astonishing chapel. He loved Henrietta, her strong, simple faith and quiet courage; he loved kind, bluff Teddy, always looking to do someone good; he loved the children, and the sensible, hardworking servants; he even loved the panting, hairy mass of dogs that hogged the fires and lavished wet embraces on anyone they met.

And he loved talking to Maria. He was racked with pity for her circumstance, widowed so young, having spent no more than a week in the company of her husband; giving birth to his child when he was already cold in the ground. She bore it stoically, though when she spoke of Frank, he knew she was still very much in love with him, and missing him painfully. He wanted to comfort her; and as talking to him seemed to give her relief, he made himself available whenever he could.

It had begun that way, at least; but now he longed for those conversations just as much on his own account as on hers. The sight of her coming into the drawing-room in the evening with a book in her hand, and veering naturally towards wherever he happened to be sitting, was not the least of the reasons he wanted to stay at Morland Place.

Though she had not been listening, Polly had heard quite a bit of what James and Jeremy were saying, one part of which was that they had visited the camp before going on to the Whin. So as it was not yet quite time for luncheon, she thought she would ride up herself and see how things were going on there.

The camp was a recent addition to the estate. As the army expanded, it needed more places to put the soldiers while they underwent training, and her father, as a prominent local landlord, had been approached and had offered a tract of land for the purpose. It was up near the Monument, in the rough area behind what had been the mares' fields. It was far enough away from the house not to disturb anyone; and the mares had long been moved down closer to the Morland stud at Twelvetrees.

Vesper objected strenuously when Polly turned her aside from the path home, shaking her head and trying to evade the bit. Polly had to use the stick in the end, and Vesper shot forward indignantly in a hard trot. Though Polly had been riding almost since before she could walk, trotting was an uncomfortable gait when sidesaddle, so she eased the mare into a canter, knowing the uphill pull to the Monument would take some of the fizz out of her. At the crest, Vesper slowed of her own accord, and it was at a decorous walk that they covered the last fifty yards.

The camp was beginning to take shape now: neat lines of white tents marched along the slope, ending in the row of wooden huts which housed the offices, the mess, the stores and so on. More huts were still being constructed, and on the far side there was excavation work going on as a work party extended the pipeline that had brought water to the trough at the corner of the mares' fields. Smoke rose from several huts, including the camp kitchen; there was a quiver of soup on the air.

Vesper's ears were pricked hard towards the strange scene, and as she snorted her interest, her breath rose in twin clouds on the frozen air. Kai had caught them up, and was wandering along the dividing hedge. Something was going on behind it: Polly could see the bare twigs vibrate, and hear muffled sounds of work and voices, but the hedge was too high and thick to see what it was. But there was a gate up ahead, which would give her a view. She noted it had been left open – something that automatically offended her country upbringing – and Kai, tracking on ahead, disappeared through it. She called him back sharply, but either he didn't hear or he chose not to. Annoyed, she sent Vesper on and went after him.

She turned in at the gate, and caught a glimpse of a fatigue party clearing out the ditch that ran along the other side of the hedge; but before she could do more than register it, a man appeared right under Vesper's nose and she gave such a violent breenge that Polly was unseated and went off over her shoulder. For once in her life she did not keep hold of the rein, and felt the mare get away from her even as the ground was meeting her (and oh! it was hard with the frost in it!). Her horsewoman's instinct drove her to her feet almost before she had begun hurting – a loose horse *must* be caught. But as her head stopped whirling she saw that someone – presumably the same someone who had startled her – had caught the rein and was in process of being towed as Vesper backed away, her eyes white with shock.

A couple of steps, and Polly had her. The man was still pulling at the rein and upsetting Vesper, and she snapped, 'Let go. I have her. Let go.' In a moment it was all over. Vesper was standing, trembling dramatically – she was always an actress. Kai was sitting on his tail smiling ingratiatingly at everyone; and Polly was twisting her neck to see if there was any mud on her clothing.

'I say, are you all right?' the man asked.

'No thanks to you,' Polly said. 'What did you jump out like that for, right under my horse's nose?'

'I'm sorry. I didn't know you were there,' he said reasonably. Behind him, the fatigue party were leaning on their shovels, watching the scene with the pleasure that comes from having physical labour unexpectedly interrupted. 'Did you hurt yourself?'

'No, of course not,' she said scornfully. 'It's not the first time I've fallen off.'

He misunderstood the remark. 'Learning to ride is really hard, isn't it?' he said, with a sympathetic smile. 'I'd hardly been on a horse before I joined the army. But an officer has to be able to ride, so they give us riding lessons. I've fallen off dozens of times, so I know how you feel. Every bit of me is black and blue. I don't know whether it hurts more being *on* the animal or falling *off*!' He laughed engagingly. 'The riding-master says it takes seven falls to make a horseman, so by that count I must be quite an expert by now.'

Polly had been staring at him in astonishment at being included in his amateur status, which had given her time to register that he was a tall young man in officer's uniform, with tightly curly brown hair, a broad, fair, pleasant face, and a slight cleft in his chin. There was nothing remarkable about him – nothing to rival the dark, romantic good looks of Father Palgrave – but when he laughed she noted that he had the nicest teeth she had ever seen, white and even, which made his smile very attractive.

He needed, however, to be brought down a peg. 'I didn't fall off,' she said haughtily. 'I was thrown.'

He didn't seem at all abashed. 'Well, whatever it was, I bet it hurt just the same. The riding-master assures me it's worth it in the end, if that's any comfort to you. And, of course, it must be much harder doing it sidesaddle. I'm full of admiration for you ladies.'

Polly felt her face redden with anger that he *would* not understand. 'I've been riding since I was four years old!' she informed him. 'I am Miss Morland, and my father is Mr Edward Morland of Morland Place.'

He responded to that by straightening himself to attention and saluting her. 'Lieutenant David Holford, very much at your service, ma'am. I'm honoured to make your acquaintance. As Mr Morland is our landlord here, I am even more delighted to have been able to render you a service by catching your very nice horse.'

'After you made her shy in the first place!' Polly said. 'She wouldn't have needed catching if you hadn't startled her.'

'I can only apologise again, ma'am, and hope that the occurrence does not put you off the noble art of equestrianism.'

She was close to exploding, when suddenly she realised that he was teasing her. 'You knew all along who I was,' she accused him.

'A beautiful young lady riding alone on a horse of that quality? I guessed you must come from the house down there, and I'd already heard Miss Polly Morland described as a golden-haired goddess. I thought there couldn't be more than one person who fitted that description.'

Polly was pleased with the flattery, and angry that she

was pleased, considering he had had the audacity to tease her when they weren't even acquainted. 'I think you are a very impudent man,' she said. 'And I should be obliged if you would fetch a box, or something of the sort, that I can mount from.'

Now he bowed and looked solemn, though his eyes were still twinkling. 'I beg your pardon for having offended you. I assure you nothing could be further from my wishes. I'm truly sorry for having startled your horse. Could you find it in your heart to forgive me?'

Polly's sense of humour asserted itself belatedly as she realised she was making a large fuss about nothing at all. And he *was* tall, and in uniform, and had a nice smile. She thought, from the way he held himself, that he would be a good dancer. 'I forgive you,' she said graciously. 'Now I must go. It's too cold for my horse to stand.'

'About that box,' he said, beginning to look round.

He was going to call to one of the men, but she forestalled him. 'You may throw me up. Do you know how to do that?'

'I think so,' he said.

She gathered the reins, took hold of the pommel, and bent her leg, felt his strong hands take hold of it, and counted, 'One, two, three!' He boosted her with such enthusiasm that she felt as if she soared into the saddle. Vesper gavotted about as she settled herself and her skirt, then Holford handed her her whip and stood away.

'Thank you. Goodbye,' she said.

'Goodbye, Miss Morland,' he said.

She was aware he was watching her – and, indeed, he followed her to the gate so that he could watch her ride down the hill. She rather liked the sensation, and despite the rule about walking the last half-mile home, she put Vesper into a canter, knowing the gait showed off her figure to the best advantage.

That evening, when her father came home, she said to

him casually, 'I wonder, when the battalion has settled into the camp, Papa, whether we shouldn't ask some of the officers to dinner?'

'I've already thought of that, chick,' Teddy said. 'We'll have them all to dine, in batches. As they'll be our very own battalion, we must be hospitable. When the good weather comes, we should arrange some entertainment for the men, too. And I was wondering whether we shouldn't give a ball, perhaps in May. It seems a waste to have all those young men out there and not give them a chance to meet the young ladies of the neighbourhood.'

Sometimes, Polly thought, her father came close to being the perfect man.

BOOK TWO

Plateau

Adieu la vie, adieu l'amour,
Adieu toutes les femmes.
C'est bien fini, c'est pour toujours,
De cette guerre infâme.
C'est à Craonne, sur le plateau,
Qu'on doit laisser sa peau
Car nous sommes tous condamnés
C'est nous les sacrifiés!

Anon: 'Chanson de Craonne'

CHAPTER EIGHT

Thomas did not like leaving Tsarskoye Selo to go into Petersburg on his regular visits to the embassy. He was afraid of what might happen when he was away. The guards amused themselves by parading their power with petty insults and annoyances. Whenever the Emperor went out walking in the grounds, some guard with a rifle and bayonet would be sure to step in front of him and say, 'We don't permit you to go there, Mr Romanov. Go another way.' Inside the palace, too, they exercised an arbitrary power, sometimes forbidding entry to a certain part of the building, sometimes ordering the Emperor to his room for no given reason. Nicholas bore it with patience. He obeyed orders without demur, spoke gently and politely to all, maintained an air of serenity and indifference to the change in his circumstances. Only his appearance gave away the strain underneath. He had aged dreadfully: his hair was quite grey, his eyes bistred, his face a web of fine wrinkles. He looked like a little old man, Thomas thought, though he was not quite forty-nine.

The guards confined themselves to petty insults now, but Thomas did not know how long that would last. Most of all, he was afraid each time that when he returned they would not let him in again. Olga and Marie were still ill and confined to their rooms. He had not seen Olga since he got back from Stavka. He was assured by Dr Botkin that she was recovering, but he knew now she had been very ill, and might have died. He had sent her a note, and received one in reply, but he longed to see her with his own eyes.

Easter in Russia fell at the beginning of April. There were church services, confessions, fasting and vigils, and on Easter Day mildly joyful celebrations. In the morning all the servants assembled in the ante-room and the Emperor greeted and kissed each one individually while the Empress handed out Easter eggs.

The next day, Thomas went in to Petersburg to see Sir George Buchanan. The difference in the city was apparent now. It was beginning to look dirty and unkempt. Rubbish blew along the streets, drains overflowed, windows that had been smashed in the revolution were still boarded up, other damage went unrepaired. There were frequent cuts in the power supply, and sometimes the water was turned off. Long queues formed not only outside the food shops but at bus and tram stops: services had never gone back to normal as attendance at work was erratic.

And everywhere there were crowds of slovenly soldiers and sailors, wandering idly about the streets, gathering on corners, frequently drunk and quite out of control. There were no police to be seen, and the only motor-cars belonged to the new officials, speeding along with horns blaring to emphasise their urgency and importance. The rich and well-dressed people who had once frequented the centre of the city were absent, either hiding away at home or having fled the capital. Only the poor and the middle class were visible, and the latter took care to dress at their plainest, for fear of provoking the soldiers. What had once been a gloriously beautiful city had become drab and dingy, heavy with an air of tension and suppressed anxiety.

But no-one accosted Thomas or tried to hinder him as he made his way to the embassy; and there, at least, there were smart guards and efficient routine, things going on in the proper way. It was a relief for a few hours to be where people could be relied on to behave correctly: such a relief that only then did Thomas appreciate how frightening the world outside had become.

When he was shown into Sir George Buchanan's room, he could see at once that the ambassador was worried.

'I've had a telegram from Balfour,' he said. 'It's marked "personal and most confidential", so this must go no further. Do you understand? You must not tell anyone at Tsarskoye Selo – not Nicholas, not anyone.'

'I understand, sir,' Thomas said, feeling a low gripe of dread. 'Is it about the evacuation to England?'

Buchanan looked away, out of the window at the frozen blue sky. 'It's all very embarrassing,' he admitted. 'There's been a great deal of anti-Romanov feeling in the newspapers at home, and among the public at large – not only in the House and the clubs, but in the pubs and workplaces as well. So much so that they're now thinking it might not be a good idea for the family to be given asylum in England.' He met Thomas's eyes reluctantly. 'I'm ordered to avoid the subject with the Russians from now on, if at all possible. Not bring it up, not mention it – and if they mention it, to answer evasively. If at all possible,' he repeated.

'But—' Thomas could not immediately find words. A week ago both sides had been eager to have the removal made as soon as possible.

'Yes, I know, and it's very awkward for me,' Buchanan said. 'I can't tell the lie direct, I can't tell the truth, and I must try to keep on good terms with the Provisional Government. Fortunately, I understand that Kerensky doesn't want them to go just yet, before he's had a chance to question them and examine their papers, so perhaps the subject simply won't come up. It may give us a few weeks' grace.'

'There won't be any papers,' Thomas said. 'They've been burning everything. Apparently Lily Dehn advised it.'

'It may be just as well. Anything written down can be

179

twisted by unscrupulous characters to mean whatever they want it to mean.'

'But surely the King must be anxious for the transfer to be made quickly?' Thomas said, following his own train of thought.

Buchanan's expression was perfectly blank. 'I believe the thinking now is that it would be better for them to go to France.'

'France?' Thomas said, with reviving hope. France would do very well.

'An official approach is being made, and I believe there's been an unofficial one from the King, as well,' said Buchanan. 'So don't despair. There are plenty of diplomatic avenues still unexplored. I haven't quite given up hope of England yet. Once the public protests have died down, things may look very different. These things can flare up one month and be forgotten the next. Now, to other matters.'

They went on to discuss the war news, the political situation and what Kerensky's intentions really were. It was becoming plain that he was the real force of the government – in so far as the power was not held by the Soviet of Soldiers' and Workers' Deputies.

Emma was enjoying her new status as an engaged person. She no longer felt any awkwardness about going around London alone: the ring on her left hand seemed to her to confer absolute safety and propriety. She had had letters from her half-brothers and -sisters, and had been down to visit her oldest half-sister Fanny in Surrey, where she had been fêted with a family dinner party.

She had, of course, written a respectful and affectionate letter to her aunt and uncle at Aberlarich, labouring over the wording, for she was afraid that the matter of it would inevitably offend. She explained that she had known Major Fenniman for some time, that he was a friend of Bertie Parke's, and that Venetia and Violet had both met him, and liked him. Yet she was aware that, since she had never been able to mention him to the Abradales, it would seem like just the sort of sudden and intemperate attachment they had feared.

The reply was long in coming, suggesting that similarly great thought had gone into it.

You are as aware as I am that I cannot any longer command or forbid you [Uncle Bruce wrote], and it seems now that you have also denied yourself my advice and guidance. I am glad at least that you have not allied yourself to someone quite unknown to *any* of your friends and family. You are very young to be embarking on marriage with no firmer guide than your own fancy, and I am only relieved that you have shown enough sense not to marry out of hand. I hope and pray you will use the period of your engagement to make proper enquiries about Major Fenniman's circumstances and family, for I cannot find anyone here who knows the name at all.

Emma read thus far with a sparkle of anger and an inner certainty that she had done the right thing in breaking away from her uncle's authority. However, the conclusion of the letter brought gentler feelings, and a knot of tears to her throat.

Having urged you to caution, I will say no more on the subject, my dear niece, only to assure you that whatever I have said and done, it has always been out of my deepest affection for you, and my sincere concern for your well-being. I should be glad to receive Major Fenniman if you can make it convenient to bring him here one day. I should like to meet the man who has succeeding in capturing my dear niece's heart. Your aunt joins me in sending our fondest wishes and blessings.

She took the letter to Venetia, and asked her to write to Uncle Bruce and tell him that Fenniman was not an adventurer, and that they really loved each other. This was an awkward request for Venetia, since she didn't know anything of the kind, though she had met Fenniman, liked him, and knew no harm of him. But Emma was so urgent – and as things stood, there was nothing anyone could do to prevent her marrying him if she wished – that Venetia in the end agreed to write. She knew how anxious the Abradales must be, and was as concerned to relieve their minds as Emma's. She wrote simply that Fenniman was an officer and a gentleman, well liked in his regiment, and from a respectable army family, and that his readiness to postpone the wedding suggested he was not trying to get his hands on Emma's money. She did not, of course, show this letter to Emma, who would have been hurt by its muted enthusiasm.

Emma, meanwhile, relieved to have that part of it over, settled down to enjoy her correspondence with her beloved. She wrote to him every day, and he replied almost as often, his letters growing in facility. And in those letters their relationship bloomed. Now she could speak to him through them as an equal, without restraint; and he could unlock to her the places inside him that no-one before had touched.

He had hardly had a mother; his father had been a cold disciplinarian; the warmth in his life had all come from a servant, with whom he could never be really intimate. He had lived since the age of eight in institutions, his life the hard life of men – satisfying in most ways, but leaving unexpressed a gentler part of him that he had hardly been aware existed.

He had proposed to Emma almost on a whim, but now he found that some instinct had known better than his conscious mind: she was what he needed. She understood him; she completed him. He saw how far from a whole person he had been; and in their increasingly intimate letters, he saw the same deficits in her life as in his own, and understood her need of him as clearly as his own of her. Now he looked forward with keen anticipation to their life together after the war, and imagined it unfolding like a flower, petal by petal, into something satisfying and lovely.

This unexpectedly lyrical bent of his even drove him to begin writing poems to her – though he didn't think well enough of them to send them to her. Perhaps one day he would write something worthy of her. In the mean time he gave vent to some of his excess of joy in song. In the house where they were billeting when out on rest there was a piano with only half a dozen missing notes, and he played and sang in the evenings, to Bertie's pleasure and amusement. Bertie wrote to Jessie: 'I have never seen old Fen so completely cock-a-hoop. He really is very much in love with little Emma. I think it will answer well – no man could be more infatuated.'

Venetia received a letter from Thomas begging her to use every influence to 'have us brought to England'. It was the use of the plural pronoun that upset her: so completely did he equate his own future with the Romanovs'. She had little hope of it, but went to see Lloyd George at the House. She had never liked him, having had dealings with him during the suffragette phase, and considering him insincere and a trimmer – a judgement not modified by the way he had ousted Asquith from power. However, he received her with all courtesy in his private office, asked her to sit down, and offered her sherry.

'I think I can guess what you want to talk to me about,' he said, seating himself too. 'I know Lord Stamfordham has told you everything.'

'He and I are old friends,' she said, 'and the King asked him to keep me informed. You may rely on my discretion.'

'I know that,' the Prime Minister said. 'Your services to the state, and your late husband's, entitle you to be told what is going on. And of course, your son—'

'It's on his behalf that I am here,' she interrupted. 'He begs me to use what influence I have to get the imperial family brought to England.'

'At the moment,' Lloyd George said, 'we cannot invite them here.'

'I know the King doesn't want it, but can't you override him?'

'That would not be at all proper,' he said, trying to look disapproving.

She shook her head. 'You would do so in a moment if you really wanted to.'

'I think you over-estimate my ruthlessness, and the cabinet's powers. But at the moment, the feeling in the country is strongly against it. There's a great deal of left-wing agitation, labour relations are bad, and we cannot risk an upheaval at a time when we are straining every nerve to win the war. A strike in the armament factories would be disastrous. You must understand that.'

Venetia did, though she didn't like it. 'And France?'

'We've heard from Lord Bertie.' He was the British ambassador in Paris. 'He says the Emperor and Empress are regarded as criminals over there, and the Empress in particular is hated as a Boche. France won't have them. Frankly, at the moment no-one wants them.' He studied her face. 'But don't despair. We shan't let anything happen to them. If all else fails, there are still – shall we say – unofficial channels which we can use.'

'You mean the Secret Service?' she said bluntly.

He smiled behind his large moustache. 'My dear ma'am, it is not possible to admit that there is any such thing as a Secret Service. But if there were – and I stress that this is a hypothetical exercise – if there *were*, plans would be being discussed even as we speak for a rescue, in the event that it were necessary.'

'And where, hypothetically, would they go, if no-one will have them?'

'Oh, one of the neutral countries – Sweden, Switzerland,

perhaps; or if those were considered too close to home, there is Japan or even South America. We have a good relationship with Brazil, and I believe it can be very pleasant there. When the war is over, when sentiment has mellowed, they might still be able to come here. I don't despair of it. But at all events, we will see them safe, don't worry.'

Venetia nodded her thanks for his reassurance; and then, of curiosity, asked, 'Why are you concerned? I can't believe you like them personally.'

'We are a constitutional monarchy. It would be very bad for all of us if we appeared to approve of Red revolution. And it would set a very bad precedent to allow anything to happen to a monarch, however little we liked him.' He paused a moment, and then said, his eyes reflective, 'And I can't help being concerned for those pretty little princesses. I saw them once. Four sweeter, more innocent girls you can't imagine.'

This softer side to him surprised her, but she left Westminster feeling a little more comfortable, and wrote to Thomas telling him what she knew. She still begged him to come home, but without any hope that he would.

Jessie and Beta were called to the matron for interview at the same time, but were seen separately. Jessie went in first and presented herself, hands behind her back and feet turned out in the approved manner, and the matron, Miss Colefax, occupied herself for a few moments reading through some pages on her desk, which Jessie assumed were her record of service. She tried to read it upside-down to see what they had said about her, but most of it was handwritten and she could not decipher it.

Eventually the matron looked up. She was a youngish woman who, perhaps in compensation for her early responsibility, had developed a hard, unfeeling expression. She looked at Jessie with cold eyes. 'You have been here almost a year, Nurse?'

'Yes, ma'am.'

'And you are – twenty-six years old?' She consulted the top page.

'Yes, ma'am.'

'Hmm. I see you have worked on the acute wards. Sister Fitton speaks highly of you. Sister Thompson, too.'

It seemed too ingratiating to say, 'Thank you' or even 'Yes', so Jessie said nothing, but she was pleased.

'And you are a widow?' Miss Colefax looked up abruptly at the question, perhaps hoping to catch Jessie out.

Jessie returned the stare steadily. 'My husband fell at Loos.'

'Very good,' Miss Colefax said – an odd response, Jessie thought; but it was explained in her next words. 'You have requested service in France, and in age, experience and marital status you are just the sort of nurse we require. However desperately we need them out there, we have a duty to take care of our nurses, and there will be many shocking sights, and situations requiring a certain . . . robustness that unmarried girls may not have.'

Jessie said, 'Yes, ma'am. I understand.'

'Do you?' Matron Colefax said, as though she doubted it. She gave Jessie another long stare, then looked down at the papers again. 'However, I am not entirely sure about Nurse Wallace. You say you want to serve together?'

'We are very anxious to stay together, ma'am.'

'It is as well for a nurse out there to have a friend at hand. But will Nurse Wallace be able to stand up to the conditions?'

Jessie knew it was not a question, but she answered it. 'She is very sensible and – and robust, ma'am.' She used the matron's own word deliberately. 'I have never seen her unsettled by anything.'

'I did not ask your opinion, Nurse,' the matron said sharply. She turned more pages. 'She has a good record. And three months more service than you. Very well, you may go, and send her in.'

Jessie stood outside in the corridor – there were no seats for waiting nurses, since most visits to the matron were of the penitential sort, and standing was considered good for the soul. It seemed like a very long wait but, she supposed afterwards, could not have been more than five minutes. She wondered what she would do if she were accepted and Beta turned down. She did not want to go without her friend; but having applied, would she be allowed to refuse? And how many black marks would it mean if she did?

But when Beta came out, she was smiling. She closed the door behind her and did a small silent jig of glee, before grabbing Jessie's arm and pulling her further down the corridor where they might not be heard. 'She said yes!' she cried. 'She says we can both go. I was to tell you. The official letter will be in our pigeonholes by the end of the day, and we'll probably be off at the beginning of next month.'

'I'm so glad! I was afraid from what she said that she wouldn't let you go.'

'What do you mean?' Beta said indignantly. 'She said yes to me right away, but she was doubtful about you. Wasn't sure you had it in you.'

Jessie realised in time that Beta was teasing. 'Fool!' she said. They hurried down the corridor together at their rapid nurses' pace.

Beta grew serious. 'You do think we're doing the right thing? It's all very well to be excited, but I imagine it will be pretty bad out there – like the convoys, only worse.'

'Of course it will be bad. That's why they need us,' Jessie said.

'You're right, of course,' Beta said. 'Forget I said that.'

'And if you're worried about the danger, just think of poor little Proctor.'

Lilian Proctor, who had joined on the same day as Jessie, had recently been sent home because she had an infected finger that would not heal. Such infections were very common, given the cracked and bleeding state of nurses' hands, the infective material they had to handle, and the poor washing facilities. But Proctor's infection had spread dangerously, her general health too low to fight it. She had been dismissed from the service, after weeks of being off sick, and there was some doubt as to whether the hand could be saved.

'I'm not worried about the danger,' Jessie said, and at that moment it was true. 'I'm more concerned about these situations we'll need "robustness" for. I think Matron sees us being assaulted by maddened patients, inflamed by months of war and the absence of females.'

'I'll be all right,' Beta said. 'My brothers taught me to box. I'll teach you if you like.'

'Thanks. It might be useful,' Jessie laughed.

'Oh,' Beta added, as they clattered down the stairs, 'and one other thing – Matron said we're due leave and we'll get it before we go. What do you think about that?'

The snow came back in April, both at home and in France, and it was through snow that the Allies made their first attacks of the new campaign season. The impetus for it came from the French. Their continuing losses at Verdun had caused a crisis of morale among the French population, and a victory was desperately needed. With the Russians now incapable of mounting a convincing attack on the Eastern Front, General Robert Nivelle persuaded Lloyd George to agree to a joint offensive. The Germans, it was known, were short of men and materials after the depredations of the Somme campaign, and if only they could be driven out into the open, a war of movement would result in an undoubted Allied victory.

The plan was that the French should make a determined attack in the section they held on the river Aisne, near Soissons, in mid-April. To draw German attention away, the British were to make a diversionary attack further north, at Arras, a week before. The British assault was to cover a broad front, with the Canadians attacking in the north of the sector at Vimy, the British in the centre at Arras itself, and a British and Australian force in the south at Bullecourt.

Lessons had been learnt from the battles in Picardy. The preliminary bombardment was to be far heavier, with twice as many shells used as on the Somme; and the quality of the shells was much better this time, with far fewer 'duds'. There was also a new kind of fuse – called a graze fuse – which caused the shell to explode when its momentum was even slightly checked. This meant it exploded when it hit barbed wire: destroying the barbed wire had been a major difficulty the previous autumn.

The troops were to advance by creeping barrage, a technique that had been used with mixed success on the Somme, but had been much refined in the six months since. The difficulty of synchronising the movements of men and artillery was overcome with much rehearsal and strict attention to timing; and the erratic nature of the barrage, caused by different guns throwing to different distances, was corrected by calibrating each gun individually for its own peculiarities. Finally, sophisticated counter-battery fire, aided by 'flash-spotting' and 'sound-ranging', was to knock out the German artillery before the advance – more than half of the British casualties during the Somme attacks had been caused by artillery fire.

All these techniques depended a great deal on the activities of the Royal Flying Corps. Scout aeroplanes were needed to photograph enemy trenches and strongpoints, to watch for troop movements, to spot for the artillery, and to report back on the effects of shell and mine explosion and the success of advances. And the fighters had to protect the scouts against enemy aircraft, while trying to prevent the enemy scouting for themselves, which meant attacking both German scouts and their covering fighters. And all this was done in the teeth of constant Archie.

It was hazardous work at the best of times, and April

1917 was not the best of times. The British air superiority of the previous autumn was over. The Germans had a new aeroplane, the Albatros, which was superior in every way to the British DH2s and Strutters, and they had them in great numbers. Their training programmes were better, too. RFC losses on the Somme had been heavy, and the lack of planning at home meant that pilot numbers had not caught up. To the shortage of manpower was added the fact that new recruits were arriving at the Front with the minimum of training. Some had had only ten hours of flying. Jack was being presented with downy-cheeked boys who could barely fly, let alone fight.

Furthermore, the Germans had developed a new technique: where before air battles had usually been one against one, they were now putting up whole flights of up to twenty aircraft that fought in formation, giving the lone British pilot no chance. To fight in co-operation was a special skill that had to be learned and practised, and there was no hope of the RFC immediately using it, even if they'd had the numbers. One particular German pilot achieved the distinction, like Max Immelmann, of being known by name: Manfred von Richthofen commanded one of these *Jagdstaffel*, as the flights were called, and personally shot down twenty-one aircraft in a month.

With too few pilots, too few aircraft – obsolete ones at that – and untrained boys being sent up against the nimble Albatros, when they had only just mastered stick and rudder and had difficulty handling a machine-gun at the same time, April 1917 came to be known as Bloody April. In four days, between the 4th and 8th of April, the RFC lost seventy-five aeroplanes, with nineteen men killed, seventeen wounded and seventy-three missing. It was the new arrivals who bore the brunt of the losses, for the aggressive policy of 'offensive patrols' imposed from the top meant that new boys were sent into combat as soon as they arrived. Few survived long enough to develop the skills they needed. It was said that the expected life of an RFC pilot that April was two weeks.

The thing pilots feared most was fire. A damaged machine, provided no essential parts had been shot away, would still glide, and a skilled pilot had a good chance of putting it down and surviving. But if your bus caught fire, you had the choice of burning to death, or jumping out to your death. The RFC had no parachutes. The High Command would not provide them, afraid pilots might 'desert' their machines too soon in an emergency. This insult was bitterly resented by the airmen, and anger was added to the pain of that dreadful month.

Jack went through the month and the battles of Arras in a state of exhaustion. Continued shortage of manpower meant he and his experienced colleagues had to fly three or four missions a day, called from their beds as soon as there was enough daylight to go up. They came to pray for a 'dud' day when the weather prevented flying. Each day passed in a confusion of shellfire and machine-gun fire, Archie and Albatros, smoke, muzzle-flash, explosion; feeling the concussion of the tortured air shake the aeroplane's body, feeling the dull impact of bullet on fuselage, listening to the engine's whine, praying that knocking noise was not serious; rolling the aching eyes back and forth across the arc of sky, looking for enemy fighters while trying to navigate over ground frequently obscured by smoke.

As tiredness took over, one day merged into another, and only blessed nightfall released the flyers to stagger into the mess and try to regain some sense of normality. Their accommodation was a series of huts along the edge of the airfield, stout, double-skinned wooden structures, roomy and snug with wood-burning stoves. The mess was the end hut, built on the slight slope at the top of the field so that one end had to be raised up on stilts to get it level, and a short, wide flight of steps gave access. Sometimes Jack thought those steps were the final joke – there were days when he could hardly get up them, and many evenings when someone, well lubricated, almost fell down them.

But in the mess there was relief. The rule was that there should be only jollity – no shop talk, and no sadness. The dead were not mourned – at least, not overtly. There were jokes, songs, laughter and – given the youthfulness of the company – horseplay. In the mess they could forget the war for a few hours.

Their cook was a man of rare accomplishment who could make a dish out of the most unpromising ingredients. He was a conscientious objector – a breed that was normally loathed, but Mears was unusual in that he was both a conchie and a volunteer. He had offered himself at once when war broke out, saying that he would serve in any capacity to help win the war, but that he simply could not kill anyone. He was open and apologetic, but quite firm about it. Jack did not know how he had come to be assigned as a cook, for it was not his pre-war trade: he had been a postgraduate reader in philosophy at Balliol in 1914. He confessed cheerfully to being self-taught, bringing his intelligence and a natural artistic streak to bear on the problem, and the results were always interesting and sometimes inspired. He could be seen in the kitchen, a cigarette drooping hazardously from his lips, throwing things into pots and stirring with fine bravado, while giving vent alternately to bursts of smoke and operatic arias – he had been a leading light of the Bach Choir at Oxford.

With Mears's good food and a reasonable amount of alcohol inside them, the airmen would settle into their evening's enjoyment. There was an upright piano against the far wall, its top marked with innumerable grey circles, and scarred all along the edge from cigarettes rested there. Sheridan was properly taught, and when the mood took him would play concertos and other serious pieces. He was listened to with respect; but Borthwick could play ragtime and popular songs by ear, with only a modicum of wrong notes, and everyone liked to sing. Worseley had a gift for making up irreverent songs to do with their own lives and the thick-headedness of those in command, and they would roar those out until the glasses on the tables rang. The songs were always wry, and favourites circulated from mess to mess. A current one, sung to the tune of 'My Tarpaulin Jacket', reflected the refusal to allow parachutes, which valued the aeroplane more than the flyer.

> *A young aviator lay dying,*
> *And as in the wreckage he lay,*
> *To his comrades around him all standing,*
> *These last parting words he did say:*

And the chorus:

> *'Take the cylinders out of my kidneys,*
> *The connecting-rod out of my brain,*
> *From the small of my back take the camshaft,*
> *And assemble the engine again.'*

As every mess added its own verses, the variations on the theme were endless.

There were other occupations by which the men took their minds off the day past and the next to come. Moody and Sheridan played chess; Hodgson sketched; White had a passion for inventing cunning devices that were supposed to improve some function, but in the event either did not work or fell to pieces or set fire to themselves. Jack was known for being a correspondent: when he had finished dinner he always tried to write a few lines to Helen – they had an agreement that they would each write a little every day and post the result once a week – and there was the rest of the family at Morland Place and Jessie to write to as well.

And when enough drink had been taken, or on those bad

days (like the one when little Shaw crashed and couldn't get out of his bus before it caught fire) when forgetting was extra hard, they would clear the floor and play polo with walking sticks, half of them being the horses and the rest riding piggy-back, or an arcane version of the Eton wall game with a coconut as the ball. Things often got broken during those games, but it stopped their hearts snapping instead.

Rug was their mascot and everyone's pet. He sat on top of the piano when Sheridan played; he joined in with tuneful howls when everyone sang, and during polo matches he would often dash in and snatch the ball, forcing them to chase him instead, to his great delight. Hodgson drew him in all his poses, and Mears made sure he ate as well as anyone on the field.

But his helmet and goggles hung on a hook by the door, for he did not go up with Jack any more. It was too dangerous. When the flight went up in the morning, Rug would retire under the mess-room steps, and wait there, chin on paws, until Jack came back. Ellis, the mess steward, said that he heard the returning aeroplanes long before anyone else. 'When 'e comes out from under the steps and stands there listening, we know you gentlemen're on your way back,' he told Jack. 'Sure enough, a minute or two later we'll 'ear the engines. But 'e can tell yours apart from everyone else's, don't ask me 'ow. Soon as 'e 'ears *your* bus, sir, 'is old tail starts waggin' fit to bust. 'E don't wag for anyone else.'

One time when Dawson came back from leave with a camera, he had taken a photograph of the whole group assembled in front of the mess hut, front row seated, back-row standing. They had got a pair of steps and put them in the middle of the back row so that Rug could sit on the top and be at the same level as the back-row faces. The photograph, framed, had pride of place on the mess-hut wall, and there he was, in his helmet, with the goggles hanging round his neck, Jack on one side and Sheridan on the other. His grin was the widest of the whole group.

The various battles of Arras went on throughout April and into May, and were counted a resounding success. The Germans were pushed back, and considerable territorial gains were made, most notably the high ground of Vimy Ridge where the Germans had been dug in to advantage. But it was hard work, and German resistance was fierce, and the advance could not be kept going. The gains were consolidated and the attacks were called off, and things settled down again while both sides licked their wounds.

The day came when Jack's squadron was told to stand down for a glorious forty-eight hours, and at once plans were made to go in to Amiens to celebrate.

'Not me,' said Tindall, languidly. 'I'm going to have a long bath, and then lie on my bed and read a book until I fall asleep, and if I get beyond chapter one I shall be amazed.'

Borthwick looked alarmed. 'Oh, rot! You've *got* to come. You're the one with the motor-car.'

Tindall fished out the key and threw it across the room to Jack, who was not attending and only just caught it. 'You can borrow the motor, but only if Compton drives. I want it back in one piece, and he's the only sane man among you.'

So Jack had to go along, though he thought Tindall's programme sounded more enticing. But they already tended to call him 'uncle' and make jokes about his great age and decrepitude, so perhaps it was as well to go along with the jaunt for once.

The evening took the usual pattern for such things, with a prolonged and noisy meal in a café down by the bridge, followed by a descent on a crowded, smoke-filled cellar bar, where a rather hoarse young woman was singing in French to the accompaniment of a wheezy accordion. Bottles of wine were ordered, which proved to be the sort without labels, and conversation had to be held at a polite scream to be heard above the noise of everyone else doing the same. Eventually the inevitable happened: a group of rather tawdry young women with sooty eyes and red gashes for mouths entered, and when they spotted the *pilotes* they started to come over, smiling seductively.

'Four of them, seven of us,' Borthwick said. 'Now, my arithmetic isn't of the *very* best, but—'

'Count me out,' White said, yawning. 'I can't do anything that involves any more energy than sitting on this chair.'

'I'm a married man,' Jack said hastily.

'But you're the driver,' Borthwick pointed out.

Hodgson also yawned. 'You can have my share,' he said. 'Compton can drive us home, and you can get a lift back. There are plenty of transports in town – someone will drop you off.'

The girls had arrived, beaming and wriggling their shoulders in anticipation. '*Bongswah*,' Borthwick bellowed, in his appalling French. '*Voulez-vous un boisson?*'

'English *pilotes*,' said the tallest girl, looking them over calculatedly. 'We like very much English *pilotes*.'

God, they were thin! Jack thought. Their *décolletage* revealed clavicles and upper ribs like soup bones. They looked as if they all needed a good square meal rather than a drink. He noticed that the smallest – and thinnest – of them was staring at him, with a troubled smile on her lips, and he was about to excuse himself hastily by telling her he was married, and was working out the French for 'I'm leaving anyway', when she said in a husky, hesitant voice, 'Monsieur Jacques? *C'est vous?*'

It took him a stunned moment to look beneath the concealing *maquillage* and recognise her. 'Marie?' he said. 'Marie Bécasse?'

Some of the others made raucous hooting remarks about his knowing a girl of her sort, but he hardly heard them. He was remembering their two previous meetings,

196

at the farmhouse near Cambrai where she and her grand-father had sheltered and fed him back in 1914. Old man Bécasse had said that such meetings always came in threes. And this was the third.

But she was so thin as to be almost skeletal, and her presence here and the company she was keeping suggested the worst.

'Your grandfather?' he asked. 'Is he well?'

'Dead,' she said. 'He is dead.' She had to shout it for him to hear, and impatiently he pushed away from the table and dragged up an empty stool, beckoning her to it. More raucous noises and remarks. She squeezed in beside him. He could smell her cheap scent, not quite covering the smell of imperfect cleanliness. Her companions had got seats between the others, and more bottles of wine were being called for. Jack noted all this vaguely in a corner of his mind, as he noticed the impatient looks of Hodgson and White, who wanted to go home.

'Tell me' he said to Marie.

'The Boche came,' she said. 'Grandpère died of rage because he could not fight them. They took everything, and destroyed what they could not take away. I was glad it was quick for him. They killed Christophe – poor idiot Christophe who worked for us. They did not understand he was an *imbécile*. They thought he was laughing at them.'

'And you? What did you do?'

'I ran away. The farm was no more, and the Boche were everywhere. I hid during the day and walked at night. Sometimes people were kind and gave me food. I thought I would go to Verdun and find my brothers and Pierre Picard, my fiancé. But it was too far. After a long time I found some English soldiers and they were kind to me. The officer enquired about Pierre for me, and found that he was dead. I got to Paris in the end and worked in a bar, and wrote to my brothers. But they are dead too, now. *Ah, cette guerre infâme!*'

At some point she had slipped naturally into French, but neither of them noticed.

'How did you come to Amiens?' he asked.

'I've been in many towns. Wherever there are soldiers. They give me food and money, but I have to—' She lowered her eyes in shame. 'One must live, *enfin*. And there is no-one left to care.' She took a sip of wine to fortify herself. 'I had to leave Grandpère,' she said, in a low voice that told him she had come to the worst part. 'I could not bury him. I covered him with a cloth and then I left him.'

'It wasn't your fault,' he said.

She raised her eyes again, and they seemed young and vulnerable behind the kohl. 'There is nothing left now, no-one and nothing. And one must live. We do what we have to.' By a glance she included the other girls in the 'we'. 'At least, they are company – and we look after each other.'

'Compton, are you coming or staying?' Hodgson interrupted. He stood up and leant across the table to be heard. 'Are you going to drive us back? Do come on! I shall end up deaf as a stone if we stay here.'

'Come now,' White added at a bellow, 'and I promise I won't write to your wife about Mam'zelle.'

There was nothing he could do for Marie. She was one of the pathetic pieces of flotsam left by the passage of the war. If he left now, she would go with one of the others, and he knew they would not be unkind. He stood up and felt in his pocket, pulled out all the money he could find and pressed it into her little bird's claw of a hand.

'Buy yourself something to eat,' he said. 'I must go now.'

She looked up, her eyes shining with tears. 'Our third meeting.'

She had remembered the old man's words, too. 'Perhaps there'll be another,' he said, thinking that if she was living in Amiens, he might see her passing, now he knew what she looked like.

But she shook her head. 'Three is all. Goodbye, Monsieur Jacques. God bless you.'

He left with White and Hodgson, feeling wretched.

Fenniman had not received a reply to his letter to his father, informing him of his engagement to Emma, so he supposed it had gone astray, and wrote again. At length he did receive a reply to that, but it brought him no pleasure.

My dear Cedric,

I did indeed receive your previous communication, and was shocked by its content. When you brought the young person to see me, I thought perhaps you were presenting her – if in rather eccentric fashion – for my approval. Since you said nothing of any engagement, I assumed that there would be other visits, followed by a longer stay after the war so that I could properly judge the young person's character and suitability. Now I learn that you have thrown yourself incontinently into an engagement, of the sort no gentleman can repudiate with honour, without seeking my approval, or even my opinion. I can only conclude that you have been 'caught'.

Nevertheless, I felt it my duty to make on your behalf those enquiries you seem to have omitted on your own. It gives me no pleasure to tell you – since, as I said, you cannot now repudiate the engagement – that this young person is unsuitable in every way to be allied to our family. Her father, Mr Thomas Weston, was a Member of Parliament, but it transpires that he was merely the adopted son of his father, and no-one knows what his true origins are. However, there are rumours, and though I find it almost incredible, I must tell you I have it on good authority that he was rescued as a child from the gutter. He was a chimney-sweep's boy!

This may, indeed, be an exaggeration, but it is plain that there is something both obscure and disgraceful in his background. The young person presumably attached herself to you in the hope of marrying into a good name – the Fennimans, as you know, go back to the Conquest – and blotting out her own unspeakable origins. Had you gone about things in the proper manner, this would have emerged before you had irrevocably committed yourself.

This marriage, were it to go through, would do you no credit and bring you and those connected with you nothing but pain. I can only recommend that you make as long an engagement as possible, in the hope that the young person – who is no doubt as flighty as the rest of her class – tires of you and allies herself to another. If she breaks the engagement, all will be well.

But I must tell you that I cannot and will not receive her into my house again, now or at any time in the future. You are all that is left to me to carry on the name of Fenniman. I pray that you will not bring disgrace and ruin on us, but unless she releases you, I fear that is indeed what will follow.

Your concerned father,

A. Fenniman.

Fenniman read at first with a sick sense of shock, and then with a dull, red anger. His father's use of the expression 'young person' enraged him – he would not even call her a young lady. To be so concerned with the Fenniman name, and so little with the loyalty and love one ought to feel for one's closest relative – one's only son – seemed a perverse distortion of values. He found his fist clenched and shaking, and the realisation made him force it to relax. Had he wanted to strike his father? What did that say about his own values? He took a few deep breaths, and drew himself up straight – which resulted in a shattering crash of his head against a beam, for he was reading the letter in the dug-out. The ridiculous accident made him first curse, then laugh at himself.

It was very bad of the old man but, on reflection, what had he expected? There had never been warm relations between them. Probably the brigadier didn't know how to feel warm towards anyone, and he was to be pitied for that rather than hated. Fenniman had wanted his blessing, but was not having it going to change anything? Only to the extent that he was more determined than ever to marry Emma, and as soon as possible.

He showed the letter to Bertie, who gave a silent whistle when he had finished it and said, 'Bad luck, old man. It's not nice to be on rotten terms with the pater – I know.'

'He's so deuced old-fashioned,' Fenniman complained. 'What the dickens does it matter who her grandfather really was?'

'Old people tend to be old-fashioned,' Bertie said. 'That's why it's called old-fashioned. You don't believe this chimney-sweeper rot, do you?'

'Of course not. And if I did, it wouldn't make any difference. It's Emma I want to marry, not her father.'

Bertie reflected that Venetia would probably know the truth of it, since she and Emma's father had been close in their youth. But he couldn't think of any tactful way to ask – and it was probably best not to know, anyway. 'You didn't see much of the old chap anyway, did you?'

'No. Visiting him is a pleasure enhanced by its rarity.'

'And once you're married, he'll probably change his attitude,' Bertie went on. 'Especially after you present him with another generation. Being crusty to a son is one thing, but to a grandson it's near impossible.'

'I sometimes think they ought to be put down when they get to the crusty stage,' Fenniman grumbled.

'Might be kinder,' Bertie agreed. 'Have a fag.'

They passed it off lightly between them. But there was a

wistfulness that Fenniman had to thrust down deep and ignore. He had always wanted his father to praise and approve and ultimately to love him, and it seemed that would never happen.

CHAPTER NINE

When Jessie came home on leave, Uncle Teddy was away in Manchester, so Polly met her at the station, driving herself in a borrowed tub-trap, with Jessie's own Hotspur between the shafts.

'I'm breaking Vesper to harness, and she's doing very well,' she explained, as they reached the rig, 'but she won't stand yet, and I wouldn't trust her with all this traffic.'

Jessie was renewing acquaintance with her darling horse. Hotspur's ears were so pointed they were almost crossed, and he was running his soft muzzle all over Jessie's hands, breathing in her scent and snorting with pleasure. Jessie was almost in tears. Strange how it was so much easier to cry over animals than people.

The porter put Jessie's bag in, Polly paid the boy who was holding Hotspur, and they climbed up and were off. Jessie was glad Polly had come in the cart. The weather had at last turned more kindly after the long, cold, wet winter. There was milder air and fitful sunshine, and sometimes when the breeze dropped it was even warm. The air was sweet and good after the staleness of London and the fug of the train; the hedges were bursting into greenness and the first starry hawthorn flowers were out. Blackbird, robin, thrush and wren rinsed the air with song, and the fields were white with lambs. May was always the loveliest month of all; and Yorkshire was so beautiful at this time of year that Jessie's heart was too full for words. Fortunately Polly was concentrating on her driving – there was a lot of traffic on the south road – so there was no need to talk.

When they had turned onto the track, on to Morland land, Polly said, 'How do you think he looks?'

With a leap of mind, Jessie gathered she meant Hotspur. 'Very well,' she said. 'And his winter coat's completely out. Someone must have put in some hard work on him.'

'Oh, well,' Polly said lightly, 'I wanted him to look nice for you.'

'You did it? You are kind, Pol.'

'I thought we could go for a ride after luncheon. You'd like to see everything, wouldn't you?'

'There's nothing I'd like better. I do *miss* riding.'

At the junction of the path, they had to wait for an army lorry going the other way. Jessie stared in surprise. She knew about the camp, of course, but it was still startling to see the physical evidence of it. 'Is there much of that?' she asked.

'Any amount,' Polly said. 'But not for much longer. Daddy's putting another road in for them from the camp down to the south road at Dringhouses. At least, he's planning it and soldiers are going to do the work. Mother and Aunt Hen were tired of lorries going past the house, and Daddy's afraid the vibration might crack the wall of the moat.'

'Do you see much of the soldiers?'

'Oh, yes, we have the officers to dinner, and the men to tea. And we're going to have some sort of outdoor fête for everyone, now that the weather's better.'

When they got home, Polly said she would see to Hotspur and the trap while Jessie went in. Dear old Sawry came hurrying to meet her, and Tomlinson was close behind him. Tomlinson had been Jessie's maid, but she had left her behind at Morland Place when she went to London to nurse. Tomlinson maided Polly and Henrietta on the few occasions they wanted it, and for the rest made herself useful in so many ways she had gradually and imperceptibly turned herself into the housekeeper.

The dogs came to meet Jessie in a solid mass, and she was thoroughly buffeted and licked. Then her mother came in from the staircase hall. The sunlight from the high staircase window silhouetted her, but was not brighter or warmer than the smile she had for her daughter. Next moment they were embracing, and Jessie felt how thin and small her mother had become. But Henrietta had always been thin and small, she told herself; Jessie was used to handling soldiers' burly bodies now.

And 'You've got awfully thin,' was Henrietta's first comment, when she released Jessie to stand back and look at her.

'I don't think I am,' Jessie reasoned. 'They give us plenty of food – you mustn't worry about that. Oh, it's good to be home! Where is everyone?'

'Teddy's in Manchester – he'll be home tomorrow. Ethel and Alice are out visiting, and they'll be home for luncheon. Maria's in the steward's room, working. Helen's away delivering an aeroplane, but she'll be home tomorrow as well. Oh, and Lennie's expected at the end of the week. He's got embarkation leave. His battalion's going out to France and he's fit to go with them. So you'll see him for one day before you go. Now, why don't you let Tomlinson take you to your room? I'm sure you'd like to wash and tidy up. Then come down when you're ready.'

As soon as they were in the bedroom, Jessie turned to Tomlinson and said, 'Now, Mary, tell me everything. How are things – really?'

'Everything's going very well,' Tomlinson assured her. 'Let me help you off with that.'

'I don't need to be helped,' Jessie said, amused. 'I don't have a maid at the nurses' hostel.'

'I know, but let me, all the same. I've been looking forward to maiding you again.'

'Well, if it pleases you . . .' Jessie said. It *was* nice, in a strange way, to have her buttons undone for her as if she were a child. A tap on the door heralded a diminutive house-maid with a can of hot water. When she had gone, Jessie said, 'She looks very young.'

'She is,' Tomlinson agreed. 'We get the young girls without any difficulty, but as soon as they're trained and useful, they seem to want to go off and work in the factories. It makes it unsettling for everyone when the faces change all the time. And Sawry has the same difficulty with the men. As soon as they're nineteen the army snatches them away. We're down to one footman and a boot-boy, and you know how the master dislikes women waiting at table.'

'And how is Mother?' Jessie asked. At least from Mary Tomlinson she would hear the truth.

'She's very well. Truly! In fact, she's been flourishing since the army camp came. The master likes to have the officers for dinner, and your mother does love all the planning and contriving. It gives her so much to do that she hasn't time to worry about the rest of the housework, which suits me because it gives me a free hand, and I can manage it perfectly well. And she enjoys the occasions so much! The young men are charming, and everything's very jolly, and like it used to be before the war. It's done her so much good!'

'I'm glad,' Jessie said. 'And how is everyone else?'

'Well, Mrs Jack and Mrs Frank get along like a house afire, and it's wonderful the conversations that go on in the drawing-room of an evening! And around the dinner-table – Sawry says he doesn't understand one word in three when those two and Father Palgrave get to their arguing. The master loves it – he always did admire intelligent conversation.'

'Oh, yes, Father Palgrave – what's he like?'

'A very nice gentleman, very quiet, as you'd expect, given his terrible experience – but Mrs Jack and Mrs Frank can always draw him out, and then he can be quite witty and amusing. The children like him, and he's brought a bit of

206

peace to the nursery, so the maids tell me. And he's very devout. Takes the services in the chapel very seriously.'

'And Aunt Alice? And Ethel?'

'Oh, Mrs Morland's just the same as always. She never changes. And Mrs Robert – well, she was upset when Mr Robert went away, and was inclined to be fratchy about everything; but now she's come out of it, and she's quite cheerful. Goes visiting a lot more, goes and sees her sisters and sisters-in-law. We were worried at first when Father Palgrave came that she might quarrel with him over the children, but in fact she leaves them to him entirely and never goes near the schoolroom or the nursery – which pleases Nanny Emma, as you can imagine, because she never did approve of parents interfering with her children.'

'So it's "all serene"?' Jessie concluded, and felt, oddly, just a little pang. Everything was going on comfortably without her, and she wasn't needed or missed. It would have been nice for her vanity if she had left one small hole that no-one else could fill. But then she shook away the thought, and reminded herself that it would make it easier to go to France, knowing that everyone at home was happy and busy.

Luncheon was a cheerful affair. Jessie got to meet Father Palgrave, a startlingly handsome man, but with a look in his eyes, a shadow, that she had learned to recognise now, after a year of nursing soldiers who had come wounded from the Front. But he joined in pleasantly enough with the conversation. Jessie was, naturally, asked a lot of questions and, as the new arrival, should have had most of the talking; but so many of the questions she could only have answered to people who knew what it was like at the hospital that again and again she was forced to make evasive answers and turn the subject. Once she saw Palgrave looking at her with keen sympathy. She remembered Bertie saying that he could not talk to people back home about his life at the Front because they simply couldn't understand. There was no common ground where they could meet. She supposed Palgrave felt the same, and was sensitive enough to perceive her similar trouble. She liked him for that.

After luncheon she changed into her old habit, which had been left hanging in her wardrobe when she went to London, and found it a snug fit. She hadn't lost weight, or put it on, but had subtly changed shape at her labours. Vesper and Hotspur were waiting for them, ready tacked up, and they clattered out over the drawbridge with a positive entourage of dogs: Polly's Bell and Kai, Uncle Teddy's young hounds Tiger and Isaac, the bitch Helle escaping from her annoying pups, the kitchen dog Roy, and Skipper the terrier, all came bustling along, glad that *someone* was going out on this fine day. Vesper curvetted about, neck arched, fretting that they might get under her feet.

Hotspur ignored them, like the sensible horse he was. He was eager to get out into the open. It was glorious to be riding him again, Jessie thought. Despite her long absences, they never lost that perfect sympathy, by which he seemed to know what she wanted almost before she did. It was like having six legs instead of two; she thought centaurs must have felt rather like this.

They rode out to the stud at Twelvetrees, which had been left to Jessie by her father, to see how things were going. Webster, the head man, was glad to see her, shook her hand heartily after first wiping it down the back of his breeches, and told her everything was going smoothly.

'We've got a batch of two-year-olds just ready: the army'll be collecting 'em any day now. And ten nice yearlings ready to be backed. We lost awd Sapphire during the winter – she were a great awd lass, twelve good foals she gave us and not a wrong 'un amongst 'em. But at least she went quiet at the end – found her dead out in the field one morning, died in her sleep. Ah were glad o' that, any road. Couldn't have borne to have to shoot her.' He pulled out his handkerchief and blew his nose briskly. 'But the rest o' the mares is doing gradely,' he concluded.

'And how is Field working out?' Jessie asked.

'She's a grand lass,' he said enthusiastically. 'Ah knaw at first Ah didn't like the idea of a female in ma stables, but it 'as to be said she works like a Trojan, and the 'osses like her. She has a way wi' 'em.'

'It's a good job you've got used to her,' Polly said, 'seeing as there's two more females now.'

Webster met Jessie's eyes. 'Aye, Miss Jessie, females was all we could get when th'army took the lads. So now there's on'y me and a couple o' boys to hold our end up.'

'I interviewed them for you,' Polly said. 'Scott and Maiby, their names are.'

'They're good workers,' Webster said. 'Aye, the army took that daft dollop Mattock at the end, can you believe it, Miss Jessie? It's to be hoped they don't give him a rifle, or we'll never win the war.'

Jessie laughed. 'So you've got enough help now?' she asked.

'Aye, well, we're managing. O' course, we don't have the establishment we had before the war, not half of it, so we don't need so many hands. Aye, we manage all right. Miss Polly helps a lot, and the Master's there to answer questions.'

So you don't need me, Jessie thought. It seemed her home was shrugging her off.

'Come and see awd Prince, Miss Jessie,' Webster said, cutting into her thought. 'Ah'll wager t'awd lad'll remember you all right.' So she went to visit the stallion in his box, gave him a handful of nuts and discussed his condition. Prince proved he remembered her by doing his old trick of opening her pocket flap with his lips. Then she spoke to the girls, looked at the stock, and – since Vesper was by now impatiently kicking the door of the box she had been put into – resumed her ride.

Teddy could not let the occasion of Jessie's being home pass without a celebration, so with Henrietta's willing agreement he announced a dinner party with dancing afterwards in the great hall. Henrietta went into a prolonged consultation with Mrs Stark, Tomlinson and her recipe books over the menu. Because of the U-boats, some things were hard to find nowadays. And May was an awkward sort of month, with no game except pigeon, very little fruit and not many vegetables. But, of course, nothing could match spring lamb; and they could scrape together enough of the first new potatoes to go with it. The first of the asparagus was ready, and the last of the stored carrots would just about do. Stewed pigeons would help the lamb, and a fricassée of rabbit, done to her old recipe with cream and chestnuts, was not an ignoble dish; and for puddings there was forced rhubarb and bottled strawberries, and plenty of dried fruit to make duffs. Flour for pastry and the duffs was a problem. It had all but disappeared from the shops, and though Morland Place always kept stocks of staple ingredients, Henrietta was wary of depleting them when there was no hope of replenishing. But they had plenty of oats and oatmeal, so they could have oat cakes and bannocks instead of bread for breakfast and tea, if necessary, and she wanted it to be a fine feast for Jessie.

The dinner was superb; and the problem of having seven females in the house and only two males was easily solved by the proximity of the army camp. Half a dozen of the officers and a few old friends from the neighbourhood made up a pleasant party; and with the long-delayed advent of the better weather and the good news from the Front, everyone was in a mood for enjoyment.

Afterwards there was dancing, and Polly was able for the first time to dance with Lieutenant Holford, and discovered that he was, as she had suspected, a good dancer – light on his feet, but with a firm grip and a good sense of direction. She enjoyed it so much that she gave him several dances although, as the young lady of the house, she was much in demand. It gave them a chance to talk, and she quizzed him about his background and upbringing.

'How could you not have learnt to ride before you joined the army?' she wanted to know.

'Oh dear, is that a terrible shortcoming in me?' he said. 'If I had known when I was a boy that I would one day meet *you*, I should have rectified the omission. As it is, I can only beg your pardon with all due humility.'

'But you didn't answer the question,' she said severely. 'I can't think how anyone can get through life without horses.'

'Easy enough, if you live in London.'

'Did you? How dreadful!'

'Not at all! We had a house in the country as well, in Surrey, if we wanted flowers and trees and so on. We went down to the country most weekends. As a lad I had a bicycle – much more convenient for getting around than a horse – and, of course, in London there were always taxicabs, and my father had a motor-car. So, no horses necessary, you see.'

'But what did you do for fun?' she asked.

'The usual things – tennis and croquet, walking and bicycling, picnics, reading groups and sketching parties. Boating and punting and swimming in the river. I'm sorry to have to say,' he added, with mock regret, 'that a large number of us were misguided enough to enjoy ourselves very well without once getting on a horse.'

'So you didn't hunt in the winter?'

'I've been to meets, and hunt balls. I like the social side of it very much. And the look of the thing, you know – the horses and the chaps in pink coats and the jolly hounds, all steaming on a cold winter day – the spectacle and pageantry of it. Like those wonderful old paintings. Very handsome. But I'm afraid it never occurred to me to join them. Surrey's not much of a hunting county – at least, not our part of it.'

Polly shook her head. 'I think you're quite, quite beyond hope.'

'Oh, don't say that! I'm sure I'm capable of improvement, with a little work. After all, I'm already learning to ride.

That must be a step in the right direction. Won't you please take me in hand, and see what can be made of me?'

'That is a very improper question,' Polly said, enjoying it very much. 'I shall ignore it. What does your father do?'

'He's a banker in the city. Holford and Holford. The other Holford was my grandfather,' he explained.

'And are you going to be a banker too? After the war, I mean?'

'I don't know. My father wants me to, but I'm not terribly keen. I just don't find finance terribly gripping. The war's been rather a good thing for me in that respect – it's taken me away and given me time to think, without all the arguments there would otherwise be.'

'I suppose you'll have to do something,' Polly said.

He smiled. 'Not necessarily. There may be something coming to me from my mother's side. I may end up as a gentleman of independent means.'

'Well, that certainly sounds more agreeable,' Polly said. 'All the bank people I know are terribly dull.'

'Yes, my father is particularly so,' he said solemnly.

Polly blushed. 'Oh, I beg your pardon! I didn't mean—!'

'Please don't apologise. My governor really *is* dull – and you look so pretty when you blush.'

'You oughtn't to say so,' Polly said, pleased.

'No, really? I was always brought up to tell the truth. But I'll change the subject if you like. You are a remarkably good dancer, Miss Morland. Do you play tennis as well? I'm ready to bet you're very good at it – the one usually goes with the other. I haven't had a racquet in my hand since last summer. Is there anywhere to play hereabouts? I would love to have a knock-up some time.'

So they talked about tennis, and he told her about rowing, and before the dance ended they were making vague plans to do both, when the summer weather came in and if his duties permitted.

* * *

The days of Jessie's leave fled by too quickly. She enjoyed riding, and went out every day, sometimes with Polly but sometimes alone, to enjoy that perfect communion with horse and nature she had so missed. For the rest she spent time with her mother, had long talks and walks with Helen, and was amused at how the life of the army camp spilled over into the house. Apart from the special dinner party, Henrietta had a tea party twice a week to which she invited five or six ordinary soldiers, and she asked Jessie to help her entertain them. The officers often dropped in on passing; and there always seemed to be a messenger coming or going between the camp and the house.

She didn't see much of Maria, who seemed to work long hours, and was often silent and distracted at meals. Her animation returned, though, when a discussion got up between her and Father Palgrave. Jessie thought that he was probably in a unique position to comfort her for the loss of Frank, for he was both a scholar and a soldier, as Frank had been – and had, moreover, been in the battle on the 1st of July that had claimed Frank's life. Jessie thought Father Palgrave was a good influence in the house for many reasons – not least that the chapel was in use again, with a daily celebration in the early morning for those who wished to take the sacrament; and evening prayers for everyone. Teddy expected everyone to attend unless there was a very particular excuse, but hardly anyone tried to get out of it: there wasn't a soul who did not have someone at the Front to pray for. Praying together every day welded the household together and made for a good atmosphere. Father Palgrave was good for the children, too; and he dealt gracefully with Polly's intermittent attempts to interest him in her.

Lennie's departure, and therefore his leave, was cancelled, so Jessie did not see him before she left, which was a pity. His battalion had been told at the last moment that they were not going to France, after all – a great disappointment to most of them.

213

On her last day everyone made a pet of her, drawing close while they could. She had a last ride on Hotspur, then said a long goodbye to him in the stable. He did his old trick of thrusting his nose under her arm and leaning his face against her in absolute trust, and she caressed his silky ears and wept a few tears into his mane. For the rest of the day she sat and talked with her family, each of them making time to be with her.

Helen said, 'I think you are doing a very good thing, a noble thing. Ned would be so proud of you. Indeed, we all are.'

Henrietta said, 'You'll write very often, won't you? And eat properly, and keep your feet dry? And if there's anything you want sent over, we'll send it.'

Polly said, 'I wonder if you'll see anyone you know? Any of our people – Jack or Bertie or Oliver Winchmore? I suppose they might come and see you – it's not as far as coming home to England.'

They gave her presents – Helen a blank book in which to keep a diary, Maria a copy of *Mansfield Park*, Ethel a muffler she had knitted herself. Henrietta gave her a neat little sewing-set with different sizes of needle, threads and darning wools in various colours, spare buttons and elastic, pins and a bodkin. Uncle Teddy gave her a leather-covered metal case containing a knife, fork and spoon, a tin-opener, a pen-knife and a compass, each sitting securely in its own indentation in the blue velvet inside – 'You never know when they'll come in handy.' Alice gave her a lovely pale blue silk scarf – 'because there are times when nothing is more comforting, dear, than a silk scarf about the neck'. And Polly gave her a bookmark in the form of a lock of Hotspur's mane, tagged at the end with tortoiseshell, 'because I expect he's who you'll miss most of all'.

Dinner that evening was a quiet occasion – not sad, precisely, but reflective. At the end, Teddy tapped his glass, halting the quiet conversation, and said, 'I think I can guess that we're all thinking about our dear ones who can't be here with us tonight, especially Ned and Frank, who gave all that a man can give. I hope and believe none of us would give less, if we had to. We're fighting for freedom and decency. We didn't start the war but, by God, we won't stop until we've won it.' He looked around the grave faces turned towards him. 'We can't all go and fight, but each of us can do our bit, according to our natures. Now our little Jessie is going to France, to do what she can, and we are very proud of her. So let's pray that the war will be over this year.' There was a murmur of agreement round the table. 'And drink to . . .' He paused, thinking. 'There's a lot of things we could drink to, but what it comes down to in the end is this family. To us!'

And everyone drank. 'To us!'

The next morning, Jessie was up very early, and attended the chapel service with her mother, then went to breakfast. Despite the early hour, Uncle Teddy had already eaten and gone, and apart from Father Palgrave, only Maria was there. Nobody spoke much.

When the meal was done, Jessie collected her bags, hugged her mother once more, and went out to where Simmons was waiting with the motor to take her to the station. The sun was up and it looked like being a fine day, though the air was morning-cold. She was going to catch a train to London, and thence to France, to a new life, and experiences she could only just imagine. Despite the large breakfast her mother had insisted she eat, there was a hollow feeling in her stomach. She was sure she would be tested out there, and she hoped she would not fail. She thought of Ned, and Frank, taking that same journey, but to even greater unknowns, and more severe tests. For their sakes, she must *not* fail.

Simmons took her all the way to her compartment and saw her settled, and said goodbye with tears in his eyes,

215

and stood at attention as the train drew out in veils of smoke and steam; and the train's whistle sounded a sad, haunted note. But once it had rattled past all the points and curves and got into the straight, it picked up speed and the wheels tattooed a more cheerful rhythm. Jessie thought of meeting Beta under the clock at Victoria, as they had arranged, and travelling with her to France, and she felt glad that they were embarking on a new adventure.

Jessie had gone back to London a day early to give herself time to do some shopping. She went to the Army and Navy Stores and bought several pairs of thick stockings, the better to withstand the hazards of nursing; and extra underwear and handkerchiefs, in case the laundry facilities were not up to standard. On Bertie's advice she went to a dispensing chemist to improve her personal first-aid kit with a supply of morphine tablets, and two pairs of good scissors, one large and one small, which he said were always hard to find. She bought soap and Vaseline, Horlicks tablets, which she had already learnt the good of in those emergencies when a meal was either missed or delayed, and Bovril tablets for late-night drinks. Finally, she bought tins of cigarettes and chocolate, which Bertie said were readily exchangeable in France for anything she might find she had run out of.

Feeling thus somewhat bolstered against the fray, she went out to pay her visits *pour prendre congé*. She went first to Pont Street to say goodbye to Maud, for though they did not see much of each other, they were cousins by marriage. She found her, to her surprise, quite animated, a very different Maud from the cool, composed creature she was used to. When the maid went up to see if she was at home, Maud came down to the hall in person to greet Jessie. Her eyes were bright and there was colour in her cheeks, and she expressed herself pleased that Jessie had called. Her usual sleekness seemed almost ruffled, which in Jessie's opinion made her look prettier.

'We have company,' she said, and when Jessie would have drawn back, she said, 'No, no, you must come upstairs. It is only my father's friend, John Manvers, whom you have met before, and I know he would like to see you.'

'Well, if you're sure I shan't be intruding.'

'Not at all. I was hoping you would call, when Bertie wrote that you were going to France to nurse. John – Lord Manvers – has been staying for two weeks, and he goes on to Ireland at the end of the week.'

'He's been staying here?' Jessie asked. She didn't mean anything in particular by the question, but Maud blushed.

'Yes, in my father's old room. But I have had my second cousin on my mother's side, Mrs Thompson, staying as well, just in case anyone should say anything. You will meet her above, as well.'

'Oh, I'm sure—' Jessie began in hasty demurral, then couldn't think of any tactful way of ending the sentence. 'He was a good friend of your father's, wasn't he?' she concluded weakly.

'Yes; and of course he and Bertie were often meeting when he lived in India.'

She led the way into the drawing-room, where two figures were seated in the chairs on either side of the fire: one, tall, powerfully built, with a lean, tanned face and thick brown hair, stood up at once, and advanced on Jessie with a ready smile and hands outstretched. 'Mrs Morland, what a pleasure to meet you again.'

The other was a plump elderly lady, fussily dressed in the style of twenty years back, with a quantity of bangles, chains and jingling ornaments about her shiny black garments, and a fine false front of grey curls. Maud introduced her and Jessie, then rang the bell. 'You will take some refreshment, won't you?'

Manvers, meanwhile, was showing Jessie courteously to the sofa, and then sat himself beside her. 'The last time we

217

met,' he said, 'I remember we had a very pleasant talk about horse-breeding. How is your stud?'

'Oh, it's doing very little now, just a handful of horses for the army each year,' Jessie said. 'Until the war is over and I live at home again, I can't do more. But what of your farm? And your racehorses?'

'All gone, alas,' he said. 'The war has just about killed horseracing, and while the wheat, millet and sugar are still crops in demand, I find I have lost heart for farming over there. So I've sold everything and bought a place closer to home, in Ireland. I'm going there now. I just stopped off to see Maud on the way.'

'Are you making a long stay in London?' Jessie asked.

'I should have been in Ireland by now,' he said with mock ruefulness, 'but I've been made so comfortable here I keep delaying my departure. I'm afraid things will be a little less polished in Ireland, until I have settled in and trained some household staff. There may be some rough living ahead for me.'

The servant came in just then with sherry, Madeira, biscuits and cake. Maud served Jessie and Manvers with sherry and biscuits, herself and Mrs Thompson with Madeira and cake.

'What sort of place have you bought?' Jessie asked Manvers, when this was done.

'It's an estate in County Wicklow: an old castle that was turned into a manor house in the eighteen eighties. Lots of rolling green acres – wonderful grazing and fertile land – and some woods and a lake, but the house is quite dilapidated. No-one's lived in it since the old lord died, which was about ten years ago.'

'It sounds romantic,' Jessie said.

'That's what Maud thought,' Manvers said, with a smile, 'until I told her about the leaking roof, the blocked gutters, the mice in the wainscot and the black beetles in the basement.'

'All those things can be put right,' Maud said, with a little of her old briskness. 'But in the photograph he showed me it has turrets and battlements, and such a pretty lake and a little island with a pagoda on it.'

'It must be charming,' Jessie said. 'And do you mean to farm, or breed horses?'

'Oh, both. It would be a crime not to farm, with such good land and food shortages getting worse because of the U-boats. But I couldn't do without horses, and the Irish are keen racegoers and hunters. It will take me time to set up my stud, but I hope by the time the war ends to have some stock established, and then I can start to enjoy myself. I hope you will come over and stay one day, Mrs Morland. It's good riding country – good hunting country, too.'

'I should like to, one day,' Jessie said. At the moment, the end of the war seemed too far off for the invitation to be more than a politeness.

He went on, 'I am hoping Maud will come, and bring little Richard. It's a wonderful place for a boy – trees to climb, a lake to swim in and row on, untouched acres to get lost in.'

'How is Richard?' Jessie asked Maud.

'Very well,' Maud said automatically, and added, 'He still has that troublesome cough I spoke of the last time we met. The doctor says it is bronchitis.'

Mrs Thompson snorted at that, as if she thought the doctor was a fool, but she did not speak, or look up from the needlework with which she was occupied.

'That must be very distressing for you,' Jessie said. 'Poor little man. What treatment does the doctor recommend?'

'He gives me his patent medicine, and he says it will go away of its own accord when the warm weather comes.'

'It has been quite warm this last week,' Jessie said.

'Yes, but still terribly damp,' said Maud. 'However, I'm taking Richard away when Lord Manvers leaves.'

'To Beaumont?' Jessie asked.

'That's what Bertie wanted, but Dr Buller thinks sea air will be better for Richard, and Mrs Thompson has a house in Folkestone.'

Mrs Thompson looked up and spoke at last. 'I've told dear Maud that I am happy to have them both there for as long as they like – for the whole summer,' she added, with a meaningful look at Maud, who ignored it. 'Much better they stay there with me as long as the weather holds, than come back to this nasty, smoky place – or elsewhere. Folkestone has the best air in the country, everyone knows that. And the war might be over by September.'

'We'll see,' was all that Maud said.

Mrs Thompson threw a look at Lord Manvers before returning to her work, and Jessie felt there was an undercurrent of some sort in the room.

Manvers said, 'I'm afraid my delayed departure has kept Maud and little Richard in Town,' then changed the subject. 'But I understand you are going to France? What a courageous decision. Do you know which hospital you'll be nursing at?'

This conversation lasted until Jessie finished her sherry and took her departure. Maud showed her downstairs again, an unexpected courtesy, and it seemed as though she wanted to say something to Jessie; but in the end she only shook her hand, wished her good luck in France, and said goodbye.

Her next visit was to Violet, who greeted her affectionately, and took her straight upstairs to see the children. 'Emma's out,' she said. 'She'll be sorry to have missed you.'

'I'm sorry too. I shan't be able to call again before I leave.'

The two elder boys, Robert and Richard, were at school, and Charlotte, who was just five, was doing her letters with Nanny Finch. She entertained them for a little while with her artless prattle, until Violet took Jessie away to look at the baby, who was asleep in another room.

'Isn't he perfect?' Violet breathed.

His eyelids were glossy, his lashes a silken fan against his velvet cheek, his lips pale pink and pursed in sleep, his hair, baby-fair, a halo of soft curls. He really was, Jessie had to admit, a very pretty baby, and she felt a pang in her stomach at the thought that she would never have one of her own. Violet had so much, Violet had everything – and then she checked the thought, remembering that Violet's love was dead and she would never see him again. She looked sidelong at her friend, and saw the thinness of the cheek and the shadow in the eyes that belied the tender smile as she hung over her baby.

'Yes,' Jessie said kindly, 'he is perfect.'

When the baby had been admired enough, Violet said she would go with Jessie to Manchester Square to call on Venetia, 'so that you can kill two birds with one stone, and I can spend longer with you'.

Venetia was working in her laboratory, but came down at once when the maid told her who had called. 'I was trying to catch up with my work,' she said, greeting Jessie with a hearty handshake. 'I've been so much occupied lately that I've hardly set foot upstairs in a month. And I want to get things in order before I leave.'

'Leave?' Jessie queried.

'Oh, didn't you know? I am going to France, too. To Paris, in my case. We are going to launch one of my X-ray ambulances, and Lord Stamfordham has arranged for the Prince of Wales to attend the ceremony. I had been hoping for the King, but I suppose the prince will do as well,' she concluded.

'Better,' Violet said. 'Everyone's interested in what the prince is doing.'

'Perhaps,' Venetia said.

'A prince of Wales is much more romantic than a common-or-garden king,' Violet said. 'Don't you think so, Jessie?'

Jessie laughed. 'Both are so far out of my sphere, I can't compare.'

'I'm glad you're going to France,' Venetia said to her. 'It is just what you ought to do. You're a good nurse, and that's where you're needed most.'

'I hope the sisters out there know that,' Jessie said.

'Yes, I've seen how the reactionaries in the nursing profession treat VADs. But I think you'll find no nonsense of that sort so close to the Front.'

'Shall you be afraid?' Violet asked suddenly, as the thought occurred to her.

'No, I don't think so,' Jessie said. 'I'm sure the hospitals will be far enough from the shelling to be safe.'

'I didn't mean that,' Violet said, though she couldn't quite put into words what she *did* mean. It was the whole thing, really – the newness, the strangeness, the unpredictability – not knowing what one might be faced with or what might be demanded of one. A place of terrifying emergencies and emotional horrors – and that was without even considering the dirt, the gore and all the other physical unpleasantnesses.

Jessie understood, more or less, what Violet hadn't said, and she answered it obliquely. 'I shall have a good friend with me.'

'When you find out where you are being sent, do let us know,' Venetia said. 'I shall tell Oliver where you are. He may be able to come and see you when he has time free.'

'I'd like that. And have you heard any more from Thomas?' Jessie asked.

'He is still at Tsarskoye Selo. He says they've settled down to a routine there. They do a great deal of gardening – they're growing vegetables on quite a large scale – and the Emperor particularly likes cutting down trees and turning them into logs. He talks of having a good stock of firewood for next winter.'

'He thinks they will still be there next winter?' Jessie said.

'I believe he has shut his mind to the situation. Thomas says he is astonishingly serene.'

'But won't they be brought to England?' she asked.

'I've heard that there was a lot of discussion of it in the newspapers.'

'These things take time to arrange,' Venetia said, and changed the subject. 'I shall send you an invitation to the launching of my ambulance. You may possibly be able to come, and it would be a great pleasure to see you there.'

'I should love to, if I can.'

Jessie was tired when she got back to the hostel, and she still had to complete her packing. She took off the rose-fawn costume she had worn for her formal calls, and wondered for a moment what to do with it. It was unlikely she would want it in France, and she could not leave it here. She ought never to have bought it, she thought. Perhaps she should give it to Nurse Cantry, in the next-door cubicle, who was more or less her size.

And then at the last minute she folded it up and put it into her trunk. There might possibly be an occasion over there when she wanted to look smart. They must *have* time off, after all, and there were restaurants in France, and presumably other amenities. She and Beta might even be sent to a hospital in Paris: now there was a thought!

CHAPTER TEN

Robert Nivelle, the French commander-in-chief who had taken over from old Papa Joffre, had originally intended to attack the German salient between Péronne and Soissons in February; but before his plans were complete, the Germans performed their unexpected retreat to the Hindenburg Line, and the salient was no more.

But France desperately needed a victory. The long and bloody struggle at Verdun had left the army and the nation exhausted and disillusioned. Casualty numbers had been devastating, and for what? After almost three years of war, the Germans were still there on French soil, and the line of the Front had barely moved.

Nivelle moved his focus to the area of the river Aisne, and planned his attack along forty miles of the Front between Soissons and Rheims, an attack that, he assured the French government firmly, would bring the war to an end in two days. British experiences, especially in Picardy, led General Haig to doubt it would be that easy – particularly as much of Nivelle's chosen ground was overlooked by an escarpment and plateau known as Chemin des Dames, on which the Germans were well dug in and would be difficult to attack. But as the junior partner in the Allied effort, Britain had little choice but to go along with the French plan, and undertake the required diversionary assault in Artois and Picardy.

Haig's preferred theatre of war had always been Flanders, which he saw as vital to the defeat of Germany; but his ambitions there had to be put aside until the French had broken through on the Aisne. When that was done, the French would pursue and crush the fleeing Germans, the British would break out of the Ypres salient, the Belgians would attack Diksmuide, and they would all meet at Ostende and the war would be over.

The reality was less clear-cut. The British attacks at Arras were largely successful, but on the Aisne the element of surprise had been lost. From their elevated position, the Germans could hardly help noticing the movements of thousands of troops down on the river plain, the stockpiling of ammunition and supplies, the building of roads and light railways and the digging of jumping-off trenches. Worse, a copy of the entire French battle plan fell into German hands in early April. They could hardly have been more prepared.

Still the attack went ahead, slightly delayed by the weather, at six a.m. on the 16th of April, in a misty, overcast dawn. Despite a two-week bombardment, German wire was largely uncut and their positions unreduced, and the exposed French troops were cut down by withering machine-gun fire. By the end of the first day they had suffered forty thousand casualties and made almost no ground: they had only reached a line they were supposed to have captured by nine thirty that morning.

The second day was attended by some success at Laffaux and in the Champagne, enough to persuade Nivelle to keep attacking. By the 5th of May the main Soissons–Rheims railway line had been cut, the French had taken some German positions in the Champagne hills, and three miles of the Chemin des Dames Ridge had been captured. But it was not a breakthrough, nor did one look at all likely. The Germans were as firmly entrenched as ever. The French Army and the French nation had been promised a victory, and the reality was a devastating disappointment. Moreover, the butcher's bill had been high: no official figures were forthcoming, but it was generally believed that there had been between 150,000 and 200,000 casualties.

Bickering broke out between the French generals and the French government as to who was to blame; Nivelle was asked for his resignation and refused, blaming his subordinates. It was an unedifying spectacle, which only increased the soldiers' resentment. Finally on the 15th of May Nivelle yielded to the inevitable and resigned, and General Pétain was appointed commander-in-chief. But by then worse damage had been done both to France and to the war effort: mutiny had broken out.

It was something that the French commanders had long feared. Anti-war propaganda had been circulating among the troops, and the situation had grown worse since the Russian revolution. Serving alongside the French there were two brigades of Russians, who were restive and talked of the 'rights' of the common man, the changes back home, and how the soldiers and workers were now in charge. Soldiers going on leave were waylaid at railway stations by pacifists and harangued on the evils of war, while Communists encouraged them to desert and offered them help to do so. Anti-war tracts called *papillons* and the revolutionary newspaper *Bonnet Rouge* were passed freely up and down the trenches. Rumours were spread that munitions workers were being paid far more than the men in the trenches, and that the soldiers' wives were being debauched while they were away.

Such things would have had limited effect on soldiers whose morale was intact, but the French Army was suffering under chronic maladministration. The conscripted soldier's pay was derisory, his food was meagre and lacked nourishment, his general amenities almost non-existent. He rarely received mail, and if he was lucky enough to be granted leave – which was unusual – he would probably not be able to get home, because the French authorities made no arrangements to transport him.

By contrast, the careful building up of the War Book before 1914 had set up an efficient system for the British soldier. His pay was better, he received regular post from home, his food, while monotonous, was ample and sustaining, and when he went on leave he was transported home and back without delay. Moreover, from the beginning the British troops had been rotated, both in and out of the trenches, and up and down the line, so that the heaviest burdens were well spread, and there were regular periods out 'on rest', during which there was a chance to clean up, more varied food, and entertainments such as football matches, theatricals and band concerts.

The French *poilus* were not rotated: they served endlessly in the same part of the line, and spent months at a time in the trenches, only relieved when they were exhausted; and when they did come out on rest, there were no facilities for them, no baths, no entertainments, bad billets, and often even worse food than in the line. The British officer had it drummed into him from his first day that the comfort and welfare of his men was his paramount responsibility, but many of them had noted with surprise and disapproval that while the French officers led their men in battle with great gallantry, when the battle was over they disappeared and left the men to their own devices.

The first mutinous act happened on the 29th of April, when a battalion of the 20th Infantry behind the line refused to turn out. The rumour of this action spread like infection, and soon refusal to leave billets and go up to the line was widespread. It was a limited mutiny – most did not desert, or ill-treat their officers, but simply refused to fight. They were tired, miserable and hungry, and sick of fighting a war that never seemed to get anywhere.

On the 18th of May, the 18th Infantry refused to go up to the line. They slashed the tyres of the lorries brought to transport them, and milled about, firing their rifles into the air, some of them singing the 'Internationale'. Officers tried to reason with them, and eventually two battalions agreed to go up to the Front; the third marched about aimlessly, lacking leadership, until the following day a contingent of gendarmes arrived and resistance collapsed.

The 41st Division came out of the line on the 12th of May, having been there continuously since the 28th of January. The billets were overcrowded, there were no facilities for cleaning up, and the food was all but inedible. Then, after a week, they were warned to go back up to the line and tempers flared. The men marched in columns from place to place, waving red flags and singing revolutionary songs. When a general tried to reason with them they stoned him and tore off his stars. They had heard rumours that black and Indo-Chinese soldiers were violating and murdering their women at home: there was much resentment of these French colonial troops, who were kept in the rear and never had to serve at the Front, and they had no difficulty in believing the rumours. They also believed that revolution had broken out in Paris and the Louvre was ablaze. The division's general managed to calm them at last by promising they would not be sent to the Front.

While the units behind the line refused to go up to the Front, the units actually in the line stayed put, only telling their officers that they would not advance or obey any order to attack, though they would resist if the Germans attacked. The exception was a battalion of the 66th, which drove out its officers, abandoned the trenches and camped in the woods behind the line. By the 4th of June there were only two divisions between Soissons and Paris still under discipline. As well as the mass refusal to fight, hundreds of individuals were deserting every week, and the largest number of them were going over to the Germans – not for treasonous reasons, but because they were men originally from the areas now under German occupation, and they were desperate to get home. While 'peace at any price' was the mutineers' overt demand, there was more deep feeling about pay, rations and leave: the political agitators wanted France out of the war, but the *poilus'* concerns were closer to home.

It was given to General Pétain to restore order. He was well liked by the soldiery, and was known to have been against Nivelle's Aisne plan, so he was listened to. He visited a hundred divisions in person and talked to the men face to face. He at once sent half the army on leave, promised leave to the rest when they returned, and instituted measures to improve the food and the pay. The ringleaders would have to be court-martialled, but in return he promised there would be no more offensives like that of April. The French Army would hold the line, nothing more, until the Americans arrived in force.

It was not until the 2nd of June that General Haig learnt of the full extent of the problem, when the French chief of staff told him that the French Army could no longer assist with the next stage of the offensive, which was supposed to start on the 10th. The news placed a great responsibility on British shoulders. Plainly, it was desperately important that the Germans did not find out about the state of affairs, and with the French Army able to do nothing but defend for the foreseeable future, any attack must be made by the British Army, and it must be prosecuted with enough vigour to keep the Germans occupied. There must be a major offensive, and it must be continued until the French were ready to fight again.

Haig's plans, before the French troubles struck, had been for an offensive in the Ypres salient, and nothing had altered his opinion that this was the vital area of the war. It was here, therefore, in the new circumstances of the second half of 1917, that he determined to strike.

At last, in May, the new aeroplanes began to come out to France, together with an increase in personnel; the RFC's flying hours began to increase and their casualties to decrease. Jack's squadron received a batch of new Bristols that were a match for the German Fokkers and Albatroses, and the mood in the mess changed dramatically. It was good to wake up in the morning without dreading what the day would bring.

In the middle of May, the squadron received just one of the new fighters from Jack's old friend Tom Sopwith. The Sopwith Camel was intended gradually to replace the Pups and Strutters, and was so called because of the hump in the fuselage in front of the pilot, which housed the guns. It was fitted with two synchronised Vickers machine-guns, where every previous fighter had only one, and the increase in firepower was very encouraging. The Camel had been tested earlier in the year and was now in production. Some friendly influence in the RFC – perhaps that of their chief, Hugh 'Boom' Trenchard himself – had ensured that Jack got one of the earliest, together with a cordial note from Tom Sopwith, inviting Jack to let him know what he thought of it, and to feel free to offer any suggestions for improvement.

Jack took it up for a test flight, and found the controls extremely sensitive, which made it very nimble, while the more powerful engine gave greater speed and height, and more rapid climbing. It had the usual drawback of the rotary-engined Sopwiths, caused by the propellor torque – the tendency of the nose to drop in a turn to starboard and rise in a turn to port. That same torque allowed the aeroplane to turn more quickly and tightly than anything else in the air, but if the turn was too tight, the machine could fall into a spin. A skilled pilot like Jack, accustomed to its vagaries, could neutralise the controls without difficulty; and he had even used the spin deliberately as a manoeuvre, to lose height quickly. But not a few inexperienced pilots had crashed in such spins, and some had been killed. It required special training to fly them in combat.

There was a further improvement in the Camel's guns: the Vickers guns in the Pup and Strutter were fed by canvas belts of ammunition, and the canvas was a weak spot. It deteriorated quickly, so that breakages and consequent jams were not infrequent; also the canvas would become damp and then, when the aeroplane climbed to the icy upper air, the belt would freeze stiff. This canvas belt had been replaced in the Camel with a belt of metal links, which disintegrated after firing and were ejected with the empty cases.

Jack was delighted with his Camel, excited at the thought of the advantage it would give him over the enemy; and the opportunity to test it was not long in coming. After several days of formation-flying practice with the new machines, Jack was ordered to take out a late patrol over the line, with Moody and three of the new boys. They took off in the mellow light of late afternoon and flew eastwards, climbing steadily to eighteen thousand feet. It had been a beautiful day, the air clear and brilliant as if polished; now the sun was declining, with little pink clouds like powder-puffs low in the west, and gold streaks above them. Jack listened to the thrumming of his engine, felt the buoyancy under the wings, heard the wind singing in the wires like an angel choir, and told himself it was good to be alive.

Soon they were over the ruined land that lay like a scar along either side of the line. The artillery was firing on both sides, but it seemed distant and irrelevant up here in the clear sky. Even when Archie opened up, it was almost like a friendly greeting: at this height they were not in much danger, and the sound was like a repeated, bronchitic cough far below, like an old man beside a pub fire. At eighteen thousand they turned north-east, and soon afterwards spotted an enemy formation of seven Fokkers below and ahead of them.

Jack wagged his wings and pointed downwards over the side, to make sure his companions, flying in a V-formation behind him, had seen, and then dived. He had given plenty of lectures to newly arrived fliers on the principles of air fights. 'Dive and zoom on to their tails. Until you're confident enough

231

to engage in a dog-fight, don't stop to argue – just dive straight through them and out, gain height again and see what's left. Then you can half roll and dive again. If the enemy fire gets too hot, hard rudder and side-slip. If you're hit, dive for home by the shortest route.'

The enemy was in V-formation as well, and as Jack dived in firing, it broke up, peeling off to left and right. Jack went after the leader, who side-slipped to port, with Jack hard on his tail. He saw the pilot turn a goggled face back to him. It may only have been the effect of the goggles, but Jack thought he looked surprised at how tightly the Camel turned, actually catching him up. Jack fired, saw a burst of flame and then thick smoke issue from the Fokker's starboard engine, and at once it began to dive out of control. No need to pursue further – and there had been seven of them, he remembered, to five. He must re-engage. He pulled up and circled, to discover that in those few seconds, both neat formations had disintegrated as each man went after the enemy nearest him, and the sky was now full of machines hurtling in every direction – like Piccadilly Circus gone mad, he thought. The lambent air was criss-crossed with vapour trails, and two darker streamers marked where his late enemy and another machine had gone down, hit.

A Fokker that had also climbed out of the fight, but on the other side, dived back in and was on the tail of Moody's Bristol, guns blazing. Jack put his nose down and went in pursuit. Again, that goggle-faced look of surprise. Moody side-slipped right. The Fokker turned left to circle and regain the rear position, and Jack went after him, seeing a thumbs-up of gratitude from Moody as he passed. The Fokker circled, but Jack could circle even better in his Camel: it responded to him like his own body, and he was hardly aware of the controls. The pilot looked back again, tried a side-slip, and Jack slipped too, hurtling down the air, firing, seeing little dark holes appear in the white canvas ahead of him. They were away from the fight now, heading back over the line on the British side. The German wanted to climb, but with Jack close on his tail he could not afford the loss of speed it would entail. Jack fired again, and was rewarded by that gout of black smoke, which turned into a tell-tale, streaming behind. The Fokker, still turning, was losing height, but Jack wanted to be sure of him, followed him down and fired again.

There was nothing but a grinding click. The gun had jammed! A series of oaths poured through his mind as he jiggled hopelessly with the trigger-release. Complete jam, nothing doing at all. But the Fokker was spouting plumes of black as the wounded engine coughed in its death throes. Seeing the game was up, the German straightened out, skimmed the trees, and put down in a field with a series of jarring bounces. Jack pulled up and circled as the Fokker jolted to a halt, and as he came in again he saw the pilot struggle out of the cockpit, take a couple of lurching steps and fall flat on his face as Jack zoomed past above him. As he circled and came in again, Jack saw the German had got to his feet and was running, clumsily in his big boots; but hearing Jack and seeing there was nowhere to hide, he stopped and turned to face him, and put his hands up, waving them in a helpless gesture, not knowing whether it was the British custom to shoot in this situation or not.

Jack passed over his head, leaning out to look down. The German saluted him bravely, and Jack waved back, then wagged his wings as he pulled up over the trees. He knew this field – it was only a few miles from the airfield. He headed home at top speed by the shortest route.

In a matter of minutes he was landing. As soon as he came to a halt he scrambled out of the machine in great haste. 'The damned guns jammed,' he said to the mechanics, to explain why he was back alone. 'We met some Huns. I downed two before I lost the guns. One's in a field just two miles away, and I'm going to get him.'

They grinned their understanding. It was a custom that

any German they brought down within easy reach of the airfield was a guest of the mess for one evening before being handed over to the Military Police. Jack ran across towards the transport lines, and Rug came hurtling from the direction of the mess, barking joyfully. Their paths converged at the line, and the dog flung himself on his master with shrill yips of adoration. 'Yes, all right, old boy, you can come too.'

One of the mechanics, Noon, was lounging by a small Crossley tender, and straightened up hastily as Jack approached.

'Is that one a goer?' Jack asked.

'Yes, sir,' said Noon.

'Come on, then – you can drive me. I've downed a Hun in a field nearby.'

Noon grinned. 'Guest of the mess, sir?'

'I want to get to him before he runs and hides,' said Jack.

But when they reached the field, the German pilot was sitting resignedly in the grass smoking a cigarette. He obviously felt that in raising his hands he had surrendered to Jack, and it would have been dishonourable after that to run away. He had pulled off his helmet, and rose to his feet as Jack came towards him, revealing himself as very tall – too tall for a pilot, Jack thought – and very fair, with a ruddy complexion, bright blue eyes and soft, floppy hair that was so blond it was almost white. His face was smoke-grimed from the engine fire, and the white rings round his eyes where the goggles had been made him look as though he were staring nervously. Perhaps he was, for he raised his hands again as Jack reached him.

'I am your prisoner,' he said. Holding Jack's eyes, he reached slowly for his pistol and held it out, butt first. Jack gulped as he took it, having completely forgotten to draw his own. Noon reached them, and started to walk round the damaged machine, inspecting it. 'You stay with it,' Jack told him. 'I'll drive the Crossley home and send it back for you with some of the others. You'll need help.' Then he turned to the German and gestured towards the tender. 'Would you please come this way?'

Rug set up a ferocious barking as they approached, standing on the driver's seat with his paws on the open window ledge and his head sticking out. He fixed the German with a fierce glare and lifted his lips in a long, rattling snarl. How on earth did he know, Jack wondered, that this was the enemy? 'Quiet, Rug!' he ordered. 'Get down!'

The German stood still, just out of range. 'Is it your dog?' he asked.

'Yes. I apologise for his bad manners. He's usually very friendly.'

'I have a little dog at home, very like him. He too is – no breed. How do you say that?'

'A mongrel.'

'*Ja*. Mongrel.' He tested the word with interest. 'But he is very brave. His name is Herakles because he is so brave.'

Jack smiled. 'My dog is called Rug, because he looks like one.'

'*Ach, so?*' The German looked steadily back at the snarling Rug, and began speaking softly in German. Jack did not understand what he was saying – he had little German and was glad this fellow spoke such good English. It seemed to work some magic on Rug. The dog's snarling diminished and became a mere growl, at the same time as a tentative wagging started up at the other end, and the rough head took on a puzzled tilt. Then the growling died away, the wagging became wholehearted, and as the German slowly advanced his fingers, Rug licked them, then submitted his head to be scratched.

'You're very good,' Jack observed.

'I like always the dogs,' the German said, with satisfaction. 'So, do we go?'

'We go,' Jack said, opening the door and pushing Rug over to get in. The German went round to the other side and got into the passenger seat, and Rug sat happily between them, as though they had all been friends for years. Jack started the engine and turned the Crossley towards home.

'Do you take me now to prison?' the German asked, and despite the great calm and self-possession he had shown so far, there was something of a tremor in his voice. Jack looked at him. He could not have been more than twenty-one or twenty-two, and the prospect of being a prisoner of war was a miserable thing.

'Not immediately. You will be the honoured guest of our officers' mess until tomorrow, and I promise you we will have a splendid time. It's our tradition.'

The man smiled. 'Then I think no more about prison until tomorrow. Is good?'

'Good,' said Jack. 'I had better know your name so I can introduce you to the others.'

'I am Leutnant Georg von Liebeswald.'

'And I am Captain Jack Compton. At your service.' He couldn't shake hands as he needed bath to steer, but he nodded and smiled, and von Liebeswald bowed and contrived somehow to click his heels while seated.

By the time they got back, the rest of the flight had come in, with only minor damage, no casualties, and a bag of three of the seven enemy aeroplanes shot down, one of which, Jack's first target, had crashed, and the other, damaged by Moody, had flown off towards the German side, apparently still in control. The youngsters were all wildly excited about the fight and the good outcome, but when von Liebeswald was explained to them, they ceased their chattering in favour of an awed silence. It was the first time any of them had seen a real live German.

Jack had to take him first to the major, who interviewed him briefly, asked for and received his parole not to try to escape, then handed him over to Ellis so that he could clean up and rest before dinner. Jack and his flight had to make their report to the major, and discuss the action, the lessons to be learnt from it, before they could do the same; and

Jack had to go and see what the mechanics had made of his gun failure, and report that to the major as well.

'It's the gun belt, sir,' said Vickery, beckoning Jack round the side with an oil-caked finger. 'Look 'ere. All these little bits 'o metal've choked up the ejection chute. There ain't hardly room for them *an'* the empty cases, 'specially with two of 'em. I've cleared it out easy enough, but there's nothing to stop it 'appening again.'

'It'll have to be modified,' Jack said.

'Be better if they wasn't both right-'and feed guns,' Vickery grumbled. 'It's tight in there as it is.'

'I'll report it back to Mr Sopwith and see what they come up with. In the mean time, perhaps we can do something with it on a temporary basis.' And they plunged into one of those arcane technical conversations that so delight the male spirit, from the age of eight onwards.

Mears had done his best at short notice to make a special dinner that evening, with clear soup, croquettes of ham, fried fillets of some nameless local fish, roast leg of mutton with curried rice, then apple charlotte and Nassau tart for pudding. Borthwick, who was mess president, got out the best wine and port, everyone donned their blues, and Jack went to fetch von Liebeswald, who had bathed and shaved, and whose uniform had been sponged and pressed and his boots polished by Jack's batman, Corrie. With Rug as the jaunty outrider, they walked back across the dark field towards the lighted windows of the mess hut, and as they stepped in through the door they were met by an enormous roar of greeting.

Borthwick came forward and pressed a silver tankard of champagne into the hand of each – on special nights, that was always how they drank champagne – and proposed the first toast. 'To flyers all, may their engines never fail, their wings never fall off, and may all their landings be happy ones.' Everyone, including von Liebeswald, drank the toast with a roar of acclaim. Then

237

Jack introduced him to everyone in turn, and he began to look rather bemused, though in a happy way, as beaming face succeeded beaming face, and his hand was wrung and his back slapped as though that afternoon they had not been firing on each other.

The mood sobered slightly when Major Wilkinson entered, and a more formal introduction was made, and then they all went through to the dining side of the hut and took their places at table. Von Liebeswald was seated on the major's right hand, with Jack on his left and the adjutant, Captain Johnson, opposite.

'This is a very nice custom of yours, sir,' von Liebeswald said. 'I like it very much. If ever you should have the misfortune to be shot down on our side of the line, I hope we shall be able to show you such good hospitality.'

The major blinked at that, but said, 'Thank you, you are too kind.'

The adjutant said, 'Your English is very good, Herr Leutnant. Did you learn it at school?'

'Yes,' said von Liebeswald, 'and also my father is professor of English at Heidelberg University, so we spoke English at home quite often.'

'I believe Heidelberg is a beautiful city,' said Wilkinson.

'Most beautiful,' said von Liebeswald. 'Have you been there?' As the major shook his head, he turned to address the same question to Jack.

'No,' Jack said. 'I'm ashamed to say I have never been anywhere apart from France.'

'I also must say that. The world is very large, and I would like very much to travel. When the war is over.'

'Yes,' Jack agreed. 'I have relatives in America – a half-sister. I'd like to see America one day.'

'Ah, yes, the Land of the Free,' von Liebeswald said wryly.

Jack said, 'Tell me, did you go to Heidelberg University too? I suppose with your father a bigwig there . . . ?'

'Bigwig? Oh, *ja*, I understand. No, my brothers Albert

and Frittie both did go, but when my turn came, I begged my father to let me go to technical school.'

'So did I,' said Jack, pleased with the coincidence. 'I went to technical school in Manchester.'

Von Liebeswald looked pleased too. 'Always I wanted to fly, since I was very little boy.'

'Me too. It was all I ever wanted to do. Was your father disappointed?'

Von Liebeswald grinned. 'It was as if the world was coming to an end. Also when I joined the *Fliegetruppe*. My brothers both joined the Uhlans. My father could be proud of this. It is for the aristocratic. But he believes the *Fliegetruppe* is for—' He searched a moment for the word, and then said, 'For the bourgeois.'

The three Englishmen exchanged a wry look. Aristocratic cavalry, middle-class flying corps. It had a familiar ring. The army looked down on the RFC as 'garage mechanics', and resented their more informal ways and easier discipline.

'But wasn't your flyer von Richthofen in the Uhlans?' Johnson said. 'We gather he's a baron in civilian life.'

Von Liebeswald grinned. 'Oh, *ja*, he is most aristocratic, and since he has been so much in the newspapers, I write to my father very often about him, to make him know it is not shameful to fly.'

'Have you met him?' Johnson wanted to know.

'Once only, when he came to our mess. He is a very nice fellow, most . . .' He searched for a word.

'Affable?' Jack suggested.

Von Liebeswald nodded, though Jack wasn't sure he understood the word. 'And a very good flyer,' he concluded. 'Perhaps our best.'

'He's certainly accounted for a good many of us,' Wilkinson said sourly, and there was a moment's awkwardness.

'It is true he's painted his kite red to be more conspicuous?' Johnson said, to get them over it.

'Kite?' Von Liebeswald savoured the word. '*Ja*, he has

painted red some part of his kite, and all his *Jasta* do the same, to honour him. Red was the Uhlans regimental colour.'

'It would make things more interesting if we did the same,' Jack said. 'Paint our buses in nice bright colours.'

'Don't you try it, that's all,' Wilkinson growled. 'The brigadier would have a fit.'

When the port was put on, Wilkinson excused himself, saying he had a great deal of paperwork, and the look he gave Jack suggested much of it had been generated by von Liebeswald. Johnson went with him, and as soon as they had gone, the atmosphere grew more relaxed. Cigarettes, pipes and cigars were lit, glasses were filled, and von Liebeswald was taken on a cheerful tour of the mess treasures and trophies, such as the wooden German propellor, the square of white canvas with a black cross on it, cut out of a downed Fokker monoplane, and not least the board on which were painted the pilots' names, with an aeroplane silhouette to denote each 'kill' alongside them. Von Liebeswald looked at this soberly, and then said to Jack, 'I will be put there, beside your name, *ja*?' Jack didn't answer – it seemed tactless to glory in his plight. Then von Liebeswald smiled. 'If it must be, I am glad at least to add to *your* success.'

And then, to lighten the mood, Jack showed him Rug's helmet and goggles, and at the general insistence put them on the dog, and Hodgson took a photograph of Jack and von Liebeswald, with Rug in the latter's arms.

Then Borthwick took his place at the piano, his foul pipe stuck in the corner of his mouth and reeking like the funnel of a Clyde puffer, and they all gathered round and started to sing the favoured wry and rowdy songs. Glasses were refilled and swung from side to side to the thumping rhythm, and von Liebeswald sang as lustily as anyone, improvising words in German and joining in with the choruses in English when he had mastered them.

> *Oh, had I the wings of an Avro*
> *Then far into Holland I'd fly*
> *I'd stop there until the war's over*
> *And laugh at you blighters on high.*

> *So gather up quickly the fragments,*
> *And when you've returned them to store,*
> *Write Wilkie a letter and tell him*
> *That his precious squadron's no more.*

Later, when the right level of frivolity had been reached, they played the orange game, where each man had to try to drink from a tankard while balancing an orange on his head, the winner being the man who drank the most without spilling or dropping the orange. Rug did his best to influence the outcome by barking hysterically and tugging at the trouser legs of the contestants – for some reason, this particular game always had that effect on him.

Later again, a more reflective mood came over the mess, and as Borthwick was almost comatose in an armchair, Sheridan took over the piano and played some of the sad songs, which they crooned in low voices and heartfelt, if uncertain, harmony.

> *We meet 'neath the sounding rafter,*
> *And the walls all around are bare;*
> *As they shout back our peals of laughter*
> *It seems that the dead are there.*
> *Then stand to your glasses, steady!*
> *We drink in our comrades' eyes:*
> *One cup to the dead already –*
> *Hurrah for the next that dies!*

> *Cut off from the land that bore us,*
> *Betrayed by the land we find,*
> *When the brightest have gone before us,*
> *And the dullest are most behind –*

Stand, stand to your glasses, steady!
'Tis all we have left to prize:
One cup to the dead already –
Hurrah for the next that dies!

Jack sat in a comfortable corner with his guest, and they talked in low voices.

'Are your brothers still serving?' Jack asked at one point.

'Frittie is with his regiment at Verdun. Albert was killed at Ypres in 1915,' von Liebeswald said.

'Oh, I'm sorry.'

He bowed. 'I think many of us have someone to be sorry about. That is the nature of war, is it not?'

'My brother Frank was killed last year, at Gommecourt,' Jack said.

'I too am sorry. We have so much in common,' said von Liebeswald. His eyes were rather red from drink, but they looked steadily into Jack's. 'I think it is that we could have been friends, if we had met in another way.'

Jack smiled. 'And our dogs could have been friends too.'

'*Ja*. Rug and Herakles.' Rug was asleep on the sofa beside him, with his rough head in von Liebeswald's lap, and the German stroked it tenderly. 'We could go ratting together. Is he a good hunter of rats?'

'I don't know, but I bet he is,' Jack said.

'But now I must go to prison,' von Liebeswald said mournfully, 'and there is an end of all the war for me. It may go on for years more. So it is *adieu* to my youth, perhaps.'

'I know how you must feel,' Jack said. 'I was a prisoner, in 1914. I was shot down at Ypres. I thought it was the end of everything.'

Von Liebeswald looked up with interest. 'You were also shot down? Also a prisoner? So, we do have much in common. But how did you come to be free?'

'I was badly wounded, and the German unit who captured me could not give me proper medical attention, so I was

242

exchanged for a wounded German flyer. Perhaps you will be exchanged, too.'

Von Liebeswald shook his head. 'I am not wounded. But I might perhaps escape.'

They were silent a moment, and then Jack said, 'I do not think the war will go on for years and years.'

'Our people think it will end this year,' von Liebeswald confessed. 'But so also they said last year, and the year before.'

'But now America has joined—' He stopped, because what he was suggesting was the defeat of Germany, and while that was, of course, what he wished, he could not say so to this young man.

'Yes, our new enemy,' von Liebeswald said with a wry smile.

Rug mumbled and grumbled in his sleep, his moustache twitching. Most of the airmen had gone to bed, only Borthwick remaining, sleeping in his armchair, and Sheridan, screwing up his eyes against the smoke rising from his cigarette, quietly playing something that sounded like Chopin.

'When the war is over,' von Liebeswald said, 'I would like very much for you to visit me in Heidelberg. I should wish to show you the city.'

'I'd like that,' Jack said. 'And you must visit me in England.'

'After the war, when once again we can be friends, as we should have been. Men who love to fly must always be friends, *nicht wahr*?'

The next morning, Jack was up early to see his guest off, when the MPs came to collect him. He looked pale in the morning light, though that might have been a reaction to the copious and varied drinks of the night before. He shook hands with the major, then turned to Jack. 'If I escape from prison and fly again,' he said, 'I will try to shoot you down if I meet you. I will try to kill you, because I must. But after the war, I hope you will visit me, and we will be friends. This is the madness of war. You will visit me, if we both survive?'

'Yes,' said Jack. 'If we both survive.'

They looked into each other's eyes for a moment, and then von Liebeswald drew himself to attention and saluted. Jack and the major saluted in return, and watched as the MPs escorted him to the waiting transport. Rug, who had been taking his early-morning constitutional round the back of the huts, ran up and stood beside Jack, pressing himself against his leg. He barked as the transport roared into life, but it was just his custom.

Teddy hated reading about shipping losses in the newspapers, but he could not help himself. Something made him read every word, while his mind bristled with horror. His experience on board *Titanic* would never leave him; then there had been *Lusitania*, then the sinking of HMS *Hampshire*, which had taken Lord Overton to his watery grave. To these constant reminders had been added the sinking of *Titanic*'s sister ship, *Britannic*, in the Mediterranean the November before. *Britannic* had been fitted out as a hospital ship, and had completed only five round trips carrying sick and wounded back to Southampton when on the sixth she went to the bottom after an explosion. Fortunately most of those on board had been saved, but thirty people had lost their lives when two lifeboats were cut up by the still-turning screw. Of the three giant, beautiful ships Teddy had been involved with, that left only *Olympic*, still serving her time as a troop-carrier – if it was *Olympic*. He remembered the ravings of the deranged crew-member who had claimed that the names of the first two sisters had been switched and that it had been, in fact, *Olympic* that went to the bottom in 1912. That was something his mind still chewed over on those rare nights when he could not sleep. There had been things that puzzled him, things he had observed . . .

But it hardly mattered now. What mattered was that the evil Germans were attacking merchant ships with their

U-boats, sinking them, killing their crews. That was against the law of the sea, which was a law as old as mankind itself. At sea, it had always been understood that while ships might fight each other in time of war, all seamen were united in one brotherhood. And for an armed U-boat to attack an unarmed merchantman was a revolting thing. The British did not do it. The Royal Navy blockaded German ports and German ships in foreign ports, and stopped and searched any ship suspected of carrying 'contraband' – something that had long annoyed America, who regarded the freedom of the seas as the beginning and end of her foreign policy – but it did not fire on non-military vessels.

And the losses were huge: since February, 875,000 tons, including American ships. Since a large part of the food supply to Britain came across the Atlantic, there was a real chance that the nation would starve by midsummer and the war would have to be given up. That, of course, was exactly what Germany was hoping for.

The answer, it seemed from the debates Teddy had read in the newspaper, was to institute a convoy system, whereby groups of ships crossed the Atlantic together and were guarded by a contingent of warships. The system was already in use, with some success, for Scandinavian shipping to east-coast ports, and for ships taking coal across the Channel from England to France: losses had been reduced in both cases. But the Atlantic crossing was far longer and more exposed, and the navy had been against convoys there, arguing that they would have to be larger to justify tying up the warships for so long, which would make them a bigger target. It would be putting all one's eggs in one basket – a successful German strike would mean far greater loss; and assembling such large convoys would choke the ports and cause delays in delivery of their cargoes.

Teddy read both sides of the argument carefully. There was much truth in the idea that a large group of shipping would be easier for the Germans to find in the vast tract of the Atlantic; but he concluded that it would at least have a chance of fighting back, and that, in the end, *something* must be done. The evidence of the food shortage was not hard to discover. Flour had disappeared from the shops, and the price of bread, sugar, butter, milk, cheese and bacon had doubled since the beginning of the year – all the staples on which the lower classes relied. A Ministry of Food had been set up in February under Lord Davenport, and he had called for a voluntary rationing system – much advertised in newspapers, on hoardings and in the cinema – asking people to eat less meat and, particularly, less bread. That was all very well, Teddy thought, but the poor in the towns ate little meat anyway, and bread was mostly what they lived on. Already margarine had replaced butter for the poor – Teddy had seen it in the back-street houses of York. In his view, margarine had no more food value than saddle-soap. He recommended dripping and lard as more nutritious replacements for butter, and even on occasion distributed them to make the point. Mrs Stark sighed over, but could not prevent, the master's depredations on her stocks, and took the precaution of hiding away her precious goose-fat where he could not find it.

In March the Ministry of Food ordered a change to bread production, to increase the quantity available without using more wheat flour. Maize, barley and potatoes were to be added to make the flour go further. The resultant bread was nourishing, but had an unpleasant marshy smell and strange texture, and it was not uncommon to find lumps of potato that had missed the crushing process inside the loaf. Slicing too vigorously could make the lump shoot out like a missile.

In towns, queuing for food became a large part of daily life, and rumours that So-and-so's had butter today, or sugar, or that Such-and-such had received a consignment of tea, or that there were sausages at Thingummy's, the butchers, could cause vast movements of the population almost akin to panic. Again, it was the poor who suffered most, for the middle class had the leisure to queue, or could send a servant, where the poor were more likely to be working. Often it was the children who did the queuing, truanting from school. It was in towns, reliant on food brought in from outside, that there was real hunger, and the old, the sick and the very young died.

Teddy went to Manchester in May to settle a strike at one of his factories – there were strikes all over the country in protest at the abolition of Trade Cards, which had exempted skilled workers from conscription – and he saw the skinny children waiting outside factory gates, begging for the crusts from the workers' midday sandwiches. The sight upset him so much he determined to do something. His own workers did not bring sandwiches from home because they already had a canteen, built and subsidised by him, to cook them a midday meal. Now he set the kitchens to making vast quantities of soup, and set up a distribution booth by the factory gate, which handed it out twice a day, morning and evening. The newly formed Women's Institute eagerly volunteered to man the booth, and Teddy was glad to accept.

Things were better in the country, where most workers had their own patch of garden to grow beans and potatoes, keep a few chickens and perhaps a pig, and there were gleanings from nature to eke things out – though early summer was not a good time, with no berries or nuts around. Teddy ordered his men to turn a blind eye to anyone taking rabbits or pigeons, unless damage to property was involved; and he mentally gave up the outer rows of every vegetable field. Morland Place grew a great deal of its own food, and none of his tenant families was suffering; but he kept a close eye on Morland pensioners and former servants. Meanwhile the presence of the army camp on his land was attracting the children of the poorest York families, for the army made sure its men were well fed, and there were always back-door pickings for the urchins willing to walk out that far.

Still, with an eye to the greater problem, Teddy decided that May to put a lot more land under the plough, and grow wheat, barley and potatoes. There was grazing land spare, because of the lower numbers of horses now kept, as well as marginal lands that had been allowed to go back twenty years ago, when the price of cereals fell too low to make them viable. And on the ings and corners that were not worth putting down to cereals he decided that more vegetables could be grown. The difficulty was in finding the manpower to do the work, with most of the male population taken up by conscription. Local women were glad of the wages to boost what their men sent home from the Front, and they took over most of the work the men had done. Teddy was able to make a start using them, but he could see that more labour would be needed in the future.

At the end of May the government made a trial of the convoy system with a large convoy from Gibraltar, and when it reached its destination without loss, the decision was taken to keep on with it. If the success was maintained, the food shortage might soon be eased, if not eliminated. And at the beginning of June Lord Davenport was replaced as food controller by the more vigorous Lord Rhondda; under his urging the government empowered the Board of Agriculture to see that all possible land was cultivated, and gave it powers to force farmers to grow staple crops on unused pasture and spare land.

Teddy was pleased that he had thought of it before the decree was issued, and reflected that if they wanted everyone to plough up their pastures, the government would have to do something about the labour shortage. He pondered on what that might be, without coming to any conclusions; but was glad that it would be someone else's problem. He had enough on his plate as it was.

CHAPTER ELEVEN

U-boats had not been much on Jessie's mind on the sea crossing from Dover to Boulogne. She had heard the other nurses in the draft talking about them, and had seen them peering nervously about at the sea and fingering their life-jackets as though at any moment they might need them. But Jessie was too interested in everything, the ship, the smell and sight of the sea, the following gulls, the activities of the crew – pretending insouciance as they hurried about their duties but eyeing the chattering women sidelong like foxes glancing at hens. And she was too excited about the adventure to come to worry about submarines, though she knew they were a possibility.

She and Beta stood close together by the stern rail and watched the white cliffs of Dover grow smaller and disappear. They seemed dazzlingly white against the dark blue sea, as if they were more than mere nature but a divine symbol of England and all it stood for. It was the first time Jessie had ever left her native land, and she felt a tightening of the throat as it fell behind her, a mixture of love and regret and determination to be worthy of it.

It was a fine day, though there was a strong breeze that made it just a little chilly on deck, and made the waves romp under the ship, and the funnel-smoke bat away sideways. The wake was a vivid pale turquoise under the foam. It amazed her that the colour of the sea could change so much just by its being broken, but she felt disinclined to voice the thought to Beta. Beta was silent, too. There seemed something very important in what they were doing, too important for light conversation: Jessie wondered that the other nurses did not seem to feel it too. They all seemed very young, much younger than her and her companion. She leant in a little towards Beta and felt her lean back for warmth against the keen wind, and was glad of her presence and her silence.

At Boulogne they were herded together and marched off the ship, through the dockyard and into the town. Because the way was too narrow for anything else, they walked two by two – like a school crocodile, Jessie thought. Boulogne looked shabby, and dirty, and crowded, with rubbish blowing along the gutter, and an indefinable air of having been knocked about, though Jessie couldn't quite put her finger on what it was that gave that impression. The breeze was blowing up clouds, and the glum light did the architecture no favour. It looked as though it would rain soon, and they were glad to reach the shelter of a large hotel that looked like it had seen better days.

The inside of the hotel had a knocked-about look, too, with worn carpets and upholstery and sadly inadequate electric lamps that flickered sulkily and occasionally went out altogether for several seconds. It smelt dusty, with a background odour of French cigarettes and something musty, which might have been mice. Here they were ushered into the grandly named Salon Grande Bretagne and handed long forms to fill in with their 'particulars', as they were called by the hatchet-faced sister in charge. While they were working laboriously on this, the sky darkened rapidly outside and a clattery rain began to hit the windows, blown by the strengthening wind.

Beta looked up and smiled at Jessie. 'Rather a muted welcome.'

Jessie said, 'But I still can't believe I'm in France.'

'Actually in a different country!'

After the forms, they had to line up for typhoid and tetanus inoculations, then made a queue at another desk where the sister in charge gave them their destinations. Beta and Jessie were told to report to the No. 24 General at Étaples, along with two other nurses, who looked very young and permanently round-eyed.

'Your train leaves at fourteen thirty hours tomorrow, Nurses,' said the sister. 'Here are your travel warrants. You will be billeted here tonight – you may get your room key at the hotel desk. Supper will be served at six.' She dismissed them with a glance and said, 'Next!' over their shoulders.

The other two nurses followed Jessie and Beta as they moved away, and one of them giggled and said, 'I'm so glad we're not on our own. Harris and me haven't the least idea how to get to the railway station.'

The other said, 'Is it all right if we follow you two? You look as if you've been here before.'

'I say,' said the first, 'what was that place she said we had to go – Heat-ups, was it?'

'Étaples,' Beta said. 'Haven't you heard of it?'

They shook their heads and giggled some more. 'Evans and I are from Shrewsbury,' said Harris, as if that explained everything.

'There's a big transit camp there,' Jessie told them. 'Practically every soldier in the British Army goes through it at some point. And obviously there must be a hospital there as well.'

'Is it far away?' Evans asked.

'I don't know. I don't think so,' Beta said.

'Is it near Hazebrouck? That's where my father wrote from last time,' said Harris.

'I really don't know,' Beta said, distracted.

They looked at her, still round-eyed, but evidently disappointed in her. But Jessie and Beta had reached the hotel desk, showed their names, and were given a room key, so they were able to shake off their unwelcome companions and hurried up the stairs, rather than wait for the ancient and, frankly, frail-looking *ascenseur*, which was struggling to cope with the sudden influx.

Their room, when they found it, high up in the building, was small, dark and bare, with two iron bedsteads, the bedding still folded on top of the mattress, and a tiny square window, which looked out on to a muddle of roofs and chimneys, onto which the cold rain was now lashing with an air of being about to turn into sleet. The smell up here was different, predominantly of soot and drains. Jessie wondered how the drains could smell this high up, but later when she went in search of a lavatory she found the answer.

They put down their bags, looked at each other, and laughed.

'And we thought the hostel was bad,' said Beta.

'I don't care,' Jessie said. 'It's only one night. And I'm in France! France, do you hear me? Let's go out and look at things.'

'In this?' Beta gestured towards the rain.

'We can't waste the opportunity,' Jessie said. 'And what's a drop of rain?'

So they went out, and walked about the streets, looking in shop windows, marvelling at the foreignness of everything, the French street names and shop names and advertisements, and the frequent notices in English that told the tale of the benign invasion. There were uniforms everywhere, khaki and dark blue, and the French civilians all seemed to be in black, which was a little depressing. The pelting rain eased off to a more gentle fall, and Jessie, tired of being wet, said, 'Do we dare go into a café for a cup of tea?'

'We're in France now. It will have to be coffee,' said Beta.

'Coffee, then. Shall we?'

'Why not? I can manage to ask for that in French.'

Jessie suddenly thought of something. 'But we haven't got any French money.'

'I have,' Beta said. 'My father had some francs from before the war and he gave them to me before I left.'

So they went in and ordered *café-au-lait*, and sat at a window table with the big, thick white cups and watched the people passing in the streets, which never seemed to grow less crowded.

'How do you feel?' Beta asked her suddenly.

'Strange,' Jessie said. She thought a moment. 'Detached – as though I were a boat and my rope had come loose. I'm floating away from everything I know towards – well, I don't know what.'

'I know what you mean. But I'm so glad we came. I feel we're doing something important at last.'

'Me too. I was getting awfully fed up in Camberwell. I was forgetting why we were there. Here, I believe we'll be allowed to serve properly.'

Beta nodded. 'It's . . .' She hesitated. 'It's a sort of holy thing, isn't it? Do you feel it?'

'I was thinking that on the boat,' Jessie said. 'I'm glad you feel it too.'

'I can see why, now,' Beta said, with a faint smile, 'they dress nurses up like nuns.'

When they left the café, Beta said she wanted to find a post office to send a wire to her brother to say she had arrived safely. 'I promised Mummy and Daddy I'd wire them, too – they were worried about submarines.'

When she was filling in the forms, Beta glanced curiously at Jessie, and said, 'Is there anyone you want to wire? I can lend you the money.'

So Jessie accepted gratefully, and sent a telegram to Bertie to tell him where she would be. Beta politely averted her eyes from the name and direction, but a glance at Jessie's face told her she had come close to the mystery of Jessie's heart. There *was* a man, and he was here, with the army. Perhaps at some point she would meet him, she thought.

★   ★   ★

It rained all night, but stopped the next morning, so they were able to go out and look around again. They walked up the steep hill to the old city with its massive basilica and mediaeval buildings, then found a café for an early luncheon. Jessie had managed to change some money at the hotel desk, and enjoyed a new sensation, of paying for her meal with what looked to her suspiciously like forged coins and notes. The café had bare dusty floorboards and crude wooden chairs, but the red and white checked tablecloths were cheerful, and the tired-looking, overworked waiter gave them a kind smile and seemed to understand their faltering school French. Though he was young, about thirty, he walked with a heavy limp, and had a puckered scar running up his neck from under his collar, so they guessed he had been invalided out of the army – a *mutilé de guerre* in the brutal French phrase. They had coarse local sausages, which took a great deal of dedicated chewing, with haricot beans, which had been cooked with onions and tomatoes and were delicious. Then they had to hurry down the hill again to collect their bags and find the railway station.

The train journey was short. At Étaples station they were told to leave their kit-bags, which would be transported for them by the next ambulance, and walk to the camp. Harris and Evans tagged along with them, asking them endless questions about where they had got to yesterday and this morning – 'We didn't dare leave the hotel, did we, Evans, in case we couldn't find it again?' – and exclaimed over everything they saw, reading out the name over every shop phonetically. Étaples looked even more grimy and battered than Boulogne, and there wasn't much of it, just a square with a church in it and a few narrow streets, and then they were out into the open country.

The previous day's rain had turned the roads to mud, and walking was precarious. But Jessie could smell the sea, and she breathed deeply and looked around with interest, glad she had on stout boots, and even gladder that they were not carrying their bags. The army camps covered a vast area of the flat coastal country, divided from the sea by the railway line and a barrier of sand-dunes and marram grass. The river that ran through Étaples spread out in several arms through the marshes on which alone the army had made no imprint. Yellow gorse colonised these rough places, and further off, where the land rose a little, there were clumps of dark sentinel pines, forbidding against the watery, uncertain sky.

The mass of tents and huts would have been daunting were it not for the helpful signposts all along the way, and they had no difficulty in finding the No. 24 General: streets of long wooden huts, and beyond them large marquees, presumably housing the overspill. The hospital had been there so long that narrow beds had been dug out along the fronts of the huts with flowers planted in them, marigolds and pinks, pansies and nasturtiums, which would be cheerful when they were in full bloom.

They had been told to report to the matron's office. Beta asked directions of a passing orderly, who told them briskly, while managing in the short time available to give each of them a comprehensive look-over, like a dealer at a horse fair. But the matron received them with a warmth that quite startled Jessie, used as she was to being treated coldly by the professional nurses.

She asked them their names and questioned them on their experience. 'You and Nurse Wallace both have more than a year's service?' she said. Beta had fifteen months, and Jessie had just won her 'efficiency stripe', a red braided ribbon sewn onto the sleeve of the uniform after a year's service in a military hospital. 'I'm glad of that,' the matron said. 'We are very busy here, and we need all the experienced hands we can get.'

Harris and Evans had only five months in a military hospital, but they had been almost a year in their local Devonshire before that. When answering the matron's questions, Jessie was glad to note that they spoke much more sensibly than their excited chatterings had so far suggested.

'Very well, Nurses,' the matron said at last. 'I'll have someone show you to your huts. You will go on duty tomorrow morning, so you had better use the rest of today to unpack and learn your way around.'

A harried-looking nurse showed them the main buildings, waited impatiently while they collected their bags, which had just arrived, and took them to their quarters. The nurses were accommodated in Alwyn huts – wooden buildings with a wooden floor and a canvas roof, about six feet square, with one small window. Jessie had been afraid they would have to sleep in a tent, and was relieved and pleased with the small but sturdy structure. Each hut accommodated two, so she and Beta would be sharing, which seemed cosy.

They spent the evening investigating the area, finding the dining-room and the mess hut, the post office, the pay office and other useful places. There was a small garden called the Sisters' Compound, where again flowers had been planted in neat beds round a square of grass, with two wooden benches to rest on. Jessie and Beta sat there a while.

'Can you hear the guns?' Beta said, suddenly.

Jessie listened. It was not quite a sound; nothing that could be identified over the trivial local sounds of people and the occasional bird and the movement of grass and leaves; but she could feel it. The air seemed uneasy with it, as though a thunderstorm were on its way, and now and then the ground under her feet seemed to tremble slightly. It was a reminder that the battle of Arras was still going on, not so many miles away; that men were still locked in the fiercest struggle mankind had ever known, and were suffering and dying. It was why they were here.

'How are you feeling now?' Beta asked softly.

Excited, Jessie thought. A little apprehensive. Awed by

the thought of those guns and what they meant. But glad to be here. After the grim, closed, uncomfortable, often meaningless privations of Camberwell, she felt as if life was opening out again, a narrow road running out into open country with a wide horizon ahead.

'Happy,' she said.

The next day they began nursing. At breakfast they were told which ward to go to, and Jessie was glad that she and Beta were sent to the same one. The sister caught the pleased look they exchanged, and said, 'We think it best for friends to work together just at first, until you settle in and find your feet. Later you will go where you're needed most.'

As they passed out of the hut, another nurse, eyeing them curiously, said, 'They must think a lot of you, sending you on Acute Surgical right away.'

'Is it a hard ward?' Beta asked.

'You'll see,' said the nurse, with a snort of what might have been laughter, and hurried away.

'That's all right,' Jessie said. 'I wanted hard work. Much better to be kept busy – then you don't have time to think.'

It was a baptism of fire. They had worked on acute wards at Camberwell, but that was a long stage removed from the battlefield, and the gravest cases never got that far. Here they were receiving men sometimes within twenty-four hours of being wounded, and half of them would never leave this place. The wounds were horrifying, worse than anything they had seen before; worse than Jessie could have imagined. With the battle still going on at Arras, there were fresh casualties arriving all the time, and the ward was so busy there were no half-days, and the daily three hours off were also forgone more often than not. But it was good, Jessie reflected at the end of the first exhausting day, to be kept so busy, for otherwise how could she have borne the horror of it? The only wonder that ever crossed her mind was of how men could cling so grimly to life in the face of such devastation, when the holding on meant such exertion and agony, when not letting go meant only a prolonging of suffering. Yet they did hold on, and as long as they had consciousness, their eyes told her they wanted to live.

In the operating theatre attached to the hut, operations went on all day, while on the ward Jessie and Beta applied dressings to wounds so gaping there seemed no beginning or end to them, struggled to staunch haemorrhages, to push intestines back into bellies and keep them in, to insert drainage tubes and keep them open, to pick shards of metal out of flesh as raw as on a butcher's slab. Often there was no time to do anything with the wads of soaked dressing but drop them on the floor; the stink of blood seemed to get down into their throats and make them raw.

When a convoy arrived, there would often be no beds for the newcomers, and they would lie on the floor on stretchers until someone lost his grip on life and a bed became vacant. Occasionally Jessie was called into the theatre to help, and then there were worse things lying on the floor than bloody gauze. And when the rushes were over, dressings had to be changed, and the pain of the process took all a man's courage to bear. However stoical they tried to be, they would always cry out in the end.

But they were always grateful for attention, however little good it might do them. Sometimes Jessie felt bitterly helpless, and wanted to stop them thanking her. On the second day, in a quiet period, the charge-sister told her to go and attend a boy around whom the screens had been drawn. He had a bubbling wound in his chest and his skin was waxy with blood loss. He turned his eyes feebly to Jessie as she came to his bedside.

'I'm dying, aren't I?' he whispered. 'That's what the screen means.' She didn't answer at once, taking his pulse. 'I'd like to know,' he said courteously, as if asking something of very little importance.

'Yes,' she said.

At once, tears came to his eyes, and he said, 'Sorry. Didn't mean to blub.'

She wiped them away, and then lifted the wad of gauze and cotton wool over his wound, which had soaked through. 'Is there anything I can get you?' she asked, reaching for more dressings.

He shook his head feebly. After a moment he said, 'You talk about dying for your country, but – I never thought I wouldn't see my mum and dad again.'

'Do you have a girl?' she asked, to keep him talking.

'No,' he said. 'There was one girl. I thought perhaps . . . But I didn't say anything before I left. I thought there'd be time. And last leave, she was going with someone else.' He was silent again.

She finished replacing the dressing, and then, seeing his hand move slightly, apologetically towards her, she took hold of it. She did not even know his name, but they were somehow locked together in this final act of the war that had to be played out; though it seemed, here in the hospital, to be nothing to do with either of them.

The charge-sister called from beyond the screen. 'Nurse Morland! I need you.'

She stood, releasing his hand. 'I'll be back in a moment,' she said.

She was not more than five minutes, but when she returned behind the screen, his eyes were empty; he had gone.

At the end of the second day, when she and Beta walked wearily into the mess hut, too tired to talk, almost too tired to eat, she found a letter in the rack for her, in Bertie's hand.

'Read it,' Beta said sympathetically. 'I'll get us both a cup of tea.'

259

I can hardly believe you are here in France [it said]. It makes me feel closer to you – not in geography, but in spirit. I dread to think of the things you will have to witness, but I know you will not falter in your duty. You are, for me, the pattern of womanhood. If that seems too much praise, remember we are living in a time of extremes – and that I know you as you are, as well as how I need to imagine you!

We are moving up to the Salient almost immediately. The very name fills me with foreboding at the thought of a third tour there. No good can come out of that poor, battered country. Well, we will do our duty, as we always have. I wish to God this war was over! Leave is out of the question for the moment, but be sure I will come as soon as I can – so much easier now you are this side of the water. I hope to get a day or so before the next show, and however short the time is, it will be yours. For now – take care of yourself. I am very proud of you.

Maud was not happy in Folkestone. Mrs Thompson's house was not at all the sort of thing she was used to, a small terraced house with nothing but two rooms on the ground floor, three bedrooms above, and the kitchen in the basement. There was no nursery: Richard and Nanny had to share one of the bedrooms and do their lessons in the dining-room. Mrs Thompson only had one live-in servant, a cook who slept in a room off the kitchen; and there was a housemaid who came in by day. It wasn't enough, but there was nowhere to put any more servants. Maud had to leave her lady's maid behind in London: there simply wasn't a bed for her.

Maud blamed Bertie for the situation. When she had told him the plan, he had said she wouldn't be comfortable staying with her cousin and had urged her to hire a house and take her own servants with her. But he had been so, frankly, triumphant that she was taking Richard out of London at last, that it had set her back up, and in her irritation she had refused to take his advice. If he had been more tactful about it, she reasoned, she would have listened to him and been much more comfortable now, so it was all his fault. Now she was stuck here. It would be insulting to Mrs Thompson to move out.

She hadn't *wanted* to leave London at all, and she was still far from believing it had been necessary. It was true that Richard's wretched cough would *not* seem to go away, and he was looking pale and worn with it; but how was sea air supposed to help? Damp was the very worst thing for the chest, as anyone knew; and the proof that sea air was damp was all around, from the peeling wallpaper and rotting window-frames of Mrs Thompson's house to the ruination of Maud's hair as soon as she stepped out of doors.

Nanny Katie hated Folkestone too. She was a Town girl. Though Irish by descent, she had been born in the East End, where her family still lived. Not being one to hide her feelings, she complained all the time, and about everything, until Maud, normally a calm and self-possessed person, wanted to slap her. It was a comfort of sorts to see how Richard loved the sea and the beach: he had never been to the seaside before, and his wonder at the sights and smells was touching. It was good to see his cheeks grow rosy, though he did not seem to put on any flesh. He ran about on the sands, made sandcastles, watched the Punch-and-Judy and pierrot shows with loud delight, splashed in the shallows, begging in vain to be allowed to go in and bathe properly, and made cautious friends with one or two other children.

Nanny Katie found things to object to in much of this programme too. The life on the beach bored her. Besides, here in Folkestone she was responsible for Richard's clothes and boots, and seawater marked, while sand was the very dickens for getting everywhere. Then she had a nanny's proper snobbery about the class of child her own could mix with, and there was no telling anything about those she saw on the beach with their boots and stockings off, their trouser legs rolled up and their skirts tucked into their knickers. And once a *dog* had run up to them and shaken water and sand all over them. She would have preferred to have Richard dressed immaculately in his sailor suit and walking demurely by her side along the promenade or through the public gardens. She made sure that that was what they did as often as possible, despite his protests.

For Maud, Folkestone was very dull, for she had been taken away from her usual occupations, her friends and acquaintances, her committees, all the things that gave her a sense of purpose and belonging. She was missing the company of Lord Manvers, too, who had been such a friend, so good with Richard, so enhancing of the family, so attentive to her. Now she had nothing to do, and no-one to talk to except Mrs Thompson – whose silence, she discovered, was just what was wanted in a companion in one's own home but did nothing to help the evenings along in someone else's.

At least Mrs Thompson had so far had better sense than to inflict her own friends on Maud: she had met two of them when she came across Mrs Thompson talking to them on the corner of the street, and thought them extremely vulgar. She had been given several introductions from London friends to local families of respectability and style, but on making the calls she found most of them still in London, and the only invitations so far forthcoming were one tea party and one bridge evening. The days and the evenings stretched before her imagination like endless deserts.

So it was almost a relief when one day Nanny Katie developed a blister the size of a shilling on both heels – from all that walking along beaches she was having to do, she complained; Maud thought it was more likely an unwise choice of footwear – and could not take Richard for the daily period out of doors that the doctor had prescribed. Maud would not trust him to Mrs Thompson, so she had to take over the task herself; and such was her state of boredom she was positively glad of having something to do.

It was a perfectly beautiful day, clear and sunny, with the gentlest of breezes rippling the calm surface of the sea. Maud enjoyed walking along the promenade with little Richard's hand in hers. He was a handsome child, and drew approving looks from passers-by. Richard had rather hoped to go on the sands, but he was so awed by his mother's taking him out that he did not dare to ask and, on his best behaviour, trotted along at her side in silence. To mark the occasion she bought him a paper windmill on a stick and, as a treat, allowed him to look through one of the telescopes fixed at intervals along the railings. (Nanny Katie never would let him, because it cost a penny, and she always said she didn't have a penny to spare for such nonsense.) Then they walked as far as the Martello tower. Richard didn't say that he had seen it already, because being with his mother anywhere at all was better even than paddling in the sea or making sandcastles.

They caught a tram back along the seafront, and she let him hand the conductor the money. It was just about the perfect morning for a small boy, and when they got off the tram he asked if he could have the tickets.

'What do you want them for?' Maud asked carelessly, as she handed them to him.

'Oh, just to keep,' he said, smoothing them between his fingers. He had a scrapbook he had been keeping for almost a year, and he thought he would stick them in as a memento of this glorious day.

Back home, Maud handed him over to Nanny Katie, and discovered that a message had been delivered by hand while she was out. It was from Lady Beezeley, one of the 'introductions' who had not been in when she called. The note was very cordial, regretting having missed her, saying that Lady

Beezeley and her three daughters were now in residence, and hoping that Lady Parke would call again whenever it was convenient to her.

Maud decided that there was no time like the present, and having taken a light luncheon alone (Mrs Thompson, fortunately, was out for the day), she changed into an afternoon dress and her newest hat and sallied forth to conquer the heights, such as they were, of Folkestone society.

Lady Beezeley was affable, her daughters pleasant and sociable girls. It was their first day 'at home' – they had arrived only the day before – and there was such a variety of interesting people dropping in that what should have been a formal fifteen-minute call seemed to extend itself quite naturally. Lady Beezeley was far from wanting any of her visitors to observe etiquette by leaving, and when Maud attempted to do the proper thing after half an hour, she said, 'Oh, no, don't go. Must you? It is so pleasant having friends around like this. Now, do stay, Lady Parke, and have some tea. I shall be ringing for it in just a minute. We'd so like to hear about your Red Cross work.'

So Maud stayed, talked more than she had in a week, made some delightful new acquaintances, and left at last feeling much more satisfied with Folkestone. She had met the better stratum of the population, and had laid the foundation for several invitations. If only she had rented a house, she might have issued some invitations of her own. She felt a spasm of crossness pass through her as she thought of Mrs Thompson's house, in which she could not entertain for herself, and to which she must now return, with the prospect of dining with Mrs Thompson that evening. But at least they would not be *à deux* – the vicar and his wife and a local councillor and his wife had been invited, Mrs Thompson having decided they were elevated enough to be introduced to her high-up London cousin.

Mrs Thompson opened the street door as she approached it (it was one of the constant annoyances to Maud that there was no servant to answer the door for her) and could be seen at once to be in a state of agitation.

'Oh, dear,' she said, 'we are in such a muddle! Everything is quite dreadful! There's been such a disaster, I don't know what to do!'

'Please calm yourself,' Maud said, avoiding the fluttering hands that seemed longing to fasten onto her. 'What's happened?'

'It's more what hasn't happened,' Mrs Thompson said, wringing her hands in lieu of grasping at Maud. 'The wretched fishmonger hasn't delivered! I asked Cook if we could manage without, but it's the salmon *and* the prawns to decorate it, besides a dozen eggs for the soufflé, and she says without both of those we only have half a dinner, and the Reverend Mr Conybeare coming, as well as the Laverys! We *can't* give them only three courses. What would people say?'

'Well, someone must go for the things,' Maud said logically. 'Send the girl – what's her name? Milly?'

Mrs Thompson looked wretched. 'She's not here. She went home after luncheon with a terrible toothache. She left a note with Cook to say she'd send her sister to wait at table tonight, but *she* won't be here until seven, and that will be too late to send to the shop.'

'Then send Nanny Katie,' Maud said briskly. 'She can walk well enough, I'm sure, in an emergency.'

'But she isn't here either!'

'Isn't here?' Maud was astonished. 'What can you mean?'

'She went out during the afternoon and hasn't come back. When I got home, little Richard was in the kitchen with Cook. Cook says Katie said she was just popping out to the chemist to get something for her sore heel, but she's not come back yet, and I've been watching the boy, because Cook said much as she liked him, he was under her feet and she couldn't cook a dinner *and* be a baby-minder, and she was afraid he'd trip her up and get something spilt on him. So I've had him in the dining-room playing Spillikins.'

Maud was furious. She had known from the beginning that Nanny Katie wouldn't do, but there had been no choice about taking her, given the other candidates. But this was beyond bearing. When the girl came back, she could pack her bags at once and leave, and she would get no character from Maud, either.

'Very well,' she said, in a steely voice. 'I'll go to the shop.'

'Oh, thank you, thank you!' Mrs Thompson cried, wringing her hands more than ever. 'And, oh dear, could you take Richard with you? Because with Milly not here, I have to lay the table and do the silver and so on, and though I love him excessively, he's very *high-spirited* today, what with everything being disrupted for him, poor little lad.'

So Maud found herself going out again into the lovely, luminous spring afternoon, with a shopping basket, Richard bouncing along beside her in a state of high excitement at the novelty of it all (this really *was* being the best day of his life!) and instructions on how to find Tolley's the fish-monger's – in Tontine Street, on the right and just past Gosnold's. Everyone knew Gosnold's, the drapers, the biggest and most popular one in Folkestone, and a shop where every woman found herself at least once a week for those essential feminine purchases of thread, pins, needles, elastic and so on.

Tontine Street was in what was known as the old town, a long street running down to the harbour, full of shops and public houses. The walk there along the front was agreeable enough, for it really was a lovely evening, and once Richard had stopped bouncing in favour of chattering, Maud quite enjoyed answering his questions and listening to his obser-vations about the sands and the cliffs and the harbour, the boats out on the water, the enormous seagulls circling over-head, the horse-drawn cabs going past (visitors used them to explore the area) and the little 'Scottie' dog coming

266

towards them on the end of a tartan lead held by a smart-looking lady.

'What's that noise, Mama?' he asked, when the dog was past. 'It sounds like guns.'

Maud listened, and heard, far away, a strange series of thuds. It didn't sound very much like guns to her. 'I suppose it might be,' she said doubtfully, 'but where would it be coming from?'

'Perhaps it's the guns in France,' Richard said excitedly. 'Do you think it's the guns in France? It might be Papa's regiment fighting.'

An elderly gentleman they were passing smiled as he overheard that and, lifting his hat to Maud, said, 'I doubt those are French guns, ma'am. What a bright little boy you have! Father with our gallant lads at the Front, hey? No, it will be the Royal Flying Corps gunnery school you can hear. That's in Hythe, just along the coast. We often hear them, when the wind is in the right direction.'

He lifted his hat again and passed on. Richard now talked excitedly about the RFC gunnery school, asking questions Maud had no hope of answering. There were lots of soldiers about, she noted: there were rest and transit military camps nearby, at Shorncliffe and Cheriton, so there were always soldiers in Folkestone, recuperating from wounds, on leave or on passes. They turned into Tontine Street, and Maud's mouth turned down, and she took a tighter grip on Richard's hand. The street was narrow in any case, and it was thronged with people: Friday was pay night, and this was the beginning of the Whitsun weekend, so both shops and public houses were doing brisk trade, and their clients had spilled out onto the street, the men from the pubs enjoying a pint of beer in the balmy evening sunshine, and the women and children patiently queuing outside the shops.

There were always queues of people at food shops, these days, she thought; but tonight the situation was exacerbated by late deliveries of goods at several of the shops. Horse-drawn drays were pulled up outside them, half blocking the road, while men unloaded, heaving and trundling boxes and barrels and sacks across the pavement, threading between the slowly moving crowds. Richard's eyes were wide with the wonder of it all, and Maud could hardly get him along, and several times jerked at his laggard hand in annoyance, inwardly cursing Mrs Thompson, the suffering Milly, the delinquent Nanny Katie, Mrs Thompson's guests – for accepting the invitation in the first place – and most of all Bertie, whose fault it was that she was here at all, having her toes trodden on and being jostled by hot strangers, in quest of nothing more elevated than fish and eggs.

There was Gosnold's at last. The shop opposite – Stokes's the greengrocers – was extremely popular and its queue had spread right across the road, while the fact that it was having a load of potatoes delivered added to the problems of getting past. She had cleared the immediate jam and was heading towards Tolley's when there was a sound of aircraft overhead, a low, growling, grinding noise, and several people stopped and looked up. Maud stopped perforce because the man in front of her did, and Richard tugged on her hand too, but she would have looked anyway. She was terrified of Zeppelins, and though the engine noise didn't sound like a Zepp, and there had been no daylight raids for many months, she gulped and looked up in dread, with the hair on the back of her neck rising.

It was not an airship, and she took a breath of relief. It was, in fact, a skein of aeroplanes: like huge insects, they buzzed past, faint in the sunshine against the blue sky, silver-white, flying in formation. There seemed a great many of them.

'Look, Mama, look!' Richard cried, gripping her hand so tightly in his excitement that he hurt her. *What* a day this was being! 'Aren't they grand! Where are they going, Mama? There are so many of them!' He waved his other hand vigorously to the aeroplanes, jumping up and down on the spot. 'Hi! Hi! Hurrah!'

'That's it, lad,' said the man who had stopped in front of them. 'Give 'em a cheer! We often get airyplanes buzzing about over our town,' he added proudly. 'They'll be from Detling, I don't doubt.' And he waved, too, at the beautiful, airy things, shining in the sun.

'Nice to see our boys up and doing,' said a woman beside Maud.

'Must be twenty of 'em,' said the first man. 'Wonder where they're off to?'

'They'll be going out to France,' said another man. 'St Omer – that's where they goos to, first off, 'fore they goos on for a crack at Jerry.'

Maud had lost interest in the aeroplanes. '*Excuse* me,' she said. 'May I pass, please? *Excuse* me!' She pushed between the men, who were still staring idly upwards, and hauled Richard along towards the fishmonger's. 'Please stop staring in that silly way, Richard, and look where you're stepping,' she said sharply to him, giving his hand a little shake.

There was a huge, heavy sound, from somewhere not far away – a monumental, weighty thud, as if something unimaginably massive had been dropped from the top of a building. Maud actually felt the ground under her feet lift slightly. She looked round, saw people turning and staring in all directions, heard someone say something, a high, frightened splurge of syllables in which the word 'bomb' was the only one decipherable.

She thought she heard a kind of high-pitched whistling noise. Then a vast, silent blow like a velvet-covered anvil seemed to knock all the air out of her, and the world went dark.

CHAPTER TWELVE

It was not slow, unwieldy Zeppelins that had attacked England, it was a flight of gigantic aeroplanes, twenty-two of them, forty feet long and with a wing span of seventy-seven feet, each able to carry a massive 600 pounds of bombs, and armed with three machine-guns to defend itself. They were the Gotha bombers. No aeroplane near as big had ever taken to the skies, and they had been designed solely to drop bombs on England, to kill and terrorise English civilians.

Being aeroplanes and not airships, they were fast and manoeuvrable. They had crossed from Belgium in the afternoon of the 25th of May, and been spotted at 16.45 by the North Foreland lightship, which had telephoned a warning to the Admiralty. Within ten minutes several RNAS home-defence squadrons had been scrambled. The rivalry that still existed between the two services caused a delay in passing the warning from the Admiralty to Horseguards, and it was another fifteen minutes before the RFC home-defence wing put up squadrons. Their effort was useless from the beginning, for their aircraft were obsolete, slow old two-seaters. The RNAS had modern Pups and Triplanes, but even these were helpless against the new enemy: the Gothas were so fast that by the time even the RNAS fighters had reached their ceiling, they were thirty-five miles away.

The Gothas, when first spotted, were heading for London,

to deliver their deadly load over the most densely populated city in Europe. But the weather came to London's defence with a heavy blanket of cloud between the city and the bombers, which made an attack impossible. Seeing that the weather was clear over the south coast, the Gothas peeled away to redirect their attack.

Because of the cloud bank, the attackers were lost to sight for a crucial twenty-five minutes, by which time it was too late to get a warning to any airfield within reach of their new position. So it was unchallenged that the gigantic bombers flew in formation over an unprepared south coast, innocently basking in the early-summer sunshine of the beginning of the Whit weekend. Bombs fell on villages along railway lines, and along the Royal Military Canal that linked Rye and Hythe. Ashford, with its railway works, was attacked with six bombs; twenty-two hit the RFC's aircraft park at Lympne. Hythe was 'blitzed', then Sandgate, then the army camps at Cheriton and Shorncliffe, killing seventeen Canadian soldiers and injuring ninety-three more.

This was the sound the peaceful citizens of Folkestone had heard as the deadly flight approached them. No air-raid warning had been given – the civil authorities had heard nothing from London, which had been taken completely unawares by the change of direction. And as the people in Folkestone looked up at the lovely white aeroplanes flying by, a deadly hail of fifty-one bombs hurtled down, most of them falling in an area of one square mile around the harbour. The central railway station, the Pleasure Gardens theatre, shops, houses, hotels and schools were all hit.

And bombs fell on crowded Tontine Street. One exploded among the queue of people waiting outside Stokes's, with horrifying carnage. The roof of the shop fell in, killing those inside, including the owner and his staff. The frontage of the shop opposite collapsed into the road, crushing those under it, and a shattered gas main exploded and sent a jet of flame fifty feet up into the air. Sixty or more people were killed or seriously injured in Tontine Street alone, the majority women and young children, many of whom had been queuing for the delivery of potatoes that rumour had said Stokes's were expecting.

The Gotha bombers flew on towards Dover, where the sound of the bombing of Folkestone had at last given warning to the batteries. A vigorous Archie barrage was put up, fierce enough to cause the attackers to give up the idea of bombing the docks. They veered away and passed out over the Channel, heading homewards. In the ninety minutes they had been over England, they had dropped around a hundred and seventy bombs and killed or gravely injured nearly three hundred people, far more than in the worst ever Zeppelin raid. Of those dead and wounded, a hundred and sixty-three were in Folkestone, three-quarters of them women and children.

Bertie stood, head bent, beside the open grave in the church-yard just outside Beaumont's gates. Since reading that first telegram he had gone through such a hellish kaleidoscope of emotions that his mind was now empty and numb, worn out with them. He did not know how to feel any more sorrow.

The few villagers and the Beaumont servants who had come to the funeral out of respect were clustered at a respectful distance, and some of the women were crying. Even the old gamekeeper, Tom Tabby, who last summer had shown Richard how to 'tickle' a trout, was moist-eyed, and had to blow his nose briskly on his big blue handkerchief. But Bertie felt as dry as an empty well.

Beside him, Maud stood rigid, her hands clasped before her, the veil from her hat hiding her face and the sticking-plaster on her forehead that was the only visible memento of the event. Maud had wept until she could weep no more. Now she was as silent as Bertie, as she watched the coffin of their only child being lowered into the hole in the earth, with that horrifying sense of finality the grave confers.

Bertie's experiences at the Front, these two, almost three years, had taught him the random nature of explosions, how one man could remain untouched while the man standing next to him was obliterated. His mind understood, but it did not come near to explaining to his bewildered heart how he had lost his boy. The blast from the bomb that had fallen on the queue outside Stokes's had flung Maud thirty feet down the street. She had been picked up unconscious by the rescuers who had hurried to the scene and was taken to the Royal Victoria Hospital, but she was suffering from nothing worse than a concussion, bruising to her back and ribs, and a gash on her forehead, either from shrapnel or flying glass.

Richard had been found under the rubble. The doctor at the hospital said it was the blast that had killed him, and that he would have died instantly, was dead before half a house fell on him. It was meant to comfort, and Bertie hoped at least that Richard had felt and known nothing. But it did nothing to ease the pain of losing him. Richard's hand was still clasped in Maud's when she was found. That was how they had known to look for a child. Bertie had overheard an orderly telling a nurse. He wished he had not. He would never tell Maud that.

At first he had felt a murderous rage towards the Germans for what they had done. For soldiers to kill soldiers was one thing; but to murder innocent civilians, to attack without warning and slaughter them as they went about their peaceful business, was an abomination. But he could not hold on to the rage, sustaining as it was. Almost three years of war had blunted his ability to feel anger about any part of it. It was as though the war had taken on a life of its own, independent of either the Germans or the Allies. It was a foul and futile exercise, and foulness and pointless death were all that could be expected of it. They were trapped in it, as in a nightmare from which none of them could now wake up. They had waged war once. Now it waged itself.

He came back from his black thoughts as the rector reached the final Collect. 'O merciful God, the Father of Our Lord Jesus Christ, who is the resurrection and the life, in whom whosoever believeth shall live, though he die . . .'

Maud gave a convulsive sound, like a sob, and then was quiet again. Bertie thought how wrong it seemed that it was such a beautiful day: sweet, soft sunshine, the faintest breeze stirring the trees, birds everywhere trilling and chirruping. The world should not go on so glamorously while his boy was being covered with heavy Hertfordshire clay. There ought to have been teeming rain, black skies, howling wind – cataracts and hurricanoes.

'Come, ye blessed children of my Father, receive the Kingdom prepared for you from the beginning of the world . . .'

Now Maud was crying. Bertie was glad, hoping it would ease her. His throat was tight and painful but he could not cry. Oh, my boy, my little son!

'The grace of our Lord Jesus Christ, and the love of God, and the fellowship of the Holy Ghost, be with us all ever more. Amen.'

And that was the last word. Amen. The villagers and servants murmured it. The rector closed his book. There was no Richard any more, only this wound in the earth.

When they got back to the house there were people waiting for Bertie, business that had to be attended to. He got rid of them as quickly as possible and went to find Maud. She was in the drawing-room, at the open french windows onto the terrace; standing just inside the door, as though outdoors might be dangerous. Her eyes were red from days and days of weeping, but she was not crying now. Her face was white and set, all planes and angles, as though she had been recently carved from a block of salt. He walked up to her, meaning to lay his hand on her shoulder, but at the last minute he somehow did not dare – almost as though he was afraid she might shatter if touched.

She spoke first, while he was still searching for something to say. 'I can't stand it here,' she said, in a low voice.

She had never liked Beaumont, never liked the country. 'I understand,' he said. 'I've got a few bits of estate business I must see to, but then I'll take you back to London. We can be there by this evening if—'

'No, not there,' she interrupted harshly. 'I mean, I can't stand it here *in England*. Nowhere is safe any more.' She turned her wounded eyes up at him angrily. 'First the Zeppelins, and then they said they'd got them defeated, they weren't getting through any more, and now this. Those aeroplanes just came, no-one could stop them, and they'll come and come, and nowhere will be safe from them. I can't stand it, Bertie, I tell you I can't! I've got to get away, somewhere they won't come.'

'We'll find a way to defeat them,' he said helplessly. 'We were taken by surprise this time but—'

'No!' she said angrily. 'They're always one step ahead. You couldn't stop the Zeppelins until they'd killed hundreds of people. Now this! And even if you stop *them*, they'll think of something else, and then something else, and always come flying over us and killing us while the government does nothing and the army does nothing, and we die, and our children die. I can't stand it any more, not knowing every minute what's coming. I can't live like this!'

'Then what—' he began helplessly.

'I'm going to Ireland, to stay with my father's cousins in Wicklow. The Germans won't come there. I'll be safe. The Carnews have plenty of room, and they're always asking me to visit. I can stay with them until the war's over.'

Bertie was too numb to feel anything about the proposal. He shook his mind into motion, made it take grip. He thought she would be safe enough here at Beaumont, but he also knew that he would not persuade her of that. It was too close to London; and it was part of the life that had betrayed her. Better, really, that she went to Ireland, if that was what

275

would ease her suffering. The Carnews were good people. And he thought of something else. 'Wicklow is where Manvers lives now, isn't it?'

'Yes.'

'Well, that's good. He can keep an eye on you too. He's a good friend.' She nodded, her head turned away, staring out at the garden again. 'If it's what you want, my dear, I have no objection. Stay there until the war's over. But you might not want to live with the Carnews all the time, if the war goes on beyond this year – which seems likely. If you want to set up a place of your own, I'm happy for you to rent a house.'

'Thank you,' she said rigidly.

'I'll try to come and visit you when I get leave.'

'Thank you.'

'Maud,' he said, wanting to say something *to* her, rather than *at* her, something that might break through the barriers that had always been between them, something that might touch the inner part of her that was suffering, as he was suffering. He put his hand out, again wanting to touch her; but there was something in the set of her shoulders that warned him against it. He realised that there was nothing he could say to her. They had both lost their beloved son, but their two griefs were entirely separate, and each would have to suffer alone.

Public anger over the Gotha raid filled the newspapers. How had the Germans been able to bomb England with impunity, free from defensive intervention? Where had the home-defence forces been? What was the government doing to protect the people – surely the first duty of any government? What further attacks could England expect? There were fierce demands for retaliation in kind – give the Huns a taste of their own medicine!

The first official communiqué suppressed the details of the raid, saying only that the south-east of England had been attacked and that nearly all the damage had happened in one town, where there had been 'considerable casualties'. It did not name the town, and as soon as the report was published in the evening papers, the telephone system became jammed, as anxious people everywhere tried to call their relatives in the south-east. What the government hoped to gain by censorship was unclear, but in any case it could not be maintained for long. On the Monday it was lifted, and a full report was in *The Times*, at the same time as the German news agency issued its own report, revealing that it had known perfectly well the name of the town it had devastated.

On the same day the government was able to publish a report that a retaliatory attack had been made by the RNAS at Dunkirk on the airfield from which the Gothas had come.

A deputation from Hythe and Folkestone travelled up to Horseguards to demand of Lord French, the home-defence minister, that adequate protection be afforded their towns in future. Questions were asked in the House, retired military men demanded to know why there were not constant air patrols across the south-eastern corner of the country, and a hasty conference was set up in the War Office on the last day of the month to consider the question of 'the defence of the United Kingdom against attack by aircraft'. Despite the eminence of the generals and admirals who attended it, there was not a great deal that could be done. The production of aircraft was still insufficient for the needs of the army at the Front, and the diversion of new machines for the home-defence wing could only be an aspiration. Flying constant patrols was too costly in men and aircraft, and Major General Trenchard had already ruled it out as being 'the least effective and most expensive way of protecting a place like London'.

What was left was more communication and co-operation between the RNAS and the RFC, better tracking of any incoming aircraft, and a quicker way of disseminating the air-raid warning. The Home Office issued a statement that it intended to introduce a new system by which coastal towns, and perhaps towns as far inland as London, should be notified as soon as hostile aircraft were sighted approaching. It had not been decided yet what form the warning to the populace should take, whether by lights, sounds or – a new suggestion – the mass ringing of telephones: those with telephones would then be expected to alert neighbours without. The report added, with a hint of self-justification, that before the Folkestone raid, people might have been annoyed at being alerted by an air-raid warning if there was no subsequent attack, but that they would be less likely to complain now.

Folkestone did not wait for the government to decide on what an air-raid warning should look or sound like: the town council installed a siren as a matter of urgency; and after the horrifying incident in Tontine Street, the people of Folkestone would need no urging to take cover if ever the siren should sound.

Venetia heard about the matter first from Henrietta, who wrote to her about Bertie's tragic loss. Venetia sent a letter of heartfelt sympathy to Bertie and Maud. She had always liked Bertie, and was appalled at the nature of the child's death. They had all had to come to terms with the death of menfolk engaged in the fighting, but this was something different, and insupportable. Henrietta also wrote that Helen seemed to have had a lucky escape. She had delivered an aeroplane to the RFC aircraft park at Lympne only the day before the raid; had she been a day later, she would have been there when the bombs fell. Indeed, the Gothas had fired at an unarmed aeroplane that had strayed into the area while being flown from the factory to the aircraft park in France. Suppose that had been Helen? The army pilot of the machine that was attacked had landed it without harm but, as Henrietta said, it made you think.

Helen was robust about the incident, having no time for 'what-ifs', and pointing out that although Lympne had been hit by twenty-two bombs, they had fallen in the outfield, and there had been no casualties, or even damage to property beyond some inconvenient craters. Her chief worry was that if anyone told Jack about it in 'what might have happened' terms, he would come the heavy husband and forbid her to go on with her war-work. So she deliberately did not tell anyone that in fact she had originally been intended to deliver the aeroplane on the Friday, but had asked to be allowed to fly it down the day before so that she could be back with the children for the Whit weekend, when Teddy had arranged several pieces of jollification, including a fair in the grounds on the Saturday, and a cricket match, the army versus Morland tenants, on the Sunday.

The second Gotha attack took place on Tuesday, the 5th of June, again in the afternoon, this time a flight of twenty-one, which had taken a more northerly course to avoid being spotted by the RNAS at Dunkirk, but were fortuitously discovered by a routine patrol of three Pups out of Bray Dunes, further up the coast. By the sheerest chance, Lord French had ordered a practice air-raid alert for the same afternoon, and was able to get a large number of defenders into the air and to alert various Archie batteries, which probably deterred the attackers from continuing to London. Instead they bombed the gasworks and the artillery Gun Park at Shoebury, then veered round to attack Sheerness. As in Folkestone, the seafront was crowded with holiday-makers, but when the dockyard sirens went off, it proved that the Folkestone lesson had been learnt, for everyone hurried for shelter. In consequence, though a large number of bombs was dropped, casualties were much lighter, forty-seven people being killed or injured.

Maud was already out of the country, having lost no time in taking herself to County Wicklow, leaving her maid, Anderson, to pack her trunks and bring them on after her.

Bertie had had to request that the Beaumont butler, Hobbs, go to London and see to the closing of the Pont Street house, for he had to get back to his battalion. Maud would not go near London, even to catch the train to Holyhead. She had travelled laboriously across country to catch the ferry to Queenstown, and the raid on the 5th of June was all she needed to assure her she had been right to get away when she did.

Venetia was also out of the country on the 5th of June, having gone to Paris for the 'launching' of her second X-ray ambulance, Hilda. It had not been possible to get the King or any member of the royal family in time for the Peggy, but Stamfordham had used his influence to persuade the Prince of Wales to be photographed at Hilda's inauguration, and Venetia saw no reason to tell the press, unless they actually asked, which was unlikely, that this was not the first of the fleet. First times were always more interesting and newsworthy, and she wanted as much publicity for her cause as possible.

She took Emma with her, for the company and as a treat for Emma who, like Jessie, had never been to France before. She was tremendously excited, and Venetia found her enthusiasm invigorating. She also found it a relief to be away from London for a while. It was not that she was afraid of what seemed to be the start of a new bombing campaign – she had reached a time of life when she was able to be philosophical about danger – but that everything about the war had become such a grim, weary, joyless grind. The privations, the shortages, the food queues, the industrial unrest, the endless stream of casualties, the bereavements and now the new fear of bombing made it seem as if the war had been going on, and would go on, for ever.

Paris, by contrast, seemed to behave as if the word 'war' was unknown to it. The Parisian's native devotion to making money meant that the cafés, restaurants, shops and theatres were always lively, always thronging; and if most of the men in the city streets were in uniform, and many of the songs were wry and sometimes even savage, that was no reason for the whirligig to stop. In fact, the current favourite sad song, '*Adieu la vie*', referring to the disastrous losses at Chemin-des-Dames, only seemed to make the populace drink more and enjoy themselves harder.

The launching ceremony was simple and effective, and there was a good number of pressmen there, mostly from the London and Parisian newspapers, but with a sprinkling of representatives of the American press, now taking an interest in the conflict they had officially joined at last. The American Army vanguard was not due to arrive for another week, but France, and Paris in particular, was getting itself ready to be Yankee-mad. Was it not France, said the French, that had exported the very notions of liberty and democracy to the New World? They were brothers under the skin; and the Yankees, when they came, would not only be fighting to rid France of the German invader, but would also be spending large sums of money. Every American soldier with a few days' leave would inevitably head for Paris, and Paris intended to welcome every one of them down to the last *sou*.

For now, however, the very handsome, very romantic Prince de Galles would do very well instead, and there were pressmen, photographers, civic dignitaries, a crowd, a band, flags and bunting to surround the moment when the slight, fair young man broke a bottle of champagne on the ambulance Hilda's rear bumper, and called on God to bless her endeavours. Venetia noticed with a private smile how already the prince had got used to being photographed, and turned automatically and politely this way and that so that all the cameras would have a chance to capture him. There was a moving news reel being taken as well, which she thought would play very well in the cinemas back home, and she was amused to be part of it, taken shaking the prince's hand, walking round Hilda with him while explaining her function, and presenting her future crew. She wondered, with a residue of vanity she was surprised to find in herself, what she would look like on the screen; and suddenly and sharply missed her husband, who would have laughed so much at the notion of her appearing in cinemas up and down the land.

She was glad to meet her nephew Eddie Vibart, who had accompanied the prince, and have a few words with him, saw that he was looking well, and said she was looking forward to the wedding, which would be the next time she saw him. The prince did not stay long, and Eddie, of course, left with him; but Venetia had something else up her sleeve that prevented the affair falling into anti-climax. She and Emma went back to the Hotel Meurice after the ceremony to change, then went out to look at the shops and, in Emma's case, to buy some charming things; and when they returned to the hotel again, Major Fenniman was waiting there for them.

Emma was overwhelmed with the surprise, and didn't manage to speak for quite a few minutes. Venetia explained: 'I invited all our people over here to the ceremony, in the hope that they might be able to get the time off to come.'

'And though I couldn't make it to the ceremony, I did manage to wangle the evening off,' Fenniman concluded for her, 'so here I am, ready to take you both out to dinner, and to whatever other form of jollity you desire. Fortunately, it's still possible to eat well in Paris, if you know where.'

'And you do, I suppose?' Emma said, finding her voice at last.

'But of course,' said Fenniman. 'In fact, the hotel restaurant here is pretty good, but I always think it's dull to eat in the hotel one's staying in, unless there's no choice.'

'First,' Venetia said, 'I must have a cup of tea. I don't know how it is that I can be on my feet all day in the operating theatre and never feel it, but as soon as I am faced with shop windows I develop two feet in every shoe.' The fact was, of course, that she had never developed shopping feet: when she was Emma's age, young ladies of her class did not go to shops – the shops came to them.

They went into the hotel lounge, found a quiet corner and ordered tea. Fenniman spoke first of all about Bertie.

'How is the dear fellow?' Venetia asked. 'It must have been a terrible shock to him.'

'It was,' said Fenniman. 'Of course, we've seen hundreds of deaths out here, thousands, I suppose, but that was quite different. It's really knocked him for six. He doted on the boy. And now Lady Parke's taken herself off to Ireland.'

'Yes, so I understand,' said Venetia.

'I don't think she'll come back before the war's over, when-ever that may be, and of course it's too far to go there on a short leave, so it will leave poor Parke rather at a loose end.'

'He is always welcome to come and stay with me,' Venetia said. 'I wish you would tell him that.'

'I will. Thank you,' said Fenniman.

They talked of other things until the tea was finished, and then Venetia said she must go and lie down for a rest before they dressed for dinner, and went upstairs, leaving Emma and Fenniman alone for a while.

'That was tactful of her,' he said, when Venetia had gone.

'Tactful? Oh, don't you think she really wants a rest, then?'

'The one doesn't preclude the other,' he said, with a smile, reaching for her hand under the table. Emma blushed with pleasure at his touch, and he smiled inwardly at the blush – she was so wonderfully fresh and innocent, despite all her efforts to appear sophisticated.

They chatted inconsequentially for a while, the sort of unimportant nothings that are so delightful to young people in love, swapping the minutiae of their separate lives. But his father's letter was always at the back of Fenniman's mind, and eventually he said, 'I'd like to talk to you seriously for a moment.'

Her eyes became round. 'Seriously? But you're never serious. Is something wrong?'

'Far from it,' he said. 'I just want to talk about the wedding.'

'Oh,' she said in relief. 'Well, I've been thinking about it, of course. I thought St Margaret's would be best, because I know Violet thinks St George's frightfully middle class. Of course, she was married at the Abbey, but that won't do for us.'

'I should think not,' Fenniman said, with a laugh. 'But that's not—'

'And afterwards there are lots of places we might have the wedding breakfast. The Ritz is safe and the Savoy is dashing – Violet had hers at the Savoy – or we might have it at St James's Square, because I rather think Violet is hoping for that – although I don't know how you feel about it, not being acquainted with Lord Holkam – or at Manchester Square. It depends a little on how many guests we invite, because there isn't much room at Manchester Square – although small, intimate weddings are the best, sometimes, as long as they're done with style. Or—'

'Emma, my dear,' Fenniman interrupted her firmly at the third attempt. 'It's not the where I want to talk to you about but the when.'

'Oh. Well, I know we haven't completely fixed a date, but there's plenty of time, isn't there? Didn't we say next spring?'

'Yes, dearest, but I've been wondering whether you wouldn't consider bringing the date forward.'

'Forward to when?' Emma asked, puzzled. Though nothing had been said, of course, and one wasn't allowed to ask, Cousin Venetia had hinted that she knew through her eminent friends that a new offensive was likely to begin some time next month. 'We don't know when you're going to get leave.'

'I'm pretty sure I can get some leave towards the end of this month,' he said. 'I was wondering if you'd consider giving up the grand wedding and having something rather more modest and wartime-ish, and a great deal more immediate?' He was watching her face carefully as he said it, and saw the flicker of consternation cross it at the suggestion. 'No, of course not,' he said quickly. 'Every girl dreams of her wedding, doesn't she? It must be all as you want it. I can't ask you to give up your dream.'

'Oh, it isn't that,' Emma said. 'Of course I'd love to have my grand wedding, and it's true, I *have* thought about it and planned it, but I'd give it up in a moment if that's what you really wanted, or if there wasn't any choice about it.'

'But? I sense a "but" in the offing.'

'It isn't the wedding,' she said, biting her lip. 'It's Uncle Bruce and Aunt Betty. I feel so guilty about running away from them – I know I didn't really, but that's how it feels – and I really, *really* don't feel comfortable about marrying someone they've never met.'

'Ah!' he said.

'I was going to ask you,' she went on, 'whether you would be so *very* good as to make time to go up and see them with me when you're next home, so that I can introduce you to them and they can see that you're not the wrong sort of person, that you're very much the *right* sort of person. And I'd like to invite them to the wedding, whenever it is. In fact, it was in my mind perhaps to ask Uncle Bruce to give me away, because it's his right, really – he has been my guardian all these years. He and Aunt Betty might even want to rent a London house for it, and have the wedding breakfast there. So you see . . . ?'

Yes, he saw. A visit to the Abradales in Scotland would take up so much time that there would not be time to get married as well in the same leave. And if Abradale did want to give Emma away, there could be no question of a quick wartime wedding – it would have to be planned and executed in the leisurely way his generation expected, which meant it could not happen until there was a lull in the war – which meant early next year – or until it was over entirely – and God knew when that would be.

Now she was examining his expression. 'You're angry,' she said anxiously. 'I've upset you.'

'No, of course not,' he said hastily. 'I just didn't want to wait too long, that's all.'

'I know, and I don't either,' Emma said, 'but we'll have all our lives together, and I don't want to start off our marriage by doing the wrong thing towards Aunt and Uncle. It isn't the wedding itself, you understand, but what it means to other people.'

He lifted her hand to his lips. 'Of course I understand, and it shall be just as you wish. As soon as I get leave, we'll go up to Scotland together and beard the lion in his den, and if I can't charm Uncle Abradale into thinking me an acceptable fellow, you have my permission to call me a turnip and feed me to a Highland cow.'

Her smile of relief was his reward. 'You are *so* good to me, John.'

It touched him ridiculously to hear her use his name. 'Who has the better right to be?' he said lightly. 'Now, let's forget the subject and concentrate on having a wonderful evening. How long do you suppose it will take you to get changed? I find myself unaccountably starving, and I know a place where they have the most heavenly *moules*. You do like them cooked in cream and garlic, don't you? Because otherwise I'm afraid I may have to call the engagement off.'

'I don't even know what *moules* are,' Emma admitted cheerfully, 'but I'm certain I adore them.'

The next morning there was another treat for Emma, and for Venetia, as Oliver arrived in the late morning to take them out to luncheon.

'Please don't thank me,' he said, by way of greeting as he kissed his mother. 'I'm looking forward to a proper meal more than I can possibly tell you. It's strange how in a war one starts off with elevated philosophical preoccupations, but after a remarkably short time it all comes down to food and dry socks.'

'Foolish boy,' Venetia said. 'I wasn't going to thank you. If you can't dance attendance on your mother once in a while, what is the world coming to?'

'You of all people don't need to ask me that. My dear Emma, you are looking positively delicious. What a charming hat! I'd know you for an English girl in any crowd.'

'I'm not sure if that's a compliment,' Emma said, receiving a brotherly kiss.

'We saw Eddie yesterday,' Venetia said.

'Oh, did you? He's sent me an invitation for his wedding. I'm pretty sure I shall be able to come. They're trying to give everyone a spot of leave before the next show, so it's only a matter of putting in for the right week.'

'It promises to be one of the main social events of the year,' Venetia said. 'With the Prince of Wales as groomsman, and the King and Queen attending, everyone will want to be there.'

'Hundreds of photographs in *Strand* magazine and the *London Illustrated*? My dear Mama, I hope you will have a new outfit for it?'

'Impudent boy! Do you think I don't know how to dress for an occasion?'

'Oh, I know you *know* how – it's getting you to care that's the trick! Dare we hope that Thomas will come?'

'I haven't heard from him yet – I know Eddie invited him and, God knows, he is due for leave. It would be a good excuse to get him home, and there's no danger to him in travelling, as things stand. But, of course, everything's so volatile out there that he may be afraid to leave the family.'

Oliver shook his head. 'I wish my good brother could get it into his head that he's not responsible for the Romanovs. I shall write to him and insist he comes to the wedding – tell him it will look like a snub to Eddie *and* the King if he doesn't – and then when we've got him home we can kidnap him and tie him up in the cellar until he comes to his senses. Now, what about luncheon? In honour of Emma's hat, I think we should go to La Tour d'Argent. Kit says it's the best restaurant in Paris since the Café Anglais closed down. It's on the Quai de Tournelle, with a wonderful view across the Seine of Notre Dame – Emma ought to see that at least once in her life. And their *canard au sang* is magnificent.'

'What's Notre Dame?' Emma asked.

'Oh, can such ignorance exist? It's a cathedral, a most famous cathedral! Personally, I think the English cathedrals much more beautiful than anything in France, but one has to know about it, though the Sainte Chapelle is prettier. And the Sacré Coeur is more interesting, with a view over the city that's quite unmatched. After luncheon, I will happily take you to all three, if we can find a taxi willing to wait for us.'

'When do you have to go back?'

'Tonight, but I don't have to be there until twenty-three fifty-nine, as the army says in its barbaric way, and there's a late train from the Gare du Nord, so you shall have me until early evening, *si l'on veut.*'

If anyone had wondered whether the two Gotha attacks were isolated incidents or the beginning of a new campaign, they had not long to wait. On Wednesday, the 13th of June – the same day on which the American General John J. Pershing landed at Boulogne with his forward party of a hundred and seventy, greeted by a civic reception, a guard of honour, a band playing 'The Star Spangled Banner', and adoring cries of '*Vive l'Amèrique!*' – a flight of twenty-two Gothas attacked again, this time in the morning. They came in over the river Crouch at around eleven o'clock and headed towards London, approaching over Romford, Rainham and Upminster. The Archie units had been alerted, but patchy cloud and the hazy conditions made sighting difficult from the ground, and the aeroplanes were at such a height that hitting them would have been almost impossible anyway.

Bombs were dropped on Barking and East Ham, and on the Royal Albert Docks at Silvertown, then the attackers wheeled over an area of the City centred on Liverpool Street station, bombing mainly residential areas like Clerkenwell, Shoreditch, Hoxton and Whitechapel. The business areas of Fenchurch Street and Aldgate were hit, then the Gothas divided into two flights. One turned north-east, bombed Dalston, then turned south-east and hit Stepney, Limehouse and Poplar. The other crossed the Thames and hit Southwark and Bermondsey.

Every strike was attended with loss of life and hideous injuries, as well as heavy damage to property, but probably the incident that caused the most outrage was the bomb that fell on Upper North Street School in Poplar, hitting the roof and passing through three floors before exploding in a classroom on the ground floor where sixty-four children were doing their lessons. Eighteen were killed outright and thirty others received appalling injuries.

In all, 162 people were killed and 432 were injured in the raid. It was not until they were approaching the Southend area that any home-defence aeroplanes were able to catch up with them. The defenders attacked bravely and several reported hits, but none of the Gothas was brought down, and now that they were lightened of their load of bombs, they were easily able to outrun the British machines and lose them in the cloud cover.

Again, the Gothas had been over England for ninety minutes and had dropped four tons of bombs, but though twenty gun stations had been in action against them, not one had managed a hit. The height of the attackers and the hazy conditions had added to the difficulty Archie had, anyway, in finding the correct range of a moving aeroplane. The failure to defend was even more frustrating for the home-defence pilots, for they were largely and publicly blamed, but in fact there was little they could do. Ninety-four aeroplanes did go up, but three-quarters of them were the old, slow, virtually useless machines belonging to the RFC; and even the more modern aeroplanes of the RNAS took so long to reach the attackers' height, they could only hope to intercept them on the homeward journey when, perversely, they were lightened of their loads and could climb higher and fly faster than ever.

The fury in the newspapers and in Parliament the next day was divided almost equally between the vile Hun, who attacked defenceless women and children, and Lord French, the home-defence minister, for not stopping them. The war cabinet met again, where it was glumly pointed out by General Robinson that the time it took the enemy to fly from the coast to London was less than the time it took for British aeroplanes to climb to the height needed to engage them. The tracking system set up for the Zeppelins could not cope with the faster-moving Gothas; and there were simply not enough aeroplanes in existence to mount any kind of effective patrols over the most likely flight-paths.

Robinson went on to propose a massive increase in the production of aircraft, even at the expense of other war machinery. The representatives of the army were in favour, though the representatives of the navy received the idea coolly. The Admiralty had always been of the opinion, since the time of the east-coast shellings, that a few civilians were neither here nor there, that all must take their chances in time of war, and that winning the war could not take second place to protecting the public. However, the cabinet agreed with the proposal, at least in principle, and ordered an inter-departmental consultation into the practicalities. They suggested also that the home secretary should set up a confer-ence for later in the month with the mayors of the London boroughs to discuss the provision of air-raid warnings.

Given the length of time these consultations would be certain to take, and the delay thereafter in implementing any decisions that might be reached, it was tempting to think that on the whole the war cabinet agreed with the Admiralty.

It was a relief of a kind for Venetia to turn for a while from the business of the war in all its detail to the question of the women's franchise. The initial stages of the Representation of the People Bill had gone through Parliament in May, and the crucial debate on the women's clause came up on the 19th of June. Venetia had been doing what she could in the past few months to speak to her friends and acquaintances in both Houses to raise support for the clause. The Prime Minister was confident, and though Venetia still found it hard to trust Lloyd George, Addison, who was very close to him, assured her that 'This time it will go through.'

For all the hours Venetia had scraped from her busy life to help the measure, it paled into insignificance compared with the work Milly Fawcett had put in. She had contrived to visit every member of the government individually and privately, as well as a large number of other MPs, besides heading deputations to constituencies of critical Members, and holding meetings and rallies, involving a great deal of travel about the country, initially in the bitterest of weather. Lord Northcliffe had used his newspapers to suggest that there was now no public interest in, or agitation for, the vote for women, which infuriated the long-standing suffragists like Venetia, because the suffrage societies had voluntarily put aside agitation in order to concentrate on war-work. It was necessary, therefore, to show Lord Northcliffe that there was quite definitely an undiminished appetite for the cause, and Mrs Fawcett criss-crossed the country, despite her age, and seemed to develop the ability to be everywhere at once.

On the 19th of June Venetia sat in the Speaker's Gallery with Mrs Fawcett and listened to the whole debate. It was stiflingly hot up there, without the slightest movement of air, but the two old friends had grown up in a tough school, and listened with undiminished concentration to every speech. Milly said very little: Venetia guessed she was more tired than she would admit after the strenuous efforts of the last few months. And there was a poignancy, even a touch of unreality, about the situation: to be sitting here within sight of victory, with the ghosts of former champions, friends and martyrs seeming close at hand, watching over their shoulders. It had been going on for so very long that the beginning, and the world as it had then been, seemed like a figment of the imagination. And if the beginning was a fiction, could the ending be any more real?

All the old arguments were rehearsed down below in the chamber, the old calumnies, the same pleas and the same fears that they had heard hundreds of times before. Yet it was somehow different this time.

'They are taking it seriously at last,' Milly said quietly.

That was it, Venetia realised. Previous debates had been conducted in an atmosphere of mockery, hilarity, even ribaldry, with the speeches of the 'pros' treated with contempt and scorn, while the arguments of the 'antis', however ludicrous, were cheered to the rafters. But today there was only serious debate, approval from most, and thoughtful opposition from a few.

'It will certainly pass,' Milly said, when the House rose to divide at last, 'but the question is, by how many?'

'We need a large majority,' Venetia said. 'That's the only thing that will sway the Lords. All our most committed opponents are in the Upper House, but they won't want to go against the will of the Commons if it's expressed strongly enough.'

They waited on, far beyond tiredness now, for the telling. Friends popped in from the Ladies' Gallery, from the floor of the House, from the world outside, to express their good will and their hopes. There was tension and a low-key excitement. It *would* pass; but by how much?

The result, when it came, was far beyond expectation.

The Commons had voted by a majority of 387 to 57 – a ratio of seven to one – in favour of the measure.

The two friends stepped out into the hot June evening to a chorus of delight, congratulations, kisses. In this very square, suffragettes had been beaten and manhandled by policemen just for being there. Now even Members of Parliament stopped smilingly on their way past to shake hands.

'The fight is not over yet,' Mrs Fawcett said, urging caution. 'We must not appear too triumphant, until the Bill is law. It would not do to provoke those who could still do us harm.'

The Bill would not come before the Lords until December.

'There are plenty of peers who will still oppose us,' Venetia said as they walked away.

'Yes, and I have no way to approach them in person,' said Milly. 'I shall do what I can, by letter and through the newspapers, but you can talk to them, Venetia dear.'

Venetia smiled. 'My nephew's wedding will be a good place to start. And you, my dear Milly, ought to have a holiday. You're looking tired.'

'I think I will,' she said. 'I shall need my strength for the next part of the campaign. I really feel we shall prevail this time – but even if we do, it's only the first step. We must fight on until women have the vote on equal terms.'

'Once they've admitted the principle, the rest ought to be inevitable,' said Venetia.

'Yes, but look how long men had to wait for the universal franchise,' said Mrs Fawcett. 'I should like to see women have it before I die.'

'Then you certainly *had* better have that holiday.'

CHAPTER THIRTEEN

The whole nation was weary, which was perhaps why there was so much attention paid to the wedding of Lord Vibart and Lady Sarah Montacute. She was very young and very pretty, he was genial and bore a striking resemblance to the loved late King Edward VII, and everyone who was anyone would be there. It touched a chord with the population. It was discussed in every pub, café and workplace in London, and the popular newspapers were full of photographs and every detail they could scrape together about the two protagonists, their families and, indeed, anyone even lightly associated with the event.

Venetia found herself prominent again, as the aunt who had brought up the orphaned Eddie, and her own past moments of celebrity, as one of the first lady doctors and a well-known campaigner for women's rights, were rehashed in the *Daily Mail* and the illustrated papers. She was somewhat annoyed by reporters as she went about her business, and missed her butler, Burton, who had had a freezing way with anyone impertinent enough to call at the house without an appointment. A housemaid, or even poor old Ash, had not the terrifying stature that withered pretension on the vine.

Violet was delighted that Freddie Copthall was able to be there, having been granted leave from his training camp by a sympathetic commanding officer. He was a Freddie subtly changed by his experience, his elegant lounge become a firmer and more upright gait, some of the genial vagueness gone from his face. He was a leaner Freddie, startlingly handsome in his uniform to Violet's eyes, which had got so used to him over the years they had hardly seen him any more; proud of his lieutenant's pips and sporting a neat but extremely virile moustache, which he had grown while he had been away, a glossy little chestnut beauty of a 'tache.

'Thought it made me look more military,' he explained to Violet at their first meeting. 'Everyone's always said I looked a bit of a fool – thought a spot of fungus would break up the vast empty spaces, what?' And he waved a deprecating hand around, to indicate the wide blankness of his face. 'Icily regular, splendidly null, and so on.'

'I never thought you either icy or null,' Violet protested. 'I think it suits you awfully well, though, Freddie. How are you liking the army?'

'Not as bad as I expected it to be,' he confessed. 'Rather a lot of gettin' up early and marchin' about, and a frightful lot of shoutin', but the others are a splendid bunch of chaps, and the men are first rate. Odd thing is,' he added, with a modest look, 'seem to be makin' a bit of a success of it. Can't think how – always been a complete idiot. My gov'nor always said the only future for me was as a doorstop. But the CO says I'm doin' all right, and the men seem to like me.'

'I'm not the least bit surprised,' Violet said loyally. 'I always thought you'd make a fine officer.'

'Did you?' he said humbly. 'Thanks awfully. I say, Violet, I've even learnt how to shoot straight. At rifle practice last week I got nine bulls out of ten shots. Of course,' he added, on a practical note, 'the bull don't move about much, not like a pheasant. Or a German,' he added thoughtfully. 'Not sure how I'd feel about shootin' a human being.'

'If he was about to shoot you, I think you'd find you could,' Violet said sensibly. 'Oh, Freddie, it's so *very* nice to have you back. I didn't realise how much I'd miss you.'

He looked confused and pleased. 'Missed you, too. Odd thing, bein' surrounded by men all the time, not a woman within miles. Changes the way you think about things.' He hesitated a moment, and then said, 'I'll be going out to France next month.'

Violet was shocked. 'So soon?'

'Shortage of officers,' he said apologetically. 'We'll all be sent out to other units already over there – seeded, I think they call it. Shame, really – got used to the chaps, awfully fond of the men. But needs must. Winning the war – that's the main thing.'

'Oh, Freddie,' was all Violet said, but there was a great deal in her eyes. Thus Laidislaw had gone, never to come back. And her mother had said that a new push was coming, probably next month – a new and determined offensive. Freddie was looking at her anxiously, probably very well aware of her thoughts. Who knew her better, after all? She tried to smile, aware that it was rather lopsided. 'You will be careful, won't you?'

'Not the stuff heroes are made of,' he assured her; and then, quietly, 'Rather wish I was. I'd like to have you think well of me.'

Violet laid her hand on his. 'I do think well of you, Freddie. And I know you'll do your duty and I'll be proud of you. I'd just rather – rather tell you that face to face, when the war's over.'

He smiled, and he looked so handsome just then it made her stomach feel hollow. 'Bargain,' he said.

As well as being grateful that Freddie had come back for the wedding, Violet was equally, though guiltily, grateful that Holkam would not be there. He had written to say he could not get leave until the next month. Violet had the secret thought that, as Holkam was a staff officer and practically in Haig's pocket, he could surely have got home for the wedding if he had wanted to, so probably he hadn't wanted to. On the one hand, the King and Queen would be there and it was the wedding of the year, at which an ambitious man ought to be glad to be seen; on the other hand, Eddie was her cousin and they had grown up together, and Holkam disliked everything about her family and was always glad to dissociate himself from it.

Whatever the reason, it added the perfect finishing touch to the occasion for Violet, that she should be able to attend it on Freddie's arm rather than Holkam's. The wedding was to be at the Abbey, and she was afraid it would bring back too many memories of her own wedding there, if she were with her husband. The wedding breakfast was to be at the Savoy, too, where her own had taken place. Altogether too many memories.

For Venetia, the greatest pleasure came from welcoming her sister Olivia and her husband to her house, to stay for a few days around the occasion. Despite being a year younger than her, Olivia had become very frail, and rarely left her home. Her husband, Charles Du Cane, had grown stout and grey, though in Venetia's mind he remained always the lean and handsome equerry her beautiful sister had fallen in love with when they were both at Court. The Du Canes had never had any children, which had been a sorrow to them, but otherwise theirs had been a blissfully happy marriage.

They arrived from Ravendene by motor-car, having driven slowly and carefully, with frequent stops, and Olivia had coped with the journey very well. She and Charlie lived in a small house on the edge of the Ravendene estate, where she and Venetia had grown up. It was the seat of the dukes of Southport, their father's title; but when both their brothers had died without issue, the title and estate had gone to a distant cousin, an extremely surprised, hard-working civil servant from Sydenham. Cousin Frederick had been a good guardian of the estate, a good landlord and much liked by the tenants, though the county had never really taken him to their hearts, much preferring his eldest son Freddie, who had celebrated his elevation by becoming wild and expensive and almost getting sacked from Eton – traits the county could understand and admire. Cousin Frederick had died in 1915; young Freddie had enjoyed the title only a few months before being killed at Beaumont Hamel; and the second son, Harry, was now duke, and serving with his regiment in France. It was a melancholy thought that if anything happened to Harry, who was still unmarried, the title would become extinct. When Venetia remembered how grand her father had been, what a seemingly immutable part of the English order, it was astonishing to think how quickly everything he had stood for might be obliterated.

But there was no room for thoughts like that in this happy reunion. Olivia and Venetia had lots to talk about and, given the family occasion, it was not surprising that they reminisced a great deal about their childhood, about their brothers, and particularly about Eddie's wicked mother, their sister Augusta. 'Gussie would have been so happy about this wedding,' Olivia said, with a sentimental sigh. 'The Abbey, and the King and Queen being there. How she'd have enjoyed it! Poor Gussie. Things never turn out the way we expect, do they?'

'I think you and I have done pretty well out of our dreams,' Venetia said.

'Oh, yes. I couldn't be happier.'

She went away to rest on her bed for the afternoon, so as to be fresh for dinner, and when she came downstairs, Oliver, her favourite nephew, was there. He had come over with Kit Westhoven to stay for the wedding. 'So we shall have a pleasant houseful,' Venetia said.

'If only Thomas had come,' Olivia said.

It was the shadow on the occasion for Venetia. The last she had heard from him, a week ago, he had still been undecided as to whether he would come or not, but there had been no further letter since then. Things were so volatile in Russia that the silence could mean anything or nothing, which only made it harder to bear.

They had a delightful and lively family dinner: Venetia, Olivia, Charlie, Oliver, Kit, Violet, Freddie and Emma. Oliver was in his best clowning mood, and made his aunt laugh so much that she got a stitch and quite worried poor Charlie, who was not accustomed to see her in such hilarious mood, and was afraid it was something worse.

'Don't worry, Uncle Charlie,' Oliver said, when Olivia was weakly recovering, wiping tears from her eyes. 'Aunt couldn't be in a safer place – there are three doctors around this table.'

When they removed to the drawing-room, Olivia was enjoying herself so much that she did not immediately go to bed, as was her usual custom after dinner, but sat talking quietly to Kit Westhoven, to whom she had taken quite a liking. He was just the sort of young man she would have wanted if she had had a son – and with his fair handsomeness and blue eyes, he even looked rather as she had always imagined her child would. Charlie watched her, glad she was happy; but always anxious for her health, he eventually went across to her quietly to say that perhaps she should turn in, after her long and tiring day. Olivia agreed it was late enough for her. Kit and Charlie helped her to her feet. Venetia had risen too, to kiss her goodnight, when the door opened, and Ash was there, looking agitated, almost shocked.

Venetia's heart jumped painfully, as it always did these days at the thought of bad news; but she turned to him with outward calm. 'Yes, Ash, what is it?'

The old man met her eyes, but for once was completely at a loss for words. They were not needed, however, for behind him a tall figure appeared, a man obviously much the worse for having travelled long and hard. For a moment Venetia didn't recognise him, standing in the half-darkness of the passage; and then, with an inarticulate sound, she was past Ash and had her son in her arms.

'Oh, Thomas!'

★   ★   ★

The weather was fair for the wedding, and it all went off without a hitch. Eddie and the prince were both in dress uniform and looked handsome and dashing. The bride wore a gown of simplicity suitable to wartime – which, however, served to emphasise her radiant young beauty. It was of ivory silk, with a V-neck, and long, plain sleeves, decorated only with pearl buttons at the wrist. It was narrow-fitting, swathed at the hips, and ended daringly two inches above the ankle, revealing plain white stockings and white silk shoes. The only hint of sumptuousness was her eight-foot veil of lace, which did not cover her face but was fitted closely to her head and fell behind, to be carried by her two bridesmaids. All the newspapers approved of the modesty of the outfit, and were eager to remark that the lace was not bought new for the occasion but had been worn by Lady Sarah's grandmother and mother before her.

Horses were in such short supply, because of the war, that there were no carriages in the procession, only motor-cars, but the happy couple drove from the Abbey after the ceremony in an open Rolls-Royce so that the crowds gathered along the pavements could get a good view. They cheered with an enthusiasm that had much to do with everyone's gladness to be forgetting the war for a little while. The rumour that Lord Vibart was an illegitimate son of dear old King Teddy was widely known and did him no harm at all, and many in the crowd waved Union flags as though this really were a royal wedding.

The Marquess and Marchioness of Talybont had chosen the Savoy for the wedding breakfast because their own Town house did not have a large enough dining-room. Privately, they would have preferred their daughter to marry from her home down in the country – they regarded London weddings as vulgar – but the royal connection made it impossible. However, everyone said the Savoy did the breakfast beautifully. It was elegantly served and ample, but again in accordance with wartime simplicity, there were no outrageous or extravagant

300

delicacies, just good, plain English food: clear soup, salmon and trout, roast lamb and roast ducks, peas and asparagus and new potatoes, raspberries and strawberries, meringues and thick cream, and fine English cheeses to finish. The menu was printed in all the papers afterwards, and everyone praised the Talybonts' good taste.

The King and Queen left after the meal, and the company retired to an ante-room where there was time to mingle and talk before the bride and groom went up to change. They came down again in travelling costume, and Eddie took a fond leave of Venetia, who was the nearest thing he had had to a mother, and of Thomas, Oliver and Violet – 'My family,' he said. 'All the family I have. I'm glad you were all able to be here.'

'Be happy,' Violet said, as she kissed him.

'Oh, I shall be,' he said. 'I love her very much.'

The couple were seen off in the motor-car that was taking them to Sandringham, where the King had lent a small cottage for their honeymoon; after which Eddie would settle his bride in their new house in Piccadilly on his way back to the Front.

When the couple had gone, the rest of the guests drifted away; Venetia only too glad to be going home so that she could have Thomas to herself for a precious few hours. On the following day, he had told her, he would have meetings with the King, the Prime Minister and foreign secretary, the Russian ambassador and other important people; and the day after that he would have to go back. Venetia wanted to protest, but there was nothing in his grim face, lined now beyond his years with worry, that she could appeal to. He *would* go back; and it would be a waste of the little time they had together to argue with him about that.

Messines Ridge was a piece of high ground to the south-east of Ypres, a natural stronghold that had been in German hands since the end of 1914, and which created a small salient that had to be reduced before the major attack at Ypres could begin. General Haig had left it to General Plumer, who had prepared for the attack meticulously by digging miles of tunnels under the German position and laying dozens of mines. On the morning of the 7th of June the mines were detonated, blowing the entire crest off the ridge. General Plumer had said to his staff at dinner the night before that they might not make history the next day but they would certainly change geography.

The explosion was so huge it was said Lloyd George felt it in his office in Downing Street; they certainly felt and heard it in Étaples. It took the Germans by surprise, killing ten thousand of them. The Second Army then advanced under the protection of a creeping barrage, and all the objectives were taken within three hours. Plumer believed in small gains and thorough consolidation – a process he called 'bite and hold' – rather than grand gestures and wild charges. He kept a steady hand, beating off German counter-attacks and creeping forward, and by the 14th of June the entire Messines Ridge was in British hands. It was a resounding success – the newspapers called it the most perfectly executed action of the war – and the cost in casualties, seventeen thousand, was modest by the standards of other battles, and in any case less than the estimated German cost of twenty-five thousand.

But it was still seventeen thousand men, and a large part of the wounded complement passed through the hospitals at Étaples, keeping Jessie and Beta as busy as they had been in the first days, with the constant arrival of convoys, the long, arduous days, the constant smell of blood, the pain and the death.

But when the rush of casualties died down, a quieter period ensued; the normal three hours off daily, and the weekly day off, were reinstated for the nurses on surgical wards, and Jessie and Beta were able to relax, rest, catch up with correspondence and explore the area. Étaples had little to offer, but there were Paris-Plage and Le Touquet, which had been popular French holiday places before the war, within walking distance, and all the wide spaces of the marshes and the beaches to amble along, with fine summer weather to make the outings pleasant. Jessie discovered, to her pleasure, that Beta liked to walk as much as she did herself, and they never ran out of things to talk about.

They felt far freer here than ever they had at Camberwell. There was no hostel, no locked door or curfew hour, no checking to see they were in bed, no inspections of their quarters: here they had privacy, and were trusted to behave themselves as adults, in a way that was new and refreshing to them. And on the wards they were treated as responsible nurses, sharing the work without differentiation, which made them feel like part of a professional team, all working together for the same end. Jessie felt properly used for the first time since the war had begun. She had work that fulfilled her, and a companion, in Beta, of whose company she never tired. She was very glad they had come to France.

Bertie had written to her about the events in Folkestone. His letter was redolent of the shock and grief he felt at the loss of Richard, and Jessie grieved for him, and wished there were anything she could do to comfort him. She had suffered bitter jealousy in the past, that Maud had a child and she did not – that Maud had *Bertie*'s child. Now she wished she could go back and wipe out those feelings. She was ashamed of them, and her only comfort was that she had never expressed them to anyone. She wrote a letter of condolence to Maud, but received no reply. Her sadness for Maud was sincere, and she expunged some of her guilt by knowing that she would have given Richard back to Maud if it were in her power to do so, whatever the cost.

Bertie told her that Maud had gone to stay with her cousins in Ireland, and Jessie could not blame her, though in any other circumstance she would have regarded as poor-spirited anyone who would abandon the dear old country at a time of need. Bertie wrote that he felt better about Maud going to Ireland, knowing that Lord Manvers would be there to keep an eye on her. 'He is a good friend and will watch over her. I'm glad she will have the comfort of his presence nearby, as well as that of her cousins.'

He didn't say much of his own feelings about Richard's death, just, 'I don't need to tell you what it means to me.' And he didn't: she knew. 'I'm only grateful he wouldn't have known anything about it. Mrs Thompson says he was excited and pleased to be going out with his mother. I like to think of him skipping along beside her, full of happiness right to the point of oblivion. He loved the seaside. I am glad he had that before he died. He had so little of life.'

In a later letter he wrote about the war:

Well, Messines Ridge is taken, and I suppose the Germans can have little doubt what our next objective will be. If we can secure the Belgian coast it will have the secondary benefit of making it harder for them to bomb London, and perhaps even cut off their submarine bases. One cannot fault the Old Man's choice of theatre. But having fought there twice already, I do not relish a third bite at it. The very name has a doomed sound to me. I hear unofficially that we move very soon. I wish I might stay here at Plug Street, sit out the war and let someone else do it. I shouldn't admit that to you, but I promised always to tell you the truth, and the truth is I am tired of it all. It seems to me that a very heavy burden rests on us now. Sometimes I feel like Sisyphus. I can hardly contemplate the boulder that we poor frail men have to push up that same hill all over again – perhaps for ever. Oh, Jessie, I am *so* tired of it.

Jessie knew what he meant. The name of doom was Ypres, of course – that tortured city at the northern end of the line that kept the Germans from the Channel ports. Bertie had fought in the first and second battles of Ypres, and now it seemed he would be fighting in the third.

And the Sisyphean task? Despite the excitement about the entry of the Americans into the war, they would be of little practical help for a long time. America's standing army was tiny – seventy thousand volunteers, none with any combat experience, burdened with obsolete equipment and hampered by the lack of experienced officers. Following the Selective Service Act, millions of American men were registering for the draft, to be chosen for service by lottery, but they all had to be mobilised, equipped, trained, transported to France and then drilled to battle readiness – a massive task.

The first division of the American Expeditionary Force had landed – rather seasick and deeply relieved not to have been torpedoed on the long Atlantic crossing – in late June: fourteen and a half thousand men, mostly raw recruits. They needed a great deal of drilling and training, and their officers were just as much in need of training themselves. Even so, the French and the British divisions would have been glad to get their hands on them. But General Pershing had decreed – and President Wilson had agreed with him – that American soldiers must be commanded by American officers only. Demands that they be used like reinforcements were roundly rejected. America had not come to France to 'help out', but to pursue an objective of its own as an independent nation. For the pride and dignity of the American People, the AEF must be a totally separate army, with its own section of the line to hold, and complete freedom of action. To this end, General Pershing told Washington, anything less than a million men was not an army. There was no difficulty in finding a million draftees, but to bring an army of that size to France and train it and its officers to combat-readiness would take the best part of a year.

So there would be no help from the Americans for a long

time yet – though the knowledge that they were coming, with all their vast resources, had done something for Allied morale. (The Germans, intelligence said, did not believe the Americans could ever be transported to Europe in sufficient numbers to make a difference.) So, with the French moping in their trenches, refusing to do more than defend the status quo, and the Russians barely holding the line on the Eastern Front, it was left to the British, with their loyal colonial friends, to wage the war alone.

Jessie had a vivid idea of what Bertie must be feeling. He had been there from the beginning, from the days in August 1914 when young men were saying gleefully that it would be over by Christmas. Bertie, as an experienced soldier, had not believed that, of course; but he must feel now, sometimes, that it would never be over.

The train from Edinburgh was rattling its weary way southwards through the long dusk of a late June evening. The yellow gaslight in the carriage made the twilight outside seem bluer than ever, and the small open section at the top of the window let in, now and then, a blue-smelling, dew-damp summer air. Fenniman was sitting very still, because Emma had fallen asleep, and her head had slipped down onto his shoulder. He rather liked it, and didn't want to wake her. He stared out of the dusty window, streaked clean by a short-lived shower earlier that day, and thought wryly about the situation. It was ironic that just as his father felt Emma was not good enough for him, Emma's guardians felt he was not good enough for her. What a farce! With the world tearing itself to pieces all around them, two sets of old people could not see further than the ends of their own noses; were obsessed with notions of blood, when oceans of blood were being poured out in France to keep them safe and free to indulge such nonsensical ideas.

He did not think he had moved, but perhaps his restless thoughts had communicated themselves, for Emma jerked suddenly awake, blinked for a moment in bewilderment, then hastily sat up, straightening her skirt and touching her hair with a blush of confusion and an embarrassed glance round the compartment. But the three other passengers were not looking. The old man at the far end was occupied with his newspaper, and the two middle-aged women – in the sort of hats that could only have originated in a respectable Edinburgh suburb – were dozing too.

Emma looked shyly at Fenniman, then down at her hands. 'I'm sorry,' she said quietly.

'Don't be,' he said. 'I liked it. You can sleep on my shoulder any time you want.'

'No, I didn't mean that. I meant I'm sorry I made you come to Edinburgh with me. I should have known it was no use.'

'It's all right,' he began.

'No, it isn't,' she said angrily. 'I wanted them to like you, and I convinced myself that they *would* if only they met you. But I should have known that they would never like anyone they hadn't chosen themselves. That's all they want – to keep control of me, to make me marry someone they can control too. I should never have put you through it. It was humiliating.'

He *had* been stung by Lord Abradale's grave aloofness, and even more by Lady Abradale's fluttering alarm at his unsuitability, as if he were a fox found sniffing round the hen-run, but he made light of it now. 'It wasn't so bad. Do I look humiliated?'

'*I* was humiliated,' she said. 'Do they think me such a fool?'

'It's natural for them to want the best for you.'

She shook her head. 'The truth is, I *am* a fool. All last year I was waiting and waiting to be twenty-one so that I could take command of my own life, and then when I *am*, the first thing I do is run back to them for approval.'

'You did it for the best reasons, and I honour you,' he said.

'No,' she said firmly, 'I was a fool, and I've wasted all this time, but I'm not going to waste any more. What does it matter what anyone else thinks about us? I should have listened to you before, John, but I will listen now. I don't care about the wedding and all the folderol. I don't care who comes or if anyone comes at all. Let's just have the banns read, and then as soon as you're given leave again we can get married right away.'

He took her hands and looked down searchingly into her face. 'Are you sure? Do you mean it? I don't want you to decide something out of anger, and then be sorry about it afterwards.'

'I'm not angry,' she said, with a faint sigh, 'only disappointed in myself. I thought I was a thoroughly modern girl, and there I was caring about things that don't matter a fig. White lace and bridesmaids and "The Voice That Breathed O'er Eden"! But all that matters is to marry you, and be your wife, and be together for ever, and I don't care now if we get married in a register office, if that's the easiest and quickest way to do it.'

The old man in the corner had his chin sunk on his chest now, and the paper fallen from his hands. Fenniman drew her to him and kissed her, then cupped her cheek tenderly in his hand. 'That's all that ever mattered to me,' he said, 'but I wanted you to have what you wanted. If you're really sure, that's what we'll do. Have the banns read, I'll get the licence, and then as soon as I have leave again, we'll do it.'

She smiled gloriously at him. 'Yes! Oh, let's! And if anyone wants to come, they can come, but we won't wait for them. Oh, John, I do love you so!'

'I love you too – darling, dearest Emma.'

They kissed again, but broke apart hastily at the sound of a throat being cleared. The old man had woken again, and though he was not looking at them, he rattled his newspaper in a reproving manner. They grinned at each other, and settled down to sit in a chaste and proper manner and look out of the window – though hidden between them on the seat Emma's right hand was locked in his left.

When Lord Holkam arrived home on leave at the beginning of July, he was pleasantly surprised to find his wife so sociable, with a well-filled diary of invitations and activities. He had thought he might find her moping at home, or even gone down to the country, but there she was, cheerful and busy, and ready to accompany him to any and every social event, from the opera to polo at Cowdray Park. There had been hardly any thinning of the Season so far, despite shortages, queues and the threat of air-raids. People were staying up longer, perhaps because, after an unsettled period towards the end of June, the weather had cleared again and it was sunny without being muggy, the best weather for London; or perhaps because, war or no war, daughters had to be found husbands.

Violet had arranged a dinner at Fitzjames House, and had accepted invitations to others, plus luncheons, morning calls, visits to exhibitions, and bridge on the only evening they were not otherwise engaged. There was no moment of his stay that was not accounted for, and if he had not got up much earlier than his wife in the mornings, he would not have had time to see his children at all. For their sake, and because of the servants, he made no distinction between Robert, Richard and Charlotte, and the baby – whom he called Henry and she called Octavian – though he managed to avoid, without actually seeming to, either touching or addressing the eleven-month-old. It was easy enough – Robert and Richard clamoured for his attention, wanting to tell him about school and ask him about his heroic exploits in the war; and Charlotte, though shy at first, was soon competing with them. She was promising to be very pretty, perhaps even a beauty like her mother, though it was hard to tell at five; but she already had coquettish ways, which her mother had never had, and clearly distinguished between the important praise of her father, a man, and the worth-less praise of Nanny and the nursery-maids.

Holkam spent the rest of his mornings reading the news-papers and seeing male friends, until his wife emerged, exquisitely dressed and ravishingly beautiful, from her bedchamber in time for luncheon. Violet was thinner than she had been before her last pregnancy, and the extreme youthfulness had left her features for ever, but to Holkam's mind the change had not diminished her beauty at all – in fact, maturity had removed her into a different category of beauty, one that was perhaps more classical and enduring. He was proud to be seen with her, and decided that the looks they drew when they went into public were of admir-ation, and nothing to do with last year's scandal, which really seemed, to his relief, to have been forgotten. Every occasion they were seen together in apparent harmony pushed that terrible affair further into obscurity.

But apart from the social good it did, he was glad for his own sake to find his wife compliant, pleasant and sociable. It was almost like a return to the first days of their marriage – though he did not detect anything of the hero-worship to which she had treated him then. Well, he could hardly have expected it, and this slight detachment actually suited him better, for he had no wish to have his wife hanging on his sleeve when the war was over. All he wanted was domestic peace and public acceptability. She was perfect as she was, and he planned before he left to reward her with a little present, perhaps some diamond earrings or a brooch – he would have Garrards send some things round tomorrow morning for him to look over.

He could not know, of course, that Violet had planned to have every minute of his leave filled with activity in the company of others, because it was the only way she could get through it. For the sake of the children, and especially of Octavian, it must appear that they were a devoted couple, but otherwise she wanted as little to do with him as possible.

She had thought time and his absence might blunt her feelings towards him, but as soon as she saw him she felt the same repulsion as before. Why was he alive when Laidislaw was dead? Despite the children – and he was fond of them, and they of him – she would have swapped his life for Laidislaw's if she could have, without a second thought. But things were as they were, and she was enough of a lady to know she must make the best of them without fuss. Her mother had been right about that, and she would not need telling again.

On the last evening of Holkam's leave, they went with a small party to a performance of *Madama Butterfly* – which almost overset Violet with its passionate exposition of love lost – and then on to supper at Claridges. When they got home, a note was waiting for Holkam that he had to deal with. Violet went into the small sitting room, where the dogs woke from the comfortable depths of their chair and greeted her with the reminder that sandwiches had been left beside the whisky and sherry decanters on the table, and that it was a long time since their supper. She petted them for a while, and broke a small triangle of sandwich in half for them; toyed with the idea of taking something herself; and then was suddenly exhausted, and wanted only to be in her bed and to shut the world away. The idea of speaking to Holkam was too much – and she was afraid that, as it was his last evening, he might want to engage her in conversation, or more.

She hurried across the room, with the dogs following, and had gained the foot of the stairs when Holkam came into the hall from the small ante-room, where he had been using the telephone.

'Going to bed?' he asked, and she heard clear disappointment in his voice. She had been right to leave when she did.

'Yes,' she said, pausing with one foot on the bottom stair. 'I'm very tired.'

He came towards her. 'I see that you are,' he said. 'Come and talk to me for a while and let me ring for some hot milk for you.'

'I want nothing, thank you,' she said. He had come close now. He was tall, big, dark – she found his closeness threatening. Laidislaw had never been like that. Everything about him had been light and delightful. Holkam had always dominated her, while her lover had led her out into sunlit meadows. *Oh, my darling*, she cried inside, *where are you?*

'But I would like to talk to you,' he insisted. 'I've hardly had a moment with you alone. Come and sit with me for a few minutes.'

She met his eyes bravely. 'I don't think we have anything to talk about. And I'm very tired. Forgive me, Holkam. I will go to bed.'

He regarded her for a moment without speaking, and she could not read his face. She was keeping her end of the bargain – surely he could not expect more than that from her? At last he said, in a neutral tone, 'Very well. I must leave tomorrow morning – I hope you will have breakfast with me before I go?' She nodded slightly. 'Goodnight, my dear.'

He bent his head towards her to kiss her, but her cheek moved backwards out of reach of his lips. It was so subtly done he did not know if she had deliberately avoided the caress, or merely swayed slightly, perhaps with tiredness. Equally gracefully – he had always been graceful in his movements, she remembered – he changed the gesture he had begun into a slight bow, and turned away towards the sitting room. Violet turned at the same moment and mounted the stairs, the little dogs leaping after her, feathery tails waving.

While Holkam was at home, an anticyclone had settled over the British Isles, resulting in clear skies and settled weather – just the sort of weather most suited to bombing raids. Nothing had been decided about how to defend against

312

them. Lord French had been loaned two squadrons of the RFC in the immediate aftermath of the last raid, but these were desperately needed in France for the upcoming offensive, and were withdrawn in early July.

On Wednesday, the 4th of July, a flight of eighteen Gotha bombers set off early in the morning and, taking a northerly course to avoid RNAS patrols at Dunkirk, crossed the North Sea and conducted a hit-and-run raid on the Suffolk port of Harwich and the naval air station at Felixstowe. Warning was telephoned to Horseguards, and several squadrons were scrambled to the defence of London, but the Gothas did not go near the capital. Having dropped sixty-five bombs, causing light damage to Harwich but serious damage to the RNAS station at Felixstowe, they wheeled round and by seven fifteen were heading home unscathed over the silvery sea.

And only three days later, on Saturday, the 7th, again in the early morning, a flight of twenty-two came in over the river Crouch, attacking Tottenham, Stoke Newington, Islington, Clerkenwell and Hoxton, then flew over the City area, unloading about thirty bombs and causing extensive damage to property, though fortunately casualties were comparatively light as the City was largely empty on a Saturday morning. In all, there were around a hundred and fifty casualties, and the most notable damage was to the GPO building in St Martin's-le-Grand, which was hit by a fifty-kilogram bomb and set on fire, destroying the wireless telegraph apparatus. Bombs fell close to St Bartholomew's Hospital, destroyed waterfront buildings and the pier to Billingsgate market, and one fell on Moorgate station, but fortunately did not detonate. Then the Gothas passed on eastwards along the Thames, bombing Tower Hill, Southwark, Bethnal Green and Plaistow, before turning north-easterly again towards the Crouch. By this time some defenders had managed to get up and into position, and the Gothas were harried in their retreat, but the attacks, though brave, were piecemeal, and the Gothas were so well defended with machine-guns – including one that fired *downwards* from a ventral port, most awkwardly for the British fighters, which were always attacking from below in their struggle to reach the same height – that there was little hope of inflicting any real damage on them.

Lord Holkam was able to see for himself, therefore, not only what the raids could do but also the resultant fury of the public that they could be attacked in broad daylight by the enemy, who seemed to be able to sail in just as they pleased and return home unscathed, with the home defence unable to do anything against them. This time, the fury was not confined to letters and articles in the newspapers or questions in the House. As soon as the Gothas were gone, mobs started to form on the streets in the East End, and began rioting. When darkness fell, they turned their wrath on any trader unfortunate enough to have a German-sounding name, of which there were many in the East End, and any number of innocent tailors and clothing manufacturers, butchers, instrument-makers and food wholesalers had their windows smashed or their premises set on fire.

The one thing that did not happen – the thing the Germans hoped for – was any call for peace. Londoners were not to be bullied or cowed by attacks of that sort – despicable attacks on unarmed civilians. Their blood was up, and what they demanded was, first, protection and, second, revenge. The cry was for German cities to be bombed in their turn; but there were no British bombers capable of such a range, even had the government been minded to undertake it.

The war cabinet met again within hours of the end of the raid, but still no ideas were forthcoming, except that the two fighting squadrons which had gone back to France might be recalled to the home-defence wing. But General Haig was of the opinion that a resounding success in Flanders was the best defence, enabling the Gotha bases around Ghent to be captured and put out of action, and that the two squadrons were therefore of more use to him in France than they would be in England. In that case, the cabinet thought, perhaps they should reconsider and *not* recall them.

The July raids – and more particularly the East End riots – did have one direct result. The hatred of all things German, the King's nervousness about Red revolution, and the unfortunate coincidence that the German bombers were called Gothas, while the royal family's name was Saxe-Coburg-Gotha, persuaded the King that something must be done immediately. On the 17th of July he executed an order-in-council, changing the name of the Royal House to Windsor. The name was selected because it had a solid, English sound, and at once brought to mind Queen Victoria. Nothing could be more quintessentially English than the old queen-empress, could it?

Venetia, reflecting wryly on the King's action, remembered that the Queen had been a monarch of the House of Hanover, that her mother and grandmother – and, indeed, great-grandmother – had all been German princesses, that her great-great-grandfather, George II, had been born in Hanover, had only come to England in maturity, and had never learnt to speak English properly. In matters such as this, it was sentiment, not logic, that was important; and what everyone felt about Queen Victoria was that she was as English as afternoon tea, and that Windsor was therefore a very suitable name for all future kings and queens of England.

315

CHAPTER FOURTEEN

'Who is that fellow I see hanging around Polly?' Robbie asked. Having just finished a bowl of porage with cream and honey, he was back at the sideboard, helping himself to large, burnished sausages. He lifted another lid and discovered some rather beautiful kidneys and fried tomatoes, and added some of each to his plate. He was very fond of kidneys for breakfast, and the Training Reserve kitchen had not quite run to such refinements.

Back in his place, he realised that no-one had answered him. He had been safe to ask the question as neither Teddy nor Polly was at the table. Teddy got up even earlier in summer than in winter: he hated to be in bed once it got light, and was about the estate by five. Polly was out riding. She had always liked riding in the early morning before the world was properly awake; and the rest of her days were so busy now that it was hard to fit in a ride otherwise.

That left Maria and Father Palgrave, at the far end of the table with their heads together as usual, arguing about Spinoza or some other such hifalutin stuff – the priest was looking much better, Robbie noted, since he last saw him – and Henrietta, who was reading a letter.

He was about to repeat the question when the door opened and Ethel came in. She looked slightly, rather charmingly, ruffled. The latest style was for curls all over the head, and Ethel had embraced it. It suited her, he thought, better than the smooth bands: she looked really quite pretty. But it was not the curls that made her look less sleek than usual. Their eyes met across the room, and a hint of colour came to Ethel's cheeks. The army had invigorated Robbie, and his absence had invigorated Ethel. They had not had much sleep last night.

She murmured, 'Good morning,' and went across to the sideboard to hide her blushes. Moments from last night kept popping into her mind and disconcerting her. Given their past record, she wondered if another child was on the way, and disconcerted herself again.

Robbie swallowed a mouthful and asked again, 'Who is that chap hanging around Polly?'

Maria looked up this time, and said, 'Half of mankind hangs around Polly. You'll have to be more specific.'

'He means Lieutenant Holford,' Ethel divined, and turned to him. 'David Holford.'

'I hope he's not some paltry fellow,' Robbie said. 'Do we know his people?'

'Well, no,' Ethel admitted.

'He's not a local boy,' Henrietta said, looking up.

'He's from Surrey,' Ethel elaborated.

'Surrey!' Rob exclaimed, as though it were the moon.

'He's from a very respectable family,' Henrietta said, wondering why she had to justify anything to Robbie, who was not even Polly's brother, let alone her father. 'His father's a banker.'

'He's very rich, apparently,' Ethel said. 'They have a big house in London.'

'So he's a City type,' Robbie concluded. 'Not our kind of people.'

Maria, amused by his tone, said, 'They have a place in the country as well.'

'In Surrey? Surrey's not the country,' Robbie said scornfully.

'I went once with my parents on a charabanc trip to the

317

Devil's Punch Bowl,' said Maria. 'The country around Haslemere and Hindhead is quite open, almost wild.'

'I think that's where Mr Holford's parents have their place,' said Henrietta, hopefully.

'No, it's at West Horsley,' Maria corrected.

'I knew it began with an aitch,' she murmured.

Robbie was not to be placated by any letter of the alphabet. 'Well, he sounds like a thruster to me,' he said.

'I'm sure Mr Morland takes every care of his daughter,' Father Palgrave said soothingly. 'From what I know of him, he will have checked everything about that young man long ago, as soon as he showed any interest in Polly.'

Sawry came in and walked up to Henrietta. 'Mr Jack is on the telephone, madam. He asked for the master but I told him he was out.'

Henrietta began to rise, but Robbie was up before her. 'I'll take it, Mother. Don't you disturb yourself.' And he was out of the room before anyone could say anything.

Maria met Henrietta's eyes and read the concern in them. 'He wouldn't be on the telephone himself if it were anything bad,' she suggested.

'No, that's true,' Henrietta said. 'But he might want something sent. I hope Rob makes a note of it, and doesn't do all the talking. Perhaps I ought to go after all . . .'

But Robbie was back before she could act on the thought. 'It's all right, Mother,' he said at once. 'It's not bad news. Jack's coming home. He's been injured – but it's nothing serious,' he added quickly, as alarm jumped to her eyes. 'He's injured his hand so he can't fly, that's all, and he's wangled it to come home for a few days while it mends. He'll be here tomorrow.'

'Oh, we must tell Helen,' Henrietta said at once. 'When is she due back?'

'Tomorrow,' said Maria, 'so that's all right.'

'But we ought to get a message to her,' Henrietta said, 'to make sure she does come home, and doesn't take on another job or anything like that. Would it be better to send a telegram to her at Downsview House, I wonder, or at the factory?'

'I'll telephone the factory and find out where she is,' Maria said, getting up.

'Would you, dear?' said Henrietta, who still hated using the telephone. 'No need to interrupt your breakfast. Afterwards will do.'

'I've finished anyway,' Maria assured her.

A swirl of dogs dashed in, heralding the advent of the master. He looked boyishly excited, and said, 'I say, everyone, you must come out and see something! Come on – right away! You can eat any time, but you won't see something like this every day of the week.'

His enthusiasm even moved Ethel, who had only just begun her ham and eggs, and who normally couldn't think of anything worth going outside for at any time of the day. They trooped after Teddy and the dogs, and the servants within earshot drifted casually after them to see what was going on.

Teddy led them across the yard, under the barbican and over the drawbridge, to where a large piece of machinery stood on the track, gleaming red in the sunshine and throwing sparks of light back at the sun from its polished surfaces. Polly was there, too, on Vesper, trying to urge the mare to approach the monster, while she goggled and boggled, snorted, sidled and backed.

'Isn't it grand?' she called out, seeing her family appear. 'Come *on*, you silly mare! It just arrived on the back of a lorry as I was coming down the hill and Vesper went into fits. I don't think she'd have minded it if it hadn't been so very red. She's getting quite good with the army vehicles now, but they're all decently khaki and subfusc.'

'Don't force her – let her do it in her own time,' Robbie called out.

Polly gave him a withering look. 'When I take advice from

you on horses, you can put me in a box. She's just being naughty.' She applied her crop briskly twice behind the saddle, and Vesper responded by bucking, and then quite suddenly stood still and dropped her head meekly, as if it had never occurred to her to object to anything in the world.

The others gathered round with differing degrees of interest to inspect the tractor.

'It's from America,' Teddy said proudly. 'A Fordson. Isn't it a beauty? It's much lighter than the ones we make over here, more reliable, too. The government's importing thousands of them, because of the horse shortage. And it's easy to drive, easier than a motor-car even. A woman could handle it.'

Teddy was walking round it with Robbie and Father Palgrave, pointing out its salient features. 'You can hitch it to anything, just like a team of horses – a plough, a harrow, a drill. I'm going to try it with the mower on the last of the hay. And it'll pull the haycarts or haul a load of mangels or whatever you want. My word, a beauty like this would make all the difference in the world to a farm. You could plough twenty acres a week with this!'

'Oh, surely not,' Rob said. A horse team would take twice, even three times that long.

'*And* uphill,' Teddy added.

'Well, it may be a modern miracle,' Father Palgrave said, 'but I think it would be a shame if it replaced horses altogether. I love to see them working the fields – like great ships on a brown sea, with the birds flying after like seagulls.'

Henrietta gave him a grateful look for having said what she felt. She disliked petrol engines, with their noise and stink. Horses were a part of farming, a part of the earth and its rhythm, and had been since man first cultivated a field. You wouldn't be part of *anything,* sitting on the metal seat of this metal monster while it roared and rattled and bellowed smoke, cut off from the sounds and smells of nature.

It would be a sort of rape of the earth, she thought, though she could not have put it into words.

But Teddy said, 'Have to move with the times. And the army needs the horses more than we do.'

Maria said comfortingly, 'Changes like that always take a long time. I'd be willing to bet there'll be horses working the fields when we are all are dead and gone.'

Jack arrived late the next morning, without fanfare, walking up from the station for the sheer pleasure of it, for the feeling of the dusty track, the dry ruts like frozen waves crumbling under his tread; the smell of the hedgerows, thick with honeysuckle and wild roses, and the meadowsweet in the ditch; the glorious embroidery of poppy and cornflower and buttercup along the edges of the leas; the arch of the trees in their noble July greenery against the blue sky. There was much he liked about France, but it was not England, and its beauties did not speak to him, did not curve sweetly about his heart as these did.

Rug was tired from the journey, or he would have cavorted about with the joy of being home. As it was, he trotted at Jack's side until they reached the junction of the track, and they both simultaneously saw a dog up ahead, snuffling about in the hedge. Rug stiffened all over and began to growl, but Jack recognised the brindle markings of Polly's Bell and gave the two-tone whistle she always used. The hound jerked his head back out of the long grasses and froze, one foot up, ears pricked; then caught the scent and came galloping joyfully down to nudge and fawn, beating his whip-tail so hard it almost unbalanced him. 'Old fool, old fool,' Jack said huskily, rubbing the big, rough head. God, he was glad to be back!

Rug had stopped growling, but he and Bell had to go through the ceremony of circling each other stiffly, whiskers bristling, before the relationship was re-established and they raced off, leaping and tussling, and disappeared round the bend. They were home long before him, of course. Rug must have told them he was coming, for Henrietta was waiting at the great door, looking out for him. When he reached her, she folded him in her arms so tightly he knew her thoughts as clearly as if she had spoken them.

Henrietta *wouldn't* say anything, of course, but she had read things and heard things and knew what losses the RFC had suffered during that terrible April. Jack felt the dampness on his neck of her tears, and released her gently to look at her, touched her eyes dry with the back of a finger, and said, 'You mustn't worry. It's the inexperienced ones who get into trouble, you know.'

It was not *entirely* true. Henrietta fumbled for her handkerchief and was smiling in spite of the tears. 'It's just the middle of the night,' she said, 'when I can't sleep.' That was most nights, since Frank. It didn't seem to get any easier. But she mustn't make a fuss. She sought for a change of subject. 'Rob's home.'

'I know, I spoke to him on the telephone,' he reminded her.

'It's his embarkation leave. His battalion's going out to Palestine. And Helen's coming home today. Maria telephoned to the factory and they said they would pass on the message, and later she telephoned too, and said she'd be home this afternoon.'

'All this telephoning,' he teased. 'The wonders of the modern age!'

'Oh, my dear,' she said, and she had to hold him again.

Sawry was there to take his bag. Alice and Ethel came next, and they were inclined to be tearful, too; and Mrs Stark popped out from the kitchen passage and was frankly in tears, especially when she saw his bandaged hand. Discussion of his wound seemed likely to set his mother off again, so to distract them he told them what he had meant to keep secret until they saw it in the newspaper, for he was not one to boast. But he had to keep from being blubbered to death, so he told them that he had been put in for a DSO. That stopped the tears as eyes flew wide with wonder.

'What did you do? Is it to do with this?' Henrietta asked, gesturing at his hand.

'No, no, this is just a scratch. A bit of shrapnel came through the cockpit and cut me on the way.' He wished he hadn't said anything now – they were all clamouring to know what he had done, except Sawry, who was looking at him with painful admiration. 'It's a lot of nonsense, really. The other chaps did the same, they all ought to have got it. They just picked on me. I can't think why.'

'Nonsense,' Henrietta said, recovering herself. 'They don't give it for nothing. You must tell us what you did, Jack dear.'

'Oh, well, I suppose you'll read about it in the papers sooner or later. They're giving it to me because I was in twenty-five combats in one month and shot down ten Germans. But it was just luck, really, you know. Any of the chaps would have done the same. They have to give these things to someone, so as to have something to put in the papers.'

Henrietta kissed him again. 'I'm so proud of you! Now we have two DSOs in the family, you and Bertie. Oh, wait until your uncle hears this!'

'Oh, don't make a fuss, Mum, please. I wish I hadn't told you now.'

'Don't be so modest,' Alice said. 'We're proud of you, and you should be proud of yourself, too.'

Ethel smiled, but she was thinking that if anyone won a medal, it ought to be her Robbie. She didn't mind Jack winning one *as well*, but she wished Robbie could have got one first – which he would have, if only he'd had the chance, because he was terribly brave. Now when he got it, it would be secondary to Jack's. Of course, those RFC fellows had all the luck and got all the attention. There'd been a big fuss in the newspapers only recently about the young man Albert Ball, calling him an 'Ace', and so on, and awarding him the VC for shooting down Germans. He got shot down himself and the VC was posthumous, so one couldn't begrudge it. And she didn't begrudge Jack his medal, either, not really: it was just that everyone had always made a fuss of him, because he was the eldest, and they never noticed Rob's good qualities.

Rob was glad to see Jack, more than glad that their leaves had coincided. They walked off together for a private talk, brother to brother, before luncheon, circling the moat, heads together. Henrietta restrained Ethel from going too. 'They want to be alone,' she told her firmly. 'Let them be, Ethel dear.' Henrietta rarely put her foot down, but when she did, even Ethel heeded her.

Teddy came in for luncheon, was told the news, and at once decreed there must be a celebratory dinner, with champagne, their closest friends and neighbours invited to hear about it. 'This is really good news!' he exclaimed, rubbing his hands. 'This is something to cheer us all up! The war's been such a gloomy business lately, but you've shown us what it's about, after all. My dear boy! I knew how it would be. I knew you would make us proud of you. So, you're a "knight of the air", like this Captain Ball chap we read about in the newspapers? Ten Germans shot down in single combat! Oh, if only Ned and Frank could be here, how proud they'd be of you!'

Helen's arrival in the middle of the afternoon took some of the heat of attention from Jack, for she came in by air, flying an unarmed FE2b from the factory. It gave the soldiers in the camp something to gawp at as she circled over them, looking for a flat place to put down. Heart in mouth, Jack hoped they had been given aircraft recognition lessons and didn't decide to shoot at her. He and Rug ran out onto the track. She flew low over him and looked down, waved to him, and he saw her mouth curve in a smile below the goggles. He gestured to her to put it down on the track.

Now the army had its own entrance, there was no traffic expected, and they could wheel it out of the way later. In a moment she was safely down, and then she was out and in his arms, and there was time for a private greeting, and a rapturous reunion with Rug, before Rob reached them and helped them turn the machine and push it over on to the grass. Helen was doubly amazed at the sight of Robbie, first, that he had actually *run*, and second, that he was not even out of breath when he arrived. The army had certainly made him fitter, but it seemed also to have made him bigger in every dimension. She hardly recognised this tall, muscular man.

'Thanks,' she said to him, pulling off her goggles and helmet. 'You're looking very well, Rob.'

'How did you get hold of the aeroplane?' he asked. 'Have they lent it to you?'

'It has to go back into the factory for modification, but the workshop is full until next week, so they said I could use it.'

'How are they going to modify it?' Jack asked at once, his interest caught. 'Are they changing the gun mounting?'

'No, they're going to make the front seat the pilot position—'

Robbie interrupted before they could get bogged down in technicalities. 'Never mind all that! Have you heard Jack's news? Isn't it splendid?'

Ethel had come originally from a large family, the Cornleighs, who were sociable and well liked around York. Polly had gone to school with one of them, Eileen, and the two were still friends. One of the best things about the Cornleighs, as far as the young people of York were concerned, was that they had a full-sized and well-kept tennis lawn, and were extremely happy to have it used. With Eileen and her younger sister Marguerite, always known as Dodo, still at home, there were frequent tennis parties at the Cornleigh house during

325

the summer. The war had taken away the local young men, but had brought others to the various military camps and airfields in the area; and war or no war, young women had to meet young men and get married, or what would the country come to?

Polly liked tennis, was good at it, and knew she showed to advantage on the court just as she did in the saddle; and more young men played tennis than rode in these horse-starved times. So she gladly accepted an invitation to a tennis party on Saturday afternoon, even though two of her cousins were home. 'It's not as if they're only here for one day,' she said.

The Cornleigh parents had expressed the wish that Ethel, Robert, Jack and Helen would come to the party as well. Ethel, for whom, with her sister Angela, the tennis court had originally been laid ten years ago, when *they* were the young ladies of the house, was not deceived. Tennis parties were for the unmarried. Mrs Cornleigh would have her particular friends Mrs Fulbright and Mrs Aycliffe there, taking tea with her indoors while the young people played, and the invitation was just an excuse to get Jack there so they could lionise him. Ethel could see her mother any time, and did not care to act as bait to her brother-in-law, so did not even bother to pass on the invitation.

So Polly went on her own, bicycling over with her racquet strapped on the carrier behind, and wondering who would be there. She was ready for a diversion, for she had been feeling rather confused and not completely happy for the past two weeks, ever since Lennie had come back on his embarkation leave. His battalion had gone out at last, not to France but to Salonika, and he had come home bitterly disappointed about it. He had wanted to be in France where the real action was. And in his disappointment, he had shown rather too clearly his dislike and disapproval of 'this man trailing about after Polly' – it was fortunate Polly had not heard Rob saying much the same thing or feathers would really have flown. As it was, he and Polly had quarrelled. She had told him it was none of his business, that he didn't own her, and he wasn't even her brother, so he should mind his manners. Lennie had taken the rebukes fairly well – he was quite aware that he had no claim on Polly other than his long devotion – but it had made him, for the rest of his leave, what Polly called 'grumpy'. In the end he had left early to go back to barracks. Ever since, Polly had been feeling a mixture of crossness with him for being 'stupid', disappointment that she had not enjoyed his leave after she had so looked forward to it, and a vague, uneasy sense of guilt at having been horrid to him. She had refused to get up on the morning of his departure to say goodbye, so he had gone away without so much as a smile from her, which must have hurt him. She knew he was in love with her, and though she told herself crossly that that was not *her* fault, she remembered the good times they had had together and how kind he had been to her, and felt bad about it all the same.

So she was ready, more than ready, for a tennis party and the hope not only of diversion but perhaps new conquest, for there was nothing like a new lover for getting an old one out of one's head. She deliberately arrived a little late, so that she could make an entrance, and so that people would be asking Eileen whether Polly Morland had been invited, setting up an anticipation of her arrival. As the acknowledged queen of the neighbourhood, she did these things quite naturally and almost without thinking, and the other girls saw it as her right. She was good-natured and friendly, so there was little resentment when she took first place in everything. Someone had to be queen, and at least Polly Morland was 'nice'.

She went in at the side gate and round the house, and entered the garden with her head high and every expectation of enjoyment. As soon as she was spotted, a gratifying rush of people came up to greet her, but she hardly heard what they said, for her eyes had gone straight past them to the vision of David Holford playing a vigorous game of doubles against Eileen and George Aycliffe, partnering an objectionable girl called Betty Newhouse. Polly liked most people, but there was something about Miss Newhouse that set her teeth on edge. She was all pretension. To begin with, she was always known, at her own insistence, as 'Baby' Newhouse. Anyone could have a nickname, but to choose your own was pitiful. And she thought herself the belle of the county and every bit the equal of Polly Morland. Most irritating of all, she had a way of claiming Polly's arm and saying 'you and I', or 'Polly and I', as though they were the greatest of friends, occupying together an eminence above the other girls and sharing secrets together no-one else would understand. It made Polly mad when other people took Betty at her own evaluation and said to Polly, 'You will come, won't you? We've asked Baby Newhouse,' as though that were the clinching argument.

And now here was Baby Newhouse playing tennis – partnering at doubles, which was worse – with *her* Lieutenant Holford. For him to be playing at all when she hadn't arrived yet was bad enough. He ought to have refused all offers with a sad smile, and stood patiently to one side, watching the gate for her to appear, having no pleasure from the occasion until she was there – not gone jumping in to play what must be, to judge from the time, just about the first game of the afternoon, as though it was tennis he had come for, and he couldn't get enough of it.

And Baby Newhouse, of all people! Polly's mouth set in a flat line as she watched Miss Newhouse leap across the court after a rather wild ball from Eileen Cornleigh. Baby Newhouse was short and too plump for her height and had a snub nose and red hair, and Polly could not understand what anyone saw in her. She had heard her called pretty, but red hair, in her view, was perfectly hideous on humans. Only chestnut horses and red setter dogs looked good in it.

Dodo Cornleigh had reached her and was eager to do the honours as hostess, since Eileen was playing. Dodo loved Polly and thought her wonderful, and greeted her in the most flattering terms, offering to fetch her a glass of lemonade, insisting she must play the next game ('We thought we'd have mixed doubles to begin with, so that more people could get to play') and asking her who she would like to partner her.

Polly dragged her eyes from the horrid sight on the court (but he *did* play very well, and looked lean and handsome and quite pantherish as he stretched for a shot) and smiled her warmest smile at Dodo and said, 'I don't mind at all, darling. But are you sure I ought to play next, when I'm so shockingly late arriving? Surely someone who was here before me should have a turn?'

Dodo looked even more adoring, and said, 'Oh, no, because we put your name down right at the beginning, as soon as we knew you were coming. Everyone will want to partner you. Who would you like?'

'You choose for me,' Polly said, and turning her back on the court, set herself to be charming to everyone around her.

Unfortunately, what a lot of the girls wanted to talk about was the new man, Mr Holford, who was so dashing and sophisticated, so unlike the local boys, with his London manners and his air of knowing about a much wider world than York and the county. He was so charming – not a bit above his company, talking to all the girls and chaffing with the men – and he was frightfully rich. Several times she was assured that his father was a *millionaire*, the horrid word that was being heard these days.

Polly made a point of being pleasant to Rupert Bayliss, who was pinkly in love with her and a nice boy, though at eighteen much too young for her (and if he'd been older, of course, he wouldn't be here to play tennis anyway), so that by the time David Holford came off the court she was ready to go on it with a partner by her side, and could avoid talking to him or even acknowledging him.

She was much in demand as a partner, and no-one minded her having more turns than anyone else, so she played a great many sets, while noticing out of the corner of her eye how Holford was always at the centre of a group of attentive females, and apparently enjoying himself very much in his languid, sophisticated way. She couldn't catch him watching her, even though she played extremely dashingly that day, and frequent cries of 'Well *played*, Polly!' and 'Oh, *shot*!' must have come to his ears.

When they finally did play together, it was as opponents rather than partners.

'I hardly seem to have had a moment to speak to you,' he said, as they stood at the net and tossed for the choice of end.

'Really? I didn't notice,' she said, with a cool raise of her eyebrows. 'I've been playing.'

'So I saw. You are well taught, Miss Morland. You have quite a backhand, though your forehand is not as strong. You don't keep your wrist quite straight enough.'

Her nostrils flared. How dare he criticise her? 'I wasn't aware you aspired to be a tennis coach, Mr Holford,' she said, the most cutting thing she could think of.

He only laughed, remaining annoyingly uncut. 'I hadn't considered that as a career, though now you mention it, it has its attractions. Do you think I would get many clients in this neighbourhood?'

'I really couldn't say,' she said loftily, and turned away.

It was a further annoyance that she could not beat him. She was a strong player, easily better than his partner, Sally Aycliffe, but her current partner, Bunny Deakes, was weaker than Holford, and even playing her heart out she could not make up for his deficiency. When they went to the net again at the end of the game to shake hands, something of her feelings must have shown, because he gave her a slightly

330

puzzled look and said, 'I say, have I done something to offend you, Miss Morland?'

Polly assembled a kindly smile with a hint of surprise in it and said, 'No, of course not, Mr Holford – how could you?'

She felt extremely pleased with herself for the rest of the afternoon for that exquisite put-down.

Robbie and Jack both turned out for the day of the last hay-harvest. Robbie looked surprised. 'Can you, with that hand?'

'I mean to drive the tractor,' Jack said with a grin. 'I can do *that* one-handed. Uncle Teddy says even a woman could drive it. And I simply can't resist, you know.' He was surprised in his turn. 'But you, helping with the haysel? I didn't think it was your sort of thing at all.'

Robbie smiled in such a natural way that Jack was taken back to their boyhood, and the fun they had had together – he and Rob and Frank and Ned. 'I wouldn't miss it for anything,' Robbie said. 'It will give me something to think about when I'm at the war with shot and shell whistling about my ears.'

There was no argument from the other haymakers when Jack announced that he meant to drive the tractor towing the mower. The assembled women grinned at him, not having any ambitions that way. They were the wives and daughters of the men who used to do the work. Their hair was held back under scarves against the dust, and they wore their husbands' old trousers, tied with binder-twine around the waist to make them fit, and around the ankle 'to keep the mice out'.

The one or two old men who had come out did not want to drive the infernal machine, either. Old Ezra Banks of Woodhouse Farm looked furious that the mower was to be hitched to the tractor, instead of to his mule team. It was hard enough that his beautiful horses had been taken for the army, and he was reduced to driving mules. But he had got used to them now, and was fond of them, and when he looked into their intelligent, humorous eyes, he thought they were fond of him, too. He had groomed them to a shine for the occasion, and plaited their forelocks with red ribbons, and now their thunder had been stolen by a petrol-breathing, soulless monster. Ezra and his team were to work in the next field, which had been cut already and was ready for carting, and it was not the same. He stood scowling, muttering to his pair about dishonour, while they lipped and nibbled at his fingers, their long ears cocked forward, listening to his every word and looking, Jack thought afterwards, as if they would answer back at any moment.

As well as the women and the old men, some of the soldiers from the army camp had come to help, a number of the men and one or two officers. The men were excited at the thought of a day away from their NCOs, doing something different from the usual routine. One of them stripped to his waist, displaying the lean but knotty physique of the countryman, and took up one of the scythes, spitting on his hands and hefting it for balance. 'This is what I'd be doing at home, if the army hadn't've taken me,' he said happily. 'Gor, it's good to be back doing what I know, after all that left-turn, right-about-face humbug. I'm a fair scytheman, I am. Known for it back home. I'll start t'other end from the mower, Master, if that's all right with you. I don't like injins much.'

It was a fine day, though the sky had an unsteady look, with large clouds passing swiftly over the blue, laying welcome cool shadows over hot shoulders. The tractor chugged up and down, creating a blue haze, and within its range there was nothing to hear but its relentless racket. Further away the scythemen, and the tedders coming behind them, worked with an older rhythm, listening to the birdsong, pausing now and then to rest their backs and watch farm cats and a dog or two hunting mice in the hedges.

Jack drove the tractor for a little while, but he found it tiring to do one-handed, and rather boring, too. He passed it over to one of the soldiers from the camp, and went to join Robbie in the next field. He found he could lift hay bundles without hurting his hand, and the two of them worked together in peaceful companionship.

Teddy came out in the middle of the morning to see how everyone was getting on, and to give encouragement and praise, before going off to York to see to business. At midday a halt was called and everyone wiped the dusty sweat from his brow and went to sit down in a patch of shade, while the house servants brought out the food, with ale and cold buttermilk to drink. Jack and Robbie sat down with their backs to a tree-trunk, and Rug appeared from the hedge and flopped down beside them. He had bits of hay stuck to his whiskers, and burrs in his coat.

'Frankly, old chap, you look a trifle *mal soigné*,' Jack told him, as he picked them out.

'How's the hand?' Rob asked.

'Doesn't hurt a bit. I say, what a perfect day. I thought earlier it was going to rain, but those clouds have gone away. Ah, here's the missus!'

He beamed as he saw Helen approaching among the bearers of 'dinner', and Rob said wistfully, 'Ethel doesn't care for the outdoors very much.' It would have been nice to have her come and minister to him, especially if she looked at him the way Helen was looking at Jack.

Because of the flour shortage, the usual harvest pies were missing, and instead of bread there were oat bannocks to go with the cheese; but there were roast potatoes, still warm from the kitchen fire, and hard-boiled eggs and thick ham, and baskets of cherries and yellow plums.

'You look hot and dusty,' Helen said, as she reached them, handing them a tin mug each and pouring from the big jug she carried. 'I must say, I rather envy you. I've half a mind to come and join you. Hay smells so delicious.'

'Spiders,' Jack warned her. 'Hairy ones as big as sparrows. And the hay gets inside your clothes and scratches abominably.'

Helen laughed. 'Now I'm more sure than ever it's delightful out here! Men never take so much trouble to keep women from doing something, unless it's something nice they want to have to themselves.'

'It *is* nice,' Rob said, 'but I think mostly because it reminds us of our childhood. Look at my hands! I've got blisters on my blisters.'

'A few months ago you wouldn't have got through the morning,' Jack said. 'The army has certainly toughened you.'

'And what's toughened you?' Robbie asked. 'You pilot-types do nothing but sit down all day.'

'It's true. Nothing but pride has kept me going this long. I couldn't allow myself to be bested by my little brother, could I? But you'll never know the effort it has taken me to hide my agony and exhaustion.'

Helen smiled down at them, glad they were so happy, seeing for the first time the family resemblance in their faces, which she had never particularly noticed before. 'Father Palgrave is going to allow the children to come out this afternoon,' she said, 'so you'll have some help.'

'At least I'll go back to France looking fit and brown,' Jack said, and was instantly sorry, seeing the flicker of a shadow pass over Helen's face. He felt Rob glance at him, too. To deflect them he took a gulp at his tin mug and said indignantly, 'I'd like to know why Rob and I only get the buttermilk, and not the ale, after our morning's toil. Buttermilk is a woman's drink. Do we look like women? Go and fetch us strong drink, slave, and be quick about it!'

Polly came out with the dinner baskets. Wearing a faded blue cotton dress, with a blue handkerchief holding back her long fair hair, and carrying a trug of cherries, she knew she looked exquisite, like an artist's dream of a country girl, and she also knew that some of the men from the camp had come to help, so she suspected there might be an officer or two there.

She was heading first of all towards her cousins, when a voice called her from the hedgerow, and she turned in surprise to see David Holford sitting in the shade with his jacket off, his shirt open at the neck and his sleeves rolled up. 'What are you doing here?' she said.

'Helping with the harvest. One reads about it, you know. I thought it would be a lark.'

'And is it?'

'In a way. It's darned hard work, though. I shall never think these country men have it easy again.'

'Is that what you thought before?' she asked, a little scornfully.

'Compared with my father, yes. There he is, bent over a desk all day, inside even in the finest weather, toiling with dusty papers and figures, racked with responsibility. And there they are, strolling about in the fresh air, carefree, working at their own pace, no-one troubling them. That's what I used to think.'

'You really don't know much about the country, do you?' she said, but less scornfully, given his admission.

'No, why should I? But do you, Miss Morland, know all the latest ragtime dances? Can you jazz? Do you know what's showing at every theatre in Town, and who's in it? We each have our area of expertise, you see.'

It was said lightly and amusingly, and she felt herself softening towards him again. He was so *very* different from the local boys, there was no comparing them.

'Come and sit down for a minute. It makes my neck ache, looking up at you,' he said.

'You could stand up,' she said, realising belatedly that he should have anyway.

Any of the local boys would have been on their feet at once, blushing for shame at the omission; but he only smiled lazily and said, 'No, you sit down. It's so pleasant here in the shade, and the grass is surprisingly springy.'

She sat, and he gave her a friendly smile, as equal to equal. *That* was different, too. The other boys worshipped her.

'What's in the basket?' he asked. 'Oh, cherries. They do look fine. Are they for me?'

'They're for the workers,' she said.

'I'm a worker. I've worked very hard this morning.'

'Have you?' she asked severely.

'Well, very hard for me,' he smiled. 'May I?' He took a pair of cherries, dark as blood, from the basket.

'I ought to take them round,' she said.

'Oh, sit for a moment. Spare me a few minutes of your company. I didn't get to speak to you at all at the tennis party.'

'You were rather busy, as I recall.'

'Busy? Well, there was a lot of company, if that's what you mean. One has to be civil. But I'd rather have talked to you.'

'I hope you didn't tell Miss Newhouse that,' Polly said tartly, and was instantly sorry. She didn't want him to think she had noticed who he was talking to.

'Miss Newhouse?' he said vaguely. 'Now, which one was she? Not the young lady of the house – they were Corfields or Corbys or something of that sort.'

'Cornleighs,' she said. 'Eileen and I went to school together.'

'Cornleigh, that was it. So who, then, was Miss Newhouse?' He popped a cherry into his mouth and looked at her with polite enquiry; but wasn't there a gleam of amusement in the depths of his eyes? Was he mocking her? She wished she had not started this now.

'Miss Newhouse has red hair. You played tennis with her twice and talked to her for ages, so it's unkind of you not to remember her name,' Polly said stiffly. 'And now I really must take these cherries round to the others.'

She began to rise, but he put out a hand and laid it restrainingly on hers, and the touch made her jump. 'Is *that* what I did to annoy you? Talk to Miss Newhouse?' he said. 'But you see how little effect she had on me.'

'Really, you are free to talk to anyone you please,' she said haughtily.

His hand folded round her fingers. 'I'm glad to hear that, because the person I really want to talk to is you. Do stay for just a little while longer.' She stopped trying to get up, and looked at him, her heart beating too fast for her to do more than wait for him to speak.

He took a cherry from the basket and put it against her lips. It was warm and smooth as she imagined his lips would be. 'Do have one, after you carried them so far.' She took it into her mouth, feeling herself blush. 'Now, Miss Morland, the thing is this: I came out here today specifically because I hoped I might have the chance to speak to you. I guessed that you would appear at some point – though I did not know, of course, that you would be looking so particularly enchanting. I love the handkerchief, especially. Just like a princess pretending to be a peasant.'

Polly was distracted from the pleasure of hearing compliments by the problem of the cherry stone in her mouth. Impossible just to spit it out – *that* would not be very princess-like – but both her hands were occupied, one held by his and the other caught under the basket.

His eyes gleamed in that mocking way again, but his face was serious as he said, 'I do beg your pardon,' and placed his free hand, palm up, below her mouth. 'Allow me.'

Feeling foolish, shy, and oddly looked-after, she ejected the stone as tidily as she could into his palm.

'Where was I?' he said.

'You came out today because you wanted to speak to me,' she said.

'That's right. You see, I have had news. The army at the Front is very short of officers, and a number of us have been told that we will be leaving soon. The rest, and the men, will be staying a while longer. But we'll be sent to other units out there, wherever there's a shortage.'

'You're leaving? You're going to the Front?'

'We don't know yet where we'll be sent. It might be France, it might be Egypt or Mesopotamia. Personally, I'm hoping for France. It would be poor sport to get sent down a backwater.'

'But – when?' she asked.

'In two weeks. Possibly three, but more likely two. So, you see, there's no time to waste, if I am to get to know you better.' She didn't say anything at once, and he regarded her face with interest and said, 'Dear Miss Morland, can it be that you will miss me?'

At the tone of his voice she jerked back from her thoughts, pulled her hand away from his, and almost scowled at him. 'You take a great deal for granted, Mr Holford. I hardly know you, and you can't miss people you don't know.'

'But that's exactly my point. Now, how can we arrange it so that we can spend time together and get to know each other?'

'I don't know,' she said loftily. 'I am very busy. I really can't spare you the time. I'm busy every minute of the day with meetings and appointments and so on.'

'What about early in the morning?' he said, unabashed. 'A little bird told me you go past the camp on your pretty horse most mornings.'

'I like to go out riding early,' she said, 'before anyone else is about.' A wicked thought came to her. 'If you really want to talk to me, you can come riding with me. But I warn you, you'll have to be up very early.'

'How early?' he asked cautiously.

'Five o'clock,' she said.

He shook his head in wonder. 'There's no such time.'

'For a city person, perhaps not,' she said. She rose fluidly to her feet. 'Goodbye, Mr Holford.'

'Wait! Wait, I'll do it.'

'*You*'ll get up at five o'clock?'

'I need the riding practice,' he said. 'The riding-master says so.' He rose too, looking down at her. 'And for you, I'd do a great deal more.'

She surveyed his face a moment, and then said, 'Very well. I'll be at the camp gate tomorrow morning at a quarter past five. But don't be late, for I won't wait.'

'My servant will get me up,' he said. 'I only have to tell him what time. Nothing could be easier. He's always up with the lark, or whatever those birds are that sing so frightfully early.'

'Is he the one who told you I go past?'

'He is. He must have had an ulterior motive, I see it now.'

'Tomorrow morning,' she said. 'With the lark.' And she whisked away to deliver her cherries.

Robbie's time was up: he was leaving to go back to his unit and then overseas. Jack was staying a few days longer. Rob's kit-bag was bulging with presents from the family, knitted things from Ethel and useful items from the others, extra soap, razor-blades, cigarettes, chocolate, writing paper. After three years of war and many departures, everyone knew what was most needed.

Jack went with him to the station, and by an unspoken agreement, they went alone. Ethel had parted with Robbie in floods of tears and had not come down to breakfast. He had told her he did not want her to see him to the train. 'There'll be such a crowd there, you'll get jostled about.' So she had stayed in bed, to indulge her tears more privately.

In the motor on the way to the station, the brothers were quiet. These days they had spent together had brought them closer than at any time since boyhood. There was a feeling of unspoken warmth between them.

'So you'll be off soon?' Robbie said at last. 'How's the hand?'

'It's all right now. As far as that's concerned I could have gone back already, but I think they wanted us all to have a rest. It's been hard this year, and some of the fellows are showing the strain. Flying three or four missions a day, you start to pray for a "dud", when the weather prevents you going up.'

'Do you still love flying?' Robbie asked.

'Oh, yes. It's still the most wonderful thing in life, to be up there in the great blueness. It's the rest of it one doesn't care for, the Archie, the dog-fights, and the killing. They're just like us, really, the German pilots.'

'But they're Huns,' Robbie said, shocked.

Jack shrugged a little. 'The ones I've met didn't want this war any more than we did.' He remembered von Liebeswald. 'Of course, they still try to kill you, and you try to kill them first. That's the madness of war.'

Rob said quietly, 'I know it's very dangerous for you pilots. The casualty figures – well, I wish there were some way to keep it from Mother. I don't think she has a moment in the day when she's not worrying about you.'

Jack managed a smile, though he knew the odds as well as anyone. 'They haven't managed to stop me yet.'

Rob nodded, his thoughts moving on. 'I wonder what it's *like*,' he said.

'At the Front?' Jack hazarded.

'You read all sorts of things, but somehow you can't make them real in your head.'

Jack searched for something to tell him. 'I think mostly it's the noise that surprises everyone at first. That's what I've heard. If you can get used to that, the rest isn't so bad.'

They arrived at the station and got out of the motor. Robbie shook hands with Simmonds and took up his kit-bag. He turned to Jack and said, 'I think, if you don't mind, I'll go on my own from here.'

Jack nodded, understanding. 'Take care of yourself,' he said. 'Write when you know where you're going, and I'll write back.'

Rob laughed. 'Oh, you know me. I'm no hand with a pen.'

'Well, see you next leave, then, perhaps.'

'At Christmas,' Robbie said. 'We're bound to get off at Christmas, aren't we? Jessie too. It'll be nice if we're all together then.'

'Yes. Let's hope for that.'

The brothers shook hands, and then Robbie was gone, blending into the khaki crowd passing through the station entrance, just one among hundreds, indistinguishable now.

BOOK THREE

The Loan

It is no gift I tender,
A loan is all I can;
But do not scorn the lender;
Man gets no more from man.

Oh, mortal man may borrow
What mortal man can lend;
And 'twill not end to-morrow,
Though sure enough 'twill end.

If death and time are stronger,
A love may yet be strong;
The world will last for longer,
But this will last for long.

A. E. Housman: 'Additional Poems VI'

CHAPTER FIFTEEN

Thomas's talks with the King, the government and the diplomatic circle had yielded nothing but frustration. The East End riots after the last Gotha raid had convinced the King that the times were too dangerous to be inviting Bloody Nicholas, the hated tyrant, to the country. His action in distancing himself from his family name would be wasted, if he now reminded everyone that the Emperor was his cousin.

On the whole, the government still felt that they should give the imperial family sanctuary, but finding a way to do it safely and tactfully was the difficulty. It would be better if they went to another country, a neutral country, and Thomas was given to understand that diplomatic manoeuvres were going on to that end, but would take time. It seemed that the family was not in any immediate danger. The recent uprising in Petersburg – referred to as 'the July days' – had been promptly put down, and the Bolsheviks were in eclipse. Kerensky was now head of the Provisional Government, and he was regarded as a civilised man. Thomas was to gather that if the situation changed dramatically, other channels would be used to get the family to safety. The government would not allow anything to happen to them.

It was strange being back in Russia, after his sojourn in small, green England. A long interview with Buchanan brought each up to date with the situation. The war was not going well. Soldiers at the front had become unreliable, forming councils and demanding a say in tactical decisions, questioning orders, sometimes trying and ejecting officers they disapproved of. Desertions were running at an intolerably high rate. On the south-western front, several units had retreated at the mere rumour of an enemy advance, with the result that the Germans and Austrians had broken through and taken a large piece of Galicia without a fight.

'And here, in Peter?' Thomas asked.

'Things have quietened down since the July days,' Buchanan said, 'but the Reds haven't been completely routed. Kerensky is having to fight to keep his head above water. God knows how it will turn out. If things don't get worse at the front, and the harvests are good, it may all settle down. We'll know one way or the other by the autumn.'

'But the family is still at Tsarskoye Selo?' Before Thomas had left for England, Kerensky had visited Nicholas to tell him that because of the hostile elements in Petersburg, it would probably be necessary to move the imperial family, perhaps to the south. Nicholas had been very excited by the word 'south', assuming that Kerensky meant to send them to the Crimea.

'Yes. Kerensky's battling for his political life at the moment. They are something of an afterthought for him.' He tapped his pencil on the table thoughtfully. 'If they do go, will you go with them? Of course, it would have to be a voluntary assignment. Horseguards couldn't order you to go, given the circumstances.'

'You mean they would order me if they could?'

'You are very useful where you are,' Buchanan said. 'It isn't only that the family trusts you – the Russkies trust you too, and you've been around so long, they won't think anything of your tagging along wherever the family is sent.'

'Wherever? It's not certain they'll go to Livadia, then?'

'We're hoping very much that it will be the Crimea. It

will be easy to get a ship across to them from there. But the situation can change from day to day. And the Reds are already making noises about all the ex-aristocrats who are getting out that way.' He tapped his pencil again restlessly. 'I wish to God some decision could be arrived at about getting them out, before the best routes are closed down. Sometimes the diplomatic service works too damned slowly.'

And this from a diplomat, Thomas thought.

But there was joy in getting back to Tsarskoye Selo, in spite of the soldiers in the town and the slovenly guards on the gate. It was at its best in June and July. The weather was perfect, hot but clear, and the park was beautiful, and from a distance the palaces looked untouched by the events that had ripped apart the fabric of life. He could pretend as he walked up the drive that all was as it had been.

Everyone was glad to see him again. Even the withdrawn, cold Empress managed to smile and speak some words of welcome; the children frisked and made a great deal of noise, and the older ones expressed themselves warmly. Olga only shook his hand, but her heart was on her face. They were all fully recovered from the measles now.

Six weeks ago, it had been found that the girls' hair had been so weakened by the disease that it had started to fall out, and the Empress had ordered their heads to be entirely shaved, so as to make it grow back thicker. When it was done, they wore wigs indoors and woollen hats outside; but Olga had insisted that they have a photograph taken of them literally bare-headed. She said it would be interesting to have a record of them like this: their albums should remember the difficult moments as well as the happy. It was a terrible thing for a woman to lose her hair, especially if she were a young, pretty girl: Thomas guessed she had done it to help reconcile them to their baldness, and he honoured her for it.

Life at Tsarskoye Selo absorbed him effortlessly again into its simple rhythms: the daily walk, the gardening, lessons for the younger ones, languages and painting for the older ones; in the evenings, needlework and music and reading, photograph albums, and endless, endless conversation. Thomas had brought them books back from England as presents. Nicholas was very taken at the moment with Conan Doyle, and Thomas brought him *A Study in Scarlet*, which he started reading aloud in the evenings while the others worked. He liked to read aloud, and did it well: he had a pleasant voice.

But Thomas had hardly settled in when a message came from Kerensky that the family should prepare itself to move: not to Livadia, but to Tobolsk, a remote provincial town in the interior, several days' journey away. Benckendorff, the Grand Marshal of the Court, told Thomas that he had been given to understand the Provisional Government was preparing to take a hard line with the Bolshevik trouble-makers, which might well mean a period of armed conflict in which the imperial family would be an obvious target. Thomas went at once to Petersburg to see what Buchanan had to say.

'It may be true that the government is planning extreme measures,' he said. 'It's certainly true that the Bolshies are giving trouble. If the Romanovs are out of the way, it will be one thing less for Kerensky to worry about.'

'But Tobolsk!' Thomas protested.

'Yes, it is a damned nuisance. Right in the middle of nowhere. Of course, that was Kerensky's reason for choosing it. He says it's an out-and-out backwater, with no industrial proletariat. The townspeople are prosperous and contented, quite old-fashioned in their views.'

'I believe there's a garrison?'

'Yes, a small one. And there's a governor's residence the family can use. The climate is fair – good clean air in summer, though the Siberian winters are damned cold, of course. But it's at the far end of nowhere. There's no railway there. Access is by river and road, and in the winter, when the rivers freeze, the only way through is by horse and sleigh. It will make getting them out much harder when the time comes. In the circumstances, you may want to reconsider going with them.'

Thomas shook his head at once. 'The circumstances haven't changed as far as I'm concerned. I will go.'

'I thought that would be your decision. It's a boon as far as we're concerned, because we haven't got anyone from Intelligence out there yet.'

'Is it known when we'll be going?'

'At the end of the month, apparently. It's the devil's own job pinning Kerensky down on anything at the moment. The Benckendorffs won't be going, by the way – too old and frail for a show of that sort. But Dolgorukov is going, so you'll have someone sensible with you. And I'll let you know before you leave who to contact there.' He stood up and held out his hand. 'I wish you the best of luck. You're the sort of chap we need, and I wish there were more of you.' He eyed him curiously, as though for a moment he was minded to ask him something personal, and then desisted. 'Don't worry,' he said. 'If anything goes wrong, we'll get them out somehow.'

It would have been better if the British Army had been able to attack the Germans at Ypres when they were still reeling from their defeat on the Messines Ridge. But there was a political wrangle going on about whether there should be an offensive at all. With the capture of the ridge, the army had eliminated the salient and the overlook, and given itself freedom to move about unmolested in the area south of Ypres. It was in a good position to attack; but it was equally in a good position to hold, and that was what Lloyd George favoured. He did not like General Haig and did not trust him; and he was afraid another offensive, inevitably costing lives, would be politically unpopular. He wanted the army to sit tight and do nothing until the Americans could take the field.

But Haig knew the French were close to complete collapse, and when the Germans discovered that, they would attack, with disastrous consequences. If the French were to stay in the war, the Germans must be kept busy elsewhere, which meant there must be a major offensive by the British. By the time the Prime Minister was persuaded of that, it was late in July, and the impetus of the Messines Ridge success had been lost.

However, the weeks of delay had been useful in preparing for the attack. Huge amounts of artillery, arms and ammunition had been moved from Messines into the Ypres Salient. New drafts of men had been brought out from England and trained in mock attacks against reproductions of German positions. Battle plans had been refined, and all the officers involved had gone over them in detail. All was in readiness when finally the authorisation came from the cabinet, and the opening of the offensive was set for the 31st of July.

The Front at the Salient was now only about two miles from the city itself, and the plan was to drive the Germans back and recapture the high ground, which formed a wide semi-circle around Ypres. The highest point was at the village of Passchendaele, which sat on the Passchendaele Ridge. Once that was taken and consolidated, the army could push on to Roulers and cut the railway line that brought the Germans the hundreds of tons of supplies every day without which they could not survive. Even more than the Allies, they were dependent on rail transport: they were far from home, and had little access to the sea. Having cut the supply line, the army could press on and take Bruges, Ostend and Zeebrugge. Then the German forces in northern Belgium would be forced either to surrender or withdraw.

In addition to this, Haig was hoping that breaking out of the Salient would let the cavalry through into the open country to fight the kind of running action he knew they could win. But at the very least the offensive would cause the Germans heavy casualties they could ill afford, and would give heart to the French and take them some way towards getting back into the war.

On his return to France from leave, Jack had been transferred to take command of a flight in a new squadron, stationed to the rear of Ypres, near Steenvoorde. He arrived one evening by Crossley tender. The other pilots, from the pilots' pool at Étaples, had been dropped off one by one at the different squadrons dotted around the French countryside, until now he was sitting in solitary state beside the driver, with Rug on the seat next to him. The driver was a raw-faced corporal with a fag permanently stuck in the corner of his mouth and the foulest tongue Jack had ever heard. Jack wondered that he could locate all these outposts, bumping down narrow, unsignposted country lanes that all looked the same to his bemused eyes. The man seemed to find his way by instinct.

To make conversation, Jack said, 'If your shooting is as good as your location finding, you're a tremendous loss to the front line.'

'Front bloody line? Don't make me bloody laugh! Why d'you bloody think I joined Ally Bloody Sloper's Cavalry in the first bloody place, mate? 'Cause I'm not bloody stupid enough to get meself caught up in that bloody lot, that's bloody why,' he said – only he didn't say 'bloody'.

Ally Sloper's Cavalry was what the men called the ASC, the service corps responsible for transport behind the lines – named after a sly and lazy comic character. What had originally been meant as an insult was now appropriated as a badge of pride.

'Here we are, cock,' he said, a few moments later. 'One tuppenny to the bloody terminus. Mind your bloody head as you get out, and don't forget to tip the bloody driver.'

Jack gave him a couple of cigarettes – on the basis that he might meet him again one day – and climbed out beside a gate leading into a large flat field, fringed on one side by the inevitable row of poplars, which seemed to tremble in the evening light, in concert with the rumbling of the guns away on the other side of Ypres. The field had a range of canvas hangars and sheds at one end, along with the transport lorries, and behind them the accommodation huts for the men and NCOs. He tramped across the grass, noticing automatically the tussocky surface and the slight slope on which he would be taking off and landing.

A corporal came out of one of the sheds and greeted him. ''Ello, sir. You must be Captain Compton. We was expecting you. I'm Jennings, sir. I saw you flying at 'Endon, once, sir, back in peace time.'

'Good to meet you, Jennings.'

'An' this must be Flight Commander Rug, if I'm not mistaken,' Jennings grinned, bending to pat him. Jack was surprised. Evidently his fame had gone before him. 'Is that right, sir, that he goes up with you?'

'Not on active duty,' Jack said. 'Only at home, or on pleasure flights.'

'I'd give a bit to see that. Well, sir, the squadron commander'd like to see you first, Major Gates, sir. I'll show you where, and take your kit and the little feller to your room, sir. Don't want to report with 'im in tow.

Beyond the field was a small orchard, with the ripening fruit visible through the leaves like gaudy red and yellow baubles, and on the other side of that was the farmhouse, with its long, sloping roof. Here the squadron had its offices, Jennings explained, and the senior officers slept in the bedrooms upstairs. A range of wooden buildings behind accommodated the rest of the pilots. The mess was in the largest of them, and was connected to the house by a marquee that held the dining area: the old farm kitchen had been adapted for the squadron's needs.

Jennings dropped Jack at Major Gates's office. As he entered, the major rose and came round his desk to greet him, swinging his left leg stiffly. 'Tin leg,' he explained to

Jack's involuntary glance. 'Fly a desk, these days. Can't bend the bally thing enough to get into the cockpit.' Jack shook hands with him, thinking how nearly that could have been his fate.

Gates explained the position, and the immediate task ahead: to fly over the German lines, and register the nature of their defences and the positions of their strongholds. It was dangerous work. Enemy Archie had improved with practice over the years, and there was a heavy concentration of German fighters here. The German strategy was not to cover every part of the line, but to consolidate their air forces in certain vital spots, which meant that, when they wanted to, they easily outnumbered the RFC.

'Most of the squadron consists of youngsters just out,' Gates said, with something like a shrug. 'There just aren't enough experienced pilots to go round, but I've wangled a handful of veterans like you to stiffen the mix. Congratulations, by the way, on your DSO.'

'Thank you, sir.'

'I believe you know the territory?'

'Yes, sir. I was here in 1914. I was shot down over Gheluvelt.'

'That's first rate, first rate,' said Gates, presumably not referring to the shooting down. 'I particularly asked for someone who knows the Salient. How do you feel about giving an orientation talk to the chaps?'

'Whatever you say, sir.'

'Capital. We'll set that up for this evening, after dinner. And I'd like you to give your flight a lecture on fighting tactics before you take them up for the first time. Make that tomorrow morning. Try to ease them into it, if you can. We probably have a couple of days' leeway – though we can't depend on the weather. We've had quite a few dud days this past week and the outlook's unsettled. So we've no time to waste; but on the other hand, a dead pilot is no use to anyone. Try to strike the right line between caution and getting the job done. I can't tell you how to do it, because it will depend on what happens when you get up, but if you make the right judgements I'll support you all the way.'

'Thank you, sir,' Jack said again. Be careful but not too careful, be bold but not too bold. Useful advice, he thought. He wondered how long Gates had been behind that desk.

'You've been flying a Camel, I believe?' Gates went on. 'Jolly good. We've just had two delivered to us, so you can have one of 'em. They take a bit of handling, I understand, so we don't want 'em pranged by a novice. Well, that's all for now. Settle yourself in, and I'll see you later in the mess.'

Jennings was waiting to take Jack to his room, where Rug greeted him with an air of never having expected to see him again. The room was in one of the huts. They were newly built, and smelt pleasantly of pine and resin, and felt snug against the rather damp evening. As Jennings was about to depart, Jack noticed something lying behind the bedside locker and stooped to retrieve it. 'Hello, what's this?' It was a leather-framed photograph of a very young woman with curly hair and a shy smile.

Jennings took it. 'Must've belonged to Mr Farnham – slipped down the back, most likely, when his stuff was being cleared.'

'My predecessor, eh?' Jack said.

'Yessir. He went west, sir, day before yesterday. Only been out here three days. One pip, one stunt, that's what they say, eh, sir? I'll take it, sir, and see it gets sent on.'

Jack handed it over, thinking it was a poor welcome. One pip, one stunt – the second lieutenants wore one pip on their shoulders, and their operational life was now legendarily short. He was feeling low enough, anyway, at having parted from his old flight, after spending so much time with them, training them and fighting with them and messing with them; and now he was being given a new bunch of babies to go through it all again. Not a happy prospect. The missing face at breakfast was something you never got used to. And he was back in the Salient, the poisoned Salient of Ypres, over which so many had fought and fallen, and which had almost been the end of him once already!

Oh, well, he told himself bracingly, you couldn't win the war unless you fought it. And this time perhaps they would drive the Germans right back and see the beginning of an end to this godawful business.

He had a quick wash, left Rug lying comfortably on the end of the bed, and made his way to the mess hut. The first thing he saw there was a friendly face. His heart lifted. 'Harmison! You here!' he said, advancing towards a grin and a warm handshake.

Harmison had been one of the first squadron Jack had joined, back in 1914.

'Compton, by all that's wonderful! I heard they'd let you come back over, but I never thought you'd turn up here. By golly, this calls for a drink! What's your poison? Beer, pinkers? Lewis, two pink gins, on my tab. Gasper?'

Jack took a cigarette and lit both. 'Thanks.'

'How's the leg?' Harmison asked. 'I heard you were out of commission quite a while.'

'Oh, it's as good as new,' he said. 'It was a long job, though. There were times when I thought they'd never let me fly again.'

'Like the Old Man.' Harmison's face turned down at the very thought of the major.

Jack guessed he was not popular. 'What's he like?' he asked.

'Oh, he's all right, but a terrible fusser. I think it drives him mad that he can't go up there with us. He feels every loss very badly, and shows it, which makes it worse. Doesn't help the youngsters when the old lags are windy.'

The steward came back with the two drinks, and they clinked and drank.

'Chin-chin!'

'Bung-ho!'

They talked about old times and what had happened in between, to them and others they knew. 'Vaughan and Flint both copped it over the Somme,' Harmison told him. 'Pettingill caught a packet and was sent back to Blighty, and Bell went missing over the sea early in 'sixteen. As far as I know, there's only thee and me left of the old squadron.'

'A short life and a merry one,' Jack said, and they drank it as a toast. He told about his latest squadron, and how he regretted leaving them.

'Me too,' said Harmison. 'I was with a very decent bunch at Hinges. Just got myself nicely dug in, and they hoicked me out and dropped me here at the baby farm.'

'What are the others like?' Jack asked.

'Nice enough chaps, but wet behind the ears. There are a few veterans like us – Kayser, Hipkiss, Cockerel, Jordan. All brought in to mind the little 'uns. Come on, I'll introduce you.'

There were more drinks, and then dinner in the mess tent, and by the end of it, Jack was feeling much more at home. When it came down to it, one mess was pretty much like another, he thought. The eager young pilots were just like the ones he had trained at Hauteville, the veterans were pretty much like Borthwick and Sheridan and crew, and the only thing his new billet lacked was the wonderful cooking of Mears. When, the next morning, he took his Camel up on a test flight, and he saw the familiar shape of the Salient below him, he felt as if he had never been away.

The Germans had learnt something about defences since 1914, and they were no longer investing large numbers of men in the comparatively vulnerable trenches. Their plan now was to have lightly manned trenches linking concrete pillboxes containing machine-guns, which covered the line with interlocking fields of fire, the whole further protected by heavy belts of barbed wire. And there were not just a first and second line, but third, fourth and fifth lines too.

Jack's squadron had three tasks: to undertake reconnaissance, to protect the two-man scouts taking photographs, and to prevent the Germans from making reconnaissance of their own. The latter sometimes involved shooting down balloons, one of the least pleasant duties. Balloons were always heavily defended with Archie, and were desperately hard to puncture – bullets tended to skip off the surface unless they were hit at close range; and a hit at close range was likely to cause an explosion in which the attacker could get caught, with horrible results. Jack lost one of his flight in his first week in just that way, when young Deacon went down in flames near Westhoek. He drank rather a lot in the mess that evening, hoping that Deacon had been killed in the explosion, and not at the end of that fiery plunge.

The coming battle was preceded by the heaviest bombardment of the war so far, with more than four million shells being poured into the German defences. After the barrage started, the squadron had new tasks: to perform artillery spotting, and to report back on the effects of the bombardment. It was heartening to see that the German positions were taking severe damage, and there was evidence of heavy casualties, too. By the time the 'off' came, the enemy would be well and truly shaken.

On the 30th of July the weather broke, and when the first waves went over the top at 0350 hours on the 31st, they had to advance through mist and driving rain. That was hard enough, but conditions worsened through the day, slowing and finally halting the advance. Most of the 'saucer' around Ypres was reclaimed marsh land, inclined in any case to be wet and always in danger of flooding after heavy rain. But the continuous shelling of the past three years had smashed dykes and sluice gates and destroyed the elaborate drainage system built up over centuries. The heavy rain had nowhere to go: ditches flooded, streams overflowed, water lay in sheets across low-lying fields. By the end of the first day, shell holes were filling up and the ground had turned into a quagmire.

The attackers had done well, advancing an average two miles on a front of fifteen miles, taking German lines and almost five thousand prisoners, and all for a relatively low cost in casualties. But the rain showed no sign of relenting. It fell like a monsoon, day after day, beyond anything that could have been expected; and by the 4th of August, Haig was forced to call a halt to any further attacks. It was impossible to move under those conditions.

Bertie had led his company through the teeming, impossible rain, and they had made two and a half miles before the failing light, the deteriorating ground and the enemy artillery had stopped them.

They had gone through two German lines almost without resistance and taken a large number of prisoners, most of whom seemed dazed by the bombardment. The pounding barrage had levelled the German defences and there were dead and dying men in number. Bertie had been here before, in 1915, and he knew where he was: what had been the village of Saint-Julien was up ahead. His objective was to capture it and use it as his next jumping-off point. But the enemy was shelling the ground in front of them, and the going was now so hard that he had no alternative but to call a halt. In those conditions, any further advance would have been so slow as to make them virtually sitting targets for the enemy guns: dry ground was necessary to move infantry up quickly, and bring the guns up behind them for the creeping barrage. Moreover, he had to consider the necessity of bringing up reinforcements and taking back the wounded. The further he went into this sea of mud, the harder those things would be, and the more cut off he would find himself.

Though he knew where he was, he hardly recognised the area. It had been fought over and shelled for so long there was very little left standing. What he could see of Saint-Julien up ahead was no longer a village, just a few broken chimneys and shattered tree-trunks rising out of heaps of rubble. He remembered being briefed in a farmhouse there by General Alderson, in April 1915, for a counter-attack on Kitchener's Wood – a do-or-die charge against the odds without machine-gun support. He had listened to the orders in a state of exhaustion close to euphoria, and the knowledge that he was almost certainly going to die had not troubled him at all. He had been eerily convinced that that farmhouse kitchen would be the last room he would ever see, and had accepted it philosophically.

Well, he was still here, and the farmhouse almost certainly wasn't. All the same, however ruined Saint-Julien was, he would have been glad of what little shelter it could afford his men. He halted at last at the remains of a farm, where there were at least some broken walls they could make use of. Furthermore, the farmyard had, sensibly, been built on an area of ground slightly above the level of the fields around it, which meant that while there was thick mire underfoot, they were not in mud and water up to their waists.

And there they dug in, further advance impossible, and tried to consolidate as the order came through from the top to stay put until the weather moderated. He wrote his report and sent it back with runners – never had there been a less apt description – and then went round his sodden, disconsolate men to see how they were faring. In the fantastic way of the Tommy, they had made the best of what they found around them, constructing meagre shelters out of bits of wall, shattered doors and timbers, mouldy hay bales, half-blasted hedges and the waterproof sheets out of their battle-order kits. He hoped hot food would be sent up to them: it would be impossible to light a fire of any sort at the moment. He praised them and chaffed them, set up defences and sentry posts, briefed his officers, spoke to the wounded, listened to requests.

When he could do no more, he went back to the shelter

that Cooper had found for him. It was little more than a hole in the ground, but crucially, it had stone walls on three sides. It had been a half-cellar under the original farmhouse, probably a root store. Rubble and rafters had fallen over the wooden hatch that had given access to it from inside the house, and the outer walls of the house had fallen down, exposing its third side to the air. But it made a space about ten feet by twelve, and five feet high, which was shelter of a sort. It had a mud floor which was going to get muddier as time went on, but Cooper said there were plenty of old floorboards and other bits of wood around, and when he had had a chance to get at them, he would put down a bit of flooring.

By the end of the next day Cooper, in his usual way, had made the major comfortable. He had discovered a broken kitchen chair, which he had roughly mended, and a wooden box to serve as a table, and Bertie had long got used to sleeping on the ground in his flea-bag. Cooper had managed to keep his cigarettes dry, and Bertie had a flask of whisky in his pocket. The half-cellar became his office, and sleeping-space for all his officers.

To the rear of his present position, work had already been going on to lay a road of duckboards over the worst places in the mud. Laboriously, supplies were moved up and the wounded taken back. On the second day, hot food in hay boxes reached them – still warm enough, anyway, to tell the difference – and the men dined on bully stew and 'floaters' – suet dumplings – with rice. There was biscuit and jam for 'afters', and tea. Cold food supplies were also brought up, with, importantly, dry firewood for cooking it.

On the third day Fenniman appeared, having come up to see for himself what the conditions were like, and report back to Hot-Water, as the men called Scott-Walter, their Colonel. He had to report the same to General Gough.

'By God, I'm glad to see you,' Bertie said, wringing his hand. 'Come inside out of the rain.' It had eased off somewhat, but still fell relentlessly. 'You'll have to sit on the floor – we haven't much headroom.'

'You've made yourself pretty cosy in here,' Fenniman said. 'Here, have one of mine.' He produced cigarettes, and told Bertie about the strategic position. 'To your left, the Guards took Pilckem Ridge and advanced practically up to Langemarck. To your right they did even better, got all the way up to the Zonnebeke road before being pushed back to the Steenbeek. They didn't do quite as well south of the Menin road, but they still advanced about a mile. The whole thing would have gone off brilliantly if it hadn't been for the rain.'

'How bad is it back there?' Bertie asked.

'It's terrible,' Fenniman said frankly. 'There are places where if you slip off the duckboards you go in up to your waist. They're having the dickens of a time getting the horses and mules out when they go in. And woe betide you if you fall into a shell hole – most of 'em are full to the top with water, and those that aren't, the sides are too slippery to climb up once you're down. They've had to call back the tanks – can't move them forward at all – and they can't bring the artillery up. And they can't do anything about the dead. Off the duckboards you can see the bodies, and bits of bodies, and dead horses and mules, all stuck in the mud, waiting for you to slip and fall in with them.'

'Too much imagination, that's your trouble,' Bertie said.

'Imagination? Me?' he protested. 'Now, as to orders, you're to dig in here for now, and as soon as the rain moderates and we can move up reinforcements, we'll advance again. It'll be "bite and hold" tactics – no dashing breakthrough for the cavalry after all.'

Bertie grinned and they went into a familiar question-and-answer routine in imitation of officers' examinations. 'Candidate Fenniman, what is the role of the cavalry on the modern battlefield?'

'Sir, to give tone to what otherwise would be a mere vulgar brawl.'

'Correct! And what is the role of the infantry on the modern battlefield?'

'To prevent random fire from the enemy, sir, by giving them a target.' Fenniman grinned back, then went on, 'But seriously, everything's gone pretty well so far, apart from the weather. Hot-Water reckons it can't go on raining like this for much longer. Bless his innocent optimism!'

'So, we're to stay put,' said Bertie. 'Oh, well, I've been in worse places.'

'I've brought up a hamper for you and the subs,' Fenniman said. 'That should warm your cockles. And there's post for the men. Oh, and I brought this for you.' He handed over a letter.

'It's from Maud,' Bertie said, looking at the writing. 'Thanks, I'll read it later. Did you get anything?'

Fenniman smiled. 'The usual delightful nothings from my fiancée, wondering when I'm coming home so we can get married.'

Bertie shook his head in wonder. 'You – old Winderpane himself – married! It hardly seems possible.'

'*Au contraire*, it's not only possible, it's inevitable. The only thing required is for me to get leave. I should say, for *us* to get leave – I can't pull off this stunt without you, old man.'

'"Marriage is a union entered into by one man and one woman,"' Bertie quoted.

'Ass! I want you to be groomsman, of course. I say, Parke, you won't let me down? I've been counting on you ever since I popped the question.'

'Of course I'll be your groomsman,' Bertie said. 'Wouldn't miss it for worlds. But we'll have to get this battle over with before they'll let us skive off.'

Fenniman sighed. 'If only rain hadn't stopped play, we might have been up to the Passchendaele Ridge by now, and be putting in for travel warrants. Well,' he said, getting to his feet, 'you'd better take me along the line, and then

I'll be getting back. If I can find Forward Headquarters again. We were in process of moving when I left, and you know what it's like, now there are no landmarks any more. Trying to find a black cat in a coal-hole at midnight would be easier.'

When Fenniman had gone, Bertie went back to his cellar. Cooper brewed him some tea and buttered some bread out of the hamper Fenniman had brought – a little stale, but infinitely better than biscuit – and he sat on his flea-bag and opened Maud's letter. It was a long one; but the opening sentences had him reading with an attention he had never given one of her letters before.

My dear Bertie,
This is a very difficult letter for me to write, so you will forgive me if I simply say what I have to say in plain language. I wish to divorce you, and marry John Manvers. I must tell you it was not with this in mind that I came to Ireland. I have always regarded him as a friend, and since arriving here I have come to rely on him more and more. But it was not until very recently that my feelings towards him changed and I desired our relationship to assume a more intimate nature.

The increase in my affection for him has corresponded with the decline in my feelings for you. I cannot forgive you for Richard's death. Had you not insisted on my going out of Town, he and I would not have been in Folkestone when the Germans attacked, and he would be alive today. His death is on your head and I can never forget that. I felt when last I saw you at Beaumont that I could never live with you again as your wife. Even had I never known John Manvers, that would still be true.

You must have been aware from the beginning of our marriage that you loved me more than I loved you,

363

but I regarded you as a good husband, and was willing to do my duty by you. I have always assumed from your demeanour that you were satisfied with that situation too. Had Richard lived, we could have continued as we were, and after the war found a *modus vivendi* for the years of peace. But without my son that is not possible. There is nothing you can say or do to make me feel anything but horror at the thought of our being man and wife again, and in the circumstances I believe I am absolved from my marital vow.

I have consulted a solicitor, who tells me that these things are usually arranged quite simply and discreetly, with the paid services of a woman of a certain class. You will, as a man of the world, no doubt understand the process better than I can. I know you will do the gentlemanly thing and allow me to divorce you in this way. You will not expose me to the horrors of the courtroom – nor insist on our remaining married, simply to deny me the comfort a second union can bring. I know that you are too generous by nature to do anything so mean or paltry.

As you are at present detained in France, I cannot expect you to act immediately, but perhaps you will at least write whatever letters are necessary to put the matter in hand, so as to be executed without delay whenever you are next in England. I wish to have things arranged as soon as possible, and you, too, will not care to delay longer than necessary. Once the knot between us is officially severed, I hope we can remain friends. This is Manvers's wish also. He sends his respects.

With sincere good wishes,
Maud Parke

Bertie was still reeling with shock when he was interrupted by a runner from one of his junior officers who wanted him to come to the line, as he believed the Germans might be readying to attack. It was late before he returned to the cellar, and by then he was cold, wet and hungry, and the letter came back to him with renewed shock, having been forgotten in the urgency of the previous few hours.

Cooper saw his look, and hurried forward to attend to him, relieving him of his wet coat, towelling his hair, and bringing him food and the remaining half-bottle of red wine from the previous night's dinner. He had read the letter while Bertie was out – of course he had: how could he look after his officer if he didn't know what was going on? Inwardly he cursed the woman, and told himself wisely that soldiers were better off not getting married. There were always enough women of the other sort around to satisfy a man's needs, and otherwise, what were they good for, except to nag a man to death and spend his money? He had been sorry to hear that Winderpane was planning on getting spliced – he'd thought *he* knew better. But this piece of the major's beat all. Writing to him like that when he was at the Front, in danger of his life and fighting for his country. She wanted slapping, that was Cooper's opinion.

He could not, of course, let the major know by the slightest look or action that he had read the letter, so he treated him with his usual brusqueness, while making sure he had everything he wanted – or, at least, everything Cooper could provide.

With the first pangs of hunger assuaged, Bertie could keep his mind no longer from the letter. It was a bitter thing to be blamed for the death of his son – as though he had not loved him as much as Maud ever could! And mourned him every bit as much! Richard's face came vividly before his mind's eye, laughing up at him as they had caught stickle-backs in the stream at Beaumont the year before. Bertie would never teach him to ride, now, or play cricket, take him hunting, show him how to manage the estate. Richard would not grow up to inherit Beaumont. How could Maud be so callously cruel as to blame him for Richard's death?

And Manvers, of all people – Manvers whom he had viewed as a friend, whom he had trusted. Had he been betraying Bertie all along, on his visits to England? Maud had said not, and Maud did not lie – or so he had always believed. But what did he really know about her, after all? This business about his loving her more than she loved him: he had always thought it was the other way round, and had tried, guiltily, to make it up to her by being a good husband. But she loved Manvers: Bertie was sure she must love him to do anything so *outré*, so dangerous to reputation, as to want a divorce – for even as the innocent party, she would find some part of the shame would stick to her. Even in Ireland there would be those who shunned a divorced and remarried woman. He could not imagine Maud loving anyone very passionately; yet Manvers had obviously roused in her something that Bertie never could. *That* was galling. That touched pride.

How could she write such a letter to a man serving at the Front, in the middle of the year's big offensive? Anger came to reinforce hurt pride. She had thought of nothing but herself and her own convenience. While he was struggling in the mud of the Ypres marshes to push back the Germans and free Belgium, she was coolly asking him to make arrangements so that she could be free to marry his friend.

But to blame him for Richard's death! That was cruel. His thoughts circled again back to grief. All through that evening, and the night that followed, his mind went round and round, like a donkey on a treadmill, unable to escape them until, in the silence of the middle watch when the German guns were stilled at last, he fell asleep through sheer exhaustion.

The following day the rain had eased to a steady drizzle. Bertie woke to a miserable remembrance of Maud's letter, but he had no time to brood over it, for while he was still going through his morning tasks, they received visitors: the colonel and his staff, including Fenniman, accompanying a brass hat from General Haig's headquarters, come to see the lie of the land and inspect the conditions.

'Ah, good morning, Parke,' said Lord Holkam, with all the arrogance of a man who had the commander-in-chief's ear, towards someone his inferior both in army rank and the peerage. There was something about him, Bertie thought, that suggested he had slept in a bed last night and breakfasted hot and well this morning before making this visit. Still, on the credit side, his boots were mired, his breeches were splashed with mud and his greatcoat was dark with rain, which was comforting. In any case, the real soldier always had his own sustaining well of contempt for the red-tab fellows.

'Sir,' said Bertie, studying this stuffed shirt that pretty little Violet had married. He was handsome, it was true, and tall, and titled; and Bertie supposed he had been less arrogant when he was younger, not Haig's darling, and campaigning in the ballroom for young women's hearts. As Bertie understood it, Haig himself was rather a stiff cove, and found it difficult to make friends, so that once he did unbend enough to like and trust someone, he was tremendously loyal to them, and they would find themselves on the inside of a very small, tight circle. It would not be surprising if a man with a propensity anyway to think well of himself should have his head turned in such a circumstance.

'The commander-in-chief asked me to pop over and have a look round,' Holkam said, and turned from Bertie to Hot-Water, who was closer to him in rank. 'See if we can't get things moving again, now the rain's eased off.'

They trudged out into the drizzle, and inspected the line, trained field-glasses on the German positions, viewed ground ahead, tested the going underfoot. Bertie did not suppose he could ever learn to like Holkam – and presumably Holkam did not care about being liked anyway – but it was evident he knew his business all right. It was to be supposed that Haig would not give this degree of trust to a man who was not a soldier, not competent – in a word, not pukka. And he was certainly fearless. He showed no interest in anything the Germans were sending over, did not even flinch when a sniper's bullet smacked into a tree stump six inches from him, as they passed their own particular 'Windy Corner', as dangerous spots were called.

'I think,' he said at length, when they walked back towards the ruined farmhouse, 'that it ought to be possible to press the attack here. It would be an excellent thing to take Saint-Julien, at least. This rain is a curse, but the ground isn't as bad here as it is on the right wing, and the 15th and 51st Divisions are both ahead of you by half a mile or so. I shall report as much to the commander-in-chief. Now, Colonel, what do you have in your support line?' With an expert and almost elegant movement, he cut Bertie and Fenniman out of the conversation and walked on with the colonel, the adjutant bustling along behind them, trying to keep up so that he could take notes.

Bertie and Fenniman watched them go. 'Quite the sweetheart, isn't he?' Fenniman said at last. 'No wonder Haig likes him. Built by the same firm – Dour and Charmless Limited.' Bertie did not speak, and Fenniman glanced at him. 'Something up? You seem a little glum yourself this morning.'

Bertie pulled himself up. He did not want to tell Fenniman about the letter, not here, not now. There was no-one he would sooner confide in, but a matter of this sort needed leisure. 'No, I'm fine,' he said. 'I shan't be sorry to get moving again. Sick of looking at the same old view.'

Fenniman nodded. 'I think we'll have to do this by small increments. Take a thousand yards, consolidate, take another.'

Bertie gave him an innocent look. 'You mean *I'll* have to,

while you sit safely in the stalls and criticise the performance.'

'You cut me to the quick,' Fenniman said with dignity. 'I was planning to lead C Company myself and leapfrog you.'

'Well, you be careful if you do. It's dangerous up here at the Front, and you're not used to it.' He parried Fenniman's mock blow to the chin.

'Got to go – the old man's calling.' Fenniman gave Bertie one more assessing look, and said, 'I've still got a couple of bottles of that claret left. I'll send one up to you with the rations tonight.'

'Thanks, old man, but I'd sooner you kept it until we can drink it together. It's too good not to share.'

'Fair enough,' said Fenniman. 'We'll make that a date.' And he raised his hand and hurried away to join the colonel.

The new orders came up that afternoon, for an attack the next morning, and Bertie was busy all the rest of the day, looking over the ground, inspecting the men and briefing his officers. He noted that Major Fenniman would be commanding C Company on his left – so the old war horse couldn't resist the smell of the gunpowder! There was a note scrawled in pencil in Fenniman's hand at the bottom of the sheet: 'And I'll be in Scotland afore ye!' Bertie smiled to himself.

Later that evening he was in his dug-out alone, sitting on his wonky chair at his box table, finishing the paperwork for the day, when he became belatedly aware of a conversation going on outside. The sentry and a pal had been talking in low voices for some time, and Bertie had not heeded it; but now another man arrived and joined in. The urgency in his voice caught Bertie's attention, and the words sprang out of the background of sound, clear and sharply etched.

'Did you 'ear? The sarge said it's just come in. Forward HQ got clobbered by one o' theirs, a big 'un. Coal-box, it was. 'Ot-Water got off with a 'eadache, but Winderpane caught a packet.'

'Blimey! Who's going to tell 'Yde Park?' Everyone in the battalion knew about ole Winderpane and 'Yde Park being best chums.

Bertie's head was up, his ears straining, but someone else had come up and silenced the group. And then Cooper was in the opening, his head ducked under the low ceiling to look at him. The truth was in his face. 'How bad?' Bertie asked.

Cooper had no option. He wished he could stand to attention, but he had to speak bent ludicrously at the shoulders. 'Dead, sir.'

Bertie tried to speak, but only a sort of click issued from his throat.

Cooper went on. 'The CO and Major Fenniman was just coming out to go along the line when a coal-box come right down where they was standing. The colonel's got a concussion – they reckon he'll be all right. Major Fenniman was killed. Blew his head and one of his arms right off.' He waited, but Bertie still could not speak; and so he added, of his pity – something Cooper rarely felt towards any living thing – 'He wouldn't have known nothing about it, sir. Most likely.'

The next day, just before four in the morning, they launched their new attack. The morning was damp and misty, though not actually raining, but cold for August. The going was heavy underfoot, and the shell holes were still half full of water, making them useless for cover; but after a brief but fierce battle they captured the German line and surged through Saint-Julien, taking a couple of hundred prisoners and clearing the entire village. The prisoners seemed as dispirited by the rain as anyone, and almost glad to be out of the fight now, with the prospect of getting dry and being fed. The colonel – who had recovered sufficiently to follow, if not to lead, the attack – thought about following up the advantage, but the rain came on heavily again, and the Germans were shelling the ground ahead from one of their lines further back, so it seemed sensible to consolidate what they had before moving again.

By evening Bertie found himself in another cellar, this time much more extensive and having proper headroom. He wondered if it was the cellar of that same farmhouse where he had been briefed by General Alderson two years ago. The upper structure was too badly damaged to be recognisable. It was wet underfoot, but the Germans, who had been using it until today, had cut a trench across the floor to carry the water away so it was not actually flooded. They had also left some furniture – a kitchen table, badly scarred, and a couple of kitchen chairs, along with some empty boxes for use as stools or lockers.

He was going through the casualty lists for the day when Cooper came in, looking uncomfortable. 'A runner just come over from the CO with this for you,' he said, and produced from behind his back a bottle of wine. Bertie looked at it blankly. 'Apparently Major Fenniman'd tole him he was going to give it to you, so the colonel thought you ought to have it.'

The bottle they ought to have drunk together, Bertie thought. He made no move to take it, and at last Cooper put it down on the table. He looked at Bertie sidelong, hesitating on the brink of some communication which, presumably, he thought would be unwelcome.

'Spit it out,' Bertie said testily. What next? he wondered.

'Well, sir, it occurred to me – the War Office won't inform the young lady, sir. Only the next o' kin.'

Ah, yes. He was right. Emma ought to be told, but the army wouldn't do it. 'Damn you, Cooper,' Bertie said miserably.

'More than likely, sir,' Cooper acknowledged. 'Pen and paper?'

CHAPTER SIXTEEN

The hour of departure from Tsarskoye Selo was set for one o'clock in the morning on the 1st of August, which meant no-one got any sleep that night. Deciding what to take, packing, disposing of other articles, saying goodbye to servants and friends who weren't coming went on all night. Knowing that they were very unlikely to see this place again, or anything or anyone they left behind, meant constant anxiety and floods of tears. At last by midnight everything was done and the family assembled in the semi-circular hall, the girls sitting on their trunks, the Empress, who could not walk far now, in her wheelchair, the dogs dozing fitfully under chairs, Nicholas walking about nervously, talking in a low voice to his attendants and constantly asking the guards when they would be leaving.

It was six in the morning and the sun was coming up by the time they finally left. The Alexander had never looked more beautiful, honey-coloured in the rising sun, reflected in the still water of the lake like a fairytale palace. Everyone was too exhausted by then to cry much. The Tsar said, 'Thank God we are all going together,' and that seemed to sum it up. After the anxieties of the past months, the repeated threats of being separated, the unspoken dread of imprisonment and trial, the insulting behaviour of the guards and the constant spying, they were almost glad to be going and, most of all, relieved to be still together.

At the Alexandrovsky station the train was waiting, disguised as a Red Cross train, and flying the Japanese flag – safety measures that proved how restless the country at large now was. The journey was desperately slow, and inside the carriages it was stifling, hot and airless. When they passed through stations or towns they were ordered to keep their curtains pulled shut; but when the train stopped in the open country they were allowed out to walk, and the girls picked berries, and flowers for their mother's compartment.

Strangely, it was a time of happiness for Thomas. Etiquette and strict chaperonage had been left behind at Tsarskoye Selo. Nicholas and Alexandra were too disheartened by the move to care about anything much other than each other, and Alexei's health; the various attendants and tutors had given up their functions for the moment, so Thomas was able to sit and talk to Olga as much as he liked, and walk with her when they were allowed out. They discussed the places they were travelling through, Russia's history and folk traditions, debated the effect of the Slavic influence on the people and the culture. Their other constant topic of conversation was England: she loved to ask him questions about it and have him tell his memories. To her it was a Nirvana: the place her mother had grown up, the place of gentleness and freedom.

'Will we go there?' she asked him, just once.

'Yes,' he said. 'I'm sure of it.'

'Are you?' Her troubled eyes searched his face.

'I am not at liberty to tell you everything – I am bound to secrecy – but they have promised me. There are ways. If the direct fails, there is the indirect. You understand?'

'I think so,' she said.

'But you must not tell anyone even as much as I have told you. No-one can be trusted – no-one at all.'

She glanced over her shoulder at the rest of her family, gathered in the parlour-car about their various pursuits. She understood him. 'I shall tell no-one. This is between you and me, Thomas Ivanovitch.'

'Thank you, Princess.'

She smiled at that. 'Not any longer. I am plain Olga Nicholaevna now.'

'Not plain – never that,' he murmured, and saw her colour.

'I'm glad you came with us,' she said, very low. 'Will you stay with us until we go to England?'

'You know I will.'

'Oh, I hope it is soon!' she said. She met his eyes, and he saw that, hope and dreams notwithstanding, she understood the continuing peril of their situation.

After several days on the train they reached Tiumen, on the river Tur, and here they transferred to a steamer, called *Russia* – inconvenient, smelly and cramped. It took them up the Tur and into the river Tobol, which was wider and more pleasant. The air was fresher, too – cool in the morning but pleasantly warm in the afternoon, and they were able to sit out on deck, which was infinitely preferable to the cabins. Two days later, at six thirty in the evening, they arrived at Tobolsk. A crowd of townspeople was waiting at the jetty, and greeted them with cheers and smiles, which was very encouraging.

'They like us!' said Anastasia, waving vigorously.

Prince Dolgorukov and Thomas went ashore and were taken by the local commissar to see the accommodation. The white, square, two-storeyed governor's mansion was to be the family's residence, with another house across the street – the Kornilov house, painted pink, larger and more decorative – for the rest of the suite. The accommodation was large enough, but the buildings had not been prepared in any way: they were dirty, dilapidated and lacking any furniture. It was impossible for anyone to move into them.

'Provincial governments were always inefficient,' Dolgorukov remarked to Thomas as they made their way back to the steamer with the news, 'and they won't be any less so now they are run by the "workers".'

'But the people seemed friendly,' Thomas said. As he

passed through the crowds he listened anxiously for their comments, but he heard nothing resentful. They seemed genuinely pleased and excited to be playing host to the imperial family. The short hair of the grand duchesses had caused some eager speculation – the leading ladies of the town had been sure this must be the new style in Petersburg. He wondered if they would all be sporting cropped heads in the near future. 'The revolution doesn't seem to have reached as far as Tobolsk,' he said.

'True,' said Dolgorukov, 'but you know, my dear Thomas, that it's the soldiers they send to guard us who really matter. They can make our lives pleasant or impossible.'

The imperial party remained on the cramped steamer for more than a week, while the rooms of the two houses were cleaned and painted, furniture was installed, and a few comforts that had been requested were acquired – such as a piano for the girls, and proper beds with spring mattresses for the Empress and the Tsar, who could not sleep on camp beds like their children. It was hotter and more unpleasant than ever on the steamer, now that she was not moving and there was no passage of air. Alexei and Marie both caught summer colds. Alexei's arm swelled, making them fear a haemorrhage; and one of the tutors, Pierre Gilliard, came down with a strange fever accompanied by a skin rash, which kept him confined to his bunk. Everyone was extremely glad when the house was ready at last and they could go ashore.

It was pleasant at first, having the extra space, a proper dining-room and drawing-room, their own things around them. Everyone's spirits rose, and they would have been perfectly happy if only they had been allowed to go walking in the woods or along the riverbanks in this hot weather: the garden of the governor's mansion was small, bare and dusty. In the first few days there was much coming and going between the governor's mansion and the Kornilov house, and everyone enjoyed the freedom. The Kornilov house had balconies on the upper floor, which caught the fresher air and were pleasant to sit out on. However, this freedom did not last. The townspeople's interest in the imperial family had not waned, and there were always crowds hanging about Freedom Street, as the main street was now called, hoping for a glimpse of them. The cheers and applause that greeted any member of the family sitting out on the balcony or seen at a window caused consternation to their guardians. After a few days, a tall wooden fence was erected around the house to keep the crowds at a distance. It enclosed a small side-street, which became, with the garden, the compound in which they must take all their exercise. Free traffic between the two houses ceased. Any of the suite wishing to visit the governor's mansion had to ask permission and be signed in and out; and the family was not allowed to pass outside the fence.

On his first visit after the fence was erected, Thomas saw the difference in their spirits. All the girls seemed tense and anxious; and Olga came to him, laid a hand on his arm, and whispered, 'They have closed us in. Now we are really prisoners.'

The days passed slowly, encircled with tedium. The girls read, sewed, drew and painted, and took lessons with the various tutors, more to pass the time than because anyone expected to benefit from them. Out of doors, in their limited space, they did what they could to keep active, walking round and round a circle until they had worn a track in the dirt; jumping on the spot and swinging their arms, sawing and chopping wood – a great deal of the latter, knowing what the Siberian winter would be like if they were still here then. Alexei was rarely outdoors, seeming to be ill much of the time. The cold he had caught kept coming back, and he suffered from pains in his joints, which confined him to bed and worried his parents constantly.

Olga did a painting of a white cottage with a thatched roof and hollyhocks and roses in the garden, and gave it to Thomas: her vision of England, and the expression of her painful hope that one day they would be allowed to go there, to freedom. All the girls were growing thin, except Anastasia, who covered her fear and confusion by eating everything she could put hand to, and by reverting to a very childish state of mind, talking in a babyish way, playing silly pranks, forgetting all she had learnt in her lessons, even forgetting how to spell. They all did their best to get on with the guards, and managed to win over most of them, so that they behaved with a modicum of kindness and civility.

The Tsar joined in the outdoor exercise, and when indoors he read, wrote his diary and many letters (which were censored), and sometimes read aloud to his daughters while they sewed. The Empress hardly left her room, shutting herself away with her memories and her photographs and her prayers. Nicholas and Alexandra grew old as the hopeless days passed in Tobolsk, grew grey and haggard and apathetic. Thomas felt, when he visited them, that they had given up: the palisade around the house had somehow finally cut them off from the hope of rescue. They expected now nothing but martyrdom for themselves, and in acceptance of their fate came a kind of peace, almost content.

But the children were young, and life was strong in them, and they suffered wretchedly from the imprisonment and the ever-present fear of what the future would hold. Thomas did all he could to amuse them, to encourage them and to give them hope, and when he was away from the house, he continued to work to bring about the rescue he had been promised. He remained hopeful: whatever the present, or any future, government of Russia might want to do with Nicholas, they could not wish harm to his innocent children. In fact, it was plainly in the government's interest to get them safely away, out of the country. Once a place had been found for them, he was sure the rescue plan would go into operation. But he was afraid of the advancing year. Once winter closed down the river, travel would be desperately difficult. He wrote his coded letters to Buchanan for transmission to London, urging them to do what had to be done to get the family out before the snows came; or, if not the family, at least the children.

A telephone call from Violet had Venetia hurrying over to St James's Square. Violet and Emma were in the small rear sitting-room. Emma looked shocked and bewildered: Venetia saw it had not properly come home to her yet. Violet was the one for whom the news was real. She had gone through it all herself only a year ago. Her mouth trembled as she met her mother's eyes.

Emma gave Venetia the letter to read. She scanned Bertie's careful words in his firm hand, saying that Fenniman had been shot through the heart by a rifle bullet and had died instantly. Of course, such things did happen, but not nearly as often as letters from the Front suggested. She knew it was the custom of the commanders in the line to make things easier for the families back home by writing of every death as instantaneous and without suffering – usually a bullet through the head or the heart. The reality was never so easy or so tidy. Venetia wondered how Fenniman had really died. She was surprised at how upset she felt, not just for Emma but because she had liked that young man very much. She hoped he really had not suffered. But, oh, God, this war!

She handed the letter back to Emma, who looked questioningly into her face as though she might tell her it was not true. 'I'm sorry, Emma,' she said. 'I know how hard this will be for you.'

'He's really dead,' Emma said, in a dazed way. 'I can't believe it.'

'My poor child, you'll believe it all too soon,' Venetia said gently.

'He wanted to marry me right away. Why didn't I do it? Why did I wait for a stupid wedding? I took him all the way to Scotland to see Uncle Bruce. I could have married him

378

in a register office right there and then. Why didn't I? Now we'll never – never—'

Her words faltered and failed, and her face seemed to collapse as realisation finally came and, with it, tears. Venetia opened her arms and Emma went to them. Her own eyes were full, for this motherless child who had lost her father, too, at womanhood's beginning, and now had lost her lover before even tasting marriage and the happiness of being together.

Violet turned away and left them, to walk to the window and stare out blindly at the warm damp day. Even the skies seemed ready to weep. The little dogs, sensing the atmosphere, ran to her and stood on their hind legs, reaching up to her anxiously. She didn't notice them. *Octavian*, she thought, and the pain in her throat was tremendous.

The children had already gone down to the country with Nanny and the nursery staff, to Brancaster for the summer. Violet had been planning to take them to the sea for a week later, perhaps to the Isle of Wight at the end of August or the beginning of September. Later that sad day, Venetia suggested the best thing for Emma was for her and Violet to go down to Brancaster right away.

'There's healing in being with children,' she said. 'London, with all its reminders of war, is no place to be just now – to say nothing of the air raids. Take Emma away, Violet, and stay away with the children for the rest of the summer.'

'I think you're right,' Violet said. 'London is horrid at the moment. And this is the best time of year for Brancaster. Would you be able to come?'

'Not at once. I might manage a few days later. I'd have to arrange my various duties, but I'm sure it can be done.'

'It would do you good. I don't think you've had a holiday in years,' Violet said.

Venetia almost laughed. 'Darling, people in my position don't have holidays. But I'm glad you're going. Of course, if you didn't like Brancaster, you could go to Yorkshire instead.' She owned a small estate, Shawes, whose boundaries ran alongside those of Morland Place.

'Yes, perhaps,' Violet said. 'I don't think Emma will want to see anyone just yet, but after a week or so, it might be just the thing.'

'That's settled, then,' Venetia said.

'But you will let me know at once if anything happens? Anything important?'

'I'll send a telegram, wherever you are,' Venetia promised.

Before Emma and Violet left for Brancaster, there were two visitors who were allowed through the barrier Violet had set up against callers. The first was Freddie Copthall.

'Oh, Freddie!' Violet cried, and was so pleased to see him she almost threw herself into his arms. 'What are you doing here?' She scanned him with quick, anxious eyes. 'You're not hurt?'

'No, no. Sound as a bell. Got a forty-eight-hour pass. Nothin' much doin' on our part of the line. Thought I'd pop home and see you. Then I heard about poor Emma's chap. Damn' shame. He was a decent feller. How's she holdin' up?'

'She's very low at the moment. We're going down to the country tomorrow, to Brancaster. I thought it would be better to take her away from London.'

'Gosh, yes. Too many chaps in khaki in London – hardly move for 'em. Frightful bad luck, Fenniman coppin' a packet like that. Rather knocks on the head the old story that HQ chaps are safe as houses. But shells can fall anywhere – and generally do,' he added thoughtfully.

'Shells? But Major Fenniman was shot through the heart by a rifle bullet,' Violet said.

Freddie regarded her steadily. 'Oh. Ah. Is that it? Must have got the story wrong. Not surprised. You know me – no brains at all, never had any. Good way to go, if you have to go – shot through the heart. Would have been instantaneous. He wouldn't have known anything about it.'

Violet nodded, relieved. 'That's what Bertie said. Come and see Emma now. It will cheer her up to see you.'

Emma was glad to see him; and as Violet invited him to stay for lunch, it was an excuse to get Emma to the table, too, where she ate a little without realising it, as she listened to him talking about his experiences in France. He kept them light, telling of the mistakes and absurdities, the jokes and pranks, and what they got up to when off duty, making it sound like a cross between Saturday afternoon at a public school and a Sunday on Southend beach. Of course, they had sent him to a quiet section of the line to begin with, in Picardy, but when he was leaving and Violet escorted him to the door, he told her privately that he expected his battalion to be moved some time next month.

'It's the way the brass hats keep us all sane,' he said. 'Everyone has to do a spell in the hot parts of the line, as well as the cushy ones. The rumour going round is that we'll have our turn in the Salient some time in September. Of course,' he added, seeing her look of concern, 'the heavy fighting could be over by then. We might just be relieving and holding the line.'

'Oh, Freddie!'

'Now, now, old thing, no waterworks. I'll be all right. Why would Fritz shoot at me? I'm no threat to anyone. As soon shoot a child's teddy-bear.'

She said, 'Oh, Freddie!' again, but this time it was with a smile. And she reached up and kissed his cheek in affection – something she had never done before – which sent him off as pleased as a dog with two tails, as he thought of it to himself.

The second visitor had rather more difficulty getting in, as the butler had never heard of him. It was a tribute to the visitor's determination that he forced the man in the end to go and mention his name to the ladies.

'Lord Knoydart?' Emma said. Heavy with sorrow, she seemed hardly able to lift her head. 'What is he doing here?' she said, without interest.

'Shall I have him sent away?' Violet asked. She wondered whether he had come courting Emma again. If so, it was terribly bad timing.

But Emma said wearily, 'I'd better see him, just for a moment. He must have come a long way.'

But it turned out that he had only come from the training camp at Aldershot. 'I was called up,' he explained. And then he went on quickly, as though he didn't want to talk on that subject. 'I came to offer my deepest condolences. I read about your engagement in the newspapers a while back, and I was happy for you. I thought of writing then, but I was afraid you might think it an impertinence. Then I saw Major Fenniman's name in the casualty lists yesterday. I can't tell you how sorry I am, Miss Weston. It must be a terrible blow.'

Emma nodded, unable to speak.

'Somehow one doesn't expect it to happen to one's own friends,' Knoydart said.

'I still can't believe it,' Emma said. 'It never crossed my mind for a moment that he might be – that he might—' She still could not say the words. Her eyes filled with tears again. 'I was such a fool,' she finished bitterly.

Knoydart said, 'I'm sorry. I shouldn't have come. I'll go now. I just wanted to tell you – well, that you have a friend in me, if there's ever anything I can do to serve you.' His words petered out awkwardly. 'I mean it with all my heart.'

Emma made a gesture with one hand, trying to control her tears. She was touched that he had called. 'Don't go,' she managed to say. 'I'll— Excuse me.' She hurried from the room.

Knoydart hesitated uncertainly, and Violet wondered what to do with him. Easiest to let him go; but Emma might come back and want to speak to him. She said, 'Do sit down, won't you?'

'Well – perhaps, just for a few minutes.'

It was up to Violet to make conversation. 'You timed your visit fortunately,' she said. 'We'll be going down to the country tomorrow, so you only just caught us.'

'I was surprised to learn you were still up,' he said, with an air of relief at this safe social topic. 'But I suppose the old habits are being changed now, because of the war.'

'Yes, a lot of people seem to be staying up,' Violet said. She was interested to see this fabled suitor of Emma's – a tall, slender young man, rather too slender, perhaps, but definitely handsome, with a fair, strong-featured face, and golden hair with a hint of red to it, cut very short, and a moustache to match. His chin was strong, his large, rather knuckly hands looked quiet and capable in his lap, his eyes were blue, with the long stare of the far country. Violet remembered that he came from a wild place of empty acres and storm-lashed coast. She could imagine him there, at one with the landscape. His voice was quiet and pleasant, and his accent was only slight – just enough to give an interest. Violet could see how he must be quite a catch in Scotland; she thought he would hold his own in London, too.

She asked him how long he had been in uniform.

'Oh, a long time, now. Since February, to be exact.' He blushed, the colour clashing with the copper in his hair. 'Well, you see, when Emma – Miss Weston – left Scotland, I had a word with some people, who knew some people in the War Office, to have my name moved further up the list,' he said. 'I felt – that is – it seemed to me . . . Well, I thought one ought to do one's bit,' he concluded awkwardly.

So Scotland had lost its savour for him? He must really have been in love with Emma. 'So what brought you to Aldershot?' she asked.

'Final training for the battalion before going overseas,' Knoydart said. 'The latest rumour says we'll be going to Egypt. There's important work to be done out there, too, but naturally everyone would prefer to be in France.'

'Naturally,' Violet said. Even Laidislaw, the gentle artist, had wanted it. They went, and they didn't come back.

Knoydart seemed to have read something of her thought.

He said gently, 'The sooner the Germans are beaten, the sooner the war will be over. We just want to get out there and do our part.' He stood up. 'I must take my leave. Thank you for seeing me, Lady Holkam. Please tell Miss Weston . . . Well, if there's ever anything I can do – if I can be of service in any way . . .'

Violet gave him her hand. 'I'll tell her. You are very kind. It was a pleasure to meet you, Lord Knoydart.'

Some time later Emma came back, her eyes red and her face swollen with tears. 'I'm sorry,' she said. 'I couldn't—'

'I know,' said Violet. 'He seems a nice young man.'

'I suppose so. I don't know.' Emma was sunk now in the lethargy of grief. After a while she said, 'If Uncle had had his way, I'd have been married to him by now. Strange thought. Oh, Violet,' and her eyes filled again, 'how do you bear it? You loved Octavian. How do you bear it when they're dead, when you'll never see them again?'

'I don't know,' Violet said. 'You just do. And one day—'

'Don't tell me I'll fall in love with someone else!'

'No. I was going to say, one day it will get easier. That's all.'

Emma shook her head. 'I don't want it to. It will mean I'm forgetting him, and I never want to forget him.' Violet took her hand, and they sat in silence for a while. 'His father doesn't acknowledge me. I have nothing of his to remember him by. I couldn't even go to his funeral. He's buried out there, like Octavian.'

Violet nodded, thinking of those lines about a corner of a foreign field being for ever England. All their men who had fallen, becoming as one with the land of France, for which they had given all a man had to give. Ploughed into the earth. What would grow there afterwards? The thought disturbed her and she shivered.

Emma looked up. 'When the war's over, can we go and visit the grave? Both of them?'

'Yes,' Violet said. 'When the war's over, we'll go.'

★　　★　　★

The next morning they went down to Lincolnshire, to Brancaster House, Holkam's seat. As they left London behind, Violet felt a lifting of her spirits. She was looking forward to seeing the children again – her mother was right, there was healing in being with them – and to tending her garden, a scheme she had started years ago and which did not get on very well, since she spent so little time there. Brancaster was an old and draughty house in the middle of fen country, and was bitterly cold in winter. But in summer it was pleasant, and she hoped that Emma would benefit from it.

Everyone at Morland Place felt Emma's loss. She had spent long and happy holidays there, and they were all very fond of her, and thought of her as one of their own. Polly was particularly shocked, having, like Emma, never allowed in her mind for such a thing happening. It almost felt as though God were cheating, killing Major Fenniman before they had even had a chance to get married. She thought of Lieutenant Holford with an alarm she had not felt before. Before he left for the Front she had agreed to write to him, though she was not sure her father would approve. Now she was determined to do it, in the face of whatever objections might be raised by her family.

Henrietta was grieved for Emma, but also for Bertie, knowing what a close friend Fenniman had been, aware that friendships like that did not come along often for men. She wrote inviting Emma to come and stay, urging her to get out of London and into the peace of the countryside. She received a reply from Violet, saying that Emma would write by-and-by, and that for the moment they were down at Brancaster.

Henrietta's letter-writing was increasing all the time – she had Robbie to write to now, as well as Jack, Jessie, Bertie, Lennie (because Polly was very erratic in replying to him) and her long-term correspondence with Venetia, and Lizzie in America. It took up so much of her time that she was glad to yield more of the household chores to Mary Tomlinson, whom she had come to value as much as Jessie had. She was tired and anxious all the time now, and was sleeping very badly, often awake all night and only falling asleep towards dawn. Then, after a couple of hours, the stirring of the household would wake her again. Helen, when she was home, urged her to have a nap in the afternoon to make up for it. 'My mother's been doing it for years,' she said. But Henrietta rejected the idea, slightly shocked. Only people who were ill in bed ought to sleep during the daytime. There was too much to do to waste the precious God-granted hours of the day.

Robbie was in Palestine, where General Allenby had recently taken over, having been moved from the Western Front after disagreeing with Haig over the conduct of the battle at Arras (this according to Venetia). In Palestine, the British troops were engaging the Turks, who were German allies, and had recently had some success. In July, the Australian Light Horse had captured Akaba, a strategic Gulf port, with the help of Arab irregular cavalry. The Arabs were rebelling against their Turkish overlords, and the British government was keen to foment this rebellion as a further way of harassing the Turks and, through them, the German Empire. The capture of Akaba had caught the public imagination because the Arab cavalry had been led by a British officer, an eccentric Intelligence major called Lawrence, a former Middle Eastern studies scholar, who had annoyed his superiors and delighted the newspapers by adopting Arab dress and riding a camel into battle.

Henrietta was guiltily glad that Robbie had not gone to France, though Maria had rather tactlessly told her that more soldiers died of disease in the eastern theatres than of battle wounds. Lennie was in Salonika, and since she tended rather to dismiss these places as not being the proper war, and therefore not so dangerous, she was glad to put them to the end of the list of people she had to worry about.

A new addition was Lizzie's son Martial, who had volunteered at the end of the college semester, along with his cousins Aubrey and Anderson Flint, and was now undergoing training at Camp Devens in Massachusetts. Lizzie had written about it to her mother in a mixture of pride and anxiety, glad that Mart wanted to fight for the old country, but half hoping the war would be over before he ever got anywhere near a German line. 'It must take at least six months to train them, don't you think? And even our boys who have already gone to France won't be ready for battle for months more, so Ashley tells me. So that means Mart wouldn't be put into a battle for something like a year, and surely the war will be over by then?'

Henrietta didn't worry too much about Jessie, for she understood that Étaples was a long way from the line. Jessie wrote regularly, and though it seemed she worked dreadfully long hours and was exposed to terrible sights, the only personal danger to her was from sickness or infection – things every person had to face no matter where they were.

It was Bertie and Jack Henrietta feared for most, Bertie in the thick of the fighting at the Salient (oh, and grieving for his little boy – what a terrible thing that was!) and Jack – well, everyone knew how dangerous it was to be a pilot in the RFC. It was Jack who kept her awake most nights, for there was never a time when they were out of the line (as soldiers regularly were) so that she could leave off worrying for a week or two. He might go up any day, and did go up most days, often several times. And flying was dangerous in itself, even without people shooting at him. She thought of him thousands of feet above the ground in one of those frail little aircraft, nothing but sticks and canvas held together with glue, which at any moment could fail and plummet to earth. A hundred times a day she saw him falling through the air, a tiny, helpless figure hurtling towards the unforgiving ground. Often when she fell asleep she would dream she saw him falling, falling, spinning slightly like a leaf as he went; and she would wake with a jerk and a gasp just before he hit the ground, and sit up, feeling sick.

The constant anxiety and the broken nights made Henrietta realise how much she lacked a friend. She was surrounded by family, but every woman needed a female friend, that one person to whom she could unburden herself with complete freedom. Jessie had Beta, and Henrietta was glad for her, knowing what a lonely life Jessie had led. At home, she saw the friendship between Maria and Helen strengthening. But for her there was no-one like that. Her daughters-in-law were of another generation; and fond though she was of Alice, there was no real spiritual bond between them. Alice, in any case, had her own friends.

No, it was Venetia she wanted. Violet had mentioned in her letter that her mother might join her and Emma for a short holiday. If Venetia was to leave London, Henrietta thought she might as well come to Yorkshire as to Lincolnshire. One morning, after a sleepless night, she came to a decision. She disliked and feared the telephone: apart from the unpleasantness of talking to someone who wasn't actually there, she could never suppress the fear that she would get an electric shock from it, through the ear and right into the brain. But nothing else would impress the urgency of her need to see her friend. She went to the steward's room and asked Maria, who was already there sorting through the post, to place a call for her.

Venetia was also an early riser so she was not afraid of waking her. The conversation was brief, but satisfactory. Venetia wanted to see her just as much, and Shawes would surely suit everyone's purposes as well as Brancaster. The children would be able to play with the Morland Place children, Emma and Violet could be as private or as sociable as the spirit moved them, and Venetia and Henrietta could talk to their hearts' content. It would take Venetia a couple of weeks more to arrange her affairs so that she could leave them, but early in September Henrietta might look for her in Yorkshire.

The battle at Ypres crept on through August, ground being gained almost at snail's pace. This was not quickly enough for Lloyd George, who wanted heroic breakthroughs and decisive victories with which to fill the newspapers and please the voters. He was a politician, not a soldier, and had no sympathy with Haig's view that the only way to win the war was to keep pounding away at the enemy. 'By these means, and only by these means, can we ensure final victory, by wearing out the enemy resistance,' Haig had told his generals, Gough and Plumer. This did not appeal at all to Lloyd George. Slow-and-steady might have won the race in fable, but Slow-and-steady did not have to stand for re-election. Why keep plugging away on the Western Front, when there might be victories to be won elsewhere? Haig, and his ally at the War Office, General Sir William 'Wully' Robertson, the Chief of Imperial General Staff, pointed out that however nice such victories might look in the official despatches, they did very little to shorten the war.

Lloyd George – and his unofficial military advisers, Lord French and General Sir Henry Wilson – felt that the British and French should merely hold the line until the Americans were ready, and meanwhile strike elsewhere – such as in Italy, where the Italian General Cadorna had been doing quite well against the Austrians. At the Rome Conference back in January, Lloyd George had promised to help the Italians; so now he proposed moving a hundred heavy guns and twelve British divisions from France to Italy.

Robertson managed to hold off this demand for the time being, but the proposal was far from dropped. And difficult as things were on the Western Front, it was only a matter of time before they got worse. Kerensky's fresh offensive of July on the Eastern Front had come to nothing, and now, in August, the Russian Army was in retreat, and suffering from wholesale desertions. How long could the Provisional Government keep Russia in the war? And when the Eastern Front collapsed, Germany would transfer its huge forces there to the Western Front. The idea that Britain could merely sit tight and wait for the Americans depended on the Germans kindly allowing them to do so by not attacking. It was a delusion.

Even if a breakthrough was not immediately possible at the Salient, it was important to keep attacking the Germans there and weakening them, and important that the high ground should be captured and the British position made stronger before the Eastern Front troops arrived. But Haig knew there had to be changes. General Gough was deeply unpopular with the other commanders and had no great reputation with the troops, and he had already told Haig that he did not believe success was possible in the Salient. Haig decided to change the roles of the Second and Fifth Armies. Gough's Fifth should take over the support role of defending the flank, while General Plumer's Second mounted the attack and advanced along the ridges to Passchendaele. But this exchange would take time, involving the removal of the heavy guns and other equipment from one command to the other; on the positive side, it would give the ground time to dry out, for now at last it had stopped raining and the sun had come out. So on the 22nd of August the offensive halted.

The West Herts came out of the line that night, and marched back to Poperinghe or, rather, stepped cautiously along the maze of duckboards and corduroy roads that transversed the sucking mud of Ypres. As soon as he had a moment Bertie scribbled a note to Jessie to say he was out and unharmed, following it with a slightly longer letter the next day, saying he wanted to come and visit her, and asking if she could get time off to coincide with it.

At the No. 24 General, the battle, though different in

nature, had been as unremitting since the 1st of August. Jessie sometimes felt like King Canute, helpless against a constant incoming tide of wounded Tommies, with shattered bodies, ripped bellies, hanging limbs, missing faces – a deluge of pain and blood. So many who came in were hopeless cases, and the knowledge that they could not be saved added an emotional strain to the physical hard work. Often they were the quietest patients, heartbreakingly co-operative and grateful. Jessie would feel their eyes following her as she moved around the ward, afraid to ask the question to which they already knew the answer. Rarely was there time to sit with them, and to their suffering was added the bitterness of dying alone, without a hand to hold or a human face to look at. Jessie, when finally released from the latest emergency, would find them gone, uncomforted, their fixed eyes staring at the ceiling.

By the 22nd of August, the flood had eased to a more manageable flow, and the matron had decreed the reinstatement of the normal off-time, for everyone was physically and emotionally worn out. When Bertie's letter arrived, Jessie took it to the charge-sister and received a considerate hearing. A cousin who was a DSO, a war hero, and who had not only lost his best friend but his little son to the Gotha bombings, was an object of admiration and sympathy. The sister was not only willing to give Jessie her day off at a time to suit Bertie's visit, but offered to make it up to a forty-eight-hour pass, if Jessie would work her daily three hours off in exchange until she had made up the time.

And the weather was warm, sunny and pleasant.

'What will you do with the time?' Beta asked her in the mess that evening. 'Take country walks, I suppose?'

'I imagine so. Or perhaps go into Paris-Plage, or walk along the beach.'

'What would you like most in the world, if you could do anything?' Beta asked. It was a frequent game of fantasy that all the nurses played – where would you most like to be, what would you have to eat if you could have anything in the world, who would you spend your day off with?

Jessie's answer was ready. 'Go riding,' she said. 'Bertie and I often used to ride together, back home.'

Beta said, 'That must have been nice. I'd love to see your home. I've never been to Yorkshire, but the way you describe it . . .'

'You must come and visit one day,' Jessie said. 'When the war's over.'

It was such a frequent suffix – 'when the war's over' – that it had almost lost meaning. On most days it was not possible to imagine that such a place existed.

CHAPTER SEVENTEEN

Bertie arrived in an open motor-car, which he had borrowed from an officer friend he had met in Poperinghe, who was going home on leave and didn't need it for a week. Jessie was waiting for him outside the mess hut as arranged. He pulled up and she came over to him. The gladness just to see him again was like a physical thing, a warmth and a rushing of blood; but she was shocked at how thin his face was, and how grim. That was until he smiled: then he looked like the same old Bertie – not exactly young again, but ageless, which was better, really.

His hand was resting on the top of the door, and she wanted to take it and press it to her cheek. Instead, she ran a finger along the chromium edging of the motor. 'How grand,' she said.

'As you've got two days, I thought perhaps we might go away, down the coast, stay in an hotel overnight,' he said. 'It would do you good to get away from here.' There was no hidden message in his eyes, but perhaps there was some reaction in hers. He added, 'They're all empty, these days, because of the war, so it will be easy to get two rooms.'

'I'd love it,' she said quickly, ashamed of herself for doubting him. But there was a word that was used here at Étaples: 'Paris-Plaging'. It referred to the custom of doctors and officers sneaking off to the resort of Paris-Plage with one of the nurses, hiring a room for an afternoon or evening.

If discovered, the nurses faced instant dismissal. The men concerned had nothing to fear, no matter what happened, so their motivation was clear; but for the nurses it seemed a case of love (or loneliness) conquering all, a great risk for so little reward – to say nothing of the tawdriness. She would not like to be thought one of them; but no-one could think badly of her for going off with the cousin with whom she had played as a child; and no-one, not even Beta, knew of her feelings for him.

'Run and pack a bag, then,' he said, smiling as if he had read her unspoken thoughts – and she would not have been surprised if he had. She hurried to the hut, put a few necessities into her valise, scribbled a note for Beta, who was on duty, and almost ran back to the motor, feeling such a lift of joy at the thought of the treat to come that she wanted to skip like a child.

They didn't talk much in the drive along the coast. Bertie drove slowly, for the pleasure of it. The white dusty road ran almost parallel to the sea, winding a little, between the sand dunes, tufted and bristling with marram grass, like an unshaven chin, and the flat green meadows where the large, placid cattle of northern France grazed among the brilliant coins of buttercups. The rising ground inland was fringed with sentinel pines, and patches of woodland, still dark green at the beginning of September, settled into the folds of the ground and spilt up the slopes – a curdle of treetops.

It was a beautiful day, with the soft, buttery sunshine of September. The sky was a milky blue, lightly fretted here and there with cloud; the sea was calm, gleaming like enamel, ultramarine fading to azure at the horizon. The tang of salt was in the air, clean and exhilarating after the hospital stinks. Jessie drew it in, feeling as if it were the first deep breath she had taken in weeks.

Beyond the dunes there was a wide strip of beach all the way from Paris-Plage to the Baie d'Authie – miles and miles of perfect, empty sands, where for generations Parisians and other northern town dwellers had taken their summer holidays. They were empty now. Summer holidays were a thing of the past. It was hard to imagine that there would ever again be anything so innocent here as children flying kites and making sandcastles.

But for now, the emptiness was a blessing for someone who spent her days surrounded by all too many bodies. Jessie drank in the peace like a thirsty plant. Beyond the quiet rumble of the motor's engine there were no sounds of humanity.

'I can hear a skylark,' she said, twisting round to see where the sound was coming from. Yes, there it was, a tiny dot hanging above the meadow. 'Why do they *do* that? So much effort from such a tiny creature. I suppose it's only we humans who translate it as joyful.'

'Perhaps it is joyful,' he said. 'After all, it must be grand to be able to fly up there in the clean air and make such a wonderful noise.'

'When I was little, I used to think they were singing to God,' she said. 'Trying to get up high so He could hear them better.'

Bertie thought of how the larks above no man's land went on singing right through a battle when the air was full of artillery shells. The thought that while they sang so desperately, their nests below were being smashed by the passage of the battle was suddenly somehow too much to bear, and he had to turn his mind away from it. In such tiny things the sorrow of war hid, and ambushed you.

Instead, he said, 'It's amazing to me, how quickly one gets away from the war.' She looked a query at him. 'All along the Front everything is destroyed for a mile or so on either side, a strip of ruined land, shell holes, tree stumps, rubble. And then there's a wider strip with army camps dotted about it, ammunition dumps, artillery parks, airfields, and so on. Villages packed with soldiers out on rest. A whole world where everything is the army. But then go a mile

395

further on, and there's no sign of it. You can't even hear the guns.'

'We can sometimes,' she said, 'when the wind's in the right direction. It sounds like someone slamming doors, over and over again.'

Bertie nodded. 'It's so peaceful here,' he went on. 'It's hard to believe that this and the Front can exist within a few miles of each other. It makes it seem even more like an insanity.'

'I know what you mean,' she said.

He glanced at her. 'You see the results of it – more, probably, than we do.' They had both seen things that no human being ought to have to see. But today was not the day to think about them. He turned off the road, bumping along for a few yards over the rough surface before stopping where the dunes rose up as a barrier. 'Let's go and walk on the beach,' he said. 'I want to see the sea.'

'Then I must take off my shoes and stockings,' she said. 'I've been longing to feel the sand between my toes ever since we started.'

He smiled indulgently as she struggled discreetly on the far side of the motor from him, then emerged with bare toes triumphantly on display. 'You have very pretty feet,' he said. 'And nice ankles.'

'You've never paid me compliments before,' she said. 'It must be the sea air, going to your head.'

'The air is wonderful, isn't it?' he agreed, as they trudged up the dune, across the top and down the other side on to the wide, flat shore.

'And the light,' Jessie said. There was so much of it, filling the whole hemisphere of sky and earth, as though it were the air itself that gave off radiance.

'Artists used to come here just for the light,' Bertie said. 'Manet, Turner, Roussel, Eugène Boudin. They called it the Opal Coast.'

'I can imagine Turner painting here. He'd have liked the skies.'

'And then there were the invalids, who came for the sea air. The Empress Eugénie opened a big hospital at Berck. There were sanatoria dotted all up and down this coast.'

'Artists and invalids. Quite a crowd.'

'And rich holidaymakers, who built the grand villas. It was a very fashionable spot before the war.'

'Before the war,' Jessie said. 'I'm not sure I believe in that place any more.'

They had walked down to the water's edge. The waves were expiring politely, turning over with hardly a sigh in a ruffle of white, like a lace edging to a petticoat. The wet sand shone as though polished, darker than the dry sand above – as a chestnut horse's coat will darken when it's wet, Jessie thought. She longed suddenly for horses, to ride as they used to 'before the war'. It would be wonderful to gallop a horse along this flat sand.

They turned and walked along parallel to the waves, leaving footprints – one set bare and toe-fringed, the other booted, square-heeled. Just above the wet sand was a line of sea-debris, dried seaweed, empty crab claws, a mass of white shells like broken crockery. She wanted one to take away with her, for a souvenir, and began idly hunting through them as they walked along, picking up and discarding. He helped her, finding unbroken specimens and handing them to her for approval. He was amused and charmed at the seriousness of her endeavour. She collected and examined them as gravely as a child. The light, salt breeze stirred her hair – the unruly curls around the edges that would never lie down tidily – and the sun shone through them, creating a blurred golden aureole. He wanted so much to kiss the crown of her head.

When she had selected four perfect shells from the multitude, she put the rejected ones carefully down, as though not to hurt their feelings. He received the shells from her and put them in his pocket for safety, then took her hand and drew it through his arm, and they walked on like that.

God, it felt good! Jessie thought. His arm under her hand, the solidness of his body close to hers. She loved him with all her heart and soul, but her body loved him too, and it had suffered a long and grievous absence. She looked up at the face she knew better than her own, and saw how the strain and sadness of the last three years had sunk deep into it. There were lines of melancholy now as well as of firmness, and they would never go away.

She supposed she must be as changed to him as he was to her. All of them at the hospital had learnt to develop a kind of mental barrier which they put up against the hideous sights and bitter suffering they daily witnessed. It enabled them to function in a world of agony, but nothing in life was without price. Youth and innocence and youth's confiding frankness were paid down and used up; and these small jewels of happiness were hard won – and the more precious for it.

As so often before, his thoughts had kept pace with hers, and when he spoke, it was to say, 'We have to make the most of moments like this. Remember how before the war we had so much – hours and days at a time, great stretches you could hardly see to the end of? Time to spare: you could spend it without thinking, because there was always more to be had. And even when bad things happened, you felt they were the exception to the rule.'

'I remember,' she said.

'Now happiness is Cooper bringing me a mug of tea, or a spoonful of chutney to make the bully beef more interesting, or a copy of the *Magnet* I've not read before. When every day brings fresh horror, you get along by such tiny things. It's pitiful for grown men to live like that. And the worst thing is that we've grown used to it, we accept it. You can't fight it, when it's all there is.' He walked on a little in silence, and then said, 'No, that's not the worst thing. What was I thinking?'

She said hesitantly, 'I'm so sorry about Richard. And Fenniman.'

He shook his head. 'I can't think about Richard. I can feel him like a piece of shrapnel in my brain, but I daren't touch it or even look at it. I'm afraid of what would happen if I did. But Fenniman – oh, God, Jess, I miss him so much! We were together from the beginning, from the first day I arrived at the West Herts barracks. Winderpane, the men called him, because of his monocle. At the start I thought him mannered but amusing – a lightweight. But when I got to know him . . .' He shook his head. 'He was the truest soul.'

'He was your friend,' she said. 'I know how you loved him.'

They walked on a little, and he resumed: 'All my luck is used up. Of all of us from the beginning, there's only me now, and Pennyfather back home, who'll never walk again; and among the men, there's Cooper and three or four others. That's all. You can count us on your fingers. They call us Mons Men, those of us who've survived from the very beginning. I catch our own Mons Men sometimes looking at each other, wondering who will be next. A man only has so much luck in his life, and when he's used it all up . . .'

'Don't say that,' she begged.

'I don't think I can survive, Jess,' he said, looking down at her. 'I've had a long run, but it can't last much longer. My luck will run out, and that will be that. I'm not afraid. I've accepted it now. I only hope when the end comes it will be quick. But ever since the beginning of this latest offensive, I've known deep down that I won't make it through to the end of the war.'

'Bertie—'

'This is my third time in the Salient. I fought at First Ypres and Second Ypres. It's not reasonable to send a man there for a third time, but there's no reason in war. So this is our little bit of time together, before the end. I'm so glad the weather is fine for us.'

It was those last words that made her cry, but only inside.

She had controlled everything for so long she felt as if there was no mechanism in her any more for crying. She pressed his arm, and he laid his hand over hers, big and warm. She did not want to think of a world in which that warm hand did not exist. Yet she knew that he was right, and that all the chances were against him.

'Bertie,' she began again, 'I—'

But he forestalled her. 'I had to tell you,' he said. 'But let's not dwell on it. Let's not be sad today. Let this be our perfect day that we'll remember – as long as memory lasts. Can we do that? Be happy, in spite of everything?'

'Yes,' she said. 'I was only going to say, I love you.'

'I love you too,' he said. 'So much.'

They went back to the motor and she put on her shoes and stockings, allowing him to crouch down first and brush the sand from her feet tenderly. It did not seem the time to worry about conventional modesty. Then they drove to the hotel. It was called Le Manoir des Pins, and was built up on the higher ground behind the village of Berck, which was at the southern end of that long, long stretch of sand and dunes and sky. Bertie explained that it had been one of the many private villas built by rich men as a holiday house, to take advantage of the sea air and bathing; but when the money had run out, there was no choice for the family but to turn it into an hotel.

The road up to it wound under the cool shade of pine and birch trees; and at the top the house sat in a sunny clearing, a typical nineteenth-century villa with mock-Tudor beams, but with large windows and a red mansard roof. Fine old trees stood around it, a cypress, a walnut, a copper beech, and the inevitable monkey-puzzle; while the top of a magnificent cedar could be seen peeking over the roof from the garden behind.

Jessie stepped into the cool, silent hall, feeling rather shy and a little defensive, with 'Paris-Plaging' still on her mind, afraid that she might meet with coldness and veiled contempt. But there were not enough guests in these hard times for the owners to look askance at any; and they had booked separate rooms, after all. The proprietor himself came out to meet them, a small, balding, bespectacled man, who ought to have been round but was not, though from the way his suit hung on him, it seemed he once had been. He greeted them and spoke to Bertie in impenetrable French – impenetrable to Jessie, anyway, though Bertie seemed to understand him all right, and answered in a French that was a long way from the schoolroom. Three years at the Front had done him *some* good, after all. When they had both signed the register, the proprietor struck the bell on the desk and a very young boy – he could not be more than fourteen, Jessie thought – appeared to carry their bags for them.

'Shall we have luncheon here?' Bertie asked her, on a thought. 'It's getting late, and the food is supposed to be very good.'

The patron cheered up at the news that they wanted to eat, and became quite animated in discussion with Bertie, ending up with a bow from the waist, and a sharp command to the boy, which he apparently questioned and had repeated.

'What was that about?' Jessie asked, amused, as they followed the boy up the stairs.

'I asked if we could have something simple, but he seemed to see it as a challenge to his culinary skills. I hope he won't go to too much trouble.'

The boy, who was dark-haired and thin, with a haunted melancholy of face that made Jessie wish she could paint, showed them silently to two rooms on the first floor. They were large, high-ceilinged and airy, and each had french windows overlooking the garden, with a little ornate railing on the outside and a balcony just big enough to put a foot on. They were furnished with Louis Quinze pieces in grand style, Jessie's in pink and white and Bertie's in green and white, with large ornate wardrobes, swagged drapes, gilt-framed mirrors, escritoire, table and chairs, sofa and chaise-longue, and in each a vast bed with a white counterpane.

'It's too much,' Jessie said.

'I didn't ask for anything this grand. I suppose it's because we're the only people here, and he thought we might as well use these as any.'

'I think he changed his mind after you spoke to him about lunch,' Jessie said, remembering the sharp command to the boy. 'You must have won his heart.'

Bertie look dismayed. 'I hope we don't have to wait hours while he produces a meal to match the room, and then have to spend hours eating it. I don't want to sit long indoors on a lovely day like this.'

But the proprietor had thought of that, for they were called to a table laid on the terrace at the back, looking over the garden, which was bright with sunshine and fragrant with pine and mimosa, busy with birds hopping in and out of the bushes and bees gorging in the lavender that grew by the old, crumbling path.

'Oh, this is delightful,' Jessie said.

It was perfect peace, with the war far away, to rest in just such a garden as they might have known in that other life, with a long lawn down to the cedar tree, and a pale pink rose scrambling over the face of the house and dropping petals on the terrace, and no sound but the chirping of the birds and a distant, muted symphony of saucepans and voices coming from the open window of the kitchen somewhere round the side. An old black dog with blue-filmed eyes came and inspected them politely, with a slow wag of the tail, then flopped down on the warm stones in a sunny patch a little way off. A striped cat emerged from the bushes and walked importantly across the lawn, tail up, stepping high like a horse between the daisies, and disappeared into the shadows on the other side.

Jessie and Bertie talked of old times, of home, of horses,

of all the good, sweet ordinary things that cousins share, and they ate with simple relish the well-judged meal the patron and his wife had prepared for them: large, tender prawns in a delicate pink sauce, an omelette *aux fines herbes* with fried potatoes, a salad of tomato and cucumber in a good, sharp dressing. The sad boy, transformed by a long white apron into a waiter, cleared the table and laid on crusty home-made bread, printed butter, a fine local cheese, and a dish of peaches and sweet white grapes. It was the perfect culmination, and they lingered over it, talking quietly as the shadows moved and lengthened into afternoon.

Afterwards they went out again, walked down to the village, or rather small town, of Berck. In the last century it had been a thriving seaside resort with trams, a theatre, promenades and restaurants, and had running water, electricity and telephones well before their time. Its clientele of middle-class French holidaymakers had come to sit on the sand and paddle in the sea, or the more energetic to play golf or ride up among the pines and lawns of the higher ground behind the town; and there were hundreds of chronic or self-diagnosed invalids who patronised the many 'medical' institutes. The Empress Eugénie's Maritime Hospital still overlooked the sea, like a huge barracks with iron balconies.

But all was quiet now, the holidaymakers missing, many cafés and restaurants closed, the trams no longer running, the sands empty, the valetudinarians apparently cured by the worse affliction of war. The theatre was boarded up, and along the promenade the strings of lights that swung gently in the breeze had many broken or missing bulbs. It felt melancholy to Jessie, and perhaps Bertie felt the same, for he turned his steps to the beach, and they walked again along its timelessness, not talking much now; in harmony with each other, but resting from words.

On the horizon, a number of red-brown sails appeared, and they stopped and turned seawards to look at them.

'Are they fishing-boats?' Jessie asked.

'Yes,' he said. 'I think they must be the local fleet. Somebody told me there were about a hundred boats still working out of Berck.'

'How so? There's no harbour, as far as I can see.'

'No, it's rather remarkable. They have flat bottoms, and when they come in they just run themselves up the beach, and unload the fish from there.'

'How on earth do you know all this about the coast and the town and so on?' she marvelled.

'Oh, one of my officers used to spend his summers here before the war. Getting him to *stop* telling you about it is the harder trick.'

'I love the colour of the sails,' she said. 'I suppose they don't show the dirt so much as white ones.'

Now Bertie laughed. 'My dear idiot, you can't think fishermen worry about having dirty sails!'

'Oh – well – I suppose not. But I do like them, anyway. They look so handsome against the blue of the sky.'

'The fishermen from Romney Marsh use red ones, too. Things like that make you realise how close England and France really are to each other.'

'And yet we've had all those wars with the French, all through history.'

'Neighbours will quarrel,' he said. 'But at least we're friends now.'

She saw his face change, and was angry with herself for mentioning war again. Now his thoughts were troubled. She stood in front of him, took hold of his hands and shook them a little to make sure of his attention. 'Don't be sad,' she said. 'Not now – not yet.'

He looked down at her, unsmiling, for a long moment. Then he said, 'There's something else I have to tell you. I didn't tell you before because – oh, it seemed too shabby and pitiful. But you ought to know.'

He told her about Maud.

She heard him in silence, hardly knowing what she felt

404

about it – what she dared feel about it. 'You had no idea?' she said at last, when he seemed to want some response from her.

'I don't think there was anything to know,' Bertie said. 'Manvers was just a friend, until Maud went to Ireland after Richard's death. She says so, and I believe her.'

'I met him,' Jessie said. 'I liked him. I thought him a nice man. Very attractive, too – strong and manly.'

'I suppose that's what she fell in love with,' Bertie said.

She leapt to his defence. 'You're strong and manly. No-one more so!'

'But I wasn't there. And she blames me for Richard's death.'

'How dare she?' Jessie said angrily.

'She's just lost her child. I don't suppose a mother in that situation thinks logically about it.'

And Jessie remembered how Ned had blamed her when she had miscarried after the bombardment of Scarborough. She turned her mind from the memory. Too much pain everywhere. 'What will you do?' she asked.

'Maud wants me to let her divorce me.'

'But how can she?'

'It's an accepted convention when couples want to divorce,' he explained to her: it was not something that had ever come in her way before. 'The man pays a girl – a show-girl or a waitress or someone like that – to go to a hotel with him, and they arrange to be "discovered" in bed together by one of the staff. There are hotels that specialise in it. Then the member of staff bears witness in court, and the judge grants the divorce on grounds of adultery.'

'But how horrible!' she said.

'I warned you that it was tawdry. But of course it wouldn't do for the man to cite his wife in these cases. It would ruin her. No gentleman would do that.'

'How could she ask it? How could she let you even—?' Her indignation on his behalf faltered at the discovery that she was hating Maud, and she had set herself never, never to do that. And was it not a case of 'there but for the grace of God'? If Maud loved Lord Manvers half as much as Jessie loved Bertie, she could understand the temptation. She, Jessie, had held out, but it had been hard, so hard, and she might have fallen at any moment. She had nothing to congratulate herself for. Violet had fallen. And there were all those Paris-Plagers, trying to snatch a little happiness out of the rubble war left behind.

Bertie was watching the struggle in her face, and now said sadly, 'I don't blame her, Jess. You know how often I've said to you that I should never have married her. I did my best and she did her best, but now she has a chance to be happy. I can't blame her for wanting to take it. And I hope she *will* be happy.'

'But you have to – do that tawdry thing?'

He shook his head. 'She wanted me to put it in train as soon as possible, but nothing like that could be arranged until I got home anyway. And I don't think it will be necessary. I shan't do anything, because I will be releasing her soon in a way that saves both our reputations.'

She knew what he meant, and her face was stricken. 'Oh, God, Bertie, no. Don't talk like that.'

'I can't help it,' he said and, taking her hand again through his arm, turned and walked along the sands with her. 'The thing that hurts me,' he went on, 'the thing that tears at me, is the irony of it. After all we've been through, you and I, after all we've suffered through being apart – now this happens, and it's too late. You and I could have had a life together after the war, if only I could have survived it. But I know I won't.'

'Perhaps you will,' she said desperately.

'I don't want to hope,' he said. 'It hurts too much. You know the odds are against it.'

She did know. Ned and her brother Frank, and all those Tommies who had passed through her hands at No. 24 General told her so. Laidislaw told her so. Fenniman – he above all – told her so.

'I'm not afraid,' he said. 'And I don't regret anything, except leaving you. I've seen too much, lost too much. I'm tired – I think it's that, most of all.' She nodded. She knew that tiredness. 'You are all there is in the world that I care for now. And it breaks my heart to leave you,' he finished quietly, 'but there's no help for it.'

They walked on the beach past the end of the village, then left the sand to come back along the road. At the end of the village, there was a large cross, raised on a grassy mound beside the road. On it hung an almost life-size figure of the Christ, the face twisted in agony, the head tilted and eyes rolled up in hopeless supplication. Many of the villages in these parts had them, and they were always depicted in the same way – perhaps even carved by the same artist. The starkness of them affected Jessie every time she saw one. For this Christ, there was no comfort or pity: never the peace of the tomb or quiet death, only the endless torment, hanging there for ever. What harsh religion was it that made this its point and focus? And yet it seemed to her sometimes it was a fit symbol for this war, in which, likewise, they must struggle on, unredeemed, the world contorted in an agony that had no end.

The little breeze had died down, and a calm, fair evening was promising. The sun was going down in a pink sky ribbed with liquid gold. Gulls were wheeling about overhead, crying plaintively. Somewhere, someone had lit a bonfire: a feather of blue haze hung on the air, and the smell of dry woodsmoke seemed a good, wholesome English smell, the essence of autumn.

'I'm sorry. I've made you sad again,' Bertie said. 'It wasn't what I wanted.'

She looked up at him. 'I'd sooner be sad with you than happy anywhere else.'

'We shan't be sad again today,' he decreed. 'Listen to those gulls! I wonder why they're suddenly so excited.'

They discovered the reason round the next bend. The fishing-boats, which they had forgotten about, had come in, and the catch was being unloaded on the beach. A trestle had been set up and some of the men and one or two women were gutting fish, throwing the offal to the quarrelsome gulls. People from the town had come down to buy, some for their own table, others in bulk for restaurants and shops. A donkey teetered past on its improbable tiptoes, pulling a flat two-wheeled cart piled high with boxes; a stout woman laboured up the sands with a massive creel on her back; a maid in a cap had a basket on her arm, with two large fish shawled in newspaper.

They stopped to watch the activity, as anyone would, leaning on the rails of the promenade, raised above the beach. An old man in workman's clothes was leaning beside them, smoking an atrocious pipe – which, however, did something to mask the atrocious smell of himself. He nodded to them as they arrived; and after a sufficient time for politeness, he removed the pipe stem from his mouth and addressed Bertie in a French so heavily accented, Jessie did not understand a word of it. She did understand one word Bertie said, since he repeated it. The old man nodded and repeated it himself; and then there was a certain amount of gesturing with the pipe, which seemed to be directions of some sort. The whole thing ended in a hearty handshake between the men, and a courtly bow of the head for Jessie, before they left him and walked on.

'What was that about sardines?' Jessie asked.

'That's what the French call pilchards. It's what most of the fishermen have been catching today.'

'Pilchards?'

'Big ones. They'll be about nine or ten inches long. There's nothing more delicious when they're fresh. The old chap was telling me about a place up there in the pines where they grill them over a wood fire.'

'I wonder if that's the woodsmoke I can smell.'

'It may well be. I was thinking,' he went on cautiously, 'that it might be a nice place to go for our supper – unless you want to eat at the hotel, or in a proper restaurant?'

'Your idea sounds much more jolly,' Jessie said. She thought of an empty dining-room, and of being the only guests there, feeling obliged to talk in whispers, with every clash of knife and fork sounding like a battle of Titans. 'Do let's go there, if you think you can find it.'

He found it easily enough. It was a pleasant walk, up the hill, on a road where the evening sun, filtering through the leaves of the trees, quivered on their eyelids, and a thrush repeated his song methodically from a high birch tree. Below, to their right, the molten disc of the sun slid into its slot on the horizon, and the sea lay calm and abandoned, rocking softly against the shore, darkening to indigo.

From the road they had only to follow their noses down a short track. It was not a restaurant proper, but a cottage in a clearing, where a number of tables had been set out, each with a lantern on a pole hanging over it. They were welcomed with enormous friendliness by a smiling woman with her hair tied up in a red handkerchief and a black apron over her dress; and were shown to a table off to one side, where very soon a pitcher of red wine was placed before them, with two tumblers. Other tables were filling up with local people, some still in their working clothes, others having hastily smartened themselves for what was obviously a customary feast. The smell of the cooking fish was making Jessie's mouth water, and she was absurdly hungry. Another, younger, woman, smiling shyly, brought a bowl of fat black olives and a basket of bread. Both were delicious, washed down with the wine, which was fruity and young.

Then the sardines came, straight from the fire, fragrant with woodsmoke, simply dressed with lemon-juice. Nothing, she thought, could have been more perfect, the flesh falling whitely from the bones at the touch of a fork, the taste rich against the wholesome simplicity of the bread, with the olives for a relish to rest the mouth. All around them people were eating and drinking with a great deal of cheerful noise, yet she and Bertie seemed to be quite private and quiet.

The sky turned to black velvet above and the stars came out, and the woodsmoke drifted up with the conversation and laughter into the tops of the silent, watching pines. Jessie ate two platesful of sardines, and regretfully refused a third – there seemed no limit to the hospitality. Then a man brought them cheese and fruit – plums this time, small purple ones – and after that coffee, very strong and bitter and sandy in texture, with two small tumblers of brown liquid.

Bertie sniffed and tasted. 'Brandy of some kind – a local grape brandy, I imagine.'

'I don't drink spirits,' Jessie said.

'Try it – it's very good.'

She sipped, and coughed, and gave hers to Bertie. He lit a cigarette. Gradually the eating all around them slowed and stopped, then someone got out a fiddle and someone else a squeeze-box, and soon people were moving the tables back and there was dancing in the middle of the clearing, to a squalling of music that sounded, Bertie said, like cats fighting. Their table was to the side, and they didn't need to move, only to turn their chairs a little so they could watch. This brought them closer together, and under the table Bertie reached for Jessie's hand and took it back in his. She could not think of anywhere she would sooner be. Happiness bloomed inside her like a fire catching hold in the grate. All the sadness of their lives had been pushed back into the shadows by the firelight, and she would not look at it or think about it.

Bertie felt her thoughts and turned his head to her. 'Happy?' he asked.

'Oh, yes,' she said. 'I'm so glad we came here to eat. This is perfect.'

'My love,' he said, and lifted her hand to his lips, and kissed it in simple homage.

410

She looked into his eyes, and read his face. Her body ached for him. She felt the colour rise to her cheeks, but she did not lower her eyes. She said, 'There's something I want, Bertie. I think you want it too.'

'Jessie,' he began, but did not seem to know how to go on.

She gripped his hand tighter. She could only say this once, and it had to be right, because she could never say it again. 'I want you to hold me, and kiss me, and love me. I want everything – everything we've never allowed ourselves to have. Do you understand?'

'I understand,' he said. 'But—'

'No, don't say "but". I want it. Oh, Bertie, I love you so much.'

'I love you too. I always have.' He examined her face, and she felt the heat in it under his eyes, but it was not uncomfortable. 'Shall we go, then?' he asked.

'Yes,' she said. 'Let's go now.'

They did not have to go back down into the town, for it turned out they were quite near the Manoir des Pins, and the hostess gave Bertie directions for a path that would take them right there, and repeated them carefully to make sure he understood. The opening to the path was marked with a white stone, and it wound, dry and level, round a spur of the hill and met the driveway of the Manoir just below the gate. It was so close that as they walked up to the hotel door they could smell the woodsmoke of the cooking fire, and hear a faint bat-squeak of the music that was still going on.

They collected their keys, and Bertie said, for the sake of the proprietor, 'I shall go out in the garden and have one last smoke. Goodnight, my dear. I'll see you in the morning,' and she went up alone.

She undressed to her chemise and waited for him at the french windows, looking out into the dark garden, smelling the smoke of his cigarette coming up to her, so that she didn't feel separated from him. She heard his voice as he refused the proprietor's offer of coffee or brandy, and thought for a moment, guiltily, that they had deprived the old man of the cost of their dinner. She heard the proprietor close the doors downstairs, and knew Bertie was on his way up. She felt tense and hot with expectation. Her door opened and closed, and she heard him lock it, and felt his quiet tread across the carpet to her.

She had put no lights on, but the moon was just rising, and he could see her white shape at the window, and went to her, slid his arms around her from behind, laid his lips against her neck and felt her quiver. He wanted her so much it was almost an agony, but it was too big a step not to ask. 'Are you sure?'

She put her hands over his, which were clasped at her waist. 'I'm sure,' she said. 'I don't know if it's right or wrong; but I know it's right. Does that make any sense?'

'It does to me.'

She went on, hesitantly: 'I think we're owed this, Bertie. We got things wrong right at the beginning. We married the wrong people. But we tried, we really tried, to do the right thing by them.'

'Yes,' he said.

'We did our best,' she said in a low voice, 'and that's all anyone can ever do, isn't it?' She turned, pulling away from him a little, so that she could look up at him, anxiously trying to read his face. 'Can we have this?' she asked.

He knew what she was asking: not, is this physically possible – which it always had been – but, can we really have the thing we always wanted, or will it be spoilt by the taking?

'I think we can,' he said.

She nodded, still gravely searching. 'Just the once. It's all there can be. This one time pays for all – everything we would have had if things had gone the way they should have. Do you think we can settle all accounts with this one time?'

No, he said in his heart. Aloud he said, 'We can try.'

*　*　*

There was no awkwardness. Nothing could break the mood, not even the necessity of taking off his clothes. She thought fleetingly of how often as a nurse she had undressed men, and the thought was only kind and comfortable. He drew off her chemise, and she lay down on the white counterpane, and he came and lay beside her. His body was milk white, except for his hands and arms and face. His skin, when she touched it in wonder, was like silk. He pushed her loosened hair gently from her face and kissed her, and she felt the heat of him, and the hardness, and she could not wait any longer.

'Please, now,' she whispered. He moved across her, and into her, and the feeling of him inside her pierced her heart with longing. His nakedness, the feeling of his flesh against hers, were the most real things in the universe, and yet it was like a dream, the sweet ache of something longed for beyond hope. They moved together strongly, like swimmers; knowing each other instinctively, knowing how to do this, as though they had done it a hundred times before. There was no more doubt. It was right. The tempo quickened, his lips found hers again, and against them as they flew out into the bright darkness together he said, *I love you!*

Afterwards they lay together, his arms round her, her head on his shoulder, and he kissed the crown of her head as he had so often wanted to.

'Now you're mine,' he said. He squeezed her closer with his arms, and she gave a little grunt, a sound so inconsequential and human that delight fountained up in him, a joy so intense he could not speak for a moment. She kissed his neck, the only part she could reach, and pressed herself into him. 'You're my wife now,' he whispered. 'In everything but the law. My only wife. For as long as I shall live.'

'I'm yours, Bertie,' she said. 'I always was.'

Time, for once, was not their enemy. This small space they had taken for themselves was a time out of time, and magically it seemed to stretch and grow so that they had no sense of haste, of approaching end. They touched and kissed, spoke a little, made love again – slowly, this time, spinning it out like silver thread, finding each other out, enjoying each other's pleasure. There was safety here, and permanence. The war was far away – the world was far away. There was only this, themselves, together at last; their breath and the touch of each other and the slow, sweet pulse of their blood.

They slept a little – there seemed time even for that – and Bertie woke at the first questioning note of the black-bird from the garden. Jessie was asleep, still on his shoulder. There was just enough light to see, and he moved carefully from under her and turned on his side so that he could look at her face, which he loved more than life itself. *My wife*, he thought, and smiled at the idea. He pushed a strand of hair from her forehead, and delicately traced the faint line of the scar down her cheek, got in childhood, almost invis-ible now, but the subject of much maternal anguish in its time. She could not have been more beautiful to him.

She was looking at him. She had woken in the passage of a thought. He smiled and saw her lips curve in answer.

'I love you,' he said.

'I love you, too.'

They made love again, while the light grew grey outside and the blackbird sang, and the thrush called again his insis-tent triplets from his high tree. Their last day was dawning.

Time was gone, time was all spent, it was over. They had walked together along the beach, lunched at Merlimont-Plage, sat for hours in the shelter of a sand dune, talking and kissing. It had been a perfect day. But at last he had driven back to Étaples, and now he had to leave her, to get back himself before his leave expired. In a few days more the offensive would resume, and he would go back into the line.

She seemed very white, he thought, when he pulled up

414

in front of the mess hut; but perhaps that was dust from the dry road. 'Well,' he said.

In her mind she was crying, *I can't bear to give you up. I can't bear the thought of life without you in the world*. But she must let him go easily, for his sake. She tried to smile.

He wanted to kiss her, but he could not, not here. He took her hand. 'I'll make sure someone tells you, when it happens. I won't leave you wondering. Cooper will do that for me.'

'Bertie—!'

'And don't be afraid. I will be somewhere, waiting for you. Nothing is ever lost.'

She reached up then, and laid her lips against his cheek. 'Write to me,' she whispered.

'As long as I can,' he agreed. 'And you'll write to me?'

She nodded. Then she got out of the motor before he could move to help her, lifted out her bag, and walked away. She didn't look back, telling herself she must not, for his sake; until she had heard him turn the motor and start off back towards the camp gates, and then she couldn't help herself any more, and twisted round, desperate for one last glimpse of him. But he had gone beyond the end of the row of huts, and was out of sight to her.

CHAPTER EIGHTEEN

Despite the terrible weather in August, the German Gotha bombers had managed to mount three raids across the Channel during the month, killing and injuring nearly seventy people and doing thousands of pounds' worth of damage. But a large number of the attackers had been destroyed, and the effectiveness of the raids had been limited by a number of measures hastily taken by the War Office after the disasters of July.

Better early warning had enabled air defences to be scrambled in time to put up a response; more anti-aircraft batteries had been established, and through sheer practice they had got better at ranging the bombers. The War Office had hurriedly diverted new aircraft from the factories to home-defence squadrons, to replace their obsolete machines: now they had new, fast Pups and Camels, which actually had a chance of climbing to the right height before the Gothas were out of range. A whole squadron of fighters had been brought over from France and stationed at Hainault Farm to the north-east of London, on the most likely approach path for the Germans, and their mere presence there seemed to have had a deterrent effect. Furthermore, Home Defence was able to call on fighters from the RFC's training, experimental and depot establishments to increase their numbers.

But perhaps the biggest factor in countering the attacks had been the improvement in co-operation between the RFC and the RNAS. Even so, it became clear that the limits of that co-operation were the chief reason success had not been greater. Rivalry between the two services was so entrenched that even the senior officers of the RFC and the RNAS were engaged in it; and only one, Lieutenant General 'Boom' Henderson, believed that a single, separate air service was what was needed.

But after the raids of July, another member of the war cabinet, Lieutenant General Smuts, had been asked to undertake a report on air organisation generally. He delivered the report on the 17th of August, saying that the Gotha attacks had proved beyond doubt that an air service could be used as an independent means of war and, unlike artillery, could operate far from, and independently of, either the army or the navy. Smuts said there was no obvious limit on the scale of such operations, and further considered that the time might soon come when air attacks would be the principal operations of war, devastating industrial and populous centres on a vast scale, while the older form of naval and military operations became secondary and subordinate.

It was clear, in that case, that Britain should and must have a separate air service, both for defensive and offensive purposes. Smuts made his recommendations in form: that an air staff should be appointed, who should undertake the immediate amalgamation of the RFC and the RNAS, transferring all personnel from both to the new force, but with their consent. There should be close liaison and co-operation between the three services, but the air staff would be wholly and solely responsible for operations, intelligence, training and, indeed, all other matters pertaining to aerial warfare.

After some inevitable wrangling, the war cabinet approved the report on the 24th of August, and with commendable promptness set the administrative wheels in motion. Henderson passed the good news to his old friend, Helen's father, Horace Ormerod, who telephoned Helen. She was

417

glad to report it to Jack: he had been fulminating for almost as long as she had known him, about the wasteful rivalry between the RFC and the RNAS. The new service was to be called the Royal Air Force, and should be instituted next spring.

Jack wrote back to Helen of his delight at the news.

Apart from the fact that its initials will be the same as those of the Royal Aircraft Factory, I can't see a single drawback! I don't doubt that some uncooperative attitudes will be carried over by the personnel transferring into it, but such things will be ironed out in time. At the moment, we RFC chaps are rather looked down on by senior army officers as being 'not quite the thing', and I don't doubt it's much the same in the RNAS. I imagine the top sea-dogs, weighted down by scrambled egg, sneering at their pilots and calling them 'mechanics'. So perhaps we'll find a community of interest that will overcome our natural suspicion of strangers. It will be a relief, anyway, to have our own Brass Hats at last, who understand us, and love us, like Nanny, for ourselves.

Despite the fine September weather, ideal for flying, there had been no more Gotha raids so far this month, and there was cautious optimism that the Germans had decided to call the operation off. An estimated loss of thirty-two Gothas and their crews might strike German High Command as too high a price to pay, especially as British air defence was manifestly so much better now, making daylight raids an undertaking of diminishing returns. Or perhaps they believed they had done their part in undermining British morale, in which case they were sadly mistaken.

Horrible though the raids had been, and shocking the losses to individuals, some good had come out of it for the country. The system of air defence was now much more robust, and should another bombing campaign be undertaken, the country would be in much better shape to repel it. And there would be a proper independent air service at last. As Jack said, 'Interesting, isn't it, that it took the jolly old Hun and his ramshackle Gothas only three months to bring about what a few of us (and all honour to dear old Boom in this respect!) have been trying unsuccessfully to do for years?'

When Violet and Emma and the children finally came to Shawes, to meet Venetia there, the harvest was in full swing, and the long-awaited fine weather that was drying out the Salient was also spreading its blessing over England.

After a year of hunger, the harvest looked like being a good one, perhaps the best in years. And other measures had improved the food situation: all over the country, people had responded to the Kaiser's reported boast that he would 'starve the British people until they, who have refused peace, will kneel and beg for it'. No nasty sausage-eating Hun was going to see the British on their knees: sleeves were rolled up, neglected allotments were cleared, lawns were dug up, gardens were planted with cabbages and beans, rhubarb and beetroot. Local councils dug up common land, parks and playing-fields; hospitals and public schools turned over their handsome acres to crops of potatoes; insane asylums had the inmates out digging, and the tranquil parkland in which they were set now provided a more active kind of therapy, as well as a surplus of food for the nation. Even the King had ordered that vegetables should replace flowers in the gardens of Buckingham Palace, and that the royal parks be ploughed up; and the Archbishop of Canterbury had issued a pastoral letter saying that in the current circumstances it was quite all right to work on Sundays.

Along with the success of the convoy system, it meant that the food situation was much eased by September, when the government brought in a bread subsidy, bringing the price of a four-pound loaf down from a shilling to ninepence, paid for out of increased income tax. But there were still problems. In rural areas, the difficulties of transport meant that shops were always running out of things, and were often shut for lack of anything to sell; while in urban areas the greatest complaint was about the incessant queuing. Women – it was almost always women, of course – might spend half the day in one queue or another, often starting at five in the morning, and not infrequently going away empty-handed at the end of it. There might be hundreds or, on occasion, even thousands in the queue, and when things ran out there were sometimes riots. Events in Russia had made the authorities nervous of the working classes gathering in large numbers, and long queues attracted a heavy police presence.

But even when all went well, it was a miserable business. Women with babies and young children were forced to take them with them, and stood, easing themselves like horses from one leg to the other, and shifting their burdens from one arm to the other, for hours, in any weather. Older children were often kept out of school so that they could 'mind the place' in the queue for a mother who had to go to work, or to conduct some other necessary business.

Morland Place did all it could to help the poor and frail and struggling in the area, and the harvest was a happy time, with the wheat and the oats looking very healthy, the barley still to come, and Teddy's new acres of potatoes promising well in another month or so. The apples were coming in, too, and with all available hands out in the fields, the women of the house, led by Maria and Helen, set to work making the cider. Even Ethel brought herself to venture outside and, once having resigned herself to the fact that apple trees in their natural state dirtied your hands, discovered an unexpected pleasure in the physical work and the company.

The children from both households had the most wonderful time, out of doors all day, getting brown as berries and developing huge appetites. The quiet, much-disciplined Holkam children took a day or two to realise the full potential of the situation, but soon they were running as wild as the Morland Place set. It was 'holiday' in the best sense for them, discovering what bliss life could be when no-one asked where they went or what they did, as long as they turned up at mealtimes, or cared how dirty they became, when they could be stripped off and thrown into a bath at the end of it all. So they held mules and carried stooks and gleaned along with the village children in the cornfields; or, for a change, went to pick and carry apples in the orchard. When exhausted, they climbed into the cool rafters of the apple barn and watched the cider-press turning, or went off with the dogs to hunt the rats disturbed by the upheaval in the barns. In between meals they ate windfall apples, blackberries and rosehips from the hedges, and chewed wheat kernels. They begged for rides on wagons and tractors. They got chased by the indignant geese, who were everywhere at harvest time, guzzling the fallen grain and apple pulp, which they regarded as peculiarly theirs, and making an infernal racket. They fell off ladders, and out of trees, and over stones, and into hedges, and skinned their knees, banged their heads, got stung by nettles and snagged by brambles, generally discovering all the ways in which the countryside could hurt you but still leave you smiling and eager for your tea.

Emma had come to Yorkshire as she had gone to Lincolnshire, not expecting any relief. She felt as though she were behind a glass screen, able to see and hear the rest of the world, but shut off from it, alone with her grief. Under general urging she went out into the fields too, and there discovered the truth others had discovered before her, that hard, physical work could distract you a little from your thoughts, and leave you tired enough at the end of the day to sleep.

She preferred to keep away from people she knew. Violet

was a loving companion, but when Violet put on a shady hat and a pair of gloves and joined the orchard contingent, Emma deliberately went off to the cornfields. With strangers she felt easier, knowing she could work alongside them and never see pity in their eyes. They knew nothing about her, and their cheerful ignorance was better than heavy sympathy. Still, she resented their laughter sometimes, and the fact that they could be happy in a world that held no joy for her. She resented sometimes the very fact that they were alive when he was dead.

And sometimes, when straightening up to ease her back, she would notice the deep colour of the sky overhead, or see a blackbird balance on a bramble spray to eat berries, or smell the rich dry odour of the earth, and then be shocked at herself for being able to feel, even for an instant, that there was good in the world. Older people told her that in time her heart would heal, and it angered her that they could think her capable of feeling differently. Her grief was all she had left of him; to stop feeling it would be to break faith with him.

In the evenings she sat apart from the conversations and laughter. She tried to read, but could not fix her mind on the words on the page. After a sentence or two, she would find herself thinking about him again, and have no recollection of what she had read. To be alone in her bedroom so that she could weep was her greatest comfort; and after tears would come sleep, the heavy, dreamless sleep that alone gave her respite.

Henrietta and Venetia spent almost every waking moment together talking. They sat on the terrace at Shawes and talked while minding babies because the nursery-maids were helping with the harvest; they stood in the kitchen at Morland Place and talked while preparing food for the harvesters; they talked while carrying it across the fields and bringing back the empty jugs and mugs; they talked while walking round the moat in the cool of the morning, and while sitting in the shade of the rose garden in the afternoon. It was balm to the soul, both of them solitary women, whose lives had been shaped by hard work, struggle and loss, and whose circumstances had given them no intimate female friend but each other. No absence or distance could lessen their affection, but it was rarely that they could meet, and even more rarely that they could be together long enough to 'have their talk out'.

'We should do this more often,' Venetia said one day, watching young Henry Octavian crawling ambitiously towards a patch of clover, attracted by the bumble bee feeding in it. She was torn between saving him from getting stung, which would involve getting out of her comfortable chair, and feeling that it was one of the necessary lessons of life, to learn to leaves bees alone. Fortunately the bee flew off, saving her from having to make the decision. Octavian sat down on his well-padded rump, picked a clover head and put it into his mouth instead, which Venetia reasoned would do him no harm.

'We should,' Henrietta agreed. 'But where would we find the time? I always imagined,' she went on, 'that when one got old, one would sit in a chair all day and do nothing. But here I am, sixty-four, and I'm busier than ever.'

'It's the war,' said Venetia, who was three years older and even busier than Henrietta. 'When the war's over, I mean to find that chair myself. We'll have two, side by side, and do nothing together.'

They looked at each other for a moment, then both smiled. 'You wouldn't do it,' Henrietta said. 'Sitting still would make you mad.'

'You wouldn't either,' Venetia said. 'But it's a nice thought.'

During this time, Helen's sister Molly finally got leave from the Ministry of Munitions and, finding things a little gloomy at home with her parents, came down by train to spend a few days at Morland Place. She arrived in high spirits, fully ready to join in anything that was going on. 'I can't think of anything nicer than helping with the harvest,' she exclaimed, 'after all these months shut indoors, toiling over a typewriter, and messing about with horrid bits of paper!'

First of all there was a great deal of talk with Helen to catch up on. There was a long gap between them in age, but the sisters had become closer since Helen married. Molly realised now how much she had benefited by Helen's pioneering. Things that Helen had established a precedent for could hardly be denied her sister. It was Helen, too, who had persuaded the parents to allow Molly to go to secretarial college, and then to take a job – something Mrs Ormerod had regarded as unthinkable before. Young ladies did not have 'jobs'. When they finished with school, they stayed at home with Mother and dusted the dining-room and arranged the flowers until a suitable man appeared and married them. Helen had broken the mould by haunting an airfield and learning to fly – bad enough, in all conscience, but at least it was not paid employment.

But Helen had talked Mrs Ormerod round by pointing out that things were bound to be different in wartime. Had there been no war, Molly might have stayed at home in the traditional manner, but with every eligible man at the Front, she might do the dining-room and the flowers for the duration, and still remain hopelessly unwed. Better she should go where men were. Mrs Ormerod came away with the vague idea of the ministry as a cross between a finishing school and a marriage bureau; and Molly, who thought all men fools and the women who married them even bigger fools, was wise enough not to disabuse her.

The sisters talked eagerly about their various experiences since they last met, went over the health and mental well-being of Mummy and Daddy, and discussed brother Freddie, his wife and their latest offspring. Most importantly, Molly had to meet and admire Barbara, now six months old and definitely precocious, and renew her acquaintance with Basil, which was a pleasure on both sides:

Molly might have no intention of marrying, but she had no moral objection to being an aunt. She liked children, and enjoyed their company a great deal more than that of *some* adults she could mention.

When it came time to go out into the harvest fields, she latched on to Emma, whom she liked the look of, and said, 'You must show me what to do. I don't want to get in the way, or seem like a fool, but you've got such a sensible face, I know you'll keep me right.' No-one had thought to warn her about Emma's mourning status; and Emma found Molly's approach so refreshing that she agreed to be latched on to. Molly was two years younger than Emma, but working in London had matured her, and she was older for her nineteen years than Emma had been for her twenty-one. So they got on very well; and unexpectedly soon Emma was talking as well as listening. Eventually she told Molly voluntarily about Fenniman.

Molly was properly sympathetic: she knew most girls wanted to get married, and did not make light of Emma's grief or tell her that time healed all wounds. But, as in everything, she favoured a practical approach to the problem. Unhappiness of any sort (and she had not led a life unmarked by conflict) was always best worked through.

'You ought to get yourself a job. Do something serious for the war effort. It won't make you forget,' she added, endearing herself to Emma by these words, 'but there's nothing like having something to do to help you get through the day.'

'I was doing war-work in London before,' Emma said, and told Molly about meeting the convoys.

'Well, I suppose that's all right in its way,' Molly said, 'but there's so much more you could do. You might get a job like mine – the ministries are crying out for intelligent women and there's lots of clerical work where you don't need to be able to typewrite. I've heard on the grapevine that there's a completely new ministry being started up next month – the Ministry of National Service. That will mean a whole new lot of recruitment. Dozens and dozens of jobs.'

She was so enthusiastic, Emma was almost tempted. But then she said, 'I don't think I'd care to work in an office.' She imagined herself in an enclosed space with a whole lot of girls like Molly, all of them asking her about Fenniman and being sorry for her. You'd never be able to get away from them. 'I think I'd rather do something outdoors.'

'Like a land girl?' Molly said. 'That would be all right in its way, I suppose, but rather a waste of one's brain. Why not join the WAACs or the FANYs? You'd have a choice of things to do there, and you'd probably get sent to France, which would be much more satisfying. I mean to join myself, if the war goes on long enough. You're supposed to be twenty-three, but I know a girl who says they'll take you younger than that, if you lie about your age. They never check. But I know my mother would have a fit if I tried it now, so I'll have to leave it for another year at least. I can talk her round to most things, given time. She gets bored with arguing, bless her, and agrees with me just so that she doesn't have to listen any more.'

'I don't have a mother,' Emma said. 'Or a father. And now I'm twenty-one I don't even have a guardian.'

'There you are, then – you can please yourself,' Molly said, making it sound like a blessing. 'And you'd easily pass for twenty-three. Which do you think you'd prefer? I think the FANYs must be the best fun.'

'I did think a couple of years ago that I might like to join them one day. Jessie was giving me driving lessons, and I thought I'd like to drive an ambulance at the Front.'

'You can drive?' Molly said, her eyes widening. 'Gosh, you are lucky! I'd love to have lessons, but Pa won't hear of it. Well, if you can drive, they'll certainly take you. You'll be welcomed with open arms. I wouldn't hesitate for a moment if I were you.'

'I'll think about it,' Emma said, and felt the weariness

come up and hit her as she remembered Fenniman again. What did it matter what she did? He was dead, and would never come back, and there would be no more joy for her in life.

Molly saw her expression change, and was wise enough to stop talking about it. Helen was always telling her she was a tiresome little jabber-monkey, and wore people out with her talking. But for her, to be alive and awake and not expressing something to someone was a waste of the precious gift of breath. However, she let the subject drop, managed a few minutes of silence, then asked Emma what school she had gone to.

The good weather in France held, and the offensive in the Salient was renewed on the 20th of September. After a heavy bombardment, two Australian and four British divisions attacked on either side of the Menin road towards Gheluvelt. The weather was fine, the ground had dried out, and the men were rested and rehearsed. Although the Germans were well dug in, with deep trenches and well-positioned pill-boxes, the attack was successful, and by the end of the first day both armies had got up to their objectives. They not only took the position but held it: over the next four days the expected German counter-attacks were beaten off, and the artillery that had been brought up, as part of Plumer's 'bite-and-hold' strategy, inflicted heavy casualties on them.

With that success behind him, Plumer could order the second phase of his offensive, an attack on Polygon Wood, with five British and two Australian divisions. The creeping-barrage system had now been perfected, and the problem of the murderous pillboxes was partly overcome by the order to outflank whenever possible, rather than attack head-on, such German strongpoints, which could then be more easily taken from the rear. By such small increments, properly consolidated, Plumer and Haig expected to move the whole army up and oust the Germans from the high ground, from which they had been able to overlook and torment the Allies in the Salient for far too long.

Jessie had been plunged once more into the madness that marked the 'big push'. Trains came in and went out at all hours of the day and night, bringing wounded men down from the Front, taking reinforcements from the camps up to it. Whenever she stepped out of doors, there seemed to be uniformed men marching from somewhere to somewhere else. These days, there were uniformed women, too: the first drafts of WAACs had arrived, to take over various duties and release the men for front-line duty. Jessie did sometimes wonder how the men felt about being released, having wangled themselves a 'cushy billet'. Perhaps at least some of them were longing to fight, and didn't mind some soft girl taking their place. The girls concerned seemed bright-eyed and eager, and their officers – though they weren't called officers but 'controllers' and 'administrators' – earnest and determined to do the right thing.

As well as the trains, there were convoys of trucks bringing in wounded, and these never seemed to stop. Each was announced by the sounding of a bugle, and everyone had to turn out. More trucks took the wounded who were being evacuated to England down to Boulogne to be put on hospital ships. And in all the bustle of coming and going, the nurses manned the wards in the face of a seemingly unstaunchable flow of blood and pain and mutilation.

In the middle of the first surge, a new ward hut was opened and Jessie, now considered a veteran, was moved to it, leaving Beta behind for the first time since they had arrived in May. In the new ward Jessie found herself alone with just one sister, facing an influx of wounded that would have been too much for a staff of ten. The sister, whose name was Parker, was a thin, handsome redhead with a sharp tongue. She was an excellent and experienced nurse, and after the first hectic day accepted Jessie as an equal, which made working together much easier and more comfortable. They quickly found each other's rhythm and made a good team – but the job they had to do was an impossible one. When a convoy came in, they received the wounded all at once and had to cope with them somehow.

Working with Parker Jessie learnt to be quicker even than she already was, and she counted it a useful lesson. When the night staff came on and released them, they would walk to the mess tent for supper. Then Jessie would retire to the Alwyn hut she still shared with Beta, and fall onto her bed, propping her burning feet on a pile of books in an attempt to get the blood out of them. She never read a book now, anyway. She was too tired to do more than eat and sleep – especially as sleep was almost always interrupted by a bugle call announcing the fall-in for another convoy.

Work, eat and sleep. In the early days of nursing, she had thought that whatever she did for one of these soldiers, she was doing for her own loved men at the Front. Now she did not think at all. There was just the next thing to be done, and there were always too many of them. She and Parker could only attend to the most urgent matters, fitting in everything else as and when they might. Wounds that even four months ago would have made her feel faint now passed before her without reaction. Only the pleading eyes of the patients sometimes got through to her; and even then she responded with briskness – a smile and a few words of reassurance were all there was time for. Once, when having tended to a terrified young soldier, she hurried on to the next task, she heard an old Tommy in the next bed say to him, 'Cheer up, chum. It's the battleaxes wot're the best nurses. Take it from me. When it comes to changin' your dressin', you want one like her what'll whip it off quick, not muck about tryin' not to hurt yer and makin' it twice as worse.'

Is that what I am now, she wondered – a battleaxe? It almost amused her.

But it was a blessing to be too busy to think of anything beyond her work. Only in the few minutes, in the morning, of walking across to the mess hut for breakfast, when the question would arise in her mind of whether there would be any post, did she think of Bertie, and then her mind would turn to him, lost and longing and tormented. He wrote often at first, more often than before, and in a way it made things worse because when there was a gap she was sure it was because he had been killed. Then she would wait in agony for the letter in the strange handwriting that would end uncertainty for ever. The sight of his firm writing on an envelope would contract her heart with relief, as painful as blood returning to a 'dead' foot. Sometimes it was just a few lines of scribble to tell her he was still all right; at others he would write from a dug-out in the silence of the night to tell her what he had been doing and thinking.

He had been in support during the Menin-road advance; but one morning she got a letter from him saying that his battalion would be in the 'next show', and that he might not be able to write until it was over. 'Oh, my love,' he wrote, 'I wish I could see you just for a moment, hold you in my arms just once more. I'm so grateful to you for giving me that joy. It was *not* a sin. Isn't it said that God "more regards the thoughts of the heart"? If this is the last I get to write to you, I want you always to remember that, that it was not a sin. And that I love you, love you, love you. There doesn't seem much else to say.'

She received that on the morning of the 27th of September, and the information had already come through that the attack on Polygon Wood had gone in on the 26th. He had been in action a whole day already, she thought. Even as she read these words penned by his warm and living hand, he might already be dead and cold.

Bertie had been at Polygon Wood before, in 1914, though it had been called Racecourse Wood in those days. Then,

430

he and his men had hunted Germans through the trees like rabbits, beating the thick undergrowth for them, ducking behind pine trunks and tripping over roots. He would not have known it now for the same place. There was no wood left, only a few broken-off stumps, two or three feet high; and one or two hopeful saplings, the thickness of his finger, trying to grow in the midst of ruination, surviving only because they were whippy enough to bend before the blasts. The tenacity of nature made him want to cry, like the thought of the skylarks. But even these slender saplings had no chance against the renewed bombardment. Sooner or later they would be blown to shreds. For the rest, where there had been a wood, there was a churned and featureless waste-land of ruts and shell-holes. The only landmark that told you where you were was the Butte, an artificial flat-topped mound. It had been the backdrop to the Belgian rifle range that had been there before the war. The Germans had invested it, with fortification and barbed wire, and in the absence of the trees it stood up noticeably in the northern corner of what had been the wood.

The West Herts went over the top in the early hours of the 26th, and advanced behind the creeping barrage, which, with the current dryness of the ground, threw up great clouds of dust as well as debris, blinding them and making them cough. Bertie was not sure whether it was more help than hindrance; but he knew the men took great comfort from it, and felt it made them invincible, no matter what the evidence to the contrary.

Advancing behind the barrage they covered the first thousand yards quickly and with little loss. In some places the barrage had both cleared the trenches and smashed the strongpoints, but unless it took a direct hit, a pillbox was a resilient object. They had a wide range of fire, and where two had been set up to create an area of interlocking fire, it was almost impossible to get past. The method of reducing them was well established by now. Bertie ordered the Vickers guns brought up – each company had an attachment – and they pinned down the pillbox with covering fire, supported by rifle grenades, while a raiding party worked its way round to the rear and took it that way.

It was hazardous work, of course, and cost many casualties. But they were making ground, slowly, through the hot, dusty morning, in the usual hell of noise. There was too much for Bertie to think about and too many decisions to be made for him to be aware of the bigger picture around him, until one of his lieutenants, Romsey, came sliding down into his shell hole to say that B Company, advancing on their right, had got held up, with the consequence that Bertie's A Company were now somewhat 'in the air' on that side.

'Should we wait for them, sir?'

Before Bertie could answer, there was a muted explosion and a gout of orange flame and black smoke from the pillbox in front of them. The raiding party had evidently got round the back and thrown in grenades; a second, ragged explosion suggested there had been a box of ammunition in there. The men cheered mightily, and started up eagerly from their positions. It would not do, Bertie thought, to check them when their blood was up: that sort of impetus could not be faked. 'No,' he said. 'We'll go on. They'll just have to catch up with us!'

Then they were out and into the hunt. A hot passage of action followed, during which Bertie noticed, in addition to all the other elements, some RFC aeroplanes wheeling about up ahead, strafing the German positions. It was a tribute to them that the German airforce had not yet been able to do the same to the British troops. He wondered for an idle moment if Jack was up there, and it gave him a good feeling.

At the end of this time A Company stormed and took a rather battered trench, killing half a dozen Germans, while one or two managed to flee and the rest surrendered. It gave Bertie a breathing space while he sorted out the men, had the casualties seen to and arranged for the prisoners to be sent back under guard. He hated losing any of his men to this duty, but the Germans did not look likely to give any trouble – they were in a poor state, dirty and hungry, and seemed pathetically eager to surrender. Rumours that the German Army was having trouble getting supplies up to its men seemed likely to be true: this lot looked as though they wanted nothing better than a square meal.

Some time later the colonel dropped into the trench to see how they were getting on. 'B Company has come up now,' he said, 'so your flank is covered again, Parke.'

'I'm glad to hear it, sir,' Bertie said.

'It's been a damned good show so far,' Scott-Walter went on. 'The dash of the men is simply amazing. They've got their tails up now, all right. But the Australians have gone ahead of us on the left flank, and we can't leave them exposed. I've got C Company coming up behind, mopping up the odds and sods, so I want you to push on up as quickly as you can, and they can take over this line and consolidate when they get here.'

'Very well, sir,' Bertie said. The plan for the day was to get to the further edge of the wood where, three years ago, he had lain in the shelter of the trees with his men, firing to keep the Germans in their trenches, fifty yards beyond the wood's margin. He supposed the trenches would still be there, but without the trees, how would he know where the edge of the wood was? It didn't much matter, he supposed. They would make a new front line with the Anzacs, and it would be where it would be.

Shortly afterwards they left the trench and advanced again, moving quickly through light and sporadic resistance, until once again they came under machine-gun fire and had to take cover. It was not a pillbox this time, but a trench and a dug-out, which, because of a fold of the land, had not been broken by the artillery. An unknown number of Germans – perhaps half a company, maybe less – was still under cover there, and firing intelligently with a well-placed machine-gun, while along the trench rifles were doing their part. A couple of rushes proved ineffectual, resulting in heavy losses, and Bertie called his men back while he considered the situation.

Cooper came up beside him. 'Got to get rid of that machine-gunner,' he commented. 'Bastard can pin us down here all day.'

'Thank you for telling me that, Cooper,' Bertie said politely. He reached for his field-glasses, but the lie of the land foiled him. 'I'm going up to that shell hole to take a look,' he said. 'There may be a way we can outflank it and clear it up from the rear.'

He gave instructions for covering fire to Captain Marchbanks, his second-in-command, and poised himself at the edge of the dry stream-bed where they were crouching. He found Cooper beside him, and gave him a frowning look. 'I go where you go, sir,' Cooper said. 'I'm the one as has to brush that uniform. I want to know what you get on it.'

'All right, but you'll have to take care of yourself. I can't let you slow me down.'

Cooper sniffed, but did not actually *say*, 'More like you'll slow me down.'

The covering fire started and Bertie slid himself over the top, got his feet under him and ran at a crouching dash across the fifty feet to the shell hole and flung himself in. It was not very deep, and full of tree roots, which hurt a good deal to land on at speed, and he rolled over onto his back to get his breath and keep under the level of firing. Cooper was there and, judging by his language, had found the landing uncomfortable too. When his body had stopped jangling, Bertie rolled over again and wriggled up just enough to get his field-glasses over the lip of the hole and survey the area. Then he gave them to Cooper, in response to his silent but eloquent request.

'No *bon*, sir,' Cooper said, handing them back. 'We'll never get round the side of that lot. It's a frontal attack or nothing.'

'Well, we can't call it a draw and go home,' Bertie said.

'You need to take out that machine-gun,' Cooper said again.

Bertie took another look. It was not much further to the trench, and once in it, a man would be out of the field of the machine-gun. And it was well known that it was harder to hit one man running alone than in an advancing party. A great calm had come over him. This was his moment: he knew it to his bones. A frontal attack on that trench with the machine-gun still in place would cost dozens of his men, and even then might fail. But with the machine-gun silenced . . .

He rolled over again and took out his pistol, checking that it was fully loaded. 'Go back and tell Captain Marchbanks to be ready to attack,' he said to Cooper. Cooper's eyes widened. 'Go on, man, do as I say.'

'No, sir,' Cooper protested automatically, but Bertie did not let him get any further.

'I hope you're not refusing an order, Cooper. That would be mutiny.' It had not been refusal, and he knew it, but he could not let Cooper argue with him. 'Go now. Keep low and run like hell.'

'Yessir,' Cooper said, but his eyes were agonised as he stared at Bertie one last second before wriggling across to the other lip of the hole.

As soon as he was away, Bertie propelled himself out of the hollow and raced towards the trench. He heard machine-gun fire, and rifle fire too, but he did not bother trying to dodge. This was his moment, and it would make no difference whether he dodged or not. He was in the hand of Fate now. He saw spurts of dust as bullets kicked up the ground around him. He heard one whine past his ear like a mosquito. He saw the white ovals of German faces, and the round black eyes of rifles staring at him, and a man – the officer, he supposed – stood up, pointing a pistol at him. Bertie fired without even taking aim and, sign that he was in the grip of something greater than himself, the man reeled sideways and fell. He shot twice more at the men to either side, and then he was over the edge and jumping down into the trench, feeling strangely exalted, as though he were flying far above it all. He did not feel his legs or feet as he landed, and he wondered if he were already dead.

Two dead men on the ground, the third he had shot holding his face in both hands and crying, blood spurting from between his fingers; white faces everywhere, and rifles, and at the far end the dug-out with the machine-gun. He felt his own face contorted in a snarl of effort, and he said something – he never knew what – and jerked the pistol round, aiming at first one then another. '*Ergeben Sie!*' He heard himself say it in a voice of thunder, while he waited in a strange place of suspended time for the rifles to swing round at him.

But first one, and then another put down their weapons and raised their hands, and then, in a little rush, all of them did it together, their eyes wide and afraid and not understanding, like young bullocks at a shambles. They were young, so young, he realised, with the callow, weakly faces of boys not yet ready to be men. One of the machine-gun team came out of the dug-out, shouting something, and Bertie turned his pistol on him, and when the man did not stop, he shot him. Every one of the boys flinched in unison, and one began to weep silently. The rest of the machine-gunners emerged with their hands up too; and at that moment the first of A Company arrived at a run, yelling as they jumped down into the trench, and started pushing the German boys back into a line against the far wall.

Marchbanks was there, his own pistol out. 'Sir! Sir!' he shouted, but could not find any further words to express himself.

'Good old 'Yde Park!' someone shouted, and there was a wild cheer.

'Silence,' Bertie roared. 'Sergeant, get those rifles picked up. Captain Marchbanks, tell off a guard for these prisoners and have them marched back.' He looked round. 'Where's my servant?'

'He's all right, sir,' Marchbanks said. 'They only winged him. Fellows is putting a field dressing on him. They'll be coming up directly.'

'He was shot?' Bertie said, aghast.

'Just clipped a piece of flesh out of his upper arm, sir. Nothing to worry about.'

Cooper, the indestructible, wounded? It was another piece of madness in a mad world. Cooper was never wounded. What bullet would dare?

'Sir, that's the most magnificently brave thing I've ever seen,' Marchbanks was saying, having reconnected his tongue and his brain by talking about Cooper. 'Stupendous, sir, absolutely stupendous show!' He was shaking Bertie's hand, and the men were grinning at him like fools.

And Bertie realised suddenly that he was still alive, and that seemed very strange and all wrong. He had given his life away to save his men, knowing his time had come; but here he was, sensation coming back into his body, his painful thoughts speeding up and taking account of reality again – here he was, not dead after all. He had made the run knowing he would die, and he had not died. He had spurned life, and life had clung to him. He shook his head slowly to clear it.

The ridiculous thing was, he thought, that it was not a tremendous show at all, not in the least brave. If he had known he was not going to die, he would never have dared do it in the first place.

He disentangled his hand, and looked quellingly round the grinning, chattering men, aware – and embarrassed by the knowledge – that this story was going to be passed from Tommy to Tommy and become a legend. 'That's enough,' he said. 'This is not a raree show. Captain Marchbanks, we shall have to disable that gun before we leave. See to it, will you? And get the men formed up. We're going on.'

Polygon Wood was taken and held, the counter-attacks repulsed. On the 4th of October the next phase of bite-and-hold went in, and Zonnebeke, Broodseinde and Poelkapelle were taken, advancing the line a splendid one and a half miles on a four-mile front. The Passchendaele Ridge was now within reach.

But on the 4th of October a thin rain began to fall, and during the night it came on harder. By dawn on the 5th it was coming down in torrents, from a uniformly lowering sky that promised no let-up.

CHAPTER NINETEEN

When Jessie came off duty, huddling into her coat ready for a quick dash through the rain to the mess hut, her eye was drawn to a figure standing under the inadequate shelter of the overhang of the hut opposite. It was an officer in a greatcoat and an extremely wet cap. His pose was elegantly negligent, one knee bent and the foot up on the wall behind him, hands dug deep in pockets, a cigarette hanging from his lips.

'Oliver!' she called. 'What are you doing here?'

He straightened up, removed his hands from his pockets, threw down his cigarette. 'Waiting for you, obviously.' She ran across to join him. 'I thought you were never coming out,' he complained.

'Nor did I.'

'Busy day?' She shrugged. 'God, you look tired, worse than I feel!'

'We've had a lot of gas patients come in. I think this mustard gas is worse than the old sort.'

He nodded. 'Yes, we've had a lot too. It's a foul business.'

Jessie remembered, without at all wishing to, how the Tommies looked when they arrived, covered with great suppurating yellow vesicles, their blinded eyes glued shut with matter. The mustard gas attacked any moist skin, so the eyes were particularly vulnerable, but it also favoured the groin and the armpit. And breathed in, it attacked the bronchial tube, stripping off the mucous membrane, then the lungs. The men came in gasping and terrified, unable to speak or breathe, and died vomiting blood from their ruined lungs. 'Yellercross', the men called it, because the German shell cases were marked with a yellow cross – their chlorine gas had been marked with a green one. There was nothing to be done for the men. They either lived, scarred and debilitated, or died. Of the nine her ward had received last night, six had died so far, and she wasn't sure they weren't the lucky ones. She recollected herself. 'But what a surprise to see you.'

'A nice surprise, I hope?'

'Of course.'

'Good. Then let me whisk you away for a slightly more interesting supper than you're likely to get in your excellent mess hut.'

'Oh, Oliver—'

'I don't like the sound of that "Oh, Oliver" business. It sounds like an objection making its way towards us.'

She was dead tired, and wanted only to fall flat on her bed, but he *had* come all this way to see her. He was watching her face as if he saw quite clearly her inner struggle – and perhaps he did: if anyone understood what she had been through that day it must be him. And that alone ought to make her want to spend an hour or two in his company, quite aside from the fact that they were friends and cousins.

'Come on, it'll do you good to get away from here for a little while,' he urged, at just the right moment.

'Well,' she said, more favourably, 'I'd have to get permission, though.'

'Already done. I went in and charmed your matron.'

'You saw the matron?'

'First thing I did when I got here. I'm a dab hand with matrons and senior sisters. None of them can resist a young, handsome doctor, particularly if he knows how to pet 'em

440

right. A little flattery and hand-feeding and they come up beautiful. As you will, my lovely, intelligent, charming cousin, when I tell you that there's no-one else I would sooner spend the next few hours with. To gaze at your beauty, to bathe in the stream of your wit, your sagacity, your radiance—'

'Stop, stop. I give in,' Jessie said, beginning helplessly to laugh. 'Anything but listen to more of your flummery.'

'The sad thing is,' he said gravely, 'that I mean every word. But fear not, I shall say no more on the subject of your perfections. I have a motor-car waiting, ready to whisk you away to Hardelot-Plage where I happen to know of a little place with excellent food and no pretensions.'

The thought leapt into her mind of Bertie, and the place among the pines where they had eaten sardines, and her heart ached. She had received a scribbled note from him to say he had been in action at Polygon Wood and was unhurt; but he was still in the line, and she had heard nothing since. Every day without word from him was an agony; and so it would go on, from note to note, until the final one came, in Cooper's unknown hand.

Hardelot-Plage was just such another seaside town as Berck, but rather smaller, and Oliver's 'little place' turned out to be a café in a back-street, which was doing a roaring trade, a mixture of local people and soldiers. Jessie was glad to see that no-one was dressed up – Oliver had been right about the 'no pretensions' – so she didn't feel out of place in her uniform drabness. The place was so full, she thought they might not get in, but Oliver charmed the proprietor and mentioned a name the man evidently knew, and in the click of his fingers a small round table was produced from somewhere in the back, and two rather rickety-looking chairs, and various already seated people good-naturedly moved their tables over to create a space. A blue and white checked tablecloth descended from the air, and was held down with a candle in a jam-jar, a *pichet* of wine and two thick, scarred tumblers, and the inevitable basket of bread.

'*Et voilà!*' said the proprietor, with the air of the conjuror who had just produced the rabbit. Where there had been no table, now there was one just right for them.

The noise of conversation meant that even given the closeness of the tables to each other, Jessie felt quite private – despite the presence (on the other side of the room, fortunately) of a nursing sister accompanied by a tall, skinny, pale-faced officer, who had glared at them as they came in. But the sister was not from Jessie's hospital – there were several at Étaples – and the officer was not a doctor, but a railway transport officer, presumably from Étaples station. RTOs were often officers recovering from wounds or sickness, or otherwise not quite fit enough for the line. This one's white face suggested he had been away from front-line duties for some time. He was at least twenty years older than the sister, stoop-shouldered and 'no oil painting', as the Tommies said. Jessie hoped for the sister's sake that he had other attractions.

The food soon came for, as Oliver explained, there was only one dish on the menu, different each day, so there was no need to order. It was a magnificent *ragoût* of pork, rich with herbs and singing with onions, which was served with mounds of mashed potato. Jessie tasted and sighed. It was a poem – no, it was a symphony! 'You were absolutely right, Oliver, and thank you for bringing me. This is perfect heaven.'

He grinned. 'I know what nurses' appetites are like, so don't stand on ceremony – dig in. I certainly intend to.'

There was little talking until they had satisfied the first pangs – Oliver, as an officer, regularly ate better than Jessie, but even he rarely tasted anything this good, and he was hungry for change and sensation.

But when the fork-work had slowed down a little, he told her, between mouthfuls, his news. 'I'm leaving – going back to England. Leaving France.'

She was startled. He had been so eager to get over here and do his bit. 'But Oliver, why?' A thought came to her. 'You aren't sick?'

'No, no, nothing like that. I'm as fit as a flea. But something's come up, back home. An opportunity I can't pass up. Have you heard of the Queen's Hospital, in Sidcup?'

'Sidcup?'

'It's just to the south of London. In Kent. That part's not important. The important part is that it's a new medical unit that's been set up to do plastic surgery – reconstructive stuff for servicemen, faces and jaws.'

'Oh, I see. I know you always were interested in that,' she said.

'This chap Gillies, Harold Gillies – you've heard of him?' She shook her head. 'My poor child, where *have* you been? To summarise, he's a New Zealander, but educated in England; joined the Red Cross when the war broke out, saw some amazing things the French were doing in reconstruction, discovered we didn't have a single plastic unit, and applied to the War Office to be allowed to set one up. At the beginning of 1916 they finally saw their way to it, sent him to Aldershot, and he set up his unit there. But it outgrew its accommodation, so they've built this dedicated place just for plastics in Sidcup.'

'And that's where you're going?'

'Yes. Isn't it splendid?' He beamed at her. 'What an opportunity! It's what I always hoped for, but I didn't think I'd get a chance like this until the war was over. I suspect Mama had something to do with it. I can't tell you how useful it is to have a medical mother who knows people in the War Office! And she knows Sir Alfred Keogh as well, and he likes me, so I wouldn't be surprised if they'd cooked it up between them.'

Keogh was the director general of the Army Medical Service.

'They're organising the staff at the Queen's by national

groups, apparently – a New Zealand team, a French team, a British team and so on – so that they can take the skills back home after the war. I'm to be part of the British team – well, obviously.' He smiled at himself. 'But Gillies is in charge of everything, of course. It will be wonderful to work with him. The hospital is only a temporary thing, just a collection of huts, but built for the purpose – and, frankly, a hut would be luxury to me, after the conditions I've been working in here.'

He paused for breath, and Jessie said, 'I'm very pleased for you, of course. Delighted. As you say, it's a wonderful opportunity.'

He frowned. 'But? Your delight seems to be tempered with something else.'

'Well – it's just that you so wanted to come to France and you're needed here. I wondered how you felt about leaving your work here unfinished.'

'How do I feel? I'll tell you, little cousin! I feel that I never want to set foot in France again. Leave my work unfinished? It will never be finished! They just keep coming and coming, the bloody wrecks of men they expect me to help. And as for being needed, a butcher's apprentice would be able to do just as well, or a country cow doctor. There's no skill involved in it. Mangled bodies and gas victims spewing yellow foam! Amputations and yards of stitching! It isn't war, it's a factory line of atrocity! I sometimes think if that's what we do to each other, it's time we had done with the human race altogether. Perhaps God will send along a nice fat plague and wipe us out. Let the monkeys have a turn at running the world. I'm sick of it.'

'We're all sick of it,' she said quietly.

'I'm sorry,' he said, in a calmer voice. 'I didn't mean to rant at you. But look, Jess, look at these.' He held up his hands. 'I can do things with these, things that matter. I have skills that aren't being used here, talents that are being wasted.'

'You save lives,' she said. 'Is that a waste?'

'Of course not. But there's lives saved and lives saved. We had an airman through our station the other day. Half his face burned away – no lips, no eyelids, and a bleb where his nose used to be. If he lives, what kind of life will it be? People will turn away from him in horror. He'll never be able even to close his eyes so he can't see their expressions.'

'But he's alive. He should be grateful for that, when so many others aren't.'

'Can't we give him something more than mere existence to be grateful for? What if that airman was Jack?' He saw her wince and was sorry, but he carried on. 'It's the waste of it all, Jess. I hate waste! Gillies gives them something more than simply a jaw that will chew their food for them. He gives them something they can face the world with, a proper life – hope. Look, it's in the nature of trench warfare that heads and faces are more vulnerable than the rest of the body. I see so many boys come through – and, yes, they are boys – with the side of their face ripped away, or their nose blown off – boys with horrors instead of human faces. Not everyone can do anything about that, but *I* can – with these.' He held up his hands again. 'Gillies is an artist. God, he's a wonderful man! He doesn't just patch them up – though that's pretty much of a miracle in itself – he uses his artistic talent to make them, well, not exactly beautiful, but he makes them look like men again. These boys have risked everything for their country, and suffered what in some ways is a fate worse than death. If the skill exists to help them, don't they deserve to be able one day to do the things other men do: to work – to marry?'

Jessie put her hand over his. 'You've convinced me. I'm sorry, I didn't mean to criticise you, or to suggest—'

'That I'm running home out of cowardice?'

She was shocked. 'I didn't mean that. I never so much as thought it. Oliver, how could you suggest it?'

'It's all right. I know you didn't. But perhaps you thought I was hoping for a cushier billet.'

'I didn't think that either – though now you mention it, you did say you were looking forward to the luxury of working in a hut.'

'Devil!'

'I only thought – well, to be honest, I thought you were letting ambition overcome your sense of duty. But I was wrong, and I admit it fully and humbly. You are right to go. This is the right thing – for what my opinion is worth.'

'It means a lot to me,' he said. 'I know Mama will be pleased – well, I'm pretty sure she's behind it, as I said – but, of course, she'd be glad of anything that brought me closer to home. You are the one person I was sure would give me an honest opinion – and one worth hearing.'

'I think you flatter me, but—' Something occurred to her. 'Oliver, you don't mean someone else has criticised you for going?'

He looked at his hands. 'Kit isn't pleased about it.'

'Kit? But what has it to do with him?'

'Well, we like working together. I suppose he feels I'm letting him down, going home and leaving him out here.'

'He didn't accuse you of cowardice?'

'No, no of course not.' He paused, then added reluctantly, 'But he did make rather a *thing* out of the fact that he'd still be here, doing his duty amid shot and shell, while I was sleeping in a comfy bed and popping up to London for shows.'

'Oh, poor Oliver!'

He grinned wickedly. 'Do you think so? I was rather fancying the London-shows part.'

She ignored that. 'But it's a shame. You and Kit are such good friends.'

'Oh, he'll get over it, I expect. In fact, I'm hoping I may be able to get him to follow me, if there's another vacancy – and the way things are going, there won't be a shortage of customers. He's quite nifty with his hands. We'll patch it up, anyway. Don't worry about that.'

They had been talking so much that by the time they had finished most of the other diners had gone and the restaurant was almost empty. The proprietor, with a conspiratorial air, offered them a real treat to follow the *ragoût* – a sweet omelette. Fresh eggs rarely came the way of soldiers or nurses and so were prized above anything. It arrived smoking hot to be divided between them – puffed, golden, and filled with hot, tart quince jam.

'Well, this is something like!' Oliver exclaimed, and they ate with a silence that was close to rapture.

Afterwards they had coffee, and Oliver lit a cigarette, and they talked some more.

'I really am pleased for you about this plastics thing,' Jessie said.

'Yes, and I couldn't get better training than working with Gillies. I was thinking that after the war I could make it my specialisation. Set up a clinic of my own in London. I'm sure the mater would help me with the capital outlay.'

'Would there be enough customers after the war?' Jessie asked.

'Some of the chaps I've seen will need treatment for years and years. And, of course, there are always accidents and fires.'

'But wouldn't they mostly be poor people – workers? They'd all be free patients, wouldn't they?'

'Well, yes, a lot would. But rich people have accidents too, you know. And rich people have children with birth defects – cleft palates and so on. And there's reconstruction after cancer – oh, all sorts of things. I think one could make a nice little practice out of it, enough to keep us in reasonable style.'

'Us?'

'You and me, dear, after we're married. I'm assuming you

are going to marry me. I know you keep saying you won't, but you only do that to fan the flames of my ardour.'

'Oh, Oliver, you're such a fool!' she laughed. 'You do me good.'

'There you are, then. Come live with me and be my love, and I will your court jester prove! Never a dull day shall we have, laughing by day and loving by night, with a little plastic surgery thrown in to spice the brew so that we don't drown in sugar. You could be my theatre nurse, and we could bill and coo over the scalpels while I'm raising a pedicle to replace some rich old buffer's syphilitic nose.'

'Really, Oliver!'

'You see, you're the only woman of my acquaintance I could say that to. And, may I remark, retain your femininity.'

'I'm glad you find me feminine. Most days I feel so old and tired it's hard to remember what sex I am. Do you think this war will ever end?'

'I don't know, love. Word is that we're biffing the Germans hard. Their losses in the Salient are much worse than ours – poor devils. And they haven't got the Americans to look forward to.'

'Oh, the Americans!' Jessie said. 'I'll believe in them when I see them.'

He drove her back, and set her down in the main 'street'. 'Thank you for this evening,' he said. 'It's been too long since we did that.'

'With you in England, it'll be longer yet before we do it again.' He took her hand and squeezed it. 'Will you write to me?' she said. 'I'd like to know how you get on, and how wonderful it is. I'm sure it will be wonderful.'

'Yes, I'll write. I'll be glad to. I'm bound to be full of it, and apart from you, only Mama will be interested.'

'I'm interested,' she affirmed.

'And that other thing – you'll think about it?'

'Other thing? Oh, you mean – yes, I'll think about it. But don't hope too much, will you, Oliver?'

'Don't I tell you I'm in the business of hope? And you'll feel differently after the war.'

Perhaps she would, she thought; but that was not something she wanted to pursue. 'I must go. Goodnight – and thank you again. I had a lovely evening.'

He drew her towards him and kissed her, chastely, on the cheek. 'Goodnight. And take care of yourself. Don't get hurt or sick. And don't let it get you down too much. Remember, one day it will be something that we look back on.'

She shook her head at him, laughing, and got out into the endless rain.

After only a few days of being back in London, Emma knew she must find some different way of spending her days. The nothing-doing of the social round had suited her before because of her sociable nature, but now she was cut off from all that. She couldn't join in with the laughing and chatting, and to sit around blankly while others did it only drove her further in upon herself. She couldn't be interested in the trivial things that before had seemed as jolly to her as to other girls, gossip and dancing and flirting. She saw now that a great deal of everything that young women did was based around falling in love and finding a husband. But Fenniman was dead. The war had taken him: the war that had been something important but distant had now come home to her, and she could see and think of nothing else. She could not undo what had happened to her, but if she could do anything to hasten the end of the war, she might help prevent its happening to someone else. She must 'do her bit', as the common phrase was.

From there it was only a short step to deciding to join the FANYs. She had been rather taken with a demonstration given by the First Aid Nursing Yeomanry that she had seen at the Morland Place Easter fair two years ago.

She thought the FANYs would be more dashing than the WAACs. They were known to be independent and free-spirited, while the WAACs, she guessed, would be regimented like soldiers. And though it didn't matter any more how she looked, she had always liked the uniform: the military tunic with smart red piping, calf-length skirt and long leather riding boots, topped with a soft cap.

So one morning while Violet was otherwise engaged, she dressed herself plainly and set off for the FANY headquarters in Earl's Court. After a short wait, she was shown into a small, dark office where the recruiting officer was seated behind a desk: a woman older than Emma, but still obviously young. She looked sharply at Emma as she came in, then got up and came round the desk to shake hands with her. She was a little taller than Emma, rather too thin, though with an attractive face in a high-cheekboned, well-sculpted way. It was a pale face, but it suited the overall rather alabaster look, which was emphasised by dark eyes and the dark hair. The most immediately noticeable thing about her, however, was that she limped heavily.

'Good morning,' she said. 'Won't you sit down? So, you want to join us, do you?'

'Yes, rather,' said Emma. 'That is, I want to do my bit for the war effort, and I thought the FANYs might suit me best.'

'The proper question is, will you suit the FANYs?' the woman said, returning to her place. Once seated, she looked Emma over with a cool and appraising eye.

Emma, blushing a little, said, 'I would have thought they were much the same thing.'

The woman smiled. 'Well done. A show of spirit – without which we women wouldn't get very far in this world of men. Now, first of all, your name.'

'Miss Weston – Emma Weston.'

'Ah, I thought I recognised you. I've seen your picture in the newspapers quite a few times.'

'Indeed,' Emma said cautiously. If this person knew who she was, she might know that she was not twenty-three.

'I'm Vera Polk,' said the young woman. 'You don't know me, but I was a close friend of your cousin Anne Farraline.'

'Indeed?' Emma said again, but with more interest this time. Lady Anne Farraline had been a leading light of the suffragette movement, but had died in a tragic road accident. She was Venetia's first cousin and they had been very close. It was Lady Anne's death that had been the cause of Emma's being sent to live with Violet, so that she should not have to go into mourning in the middle of her first proper Season. But though she had never met Anne Farraline, it would have been impossible for Emma not to know a great deal about the cousin who had been in gaol many times, had survived forcible feeding, and had been constantly in the newspapers. She had been a headline even after her death, when her brother and the women's movement had quarrelled scandalously over who should have the right to bury her.

'I didn't know her,' Emma said, 'but I admired her. She was tremendously brave.'

'She was,' said Vera Polk. 'Not enough people appreciated that.'

'Were you a suffragette too?' Emma asked.

'I was. Of course, we all gave up militancy when the war began. Now I'm doing my bit this way. Didn't you use to live with Lady Holkam?'

'Yes – I still do. She chaperoned me when I was coming out. Now we're friends. Do you know her?'

'I've met her; and her mother, Lady Overton.' Miss Polk subjected Emma to another of those detailed scrutinies. Emma thought her manner a little odd, but decided perhaps it was a test to see if she was sufficiently determined to join. She squared her jaw and returned the stare steadily.

'Why do you want to join the FANYs?' Vera Polk asked abruptly.

'As I said, I want to do my bit. And – and I hear great things about your organisation.'

That touched a spot. 'We're doing tremendous work in France,' she said proudly. 'When our first detachment went to Calais in 1914, there was no-one caring for the wounded soldiers evacuated from the battlefield. Right there and then we took over a convent school and set up a hospital, and now it has a hundred beds.'

'I wasn't really thinking of becoming a nurse,' Emma said carefully. 'I know it's important work – I have a cousin who's nursing at Étaples – but I don't think it's really in my line.'

'Mine neither,' said Miss Polk, with a look of complicity. 'Of course, we are the *nursing* yeomanry, and everyone has to do a first-aid course and get the certificate, but nursing isn't all we do by any means. We drive ambulances and run soup kitchens and mobile bath units, and take food and clothes up to the front line. It's pretty dangerous work, of course. Sometimes you're in the firing zone, and you have to get through despite shells falling all around you. You noticed, I suppose, that I'm lame?'

'Um – well . . .' Emma blushed.

'I was driving blankets and winter clothes up to the line when a shell exploded and turned my vehicle over. Broke my leg pretty badly and it's left me like this. I'm not fit for the front any more, so they made me a recruiting officer instead.'

'I'm so sorry.'

Miss Polk shrugged that away. 'Do you think you'd have the spirit for that sort of thing, driving under fire?'

'I think so,' Emma said. 'I suppose one can't be sure until it happens, but I think so.'

'Sensible answer,' said Vera Polk.

'And I can drive a motor,' Emma said, encouraged. 'My cousin taught me.'

'Better and better. Have you passed the BRCS test? No?

Oh, well, you will need the certificate, but that's just a formality if you already know how to drive. We desperately need drivers and mechanics. Do you know anything about fixing broken motors?'

'Nothing at all, I'm afraid.' Emma saw her chance slipping away. 'But I'm willing to learn.'

'That's the area where we most need recruits. Much of the motor-pool work in France now is done by women, and the more mechanics we can get out there, the more men will be released for front-line duty. Do you think you'd like to become a mechanic? It's pretty dirty work. You won't keep those dainty hands of yours soft and white for long.'

'I don't care about my hands,' Emma said.

'Have you got a fiancé? A lover? Any man you have an understanding with?'

Emma thought this an impertinent question, but she answered quietly, 'My fiancé was killed in the Salient in July.'

'Good!' said Vera Polk, watching Emma's face. Having observed her expression of hurt and surprise, she went on, 'Not good for you, of course, but good for us. Men sometimes object to their females joining at all. Don't want the little woman to do anything dirty or dangerous. Fathers and brothers are bad enough, but fiancés are the worst. I've had fiancés march the woman back in here and make her take back her application. So, your fiancé was killed, and you want to do something for the war effort as a tribute to his memory, is that the idea?'

'Something like that,' Emma said, still bewildered by the abrupt young woman's approach, but managing not to cry.

Miss Polk seemed to have observed that, too, because she said, 'Good for you. I think you've got what's needed. And I'll tell you what, it's the best thing you could do to help you forget. You'll be kept so busy, learning new things and making new friends, and then over in France having such an exciting life that you'll have no time to think about the past at all. Well, Miss Weston, I think we can take you on. Unless, of course, I've put you off the whole idea?'

Emma faced her bravely. 'I suspect that you have been trying to put me off, to see what I was made of. But I want to join more than ever.'

'Well done.' She stood up and offered her hand again to shake. 'I'd like to take you right away. You'll have to do a first-aid course, as I said, and I'd like to put you down for a motor-mechanical course, too, if you're willing.'

'Yes, I think I'd like that,' Emma said, though unsure what it meant. But she didn't want to be thought to care more about her white hands than the war effort.

'Good. The probationary period is usually four months, but we need mechanics in France so desperately that I'm sure we can get you out there sooner if you do well at it. I'm assuming you want to get to France as soon as possible?'

'Oh, yes,' said Emma.

A little while later, as she walked out into Earl's Court Road and the grey, steady rain, she felt rather breathless, as if she had been hurrying, and hollow inside with a mixture of excitement and apprehension. What had she let herself in for? But then Fenniman's death, which had been absent from her mind, came rolling back like a boulder, and she thought that in the first place, it really didn't matter any more what happened to her; and in the second place, given that she had forgotten him for several minutes, it might indeed prove to be something that would keep her mind off her unhappiness, as Vera Polk had promised.

As she started to walk back towards the taxi-rank, she realised Miss Polk had not asked her age. But perhaps she really had known that Emma was only twenty-one, and that was why she hadn't asked. She had really been most obligingly anxious to help Emma get in.

In the whole of October, there were only a few days in the Salient when it didn't rain, and even those were cool and overcast, with no drying power. Conditions deteriorated far below what they had been in August. The whole area was a swamp, a lacework of shell holes filled with filthy water, whose lips formed narrow peninsulas across which all traffic had to pick its way. It was a wilderness of mud that even the rats and birds had deserted, from which all landmarks had gone, featureless except for the bits of debris that stuck up from the mire that gripped them – the shafts of a wagon, the muzzle of a field gun, the remains of a tree-trunk, the wreck of a pillbox. The dead were in there somewhere, sunk and gone and sinking further all the time, lost for ever. Duckboards and corduroy roads were the only means to pass from the rear up to the line. Artillery and ammunition supplies were stuck fast in the mud, and any forward movement for the infantry was slow and exhausting, often without the protection of the creeping barrage. It was equally slow getting back, and the wounded suffered terribly. It took sixteen men to carry a stretcher case through the mud, and if a man slipped off the duckboards he was in danger of drowning in the mud unless he was dragged out quickly.

Passchendaele, the shattered and wire-girt village up on the ridge, was just ahead, the tangible reward for the long labours and losses of the summer. At the end of October the last great push went in, spearheaded by the Canadian Corps under General Currie, with the Fifth Army in support. Slowly and with agonising effort, sometimes struggling through knee-deep mud, the attackers inched their way forward in the still-teeming rain. But at the beginning of November the rain stopped, and on the 6th the Canadians at last heaved themselves up onto the ridge, a hundred and eighty feet above sea-level, and took the mass of slaughtered masonry that was Passchendaele village, so shell-swept that the only visible landmark was the ruin of its church. From the far side of the village, the astonished men could see the untouched country beyond, a strange and wonderful land of tall trees and whole, undamaged buildings, of green fields and hedges and barns: the most complete and heartbreaking contrast to the wasteland of the Salient behind them.

The third battle of Ypres was now officially over, its objectives met. The high ground was taken, the position vastly improved. The Germans had been severely weakened with heavy matériel and manpower losses, and they had been kept occupied while the French slowly rebuilt their army. British, Canadian and Anzac losses had been heavy, but the butcher's bill was nowhere near as bad as it had been in Picardy. But the men and officers were exhausted, and the hell of fighting and living in the mud for a whole month had ingrained in their minds a greater horror than any other battle in the previous three years.

Matters were made worse because the units in the Salient were desperately in need of reinforcements. Battalion numbers were down, and men were having to spend longer in the lines because there was no-one to relieve them. Normal rotations were being lengthened at the very time when, because of the appalling conditions, they needed to be shortened.

There were tens of thousands of soldiers fit and ready back home in England, but they were not being sent out because the Prime Minister was trying to destroy Haig and force him to resign. Lloyd George had never liked Haig, and as the war went on he came to hate him. He didn't like the Western Front, with its endless deadlock, no good news to put in the papers, and casualty lists with nothing tangible to set against them. He wanted to fight the war on other fronts, where there was a chance of having something to show for the effort; but Haig, and his supporter in the war cabinet 'Wully' Robertson, kept saying – and the French agreed – that the only place the Germans could be defeated was in France. Lloyd George would have liked to sack Haig, but he could not. Haig was liked and respected by the army, the generals, the French, the King and the people; even the press was broadly supportive of him. And, in any case, who would replace him? Hamilton had been disgraced over Gallipoli; Allenby over Arras; Byng, Plumer and Horne were all Haig supporters; and Lloyd George's personal favourite and private adviser, General Sir Henry Wilson, was deeply unpopular with both men and commanders, and was seen by staff to be too volatile, and something of a schemer and back-stabber.

Unable to get rid of Haig, Lloyd George settled for undermining him at home, and starving him of reinforcements, calculating that without sufficient men Haig would not be able to mount offensives, and would have to settle for holding the line until the Americans arrived, as Lloyd George wanted. To make doubly sure, in November he agreed to a French request for the British to take over more of the line from the French, thus thinning out the British manpower and further tying Haig's hands.

This scheming at home, which Venetia heard about from her friends at the War Office, had its main effect on the men at the Front, and particularly in the Salient. Even after the offensive was officially over, the lines had to be held, and there were always casualties. In normal times, the British Army as a whole could expect to lose two thousand men a week through snipers, shelling, accidents and sickness; and with winter coming on and after an exhausting summer and autumn in terrible conditions, the sickness count was likely to go up. And at the end of October, the war cabinet ordered five divisions and General Plumer – men and a commander Haig could ill spare – to Italy to shore up the Italian Front against Germany's ally Austria, after the defeat at Caporetto.

Bertie wrote to Jessie:

We are all wet, cold and tired, and the men are desperately in need of relief. They keep amazingly cheerful in spite of everything, but there is almost something of hysteria in their high spirits. Their rude songs are more cynical and more obscene than ever, but if it

457

keeps the poor things going, so be it. The next ten men on the list for leave have been out here for twelve months continuously, and the draft of reinforcements we have been expecting are now not coming until next week, and will only number twenty men, though the battalion is down to a rifle strength of not much more than six hundred. The greatest subject of conversation is the rumour that a mobile bath unit is coming to Battalion Headquarters and that everyone will be sent off in turn to have a hot bath. I don't know where they think so much hot water is going to come from, given that Bttn HQ is a collection of leaky tents in a sea of mud, and the CO's servant makes his tea by heating a tin mug of water with a candle. But we are getting cases of trench foot for the first time in two years so I suppose the wish is father to the thought. Oh, my love, I long for you so much that sometimes, half waking in the night, I see you for a moment before I wake fully to the grim truth of my surroundings. But each morning that I am still here – still alive – is one more when I can share the world with you, even if you are miles away and out of sight. Write to me, you must write while you can. The silence will be long afterwards.

The Bolshevik leader Ulyanov, who now called himself Lenin, had been aided and funded to return to Russia by the German government after the abdication of the Tsar, with the promise on his part that if – when – he came to power, he would end the war between Russia and Germany. After the failed coup of July he had fled to Finland; but with the gradual descent into anarchy of the autumn, he returned secretly to Petersburg in October to plan his takeover.

On the 25th of October the Second Congress of Soviets took place at the Tauride Palace, its purpose to debate how to replace the Provisional Government with a Soviet government. This had to be done before the elections that the Provisional Government had promised for November, based on a universal franchise: free and fair elections might not give the Soviets the majority they needed. But even urgent Soviet debate was no match for Bolshevik action. On that same night the Bolshevik *coup d'état* took place, on the signal of a blank shell fired from the warship *Aurora*, lying at anchor in the Neva opposite the Winter Palace. At the signal, key positions in the city, such as railway stations, the general post office, the telegraph office and the main bridges, were seized, and the newspaper presses were all closed down. There was little resistance from the populace, worn out by months of revolution and years of war and hunger, who hardly cared which group was in power, anticipating no relief from any change at the top. The Red Guards, as the Bolshevik-loyal troops were now called, swept into the Winter Palace and arrested the Provisional Government, though Kerensky managed to escape in disguise, hoping to raise a force to regain power.

The next morning Leon Trotsky, Lenin's second-in-command, announced to the Congress that power had been seized in the name of the Soviets. The Mensheviks and other moderate socialists had no doubt in whose name power had really been seized. They denounced the Bolshevik leaders as criminals and walked out. The chairman, Kamenev, tried to stop them, but Trotsky shouted, 'Let them go. They are just so much refuse to be swept into the garbage heap of history!'

News of the coup took more than a week to reach Tobolsk, and though Thomas had been half expecting something like it for months, it was a blow nevertheless. He took the news to the Tsar, who was so shaken he could not speak. Life had suddenly become much more perilous for the prisoners in the governor's mansion. No-one knew what a Bolshevik government might do with them. Later, when more details of the coup came through, Nicholas seemed more puzzled than afraid, not understanding why Kerensky, who had been put into power by the people, should have been ousted. And he was upset that the beautiful Winter Palace had been looted and badly damaged, the wine-cellars broken into and thousands of bottles of priceless wine smashed or poured down the drains.

'Couldn't Mr Kerensky have put a stop to it?' he asked plaintively.

'Obviously not,' Thomas said. 'A mob is always a mob, Nicholas Alexandrovitch.'

'But Kerensky was such a favourite of the soldiers. Surely he could have restrained them? And, regardless of what happened, why tear apart a palace? Why destroy things? It makes no sense.'

There was no immediate change in their circumstances. No doubt, Thomas thought, the new dictator, Lenin, had many things to settle in Petersburg before he could turn his attention to the household in Tobolsk. But when he did – what then? It was not talked of, but everyone in the household knew that their position had become much more precarious, and there was an underlying tension like the smell of brine in the air before a thunderstorm.

On the 3rd of November, when the news of the coup was still fresh in their minds, Olga had her twenty-second birthday. It was hardly true to say she celebrated it, though everyone did what they could to make an occasion of it, with little presents they had made for her, and wrapped as best they could, set out on a table, and kisses and good wishes, and music and games in the evening. Thomas had found a woman in the town who could bake, and by various contrivances had managed to get to her the ingredients for a small cake, which he produced as his gift. Everyone expressed surprise and delight, and the cake was meticulously divided into enough tiny slices for everyone in the household to have a taste.

The next day when he went to visit, Thomas found Olga

hiding away behind the woodpile in the garden, weeping forlornly. She tried to cover up the fact as soon as she saw him – it hurt her dignity for anyone to see her cry – but she could not immediately stop the tears. She made gestures for Thomas to go away, but for once he disobeyed. He drew out his handkerchief, which was more serviceable than hers, and put it into her hands, and then, when a fresh burst of tears followed, he threw caution to the winds and took her into his arms. She went rigid with resistance at first; but then relaxed and let her hot tears fall on his shoulder.

It was too violent a storm to last long, and in a moment she was pushing herself away from him, turning her back while she wiped her face and blew her nose. 'I'm ashamed for you to see me like this,' she said, into the handkerchief.

'Don't be ashamed. I am your friend, aren't I? Friends may comfort friends, Olga Nicholayevitch. Let me see your face.'

She turned to him at last, her eyes red and wet, her face pale. 'There's no hope for us, is there?' she blurted out.

'There is always hope.'

She shook her head. 'I thought about it all day yesterday. My birthday! Oh, Thomas, I thought I should burst into tears when you brought the cake. How could you do that? It was hard enough with the presents from the others, but – a cake! Too much like the real world. And for whom? A condemned prisoner, forgotten by the world.'

'You mustn't say that. You have friends who will not let anything happen to you. I am in touch with people. You know I may not say any more, but you are not forgotten.'

She looked straight into his eyes, and he met her look steadily. She sighed, and a frail smile touched her lips. 'You say we have friends. I only know I have you. I am so glad of you, Thomas Ivanovitch. I don't know how I should have borne it here if it weren't for you.'

Of them all, Olga was the one who had suffered the most from boredom – confined day after day, with nothing to do, when she had always been active, busy, useful; but most of all, she had told him, it was the tedium of being locked in the present that gnawed at her. 'Nothing changes. I can't look forward and say, "Next week I will do so-and-so", or "Next year such-and-such will happen." I can't plan and work towards any conclusion. I can't move forward. There is no forward.'

Now she said, 'I'm afraid the day may soon come when I shall look back on the boredom with regret. What will your government do about this?'

'About?'

'About the Bolsheviks taking power.'

'I think – at first, not very much. Forgive me, but things have been volatile for some time, and I expect they will wait to see how it settles down.'

'You mean, they will wait to see if some other party makes another *coup d'état* and throws the Bolsheviks out?'

'His Majesty's government does not like to make itself look foolish by bowing to the wrong person.'

She nodded, thoughtfully. 'Your prime minister?'

'Lloyd George? He's a pragmatist. If he thinks the Bolsheviks will keep Russia in the war, he may well feel it useful to deal with them. But I assure you, one condition will be absolute, and that will be the safety of your family. Lenin may or may not make peace with Germany, but he won't want to make war with England.'

She looked at him sadly. 'You think your country will go to war to protect us, when they would not even offer us a home?'

He was uncomfortable with that. 'They want you to be sent to a neutral country. But it would be a very different matter, if anything should happen to you.'

She seized his hands suddenly, fear leaping up in her eyes – the fear that she crushed down day after day and tried never to acknowledge. 'Write again!' she begged. 'Write to the King, beg him to help us. Oh, please, Thomas, before it's too late! Write and say things are desperate now, and he must help us. If you write it, I know it will get to him. Do it quickly! Please, please.'

'I will, I will,' he said. 'I'll write again and send it by diplomatic bag. Even the Bolsheviks won't dare interfere with that. But try not to be afraid. I know my government is working behind the scenes, but these things take time.'

'I don't know how much time we have,' she said. She was still holding his hands, and seemed suddenly to notice the fact. She began to blush, but she did not release them at once. She said, 'I wish I had not been a grand duchess. I wish I had been anyone else. But if I had been an ordinary girl, would you have even noticed me?'

'In any place, in any crowd,' he said. 'I was meant to know you. I would have found you wherever and whoever you were.'

'I wish we were in our little white cottage now.' She meant the one she had painted for him. She sighed, looking round her, and drew back her hands. 'Instead I see this desolate place, this prison, these walls.'

'Don't be afraid,' he said again.

She smiled faintly. 'But at least being afraid is a relief from the endless boredom.'

On the night of the 10th of November there was the first heavy snowfall of the winter – before that there had only been light sprinkling, interspersed by thaws – and in the morning the four girls ran out into it, excited as puppies with the change. Two swings had been put up for them in the garden by the soldiers some time before, and they took turns on them, working themselves up as high as they could, then jumping off at the high point into the snow. Nicholas, who was writing a long letter to a friend, saw them from the window and was worried for their safety. He called Thomas, who was the nearest, and asked him to go out and tell them not to swing so high. Thomas went out, but seeing the brightness of their eyes and cheeks, could not bear to

463

spoil their fun, and said nothing. He went indoors again, and finished his letter. He had decided to write to his mother rather than directly to the King, thinking it a safer route. He included a description of Tobolsk and the position of the house, and a rough sketch of the ground plan of it, which he had been working on for the last few days. His mother would make sure it got to the right person. They could not depend on Lenin being preoccupied for ever.

CHAPTER TWENTY

On the 20th of November, the last offensive of the season went in at Cambrai, which lay about fifteen miles east of a line between Arras and St Quentin. Here, early in the year, the Germans had retreated, abandoning a large salient of ground, to a new defensive position generally known to the Allies as the Hindenburg Line. Before the town of Cambrai – an important railhead – there were two lines of fortifications, with barbed-wire belts fifty yards thick, and the trenches were dug deep, reinforced with concrete, and protected by concrete gun emplacements. A third defensive line was under construction: the Germans never intended to move from here again. So strong were the defences that intelligence suggested German troops exhausted during the battle at Ypres were sent there to rest and recuperate. German High Command regarded Cambrai as impregnable.

The action had been mooted as far back as August, by General Sir Julian Byng, whose Third Army held that part of the Front, in concert with Colonel Fuller, the commander of the Tank Corps. Tanks had not had much of a showing since their début on the Somme. Conditions at Ypres had been too wet even to think of them, and in many other sectors shellfire had by now turned the ground into Swiss cheese. But the Cambrai sector was so far untouched, an area of downland and open fields, firm and dry – perfect for tanks – interspersed by copses, and only lightly invested by the Germans, who were relying on the Hindenburg defences to economise on manpower.

The Tank Corps envisaged a quick, sharp tank raid, there and back in eight hours, to damage German defences and spread alarm and despondency through the enemy; but General Byng added to the idea, believing it could be a major penetration of the German line, releasing the cavalry into the open land to the east. And capturing Cambrai itself would be a serious blow to German mobility.

The plan had been rejected originally on the grounds that the British armies had not enough manpower to mount two major offensives at once. But by October, when the battle in the Salient was foundering in the mud, it was clear that an attack at Cambrai might not only raise general morale with a quick and decisive victory, but also draw German resources away from Ypres and give some relief to the Fifth and Second Armies. Byng was authorised to make his plans for an attack in November.

Byng had the advantage, in planning his assault, of being able to use surprise. Usually a long bombardment was needed to destroy enemy wire, which also alerted the enemy that an attack was coming, and where. But with the tanks to crush the wire, this was not needed, and it was possible to plan the whole thing in deepest secrecy, and take the Germans unawares, before they had been able to bring up reinforcements.

At 06.20 on the morning of the 20th, the artillery began a bombardment of shells and smoke into the area behind the line, and under cover of this, the tanks went forward with the infantry behind them. Leading tanks would crush the wire, while thirty-two of them were equipped with hooks and chains to drag it aside. The leaders also carried huge fascines of timber to drop into the enemy trenches to make a bridge for the machines to cross them; other tanks carried ammunition, food and water, fuel and communications equipment – telephone cables, carrier pigeons, and wireless for speaking to Headquarters and the supporting aircraft.

Fourteen squadrons of the RFC were involved, not only with flash spotting and reconnaissance before the attack, and bringing back photographs and information during the advance to keep Headquarters in touch with developments, but bombing and machine-gunning enemy positions as well. The Germans had few aircraft at Cambrai, and only a dozen Albatros fighters, so for once the RFC had massive air superiority.

The attack was an immediate success. By eight o'clock the Hindenburg Line had been taken on an eight-mile front, trenches and strongpoints had been destroyed, and hundreds of discouraged prisoners were heading towards the rear. By eleven thirty a large part of the second line had been taken, and the British had advanced over two miles on a six-mile front, defeated three German divisions, taken two thousand prisoners and captured dozens of guns. Cambrai itself lay ahead, its population fervently hoping for liberation.

As the short November day turned to dusk, it began to rain, and it continued to rain all the next day, severely hampering the vital support work of the tanks and aircraft. At ten thirty the Germans mounted their first counter-attack, and there was fierce fighting up and down the line all day. It became apparent that it would not be easy to hold the ground won. There was no water up there for the cavalry, who were reduced to fighting on foot; half the tanks that went into battle were now out of commission, either through ditching, engine failure, or enemy action; and German reinforcements were arriving in number. The decision was made by the end of the day to dig in and hold the line along most of the front, while attacking only at the Bourlon Ridge in the north, which, if taken, would greatly improve the British position overall. Two divisions were hurried down from Ypres to reinforce the action, and a day was taken to prepare, get the men into position and muster and refuel the tanks. The new attack went in at dawn on the 23rd.

The Bourlon position was formidable, a wood on a ridge, with a heavily invested village on the reverse slope. Nine more German divisions had arrived since the battle began, and they had learnt something about fighting tanks: the trick was to hide until they had passed, then jump out and attack their more vulnerable sides and rear. Fighting was fierce, and though by mid-afternoon most of the wood had been taken, the village had not, and from there the Germans mounted a counter-attack. It began to rain heavily, and there was sleet in it. More German aircraft squadrons had arrived, including the famous Baron von Richthofen's, and the RFC were losing aircraft. And now there was a shortage of tanks, on which the infantry had come to rely perhaps too much.

The battle went on for several days, swinging back and forth, until by dusk on the 27th the British were out of reserves, and there was nothing for it but to call the battle off, holding at a line along the Flesquières Ridge, which General Byng felt confident they could defend. Cambrai had not been taken, but much ground had been gained, and the position, on high ground commanding the area before the town, was a vast improvement.

But on the 30th of November the Germans mounted a massive counter-offensive, which reeled up and down the line as they employed a new tactic: where they encountered strong resistance, they did not keep pushing, but moved away to try to find a weaker spot elsewhere. The fighting went on until, on the 7th of December, the deteriorating weather closed down the battle with snow and heavy rain. Battle honours were about even, with the British having taken and held a section of German line, but having lost a section of their own line almost as long to the Germans.

Jessie was working with Beta again, for they had both been sent on night duty in one of the surgical huts, a busy ward with fifteen beds a side and an operating room at the end. The sister was a middle-aged woman of amazing, wiry strength, with wrists like whipcord and a face hardened to the likeness of timber by foreign suns. She was an old campaigner, had nursed in all sorts of wild places, and cared nothing for anyone. She discarded rules that didn't suit her and even told the doctors when she thought they were wrong; but she was such an excellent nurse she was tolerated by the army establishment on her own terms.

It was unusual for there to be two VADs in a ward on a night shift, but Sister Rankin 'knew the ropes', as the Tommies said, and had 'wangled' herself the extra staff from the matron. With the battle at Cambrai in full swing, they were busy again, with convoys coming in sometimes two or three a night. To Jessie, the battle injuries were a relief in a way after the gas victims. Though the wounds were appalling, at least there was something that could be done, even if in some cases it was not enough. And she was very glad to be with Beta again.

They had gone into winter quarters now – wooden huts divided into small rooms of two beds each. The Alwyn huts could not stand up against the winter weather – the heavy, salty wind blattering in across the marshes from the sea, the bitter cold, the snow. It was so cold that when they slept during the day it was with several layers of clothes on top of their nightwear, and everything else heaped on the bed. Even on the ward they wore a couple of woollen jerseys over their uniforms and under their aprons. Sister Rankin shrugged and told them to wear what they had to to do the job. She had four other wards under her charge and to go from one to the other she wore an officer's greatcoat and a woolly hat, which she hardly ever took off. She said if it got any colder she would go into trousers – a prospect that thrilled Jessie and Beta, who could just imagine the outrage it would cause.

Everyone said it was going to be the coldest winter ever,

colder even than the last. The symptoms were there already. There were icicles on the *inside* of the windows, and outside, the going underfoot was treacherous with black ice under the snow cover. Taps froze, creating a water shortage on the wards. The sponges and flannels they washed the men with would freeze solid if they were not thoroughly squeezed out, and any trace of water left in a hot-water bottle, bowl, kettle or cup would turn to solid ice.

Even items of clothing taken off became stiff in a few hours when left out. Often it was easier simply not to undress; sometimes they went several days without undressing, or washing more than face and hands. Jessie remembered with fondness the days when she had bathed daily after coming off duty. Now the water shortage meant everyone was rationed to one bath a week, and even then the water was rarely more than tepid. At least rushing about on the ward – there was always too much to do – kept your temperature up; and in the mess hut there seemed to be cocoa on the brew at all hours of the day and night. Jessie thought they could not have got through the war without cocoa.

She had not heard from Bertie for weeks now. She suspected he might have been at Cambrai – she knew two divisions had gone there from Ypres, and she knew also, from some of the Cambrai wounded, that they had been forced to maintain strict silence before the battle to keep the Germans from finding out anything about what was planned. Letters home had been stopped, just to make sure nothing was let out. The same embargo might have been placed on the reinforcements.

He had promised he would make sure someone told her when the worst happened. But what if the person charged with telling her was also killed? The army machine would tell only Maud, and Maud would never think to tell Jessie. She might eventually write to Morland Place, and then Mother would pass on the news. But that might take weeks. Jessie tried in the black depths of the icy nights, in the small hours when sometimes the ward was quiet, to search her feelings to see if she 'knew' he was still alive – or the opposite. But she could come to no conclusion. She was too tired and war-weary to have 'feelings' of that kind any more. She wished she could have talked about it to Beta, but she was afraid of giving herself away if she tried to talk about him as merely her cousin. So she suffered in silence, waiting for the axe to fall.

Violet thought she would miss Emma more than she did, when she went away to training camp, looking alien and somehow taller and stronger in her new uniform, topped off with the fur-lined greatcoat with a big fur collar that Violet had urged her at the last minute to buy. It was already turning cold, and everyone said that the winters in France were far colder than in England. Better to be prepared, Violet said, than have to send for something afterwards and be frozen until it came. The coat's fur collar was an ingenious thing that was fixed on with patent fasteners and could be removed if not required (or, Emma thought, if the FANYs proved not to be so independent-minded after all, and strict uniform rules were adhered to).

But though the house was rather quiet for a day or two, and the dogs ran about in a puzzled way, sniffing under the bottoms of closed doors in case the missing Emma was hiding within, it was different now from the way it had been back in February when Emma had first arrived. Violet had got used to going out in the world again, had found it ready to accept her and never to mention the wild affairs of last year. Since she had always been more of a listener than a talker, she did not find social events too much of a drain on her. And having the children living with her meant there was always some little thing going on at home, something she could occupy her mind with in dull moments, and someone who was glad to see her whenever she appeared at the door.

Holkam came home for a short leave after the meeting in Paris on the 4th of November between Haig, Lloyd George and Smuts. He raged and fulminated for the first few hours after he arrived about the suggestion Lloyd George had made for an inter-allied Supreme War Council – a unified command structure with a single supreme commander at the head to rule the Belgian, French, British and, ultimately, American forces. This idea had been mooted at various times since 1914, and had always been rejected. The suggestion had always before come from the French, on the basis that the supreme commander would be a Frenchman. The French generals would never accept an English supremo, given that it was 'their' war, after all; and the English generals had had all too much experience of trying to work with the French and being let down by them to want to be under their thumb.

But on this occasion it was Lloyd George who had made the suggestion, and asked Haig for his view on the matter. Haig told him the thing had always been rejected as unworkable, and that it was unworkable still. Lloyd George had then told him that the decision had already been made and that the council was to go ahead.

'Haig was furious at being humiliated like that,' Holkam said. 'He didn't say much – he never does – but I could see how he felt. If he'd wanted a supreme commander he could have taken the job himself this summer, when the French Army collapsed, but he's never wanted it. And he certainly doesn't want a French commander appointed over his head! Half the problems we've had in this war have been caused by the French telling us where and when we could attack – not to mention waiting around for them to get on with their part of a joint action. Damn it, we could have beaten the Huns a year ago if we'd had a free hand! Sorry, my dear.'

Violet waved away the 'damn' graciously. 'But if no-one wants it, why is it going ahead?'

'The French want it because they'll be in control and "boss" the whole show. And Lloyd George wants it because he means to undermine Haig until he gets fed up and resigns. He's a damned, twisty, scheming, conniving, sneaking dog! And there was worse to come!'

'Oh dear,' said Violet under her breath.

'The council is to consist of the two war cabinets, plus a general from each of the Allied commands. Foch is to be the French general – and who does our beloved prime minister appoint as the English general? His damned puppet, Wilson! As much of a schemer as his master and with no more idea of how to run the war than your dogs! If anyone goes to Versailles it should be the CIGS – that would be obvious to a schoolboy. But Robertson is Haig's man – his only supporter back home. Lloyd George wants to be rid of them both.'

Eventually he calmed down, though the matter was evidently much on his mind, and he tended to lapse into *sotto voce* fulminations at odd moments. He did the rounds of society, both on his own – at the House, Horseguards and his clubs – and in company with Violet, in the various drawing-rooms. They gave a dinner together, hastily arranged but with no refusals, since an invitation to Fitzjames House was one you cancelled other people for. Venetia was among the guests, and Violet witnessed the unusual spectacle of her mother and her husband publicly agreeing with each other over the business of Haig and Lloyd George. Over all, Violet found her husband's visit home much less trying than she had expected.

To counter-balance the loss of Emma, there was the return of Oliver, not only safely out of the firing-line but living at home again. Sidcup was reachable from Town, so he had moved back into Manchester Square, much to Venetia's delight, with a room of his own in a hut at the Queen's for when it was needed. Since reconstruction work was long-winded, slow and fairly predictable, he was able to arrange regular hours for himself, and when off duty could enjoy the delights of London, and be on hand to escort his women-folk. It was lovely for Violet to have him home again, and she let him take her to the silliest revues, and borrowed his arm so often on formal occasions that soon, where she had once always been invited with Freddie, now she was invited with Oliver. He was also able on occasions to help Mark Darroway with his free clinic, especially when there was a burns case or anything else reconstructive, which salved his conscience when it bothered him for enjoying himself in the middle of a war.

If only Thomas would come home! But there seemed no more chance of it now than at any time this year. Violet knew her mother was worried about him, though she rarely mentioned him. Indeed, she seemed to talk about him less now than ever. Was it, Violet wondered, because she had given him up for dead? Oh, surely not! The Red Russians were mad and bad, but even they would never harm a British Army officer, with diplomatic status to boot.

As a preliminary to passing on Thomas's message, Venetia asked Lord Stamfordham to call. He came to her house, as before, at teatime, one day in early December, but this time he did not come alone.

'I hope you will excuse the liberty, Venetia my dear, but I think I know what your summons is about, and I would very much like you to meet Colonel Frederick Browning, of MI 1C.'

'Your servant, ma'am,' said Browning, with old-fashioned courtesy, bowing over the hand she offered him, but scanning her face all the same with a very sharp and experienced pair of eyes. It was obvious that Stamfordham must have told Browning beforehand a great deal about the Lady Overton he was to meet, but he plainly wanted to make his own judgement about her qualities. It seemed his first impression was favourable, because as he straightened up, he smiled and said, 'I'm delighted to meet you. I've heard so much about you. I knew your husband slightly – and your late father was well known in intelligence circles. His name is still spoken for his work in the Crimea.'

Venetia's father, the duke, had been in the intelligence section of the army during the Crimean war; and her husband, Overton, had been on the fringes of it too. But MI 1C Venetia only knew by reputation, and she oughtn't even to have known that much, because it was the section of the Secret Service that dealt with overseas operations.

Stamfordham watched her taking all this in, and said, before she could speak, 'You see, Venetia dear, we are admitting you to state secrets of the highest order, and I am sure I need not tell you that utmost secrecy must be maintained. You must not tell anyone about this meeting.'

'I understand that, of course,' she said. 'Won't you please sit down, Colonel Browning? Arthur?' They took their seats, and without further preamble she produced Thomas's letter and the diagram and handed them to Stamfordham. He read the letter carefully and handed it to Browning while he looked over the plan. While this was going on, Ash and one of the maids came in with the tea things, and Venetia was interested to see how Browning, who had both pieces of paper by then, made them disappear from sight quite effortlessly and naturally, in a way that would not have provoked the slightest curiosity from either servant. When they had gone, the papers reappeared, and Venetia poured and handed. What a pleasure it was to be able to serve bread and butter again! There was currant cake, too, and the inevitable macaroons. She really must do something about persuading the cook to stop making them. They still made her think every single time of her husband, and thinking of him made her miss him as freshly as the first time.

'This is very interesting,' Browning said, when he had finished, handing the papers back to Stamfordham, 'and will prove very useful, I have no doubt. Particularly the ground plan. And if your son could find a way to let us know the strength and usual whereabouts of the guard, it would be even more helpful.'

Venetia's heart jumped. 'Then you are planning a rescue!'

'We haven't got quite that far yet,' said Browning. 'I'm afraid these things take time – too much time, in truth, but some people can't be hurried.' He glanced at Stamfordham as he said it.

Stamfordham smiled. 'He means royalty in general and politicians in particular. One has to be so careful whom one trusts. I can't tell you how refreshing it is to be able to talk to you, knowing you are both intelligent and discreet. All too often people are one or the other. And sometimes neither.'

Venetia shook her head at him. 'Don't waste time on idle flattery, Arthur. Tell me what's going on. I thought the King was dead set against a rescue.'

'Not quite true. He would be glad to see them rescued, as long as they don't come here. Since this second revolution, things are even more unsettled. You know, don't you, that this Lenin fellow and his supporters see their Red revolution as the beginning of a movement they hope will spread all over Europe? France is already riddled with Communists.'

'Germany too,' Browning added.

'Which many would say serves the Kaiser jolly well right,' said Stamfordham.

'Amen to that,' Venetia said, with a smile so impish it was almost a grin.

'And I'm afraid there are far too many Bolsheviks in London. We're too civilised to arrest them, of course. Free speech and all the rest of it.'

'My father always used to say, "Better to have them where you can see them than drive them underground",' said Venetia.

'There's a lot to be said for that,' said Browning. 'But now, to the matter of the guards: presumably it would be easy enough for your son to make the observations. He has free access to the house?'

'Yes,' said Venetia.

'The difficulty is getting his answer back – and transmitting the request to him in the first place. He used the bag for this letter? Hm. But we can't be sure it is *not* scrutinised at some point along the way. In fact, I imagine that Comrade Lenin will be doing quite a lot of that sort of thing when he gets round to it. At the moment he's rather busy consolidating his grip on the country.'

'There's a code,' Venetia said. 'Thomas showed it to me years ago, when he first thought there might be trouble. It can be made to look like ordinary writing, though it would make no sense until it was decoded, of course. But someone who didn't speak English might glance at it and dismiss it.'

'Now that is a piece of extraordinary good fortune,' said Browning. 'To have a man on the inside is fortunate enough, but to have a man on the inside with a code and a transmission route already established is like a miracle. You would be willing to be our intermediary in this?' Venetia nodded firmly. 'I think a letter from a distinguished diplomat to his mother, and sent in the bag, would not draw more than a cursory glance as long as it looked all right. We're getting somewhere, Arthur.'

'But now,' said Venetia, 'tell me what this plan is that isn't a plan. What have you gentlemen in mind?'

Browning took up the story. 'There is a man, a very useful Norwegian of impeccable antecedents, who made his fortune in Russia – and in Siberia in particular – through timber and minerals. He was given Russian citizenship by Nicholas himself, and as Norwegian consul for Siberia he has diplomatic status, so he comes and goes freely. Even more important for our purposes, back in 1913 he pioneered a new trade route from Siberia to western Europe, through the river system from Tobolsk to the Kara Sea, and he owns his own steamship company. He's travelled every yard of it himself, and charted it in detail, and his steamers go up and down all the time, so no-one gives them a second look.'

'And he speaks perfect English, he likes the English, and he feels a sense of obligation to the Emperor for his past kindness, and for allowing him to make his fortune,' Stamfordham finished.

'My God, Arthur, that's perfect!' Venetia breathed. 'It can't fail!'

Browning lifted his hands at such impetuosity. 'Please, Lady Overton, it isn't even a plan yet. It's – an aspiration, no more. We have yet to put the idea to him – he may not be willing to do it – and before we do that we have to check up on him, make sure he's sound. It wouldn't do to have him betray us to the Reds. Then it will all have to be meticulously planned, down to the last detail. You understand that if something like this were to be attempted and to go wrong, it would be the end? We will have one shot at it, and one only.'

Venetia nodded soberly. 'And, of course, it couldn't be attempted until next spring, anyway. The rivers and much of the sea will be frozen solid by now, and the thaw doesn't come until May or even later. The route won't be open until then.'

Browning nodded. 'The Russkies chose well, putting them in Siberia. For half the year, the weather is a most effective gaoler. Hardly anything moves once the snows come down. Everyone uses the rivers to get about, and once they freeze, long journeys are out of the question. To move the entire family by sled would not only be impossible, it would attract the attention of every official and informer in the country. It has to be the rivers or nothing.'

'And that means Thomas will have to stay there for another five months, perhaps even six,' Venetia said. She looked up sharply. 'Does the imperial family *have* six months?'

'That we can't know,' said Stamfordham. 'We don't believe

Lenin wants to harm them – I fancy he sees the family as a bargaining counter he can use in his dealings with European governments. But with the state Russia is in—'

'It isn't Lenin, you see. Extreme socialist as he is, he's a moderate compared to some. Just as Kerensky ousted the Emperor and was ousted himself by Lenin, there's always the chance that some even more revolutionary group will oust Lenin. If he can get to grips with the country soon enough, he may form a government stable enough for us to deal with. But revolution is like the snowball rolling down the mountain. It tends to keep going, and get bigger and more dangerous all the time.'

Venetia gave a crooked smile. 'That doesn't reassure me very much, Colonel. Well,' she pulled herself together, 'what do you want me to do?'

They talked a little more, before the men left. Once, they had urged her to persuade her son to come home before it was too late; now they were hoping he would stay. She no longer cared what happened to the Emperor and Empress, but though she had felt desperately sorry for the children, she began to wonder whether the chance of rescuing them was worth the hazard of her own child. Let some other country do it! she cried inside herself. Let Switzerland, let Japan, let Norway or America! Don't involve my son! Let my son come home!

But, of course, he had involved himself, and she knew he wouldn't leave. And she felt vaguely comforted to know not just that 'someone' was thinking of doing 'something' but who the someone and what the somethings were. She thought the plan had a good chance of succeeding – there was nothing more innocent, for some reason, than a steamer chugging down a river. It was a sight that required no action from the authorities – especially the kind of uneducated, lacklustre, indifferent authorities that would exist in rural Siberia.

But there was so much time for her to get through before

anything could happen, and no-one to share the burden with. She could not tell anyone, not even her own family. Not for the first time she missed Beauty bitterly. *Him* she could have told – in fact, probably they would have approached him first, and *he* would be telling *her*.

On the 3rd of December, at Brest-Litovsk near the Polish border, a Russian delegation headed by Leon Trotsky met the representatives of the German and Austrian governments to discuss a separate peace between Russia and the Central Powers. The Bolsheviks needed time to bring all of Russia under their iron fist, a breathing space while they concentrated on their own problems. The Bolsheviks were in control in the capital cities and most of central Russia, but the Don Cossacks had set up a rival government in southern Russia, claiming independence, as had the Ukrainians, the Poles, the Finns and the Baltic nations. The war was a distraction and a nuisance. It was, in any case, almost impossible to wage any more, with wholesale desertions from the Front, and a crippling lack of food, fuel, ammunition and transport.

But Germany was there on the border in force and under discipline. They would not just go away for the asking, and the Bolshevik government anticipated an unhappy series of demands for territory, which would hurt Russia and, more importantly, themselves in the granting. There were two possible mitigating factors. In the first place, the Germans might be glad to conclude a peace that allowed them to transfer their Eastern Front forces and defeat the Allies before the Americans joined in. And second, if the peace talks took long enough, the worldwide Red revolution, which the Bolsheviks hoped they had started, might spread through Germany sufficiently to topple the regime before concessions had been granted. A socialist-revolutionary Germany would not make the same demands on a sister Bolshevik state. So, there were two requirements of the peace conference – that it should start soon, and that it should go on for a long time.

After a mere two weeks of talking, an armistice was signed on the 16th of December. Then the real haggling began. The Germans made their expected demands for territory, which the Russians refused. It looked like being a long session.

Jessie heard from Bertie at last on the 12th of December. The letter, much watermarked from travelling in the snow-storm that was raging outside, was waiting for her in the mess hut when she came off duty in the morning, and she took it with her to the dining-room to read over breakfast. Seeing his handwriting on the envelope, a great peace took hold of her, and she was in no hurry to tear it open there and then. He was alive!

It was a good breakfast: there was porage, and bacon, and fresh bread that morning, and coffee for a wonder – so unusual that she and Beta had it instead of their usual comforting cocoa – but it was the letter, the letter, the letter, which sat there in her mind like a patch of sunshine, warming her all through. Only when their plates were empty and they were sipping their coffee did Jessie draw it out of her pocket.

Beta said, 'Oh, you've got a letter? Do read it if you want. Don't mind me. I'm not in a chatty mood this morning anyway.'

So she opened it. It was as she had thought – he had been at Cambrai. The silence enforced on them before the battle had been extended by the simple inability to find a moment to write.

We were short-handed all through, and I was never able to get back. We were engaged the whole time. Even when the action was ended on the 7th, we had to stay in the line because there were no reinforcements to relieve us. The men who finally came are the rawest

481

recruits we've seen yet – they have the minimum of training and have only been in France a month. Just one month of trench training! But the weather has closed in and I doubt they will be called upon to do much but keep their feet from freezing. We came out of the line on the night of the 9th/10th and marched back to billets at Bertincourt, from where I now write to you. The Bosch fought better than I've ever known, and they kept coming and coming. I count it a high success that we hung on as we did, though it's a pity we didn't manage to take Cambrai. The men are very tired, having fought at Ypres and then here, and I am hoping we will be marched right out in a day or two. They need a long rest, recuperation, and when the next draft comes out, retraining as a unit. However, it seems for the moment that we must stay here in case we have to go back in for a short time. So, my love, I came through again by some miracle. Be comforted that I am unhurt, only very, very tired and dirty. I have all your letters waiting here to be read, but thought I would send you this line before I read and answer them. Thank you for them. I'm sorry you had to wait through such a long silence. I can guess what you must have been thinking. I love you, my very dearest.

Jessie felt tears welling over her lashes, a mixture of relief and anguish. He was safe; now they had it all to go through again. The war would never end. And the wounded from Cambrai were still coming in.

The next news came from home. Her mother wrote to say that she had heard from Venetia, who had heard it from a friend at the Palace, that Bertie had been recommended for the Victoria Cross for his action at Polygon Wood, in single-handedly taking the trench and saving his men from the machine-gun:

You can imagine how immensely proud we are. The VC – the highest award for gallantry. Teddy says it is only given for quite exceptional acts. We all knew Bertie was brave – and, after all, he already has the DSO – but this is something so special we feel quite light-headed about it. We have all written to him – and, of course, it occurs to me that you probably already know about it, faithful correspondent that you are! Venetia thinks the ceremony may take place in January, which would mean that he would have to come home for it. I don't know how long they give for such a thing but it would be wonderful if he could come and visit us. I suppose Maud will come back for it. What a long time she has been in Ireland, poor thing. With December half over I am beginning to wonder which of my chicks will be coming home for Christmas, and when. Have they said anything to you yet?

Soon afterwards she heard from Bertie again.

I remember that you made me promise to tell you if I was ever decorated again, and I'm ashamed to say I forgot. I knew about it some time ago, but in the balance of things it didn't seem very important. And it isn't as though I deserved it. It wasn't a matter of being brave at all. Courage is grinding on day after day in the face of fear and cold and discomfort, the way the men do, not a few seconds of hot-headed, hot-blooded running. It was over in no time. I felt no fear – and without fear, there can be no courage. However, my own men are so fiercely proud about it that for their sakes I would not refuse it even if I could. But the next man to call me a hero goes on a charge!

A week later, Jessie was told by Sister Rankin that her leave would not be until the middle of January. 'I'm sorry,

Morland,' she said, and though her face showed no feeling, the fact that she had said it at all betrayed real concern. 'I know you qualified for leave in November – Nurse Wallace too. But you know as well as I do that the sisters get first consideration for leave with Christmas coming, and that's just the way it is.'

Jessie nodded. She did know it, and accepted it. Beta's leave would be at the same time as hers. But while that would once have given her great pleasure, she had something else on her mind now that made this news quite irrelevant. The following morning, when she came off duty, she changed her apron, went to the matron's office, and asked permission to see her. She was told at first to make an appointment, but when she said it was urgent, and refused to tell the secretary (it was a WAAC now) what it was about, she was told she would have to wait until Matron was free.

So she sat in the ante-room, where the unexpected warmth and the gentle monotony of the sound of typewriting made her doze off, jolting awake unrestfully every few seconds. The clock on the wall said almost ten when the inner door opened and the matron came out. Jessie scrambled to her feet, and the matron eyed her askance, and said to the secretary, 'What is this?'

'Oh, Matron, Nurse Morland asked to see you, and said it was urgent.'

'Very well. What is it, Nurse Morland?'

'I need to speak to you in private, ma'am,' Jessie said, forcing herself to meet the cool gaze steadily. The warmth of her initial reception at the No. 24 General was not matched now that she was a nuisance and delaying the matron's business.

The matron came to some conclusion, sighed, and turned back. 'Very well. Come in.' When Jessie closed the door behind her, the matron sat down in her chair behind the desk, laid her hands before her, and said, 'What do you wish to say to me? Be brief. I have a great many things to do and you are making me late.'

Jessie had rehearsed the words, but they still did not come easily. 'I wish to break my contract, ma'am, and go home.'

'Indeed?' said the matron, frostily. Breaking contract was a serious matter and not allowed unless there was a really good reason. 'And why do you wish to go home, may I ask? I can guess the reason – you were told this morning about your leave dates, I suppose, and you are annoyed that you will not be going home for Christmas. But what makes you think you are a special case, Nurse? Everyone in this hospital has worked exceptionally hard in the last six months, just as hard as you, and most of them have been here longer. You came out in June, didn't you?'

'May, ma'am,' Jessie said. 'But—'

'Don't interrupt me, Nurse. Everyone is tired, everyone needs rest, and everyone wants to go home for Christmas. But the sisters have priority when it comes to leave. You VADs must fit in as and when possible. I had thought rather well of you up till now, Nurse. I had good reports of you. I am very disappointed that you should take up this self-pitying attitude, and I may tell you that it will not work with me, any more than it did for the previous three VADs who came to me with the same request.'

That accounted, at least, for the hostility of her reception. Jessie stood her ground, her face hot, and said, 'I beg your pardon, but you misunderstand me, ma'am. This is not about leave, or Christmas. I must break my contract and go home, and I shall not be able to come back.'

'And why is that?' the matron said, tapping a pencil irritably against the table. 'Contracts cannot be broken without a very good reason.'

Now she had to say it. Her mouth was dry. Desperately she gripped her hands together behind her back, and said, 'I'm going to have a baby.'

It was terrible to watch the surprise on the matron's young, handsome face give way to contempt. For a long moment she looked at Jessie, while Jessie's cheeks flamed, and she thought the word 'Paris-Plage' over and over, like a sing-song of mockery.

'Are you sure?' the matron asked at last.

'I was married,' Jessie said. 'I have been pregnant before. I am sure.'

For a long moment the matron stared, not at Jessie now but through her, in thought. 'Very well. In that case I shall not require you to have a medical examination. You cannot, of course, remain here in your condition. It would be both dangerous and unsuitable. I shall release you immediately and arrange for your passage back to England. I shall try to get you on a train tomorrow. The sooner you leave the better for everyone.'

'Thank you, ma'am.'

'But I must say, Nurse, that I am very, very disappointed in you. I had thought you a superior girl. How you could let yourself down in this way, how you could let *me* down after all the confidence I have placed in you, is beyond me. This sort of thing disgraces the whole nursing profession. It is an insult to our brave men fighting at the Front. Your family will be very disappointed and ashamed, and I hope they will give you a proper sense of the heinousness of what you have done. You may go and pack now, and I will have your travel warrant sent over to your hut as soon as possible. And if I were you, I would not tell anyone about this. You may say you are going home through ill health. *I* shall not divulge the details to anyone, though of course it will have to go on your official record. Dismissed.'

Jessie turned and went out, feeling scoured by the woman's dislike and contempt, knowing it was only the beginning.

CHAPTER TWENTY-ONE

The journey home was long, cold and miserable, and Jessie had plenty of time to think about her situation; plenty of time to go over in her head the unhappy last words she had shared with Beta. She could not wipe from her mind the change in Beta's expression from smiling interest to blank shock and then pain.

'I can't believe it of you,' she had said, in hurt tones. 'After all we've said about – that sort of thing. I thought I knew you, but it seems I didn't after all. How *could* you?'

'I love him,' was all that Jessie could say.

'Then why don't you marry him? Doesn't he want to marry you?'

'He's married already.'

Then Beta had turned her face away, and that was the most wounding thing of all. 'It's wrong, Jessie,' she said. 'No matter how you look at it, it's just plain wrong.'

'I know,' Jessie said.

'Then why did you *do* it?' No answer to that. Beta got up from her bed, where she was sitting, and walked over to the tiny window, and said, with her back to Jessie, 'I don't think we can be friends any more.'

'I know,' said Jessie again. 'I'm sorry. I'm going home today or tomorrow, so you'll have a new person to share with.' Beta made a vague sound of agreement, and Jessie realised she was crying. It hurt Jessie worse than her own tears; but there was nothing she could say to comfort her or retrieve the situation. They had lost each other.

The matron had evidently wanted to be rid of her as soon as possible, for the travel warrant came over for the noon train. Jessie was not sorry, though she only just had time to pack before the Crossley left for the station. To wait around would have been painful; and there was no-one else to say goodbye to. She sat as far away as possible from the other dozen passengers on the tender, and stared out of the window for the last glimpses of the No. 24 General, the sand dunes, and the forbidding sea. Canvas flapped sharply in the icy wind, the marram grasses bent and trembled, the sea was gunmetal and white-flecked under a lowering sky.

The train to Boulogne and the boat to Dover were both crowded with Tommies going home on leave, and the atmosphere, which began muted with weariness, gradually grew more and more hilarious as the prospect of freedom drew closer. The men wanted to be friendly, and offered the lone nurse sweets and cigarettes, secret nips of this and that, and told her jokes – the Bowdlerised versions. They were happy and relieved to be going home, excited at the prospect of seeing their families again; they had done their duty and their consciences were clear, and they could look forward to untrammelled pleasure for the next seven days. They laughed, and wanted everyone else around them to laugh too. Jessie had never felt so utterly alone.

One Tommy, with hands the size of hams, red and cracked and swollen with the cold, offered her half his rissole sandwich, and she discovered that she was hungry – she had not had breakfast that morning. She checked her automatic refusal, remembering that the baby needed nourishment.

'You're a quiet one,' the Tommy said, watching her take a first bite with proprietorial pride.

'I've just come off night duty,' Jessie said, only realising it as she said it. She was very tired.

'Wot? You bin awake all night? Cor! That's rough, that is,'

he said. 'Well, you just 'ave a sleep when you've finished that. I'll make sure this mob don't disturb you. Like it?' He nodded towards the sandwich.

'It's very good,' she managed to say.

'Made it meself. My special. Comp'ny cook, me. That's where I get these.' He displayed his ruined hands. 'Spud bashing. You bin at Eetaps?' She nodded. 'I bin in the Salient. Cor, that was a picnic, that was! Shit up to our elbows, pardon my French. And it stinks, not like proper mud. Ah, well, San Fairy Ann, eh? Goin' on leave now. First thing I'm goin' t' do when I get 'ome is get the missus to put the copper on and 'ave a bath. Feel as if I'll never get that smell out. You finished? Go on, then, you 'ave a kip, love. I'll shut me cake'ole.'

With her eyes shut she could avoid talking to any of the friendly Tommies, though not hearing them, as they chattered, laughed, joked and swore the journey away. But she did not sleep. Her weary mind went over and over things. She didn't even know what she was going to say when she got home. She couldn't bear to tell them the truth, but she would have to account for her sudden appearance somehow. She thought of Bertie. She could not yet think about the baby. It didn't seem part of Bertie to her yet. It didn't even seem part of her. It had no reality at all, though she knew she was pregnant. She had not menstruated since the end of August. Her breasts were swollen and tender, and she had been sick in the mornings. Fortunately it had happened while she was still on the ward, so she was able to slip away to the sluice room to vomit. Had she been on day duty, it would have been hard to keep the secret from Beta.

She was pregnant. She had been pregnant before, and each time had lost the baby. What were the chances she would keep this one? She was too tired and miserable to be afraid. She had more immediate problems to think about.

The crossing was rough. Some of the men went quiet, though most didn't seem to mind the new motion, only made raucous jokes at the expense of the fragile. It didn't trouble Jessie, who was only sick first thing in the morning. At one point two orderlies came round with a bucket of tea and, feeling desperately thirsty after the rissole sandwich, she 'woke up' and accepted a mug. It was so strong it made her feel slightly drunk, but it restored her a little. She looked out of the small rusty window at the choppy grey sea. The sky was heavy with snow, and it looked bitterly cold out there, though it was fustily warm in the crowded cabin.

At Dover she managed to get into a 'ladies only' carriage with four other nurses going on leave, and two rather quiet WAACs, who, the nurses soon winkled out of them, were going home permanently, having found service in France not at all what they had expected. One of them was very pale and subdued, and Jessie found herself wondering if the girl had 'got into trouble' and was being sent home in disgrace. The other nurses seemed eager to get to the bottom of it, and Jessie closed her eyes and slept determinedly all the way to London, while the snow began to fall.

She crossed London on the Underground, emerging at King's Cross in the dark, the natural dusk made blacker by the heavy clouds and the whirling snow. She turned her eyes away from the ambulances pulled up in the goods approach, and the nurses escorting walking wounded and the stretcher cases to various trains. She was not a nurse any more. Probably she never would be again.

She could not get into a ladies' carriage this time, and found herself squashed in with half a dozen Tommies going on leave, and two RFC privates in very new uniforms, on their way to Marske, who made her think sharply and painfully of Jack. Oh, what would he think of her when he knew? By this time, her night on duty was catching up with her and she did not need to feign sleep. She woke briefly when the train stopped at Doncaster, to discover to her chagrin that her head was resting on the khaki shoulder of one of the RFC boys. But it was comfortable, and comforting, and he didn't seem to mind, so she let herself slide back into sleep again.

Instinct woke her at York, by which time her head was resting against the cold, smutty window. She straightened up, and her former pillow, who had stood up to get his bag down, smiled at her and said, 'I was wondering whether to wake you. Is York your station? Oh, then let me get your valise down for you.'

He was a nice-looking boy with curly, ungovernable hair and a sweet expression, the sort who had a mother and sisters who loved him and were proud of him. 'Thank you,' she said, and managed to find a smile for him.

'Is someone meeting you?' he asked tentatively. He was being kind, wanting to look after her as a nice boy should. It would be fatally easy to get into conversation with him, to mention that she had a brother in the RFC. If he was plane-nutty, he would probably even have heard of Jack, and would delight in telling her his own story.

'Yes,' she said. 'Thank you. I have to wait for them over here.' Out of the corner of her eye she saw his philosophical shrug at the snub; and she waited by the clock until he had disappeared, before going out to join the queue at the taxi-rank. Everything seemed to be contriving to bring it home to her that she was now a pariah; and she hadn't even thought what to say to the family.

In the end, with everyone's surprise and pleasure and excitement at seeing her, and all the exclamations, and so many people talking at once, and so many dogs demanding attention, there was no need for her to say anything.

'What a surprise!'

'We had no idea!'

'Get down, Bell! Tiger, get off it! Lie down!'

'Jessie, darling!' This was her mother – and, oh, it was good to feel her mother's arms around her again, so good it was all she could do not to cry.

'Why didn't you tell us?'

'Have you had a terrible journey?'

'We'd have met you at the station.'

'You must be frozen. Come to the fire.'

Her coat and hat were taken, her bag whisked away, her frozen hands rubbed as she was drawn lovingly towards the drawing-room.

And then, lifting clear of the flow of words, one question she had to answer. From her mother: 'Is it leave? How long can you stay?'

Everyone stopped what they were doing and saying to hear the answer. Seeing her mother only through a mist of weariness and shock, Jessie heard herself answer, 'Not leave. I'm home for good.'

There was a little silence, in which she could feel her heart beat like a trapped bird; she heard Ethel draw a breath to say something, only to let it out in a tiny, muted yelp as Maria pinched her. And then a vast, loving blanket of tactfulness came down, like disguising snow-cover over the spiky ruined landscape of what her reasons might possibly be.

'Poor darling, you look so tired,' Henrietta said. 'When did you last eat?'

'I don't know,' Jessie said. When had that rissole sandwich been? Could such things exist? Here in the ancient hall of her childhood home, with the stillness of centuries deep in the walls like a patina, the noisy, insistent idiosyncrasies of the army, and the life that surrounded it and everything it touched, dissipated like mist. Only this was sure, only this was lasting – home, Morland Place, the family and its history: set deep in its foundations, a tower unrocked by the eddies of time, rooted in the utter sureness that was England. Oh, God, she was so glad to be home!

'I'll go and see Mrs Stark and arrange for something to eat,' said Maria.

'But do you mean you aren't going back?' Ethel's voice lifted again.

'Jessie doesn't want to answer any questions now,' Henrietta said, in that voice, rarely used, that commanded obedience, the Voice of the Mistress.

'I'll go to the kitchen,' Alice said, giving Maria a meaning look. 'You go with Jessie. I'm sure her shoes and stockings are wet – you should make her take them off. Ethel dear, come with me and help me carry.'

She hustled Ethel away, and Jessie heard her saying, 'I don't see why we can't ring for Sawry,' and being shushed by Alice.

But after that there were no more questions, just comfort being applied to her weary body, and love and reassurance to her hurt mind. Even Ethel, when she came back, helping Alice carry a tray of food and drink and warm towels for the rubbing of wet feet and damp hair, had been chastened into silence, and held her tongue in the most noble effort of restraint that had ever been asked of her. The fire was stoked up, there was cocoa, blessed cocoa in a mug to wrap her hands around, and good hot soup that Henrietta would have spooned into her mouth for her, given any encouragement, and oatcakes, and cheese from their own dairy – a taste of heaven. Maria knelt down and removed her boots and stockings and chafed her feet dry and warm, and Polly, surprisingly gentle, dried and then combed out her hair with a slow, deft touch. The dogs sat round staring at her, making her sure of their welcome by displaying their dripping tongues, and beating their tails and licking their lips whenever her eye drifted over them. And when the food was finished, Ethel's white cat Snowdrop jumped from nowhere onto her lap, and kneaded bread, purring like an engine.

No-one asked her anything, only made solicitous comments and chatted around her, giving her snippets of local news and household affairs. Uncle Teddy and Helen were both away, she was told, Helen visiting her mother, and Teddy in Manchester settling something at the mills.

Finally Henrietta said, with concern in her voice, 'Darling, you're quite dead on your feet. Are you well?'

'Just tired,' Jessie said. 'It was a long journey.'

'You'd better go up to bed straight away.'

'I told them to make it up when I was in the kitchen,' Alice said, proud of herself for having thought of it. 'And to put a hot-water bottle in.'

A hot-water bottle! The thought of it made every part of Jessie's body ache with yearning.

'Do you want a bath first?' Henrietta asked.

'Tomorrow,' Jessie said. She could hardly speak now for tiredness. 'Just sleep now.' It took quite an effort for her to get to her feet.

'I'll see you upstairs,' Maria said quickly, to forestall anyone less tactful.

Jessie managed to smile. How kind would Maria – would any of them – feel towards her when they knew the terrible truth? 'Thanks, but I'd rather go alone. I'll be all right. I'm used to taking care of myself.'

They let her go, and Polly pulled the dogs back from following her. The house away from the fires was cold, but nowhere near as cold as the huts in France had been. Still, she was shivering by the time she reached her room. Inside, though, there were candles lit, and a leaping fire, and Tomlinson, dear Mary Tomlinson, who knew exactly what to do for her.

'Welcome home, Miss Jessie. There now, don't say anything, just let me look after you.'

She did. She washed Jessie's face and hands in hot water, and held a bowl before her while she cleaned her teeth – 'You'll sleep better for it!' – then undressed her, and slipped her into a nightgown that had been warming before the fire, and helped her into the bed, where two hot-water bottles had taken the chill off the sheets – fresh sheets from the linen-room, smelling of lavender. She drew the covers over her, blew out one candle and picked up the other to take with her. And just before she left, she said gently, 'Don't worry about anything. You're safe home now.'

Then she was gone, and in the firelit darkness Jessie felt her aching body relax into the utter bliss of a warm, clean bed, and her mind yield to the soft, blessed billows of sleep. She would have liked to cry with relief, but she was too – far – gone . . .

Whatever family conference had gone on while she slept – and she could imagine her mother saying, in that same commanding voice, 'She'll tell us when she's ready. No-one is to ask her any questions' – she woke to a world where her presence was accepted and the subject of why she had come home was forbidden. When Teddy returned from Manchester, Henrietta made sure to get to him first and talk to him, and Maria did the same with Helen – not that Helen had a tactless bone in her body. Jessie was allowed to rest, recuperate, and get clean without being troubled; but she could not be happy. The thing hung over her, the thing they would all have to know some time, and which would ruin everyone's lives. For the moment, her whole purpose was to keep it from them while she could, not in the hope that some way out would be found but simply to put off the misery for as long as possible.

One morning, early, she had just been sick a little, when her bedroom door opened, startling her. She hastened to thrust the chamber pot back under the bed while trying to appear unflurried, and pulled the covers back over her – she was beginning to show just a bit. She had been having to choose her clothes carefully.

'It's all right, Miss Jessie,' said Tomlinson. 'It's only me.'

She had brought a tray, on which was a cup of tea without milk, and some dry toast. She placed it on Jessie's lap, and Jessie looked askance. It was not how she took her tea; and butter was not scarce in *this* household.

Tomlinson met the look steadily. 'It'll settle you. Best not to have any grease while you're feeling queasy.'

'What makes you think— I mean, it was nothing, just—'

'It's all right,' Tomlinson said again. 'I know.'

Jessie stared, hardly knowing what to think.

'Oh, Miss Jessie, how long have I been with you? I *know* you. Don't you think I knew why you dressed yourself, and wouldn't let me see you in the bath? Why do you think I've taken to emptying your chamber myself, instead of letting the housemaid do it? Now, don't worry, I shan't say a thing. You can trust me. Oh, Miss Jessie!'

This last, because Jessie had begun helplessly to cry. Tomlinson sat down on the bed and took her mistress into her arms, and held her while she wept onto her shoulder. And all she said was, 'That's right, let it go. Don't worry, no-one will come in. I've given orders that only *I'm* to come in in the mornings. You have your cry out.'

Eventually the tears were spent, and Tomlinson produced handkerchiefs, and stroked her hair. 'You don't hate me?' Jessie said at last, blowing her nose. 'You ought to. Why don't you hate me?'

'Why ever should I hate you?'

'Because I've done a wrong thing.'

'There's a lot of it about, Miss Jessie. Two girls in the village that I know of. It's the war, I suppose.'

'I know what you mean,' Jessie said, thinking of the WAAC in the train, and the rumours that had always gone round in Étaples about girls 'getting into trouble' and being sent home. 'But that's village girls. Working-class girls. It doesn't matter so much for them. But for me . . .' It hadn't mattered, in the end, for Violet, either. At the very top, and at the bottom, things got arranged, and the matter was covered up or ignored. But for people in the middle, like her, there was no escape.

'Your mother would understand, I should think,' Tomlinson said thoughtfully.

Jessie shuddered. 'No. I can't tell her. She'd be too shocked and ashamed. I couldn't bear her to be ashamed of me. And Uncle Teddy . . .'

Tomlinson only nodded. It was true, that it was different for village girls. Jessie would face a world of shame and scandal. The family would be hurt and shocked and disappointed in her. The household would get to know, and the tenants, and the villagers, and then all the fine people in York, where the Morlands were looked up to and sometimes envied. Then people would talk and whisper and point the finger. And there would always be some who would be gleeful at the fall of a high-up family.

'It would hurt the whole Morland name,' Jessie said. 'Remember when people cut Uncle Teddy because of that *Titanic* business? It nearly killed him. This would be such a terrible blow to him. He'd never get over it. And the family would never live it down. It would ruin everyone. Think of Polly! I can't tell them, Mary, I just can't. You do see that.'

'Yes, Miss Jessie. But they'll find out sooner or later.'

'I'll have to go away.' Tomlinson did not deny the necessity. 'But where? Where can I go?'

'Well, miss, you've money, haven't you, from the stables and so on? Enough to rent a place.'

'But what would I tell the family? I'd have to give a reason for going.'

Tomlinson nodded. 'It's a difficult one. It needs thinking about, does that. But there's still time. You can stay until Christmas, at least. You can't go before Christmas, Miss Jessie – it would break your mother's heart. We'll make sure no-one finds out anything, don't you worry. I'll look after you, and we'll work out where we can go, and what we can say.'

'We?' Jessie queried, with faint, shaky hope.

'Of course I'm coming with you,' Tomlinson said, in a voice so matter-of-fact there could be no arguing with it. 'You can't go on your own. Who'd look after you?'

'But Mother needs you here.'

'I'm your servant, miss, not hers – and your mother has plenty of people now to take care of her. Wherever you go, I'm going with you, and that's it and all about it.'

Jessie pressed her hand. 'Thank you, Mary.' A few more tears squeezed out.

'Eh, miss! We'd just got you dry.'

'It's only relief. And gratitude,' Jessie said, blotting them, and blowing her nose again. 'My face must be horribly swollen.'

'I'll pat it with cold water, miss. It'll soon go down. But try not to cry again now.' She got up from the bed, but Jessie still had hold of her hand, and she turned back, to meet a pleading, anxious look.

'It's not—' Jessie began, and swallowed. 'Mary, it was only because I love him.'

Tomlinson patted her hand. 'I know that, miss,' she said gently. 'It's took for granted.'

Though no-one asked anything or said anything, it was not possible to stop them thinking, and it was obvious that they thought that, for various reasons, she simply could not take any more of the strain of being out there, and had given up and come home. It was galling in a way, because however tired she had been, she would not have thrown up the sponge. But it was her punishment, as the days passed, to live with her mother's worry that she was secretly ill, or had simply outrun her strength. She had to accept Uncle Teddy's ever-so-faint disappointment in her, that having done the brave thing and gone to France to nurse and made him proud of her, she had now let him down by not seeing it through to the end. She had to put up with Ethel's barely concealed triumph that she had been right all along in telling Jessie, and everyone else, that nursing was not a nice thing for a lady to do, and that she should never have attempted it. She knew that Polly thought her poor-spirited, and compared

Jessie's lack of courage with that of the Morland men, facing death on various fronts every day without complaint. What Maria thought she could not imagine; and she did not suppose Aunt Alice thought at all, being happy to assume that things were always the way they were because they could not be any different.

What Helen thought, she was soon to find out. The snow had stopped and she had put on thick clothes and her heaviest boots and gone for a walk with all of the dogs who could be coaxed from the fireside. She wanted to get away from the tension she felt at home, with everyone's unanswered questions swooping above her head like bats, and the worry of how to conceal matters long enough, and where to go and what to do afterwards, which still seemed insoluble. Christmas was fast approaching.

The track had been cleared from Morland Place to Twelvetrees, and it made a good walk, far enough to stretch her legs and her lungs and make her pleasantly tired; and at the other end was Hotspur, who was always glad to see her. When she had come home, Webster had got him in from the field and groomed and fed him so that he would be ready for her to ride. But she dared not go riding, after her previous miscarriages. Fortunately the weather had been too thick for the omission to need explaining.

She had brought apples, and he whickered and pricked his ears over them, and tossed his head up and down in approval as he munched. When they were gone, he lipped her softly all over her face and hair to check that she was all there, then rested his head on her shoulder with a sigh of content. She caressed his cheeks, glad to be with him again, talking to him quietly, apologising for not riding him. Probably she would not be able to take him with her when she left. Then she wondered again, hopelessly, where she could go and how she could possibly explain it to the family.

Hotspur snorted, and a shadow fell over the doorway. Helen's voice said, 'I should have guessed I'd find you here.

Polly said you started in this direction, but I couldn't be sure where you'd gone. I met the dogs coming back, but they weren't telling.'

'Oh, you startled me,' Jessie said, disengaging herself from the horse.

Hotspur reached over to blow at Helen's hands. 'No, I haven't got anything for you, old boy. I want to talk to you, Jessie. Can we go somewhere quiet?'

'Isn't it quiet here?'

'Someone may come in, and I don't want to be overheard. Shall we start walking back?'

Her heart thumping uncomfortably, Jessie went with her. They trudged in silence for a while, until they were clear of the stables and yards and out into the open fields again. Then Helen said, 'I know you are in trouble, Jessie. I know it's something serious, and I wish you would let me help you with it.'

Jessie didn't answer, her stomach churning. Part of her longed to tell, the other part was too terrified of being found out even to speak.

'We're friends, sisters. You've always told me things. Let me help you. Whatever it is, I promise you it won't seem nearly so black if you share it with me. Two minds on the problem can solve it.'

'Why should you think there's something wrong?' Jessie said, trying to sound light, but even to herself only sounding defensive.

Helen sighed, just audibly, as if she did not want to waste time on this part of it. 'You don't take Communion any more. That's the biggest thing. You always do when you're home, but now you never go near the chapel. You don't talk, you don't laugh, you don't join in. You hardly eat; and then I see you suddenly realise you're not eating, and start to force food down as though it's a duty instead of a pleasure. You always enjoyed your food before, and Mrs Stark hasn't lost her touch. And Tomlinson won't let any of the other maids go near you – oh, yes,' she said, as Jessie looked at her in surprise. 'There isn't much I don't hear. The nursery-maids are terrible chatterers, and seem to work on the assumption that members of the family are stone deaf, or speak a different language.'

She stopped, and Jessie stopped too, perforce. They faced each other, and Helen examined her gravely. 'I think I know the answer, but I wish you would tell me yourself. Please, Jessie. I promise you I'll understand. I want to help you. Jack would hate it if I let you struggle on alone.'

The mention of Jack brought the tears, which always seemed so ready these days, to her eyes, and she pressed them back angrily with her fingers. 'You won't understand,' she said. 'You'll hate me. You'll think I've done something terrible, and—' The sentence ended in a sob as she tried to force the tears back down.

'*Have* you done something terrible?'

'No! Yes, in a way, but no. At least – I know it was wrong, but I'm not sorry, and that's why I can't take the sacrament. If it was wrong, I don't care – but everyone else will, and they'll hate me for it or, at least, they'll be ashamed, and I can't bear for them to be ashamed of me.'

'Oh Jessie – dear – what is it?' Helen said gently. 'Is it a baby?'

Jessie's gasp was all the confirmation she needed. 'How – how did you guess?'

'Deduction.' Helen got out one of her capacious handker-chiefs. 'Here, take this. Look here, darling, I don't hate you and I'm not shocked and I do understand, and you'll have to let me help you because, frankly, there isn't anyone else. I quite see why you can't tell the family, especially not your mother and Uncle Teddy. They won't hate you, of course, but they will—' She hesitated. 'All right, they will be ashamed.'

'Oh, Helen, what am I going to do?' Helen had given her her hand, and there was such strength and comfort in it. Helen was such a *rock*.

'First things first,' Helen said. 'Can't you marry him?' A thought came to her. 'Oh, God, he isn't dead?'

'No, but he may be soon. He's still out there. *You* know the chances.'

'Yes,' Helen said, thinking of Jack. 'Well, can't you marry him?'

'He's married already.'

'Ah. I was afraid that might be it.'

'But I love him. I love him so much, Helen.'

'Well, I was assuming that. You wouldn't have done it otherwise,' Helen said. 'Does he know?'

'I haven't told him yet.'

'Are you going to?'

'I don't know. I don't know if it would make it harder for him.' She thought of Bertie facing death, and suffering more because he would be leaving behind not only her but their child, too. 'I don't think I can,' she said. 'But, in any case, there's nothing he could do to help me.'

'I see,' Helen said thoughtfully.

'I can't stay here,' Jessie went on. 'Tomlinson persuaded me I must stay for Christmas, because Mother will expect it.'

'Ah, Tomlinson knows, does she?'

'She guessed. She's been with me a long time, through the other pregnancies.' That was another thing, something she could not articulate even to Helen. She had lost those other babies. Suppose she told Bertie, and then she lost this one, too? That would surely break his heart. No, better to say nothing.

'I'm starting to show now,' she went on, 'so I must get away before anyone guesses. But I don't know where to go.'

'Wherever you go, you can't go alone.'

'Tomlinson said she'll go with me.'

'She's a good person. But how will you explain it away? Everyone expects you to stay at Morland Place now. What would you tell them?'

'That's the hardest thing of all,' Jessie said. 'I'm at my

wits' end. Sometimes I think it would be best just to disappear one day.'

Helen looked startled. 'No, you can't do that. It would be too cruel, leaving them to wonder. Poor Uncle Teddy still thinks Ned is alive somewhere. You can't have him searching for you as well.'

'No, I suppose not,' Jessie said despondently. She shivered.

'You're getting cold. Let's walk on, while I think.' They walked a while in silence, and then Helen said, 'Well, I see nothing else for it. You must come home with me, to Downsview House. No-one there knows you, so there'll be no questions asked.'

'But – I didn't realise you were going back.'

'I wasn't, but that isn't a difficulty. I have been thinking I'd like to go home for a while, and it would certainly make my work much easier. All this travelling up and down is wearing. Of course, I'll have to take the children, and Basil will probably never forgive me – he loves it here so much. Oh, that's it, of course!' she said with a *eureka* face. 'I shall say I want to go home, and you've said you'll come with me to help with the children. After all, the reason I brought them here in the first place was because I couldn't leave them with only the servants while I was on a job. I shall be very grateful to you for offering to help. You need a change of scene, and you love children, and I need you more than Morland Place does. It makes perfect sense.'

'It does,' Jessie said slowly, seeing the thing before her like a cage door opening.

'We'll stay there until you have the baby, and then we'll decide what to do next. No need to worry about that now,' she said, seeing the look on Jessie's face as she realised that hiding the pregnancy was not the end of her troubles. 'One step at a time. Now, what do you think of the scheme? It seems to me to cover all the points.'

'Thank you,' Jessie said. 'You've saved me, Helen. I shall never be able to thank you enough.'

'No need for thanks. I've been missing my little home, and I shall be grateful to you for making it possible for me to go back. Shall we tell them straight away? Better get it settled, so you don't fret any more. I'll do the talking, don't worry. I'll announce that we've talked it through, and that we'll have Christmas here, and then you, I and Mary Tomlinson will take the children home to Wiltshire.'

Violet remained in London for Christmas. If Holkam had been home, he would have expected them all to go down to Brancaster, but he wrote to say he was staying in Paris and would not be home again until January. With the snow down, Brancaster, on the edge of the Lincolnshire fens, would have been positively Siberian, so Violet was glad to be excused it. Also Freddie got home, and she would have missed him if she'd been down in the country. It was good to see him back and unharmed. Furthermore, her mother wanted to stay in London – Violet guessed it was something to do with Thomas, but everything to do with Thomas seemed shrouded in secrecy, these days. So it was pleasant to have the celebration at Fitzjames House, and have the family come to her.

Oliver was in fine form, bubbling over with enthusiasm for his new job and his new boss. Gillies was an artist – literally and metaphorically. He would sketch each new face before he created it, working over the drawing for days to get it just right. His medical and manual skills were exquisite, and he was always improving on the established techniques: for instance, on noting that the edges of a pedicle – the raised flap of skin that was grafted to a wound to create new flesh – tended to curl inwards, he followed nature and sewed them together, making a tube of flesh rather than a flap, which improved blood flow and helped avoid infection. But, said Oliver, he was a wonderfully down-to-earth and practical man, too. When the government had first said he could set up his own plastic unit, he had gone out and bought a whole lot of luggage labels and had them printed with the address. Then he sent them to the Front with the instruction that face and jaw cases should be labelled so they would come direct to him.

A further comfort for Oliver was that his friend Kit had managed to get his leave at Christmas, and had overcome his pique at being left behind sufficiently to agree to spend Christmas with Oliver's family. Violet was tactful enough not to point out that he really had nowhere else to go. But it made a pleasant houseful: to save on fuel – still short this very cold winter – Venetia agreed to close her house for a few days and everyone stayed at Fitzjames House. The children loved having company and, released from the restraints of school and lessons, rushed about the house shrieking with pleasure, racing the Pekingeses up and down the stairs. Little Octavian was crawling now, and could make pretty good speed on the level, though stairs and the marble floor of the ante-room defeated him. All the children loved Uncle Oliver, who was much jollier than Mama and not frightening like Papa, and who had a fascinating way of discovering magic pennies hidden behind one's ear, or sweets in a pocket previously proved to be empty.

The final touch of pleasure for everyone was that Emma was able to join them; and she came with the news that she was to go out to France in January, wonderfully early, as she would only have had three of the normal four months' probation. 'I'm sure Vera has pulled strings for me.'

'Vera?' Venetia enquired.

'Vera Polk. She's the officer who recruited me.' Emma surveyed Venetia's expression. 'Do you know her?'

'Yes, I have met her,' Venetia said tersely. 'I'm sorry to say she was a very bad influence on my cousin Anne. I hope her connection with the FANY is a sign that she has mended her ways.'

She said it in a tone that suggested it was a forlorn hope, and Emma realised there must be more to this than she knew about. Obviously Cousin Venetia disliked and disapproved of Vera for some reason, and the best thing to do was to drop the subject, which Emma did forthwith. She found another topic, and decided not to mention that Vera had invited her to stay for a few days before she went overseas. There was no need for older people to like *all* one's friends.

Venetia enjoyed that Christmas more than she had expected to, for despite Thomas's continued absence, at least now she knew that something was being done about it. Better than that, she was directly involved in it, and did not need to trust other people to let her know how things were progressing – which was slowly, of course; but nothing could be done until the thaw, anyway. Meanwhile, she had Oliver home, and doing interesting, useful work – she meant to ask him to arrange for her to visit and observe some of the techniques in the New Year – and Violet was more settled and happy, and seemed to be getting on better with Holkam.

And in January the Women's Suffrage element of the Representation of the People Bill would come on in the Upper House, and things were looking good. Even Lord Curzon, the arch-enemy, had been saying that while he still thought votes for women would be a disaster and spell the ruin of the country, he supposed they were now inevitable. There had recently been a flurry of anti-suffrage protest from the diehards in the press, but to Venetia's ear it had the ring of desperation, not of confidence. That dreadful Mrs Humphrey Ward (the most annoying of the antis because she was a woman, which allowed the press to claim she spoke for all women) had accosted her on the street one day and had had the temerity to ask her to support the idea of taking the women's vote out of the Bill and putting it to a referendum. Venetia had been so startled she actually laughed. 'Who would you address the question to?' she asked derisively. 'The men, who elected the House of Commons, which has already passed the clause with a huge majority? Or perhaps the women, whom you don't believe are capable of voting rationally on any subject?'

Mrs Ward had looked annoyed and discomfited, which Venetia took to be a good sign. If she was prepared to put up such a ridiculous red herring at this late stage, it must be because she was afraid the clause was going to go through this time.

All in all, things were better than she might have hoped, and she was prepared to enjoy Christmas to the top of her bent, even if it did mean sleeping in a strange bed – something that, at her age, was to be endured rather than looked forward to.

Bertie wrote,

Don't feel guilty about going home. You have done your bit and more, and I know what you will have been facing day after day, without relent – sights no woman should ever have to look on. You must be exhausted. I honour you more than I can say for what you have done, and there is no shame in letting someone else take up the slack now. I am glad to think of you being at Morland Place for Christmas. I wish to God I could join you, but there is so much to do out here I don't anticipate being able to get away for at least a month more. We are still desperately short-handed and reinforcements are arriving only in dribs and drabs. Fritz, of course, does not take a holiday, and is probably feeling rather uppish now some of the Eastern Front soldiers are coming back. At all events, we are having a lot of their toys thrown over, and it seems to be the hardest thing in the world to make the new men keep their heads down when they can't actually *see* the enemy. I wish I knew why the government won't send us more men – I've heard there are plenty held in England, fit and ready. Why aren't they here? For most of this year,

507

since the French collapsed, we have been fighting the enemy on our own. Our chaps have done marvels, but if only we had been given men enough we might have got a lot further than we have. The men are all making the best of being here for Christmas and looking forward like children to a bit of fun. We are doing our best to make it festive. There will be goose or turkey for everyone, and a positive excess of plum pudding, since we get sent several every week by charitable ladies back home, and the men will get beer with it, while the CO has very kindly donated a case of wine to swell the officers' feast. D Company, which is in reserve, has worked up a concert party, which they'll be taking round, and I understand that a company of FANYs called the Fanytasticks is to be touring with a revue of some sort. So Joy, if not unconfined, will at least have her stays loosened. Think of me sometimes, and write when you can. You are never far from my thoughts.

Jessie did not quarrel with her decision not to tell him about the baby. Given her past history, she was more likely to lose it than not, and then the problem would be solved, and there would have been no need to add to his burdens. But even as she thought about this way out of her troubles, she knew that she desperately did not want to lose the baby. However hard her life would be afterwards, whatever difficulties she would face, she wanted Bertie's child with all her heart. With the coming of that knowledge, she became sharply aware of her body and of every possible hazard surrounding it. She began to take care of herself, ate sensibly, avoided lifting heavy weights – which included all the children except Barbara – and kept the dogs from jumping up at her, and when she walked downstairs, she kept a firm hold of the baluster and watched her step carefully.

The sickness had stopped and she was feeling well now, and with the decision about leaving taken, and the knowledge that she had two good friends who were going to stand by her, her mind was easier too. Christmas was not going to be such a trial after all.

Henrietta watched her daughter with anxious eyes. She knew Jessie was concealing something, some secret trouble, and had been afraid to begin with that it was an illness. Jessie had looked so shocked and ill when she had first arrived that Henrietta had feared she had come home to die. But that look had passed, and she was now a better colour, and was eating well – she even seemed to have put on weight. Surely she could not be mortally ill and still look so strong? But there was still something troubling her, and Henrietta now guessed it must be a mental or spiritual trouble. She wished Jessie would confide in her; or failing that, in Father Palgrave. But though Jessie went to chapel when it was a family service, she did not go up to the altar any more, which upset Henrietta more than anything, because it suggested she had shut herself off from God. She was very glad that Helen was going to take her to Wiltshire, even though it meant losing Helen and the children, which would be a sad depletion of the household. But she was sure Helen had hatched the plot purely to get Jessie away, and that this was the best thing for Jessie. She needed a change of scene and a change of air, and perhaps she would confide in Helen where she would not confide in her mother.

So Henrietta presented a tranquil appearance to the family as Christmas approached. It was good, anyway, to know that her daughter was out of the danger zone, though Robbie and Lennie would not be getting leave, and would be having their Christmas in the East. Robbie, indeed, would be in Jerusalem, which one ought to consider a very appropriate place to be. Bertie was still in France – they were so proud of him for winning the VC – and she and Teddy, with Maria's help, had made up a Christmas parcel for him, as they did for the other two.

And at least Jack came home, having got his leave to

coincide with Christmas. Henrietta was shocked at the sight of him, too: so thin and worn, with that not-attending look in his eyes she had seen in Jessie's, too, and in the eyes of other men back from the Front when she met them in the village – a look that said they had been experiencing things they would never be able to talk about. But being Jack, he cheered up at once, and though the look never completely went away, he was there, and he was glad. He ate enormously, played with the children, and told them funny stories about life in the squadron. Henrietta simply wanted to be close to him, touch him and look at him as much as she could while she had the chance. She knew the casualty rate in the RFC was worse than in the infantry, and she had already lost Frank and Ned. If this was Jack's last Christmas, she wanted not to waste a moment of it.

Helen told Jack about the plan to go home after Christmas and take Jessie, and while he was sorry she was leaving Morland Place – he had liked to think of her safe there while he was away – he quite understood her desire to go back to the house they had chosen together, and equally saw the convenience of it for her. At least she would have Jessie there to help with the children and keep her company, and Jack was always glad to see his two favourite women together, happy they were so particularly fond of each other.

'Is there something wrong with Jessie?' he asked Helen in bed one night.

'Why do you ask?' Helen countered casually.

'She seems very quiet – doesn't join in things the way she used to. Why did she give up the nursing, anyway?' And before Helen could speak, he answered himself. 'Had enough of it, I suppose, and who can blame her? I hate to think what she must have been going through these past months – with Arras, and then Ypres, and then Cambrai. It's enough for anyone. I've seen battle casualties, and I tell you, *I* wouldn't want to have to deal with them. It's a good thing for us men that you women are less squeamish than we are, or what would we do for nursing at all?'

'You managed before there were female nurses.'

'I'm not sure it was managing. From what I've read, we had to get better or die on our own. Poor old Jessie! She was such a brick, going into nursing and sticking it out all that time. She's done her bit.'

'I think she's tired,' Helen said. Jessie had begged her not to tell Jack unless it was absolutely necessary, and it seemed as though it was not – not yet, at any rate.

'We're all tired,' Jack said shortly.

'Oh, Jack,' Helen said, turning into his arms; and then there were other things to think about than her sister-in-law.

Later, as she was drifting off to sleep, Jessie came back to her thoughts. For Jessie's sake, Helen had made light of the difficulties ahead, but she did not take the situation lightly. She had been profoundly shocked when she guessed what was wrong, and had hoped against hope that she was mistaken. It seemed against all reason that Jessie should have done such a thing. Bad and sad as it was, everyone lost by it; and if the family ever found out . . . Well, it didn't bear thinking about – though thinking about it was exactly what she would have to do, if Jessie carried the baby to term. What on earth would they do then?

She wondered sleepily who it was that Jessie had fallen in love with so badly that she was willing to sacrifice her pride, her decency, her reputation and even her family for him. Someone she had met out there – some officer with all the glamour of the war behind him? *Morituri te salutamus.* How many men had seduced how many women on the eve of battle with that very thought, that it might be the last chance? Jessie wasn't the first and she wouldn't be the last. But Jessie had always been so level-headed. And she was not a romantic girl. She'd been married. Poor Jessie . . . Poor Ned. Perhaps it was just loneliness . . . Women had to take love where they

511

could find it, especially in war . . . Maria and Frank . . . Jack . . . Oh, Jack . . . !

She turned over towards him and was taken in his arm, onto his shoulder, and was instantly and blissfully asleep.

It was the 6th of January when they set off. Jack had gone back the previous day, bearing a letter to post over there to Bertie from Jessie, telling him that she was going to Wiltshire for a while, so that Helen could go back to her own home. Uncle Teddy was distressed that Helen was going and taking her children with her, and inclined to see the situation upside down – that if only Jessie had not agreed to go with her, Helen wouldn't have been able to change the situation, which he regarded as so comfortable for all concerned.

He couldn't have lamented the change any more than Basil, who was unhappy enough about his father's renewed disappearance, and thought it quite unreasonable to be taking him away from the nursery and all the cousins he liked to play with and torment, and all the billowy nursery-maids he liked to snuggle up to. Aunt Jessie was no substitute, and he relieved his feelings by telling her he hated her, kicking the nearest valise, and bursting into the loudest tears he had ever yet managed.

Henrietta took Jessie in her arms and held her close for a long time, then kissed her and said, 'Don't stay away too long. I've had to do without you too much since the war began.'

Jessie could only nod, biting her lips to stop herself crying.

Polly gave her a brief, businesslike hug and said, 'I'll look after Hotspur for you. Don't worry, he'll never even miss you.'

And now they were driving away in the motor, under the barbican and over the drawbridge, and turning out on to the track, kept clear by a detail of soldiers as a courtesy to their landlord. There was a new battalion in the camp, the first batch now being down at Aldershot and waiting to be sent

512

to France – or anywhere. The war went on, and Jessie felt suddenly, oddly, lonely for it. She had been a part of it, on the inside, 'in the know'. Now it went on without her, and she was just a supernumerary, one of the mass of ignorant civilians for whom the army was a closed world.

She could never go back to it. And as the motor took her away to face a new and difficult life elsewhere, she looked back at Morland Place, grey stones under a grey sky – her home – and wondered if she would ever be able to go back there, either.

Dynasty 30: The Measure of Days
Cynthia Harrod-Eagles

1916. England is at war, and the Morland family is in the thick of it, with two men already in France and three more soon to go.

Tragedy strikes Morland Place when Jessie's husband Ned is reported missing on the Western Front. His father launches a desperate bid to find him, but the family fears the worst. Jessie, in mourning and frustrated by her job as an auxillary nurse, goes to London to work in a military hospital. There she is reunited with her old friend Oliver, posted to the capital under the RAMC. Also in London is Violet, whose affair with the brilliant artist Octavian Laidislaw is about the erupt in scandal . . .

The Measure of Days paints a portrait of a family and a nation at war at a pivotal point in history. With the onset of conscription, no one is left unaffected. Every man must hold himself in readiness; and every woman knows that when she says goodbye it might be for the last time.

978-0-7515-3347-7

The Complete Dynasty Series by Cynthia Harrod-Eagles

1. The Founding	£8.99	17. The Poison Tree	£7.99
2. The Dark Rose	£7.99	18. The Abyss	£7.99
3. The Princeling	£7.99	19. The Hidden Shore	£7.99
4. The Oak Apple	£9.99	20. The Winter Journey	£7.99
5. The Black Pearl	£6.99	21. The Outcast	£7.99
6. The Long Shadow	£9.99	22. The Mirage	£9.99
7. The Chevalier	£9.99	23. The Cause	£9.99
8. The Maiden	£9.99	24. The Homecoming	£7.99
9. The Flood-Tide	£7.99	25. The Question	£7.99
10. The Tangled Thread	£9.99	26. The Dream Kingdom	£8.99
11. The Emperor	£7.99	27. The Restless Sea	£7.99
12. The Victory	£9.99	28. The White Road	£7.99
13. The Regency	£7.99	29. The Burning Roses	£8.99
14. The Campaigners	£7.99	30. The Measure of Days	£7.99
15. The Reckoning	£7.99		
16. The Devil's Horse	£9.99		

The prices shown above are correct at time of going to press. However, the publishers reserve the right to increase prices on covers from those previously advertised, without further notice.

—— sphere ——

Please allow for postage and packing: **Free UK delivery.**
Europe; add 25% of retail price; Rest of World; 45% of retail price.

To order any of the above or any other Sphere titles, please call our credit card orderline or fill in this coupon and send/fax it to:

Sphere, P.O. Box 121, Kettering, Northants NN14 4ZQ
Fax: 01832 733076   Tel: 01832 737526
Email: aspenhouse@FSBDial.co.uk

☐ I enclose a UK bank cheque made payable to Sphere for £. . . . .
☐ Please charge £. . . . . . to my Visa, Delta, Maestro.

Expiry Date ☐☐☐☐   Maestro Issue No. ☐☐

NAME (BLOCK LETTERS please) . . . .

ADDRESS . . . .

. . . .

. . . .

Postcode . . . . Telephone . . . .

Signature . . . .

Please allow 28 days for delivery within the UK. Offer subject to price and availability.